VOLUME III

Great Stories from the World of Sport

EDITED BY

PETER SCHWED and

HERBERT WARREN WIND

19 58

SIMON AND SCHUSTER · NEW YORK

ACKNOWLEDGMENTS

For arrangements made with various authors, their representatives, and publishing houses where copyrighted material was permitted to be reprinted, and for the courtesy extended by them, the following acknowledgments are gratefully made:

Brandt & Brandt, Inc., for *See How They Run* by George Harmon Coxe. Originally published in *The Saturday Evening Post.* © 1941 by The Curtis Publishing Company.

Doubleday & Company, Inc., Mrs. George Bambridge, and The Macmillan Co. of Canada, for *The Maltese Cat* from THE DAY'S WORK by Rudyard Kipling.

Messrs. John Farquharson, Ltd., on behalf of the Estate of the late Dr. E. OE. Somerville, for *Lisheen Races, Second-Hand* and *A Misdeal* from EXPERIENCES OF AN IRISH R.M. by Somerville and Ross.

Samuel French, Ltd., on behalf of the Executors of the late Captain Robert Marshall, for THE HAUNTED MAJOR by Robert Marshall.

Alfred A. Knopf, Inc., for RACKETY RAX by Joel Sayre. © 1932 by Joel Sayre.

Littauer & Wilkinson, for *The Zealots of Cranston Tech* by Archie Oldham. Originally published in *Bluebook* Magazine. © 1956 by The McCall Corporation.

The New Yorker Magazine, by permission of the author, for *Tennis* by Roger Angell. © 1950 by The New Yorker Magazine, Inc.

Thomas H. Raddall, for his story *The Man from Cap d'Amour*, 1943, *Blackwood's* Magazine.

Random House, Inc., for *A Session in Stillman's Gym* from THE HARDER THEY FALL by Budd Schulberg. © 1947 by Budd Schulberg.

Rinehart & Company, Inc., for *Light Tackle* from THE BEST OF CRUNCH AND DES by Philip Wylie. Originally published in *The Saturday Evening Post.* © 1940 by The Curtis Publishing Company.

Charles Scribner's Sons, for *Alibi Ike* from HOW TO WRITE SHORT STORIES by Ring Lardner. © 1915 by The Curtis Publishing Company; renewal © 1943 by The Curtis Publishing Company and Ellis A. Lardner.

Simon and Schuster, Inc., for *Ali the Terrible Turk* from NIGHT AND THE CITY by Gerald Kersh. © 1946 by Gerald Kersh.

Simon and Schuster, Inc., for *Fifty and Eight* from EQUINOX by Allan Seager. © 1943 by Allan Seager.

James Thurber, for his story *You Could Look It Up*. Originally published in *The Saturday Evening Post.* © 1941 by The Curtis Publishing Company.

TABLE OF CONTENTS

VOLUME THREE

Complete Novelettes

Short Stories

Excerpts from Novels

RACKETY RAX

by *JOEL SAYRE*

(1932)

The colleges which are little more than football factories had not yet begun to stud the plains of this country when Joel Sayre's buoyant farce was written. There were some suspicions then that in certain institutions of lower learning athletes worked their way through by winding clocks once a week, but that was about all. But the cycle was under way and today the annual national ratings of college football teams invariably wind up with a few leaders that haven't much more scholastic stature than Old Canarsie U, the home of the puce and the green. The explanation is simple: the gates increased, and the colleges have been able to buy more clocks.

I

I'LL NEVER FORGET what a tough time I had getting the Chief to that Yale-Army game.

Six of us—the Chief, Mike, Councilor Sultsfeldt, two of the gorillas, and I—had gone up to Hartford to fix up the fight between Slat Saltorini and our guy. A friend of mine slipped me six tickets to the game. I am a great football bug myself: played on the freshman team at college and in high school; and I used to cover it every fall when I was a sports writer. Besides, I get a great wallop out of seeing the West Point Kaydets march. So I wanted very much to get everybody over to New Haven.

At first the Chief wouldn't hear of it. He had the idea that football was a pansy game, probably played with sofa pillows and watched by people who sat around nibbling ladyfingers. Fights, wrestling, horses, baseball, racing dogs, pigeons and ferrets, he knew everything there was to know about: rules, form, and how they could be framed. He even figured out a way to frame ferrets by betting on the second rat. You know, after the first rat, a ferret would be a setup for a rabbit. But football—well, football didn't mean anything to him, or rather, it meant only one thing and that was collegiates. As far as he was concerned, all collegiates were goofy punks in big fur coats who'd come into his joints and bust furniture and insist on playing the trap drums and probably end up by being sick. So when I tried to sell that Yale-Army game to him, he just curled his lip at me.

But the Councilor, it seemed, studied law at the night school of some college that had a football team in the daytime; and Mike had had a West Pointer for a company commander during the war and thought he might like to go and give the Army team the bird just for old times' sake. So we finally won the Chief over. But on the way to New Haven in the car, while I sat beside him in the back seat, he would look at me every now and then and shake his head from side to side and go "Tch, tch, tch," and then say: *"Football!"* as though there were no more hope for me.

When we got to New Haven the streets were full of kids in coonskin coats parading around with their girls, and at the sight of them the Chief got the collegiate horrors and almost climbed out of the car.

"Nuts!" he said. "Let's scram back to New York before they all start to playing the traps at oncet."

However, we held on to him until we got to a joint in Church Street that a friend of mine runs and had lunch and drank some pretty good rye until it was time to go to the game.

When he caught sight of the Bowl from the car, the Chief turned to me with a funny look on his face.

"Am I cockeyed or something?" he said. "This ain't Soldier Field ahead there, because I know we ain't left Hartford only a while ago. And they don't have only bush fights in New Haven. What the hell *is* this, anyways?"

"Just you wait and get a load of it," I told him.

Well, it was a great game. The Army had the whole Leland Stanford backfield of two years before, and the Elis had one of their wonderful lines, so that it was a terrible battle all the way. You'll

recall that Yale won when George Weston Harpinger, Jr., of Broken
Cloud, Neb., the sophomore sub halfback, intercepted an Army forward pass with fifteen seconds left to play and pulled the game out
of the fire by one point, 20 to 19.

At least it said so in the sports section of the Sunday papers. I
didn't see much myself on account of the trouble I had with my party.
In the first place, Mike, who had stayed a little too long at my friend's
joint in Church Street, caused a lot of attention and comment (we
were sitting in the Yale stands) with the horrible Bronx cheers he
gave when the entire cadet corps marched to our side of the field.
This company commander of his in the war made quite an impression
on him, and every once in a while he would let out a roar and
challenge him to come out and fight.

"Where's Captain Robert N. Smiley?" he would bellow whenever
there was a quiet spell. "The such-and-such of a so-and-so! Tell him
to come over here and I'll knock his this-and-that face off for him!"

And then the Councilor kept turning around to look at the ankles
of the dames sitting in back of us and nudging me and pointing whenever he saw a pretty pair, until finally a couple of guys came down the
aisle and threatened to punch him in the nose. The gorillas thought
they meant the Chief and were going to give them a tossing around,
and I had to go to work and straighten that out.

But the worst of all was the Chief. He kept standing up and counting the house. I guess he hadn't seen so many people all in one place
since the second Tunney-Dempsey fight, and he'd grab me by the
arm (and maybe you think he hasn't got a grip!) every time I would
be trying to follow the players and he'd have some question. If he
asked one he asked a thousand. He wanted to know if these were all
paid admissions. And then he wanted to know what the seats cost.
How much the *ringside* ringsides, and how much just the ringsides?
And how much did those mugs back there in the bleachers pay? What
became of the dough? How was it cut up? And then he'd stand up
(always right in front of me, it had to be, just when something interesting was happening down on the field) and start to count the
house all over again.

"Geez!" he kept muttering, over and over again, "geez!"

II

The Chief was a remarkable person. His name, Francis X. (Knucks) McGloin, is probably unknown to you unless you happen to be an old-time Broadway regular; but if you were ever in New York for pleasure you must have drunk some of his beer, or spent an evening in one of his night clubs, or seen some of his fights or wrestling matches. Even if you are a teetotaler and never went near Broadway, but just lived in the town as an ordinary chump, he had quite a lot to do with your existence. That extra cent your missus paid for a loaf of bread or a quart of milk, the nickel increase for that embalmed chicken at the corner delicatessen on the maid's day off, or the sudden reduction from fifty to thirty-five cents when you went to settle with your neighborhood tailor for pressing your suit —the Chief was behind them all.

You didn't know it, the cops and the D.A. didn't know it, even the baker and the milkman, the chicken puller and the tailor didn't know it. Of course, all of them, including even you, knew that there was racketeering going on. And every once in a while there would be "exposures" of it in the papers and some arrests. But you know and I know and we all know that it's the punks that get arrested in cases like that; they never get the main guy.

The Chief was smart that way. He ducked publicity. He let Al Capone and Legs Diamond get their pictures and their life histories in the papers. He himself avoided publicity like the pox. And that's where he was smart. If you have your name in the papers all the time, it gets the young cops so excited that one day you'll be trying to get a piece of chewing gum out of a slot machine in the subway and you'll be pinched for clipping the Prince of Wales.

Another contact you may have had with the Chief without knowing it, if you lived in New York at the time, was on Election Day. Maybe you had your mind all made up to vote one way, but after you got to the polls and took a look around, you voted the other way. Well, it was the Chief who persuaded you. Perhaps you were a workman in a pants factory where there was a strike. The employers put in strikebreakers and you, as a member of your union, went on picket duty. Somebody tapped you over the head with some blunt instrument, and when you woke up you didn't have a very clear idea of who did it. Well, it was the Chief, although you couldn't have proved it if you had had slow-motion pictures made of yourself getting slugged. On the other hand, maybe your union won the strike all of a sudden, much more quickly than the most optimistic of your leaders expected. The chances are that it was the Chief who helped you to win it. Don't ask me how. Those things just happened, that's all.

In appearance, too, the Chief was remarkable from any angle you looked at him. From the front he resembled a determined fish, because he had hardly any chin to speak of and his forehead was low and narrow; in profile, his nose made him look like a little eagle; from three-quarters you noticed that not only his eyes but his whole face seemed heavy-lidded; while from behind you wondered how anybody could be so smart and have so little back to his head.

I could sit and look at him by the hour, fascinated by his hideousness. His hair was jet-black and plastered down, and he had neither brows nor lashes. The most terrible part of him was his eyes, which were blue and, in clear weather, visible for a city block. That is, when he was angry or smoked-up about something. When he was amused or just kind of mentally lying back, they seemed clouded over. Down his left cheek, from about an inch back of his eye to the corner of his upper lip, was a scar. The tip of his right ear was snipped off. (No blunt instrument there, you thought to yourself when you saw it for the first time.) He was just five feet two inches tall, but between shootings weighed around 170. Somehow, after a few minutes in his presence, you got over the idea that he was a runt; not only was he built like a fire plug, but from the way he panthered about when he moved, you got the impression of tremendous physical power. And there was none of the banty rooster about him that goes with most short men. Just from seeing him come into a room full of people and lay his hat on a table, you knew he was a killer. You did if you were smart, anyway.

When I think back to those days when editorial writers used to thunder about Legs Diamond and his twenty-five arrests and bellow for action by the authorities, I have to smile. Why, when he was going through what you might call his apprentice and journeyman periods, the Chief was pinched fifty-seven times by actual count. And except for a couple of months on the Island for ringing doorbells or breaking windows or being cruel to cats or something like that, he never did any time behind the bars except maybe a few minutes waiting for a bondsman.

The first three things a smart operator learns is: don't kill a cop; keep your racket clear of the U. S. mails; and stay out of the papers.

The wops have taken over Chicago, but New York has always been an Irish town. If you dig into its history for the last hundred years, you'll find that there's been a harp on the heap pretty near the whole time. And so, naturally, the Chief was a West Side fellah, as the boys say, for the West Side is where all the big shots come from. Born in West Street, he naturally joined the old Wiper gang after having brought notice to himself, first as a kid package thief and pickpocket, and then as the leader of his own little mob that specialized in kicking in docks and warehouses and the boxcars in the old New York Central yards. At sixteen he had killed his man. By the time he was eighteen he was leading the Wipers in their never ending skirmishes with the Ground Hogs.

Those days before the war were the Golden Age of Hoodlumry. Gangs went around fighting each other out of sheer joie-de-vivre and were happy to live on the shakedown from little gambling houses, intimidation of small merchants (mostly under the guise of "watchman service" or a "protective association" with a fancy name), strong-arm labor in a precinct or two on Election Day, and the petty cash from robberies and holdups. It was really a very innocent era.

III

Like Monk Eastman, Wild Bill Lovett and a number of other Manhattan and Brooklyn gangsters, Knucks McGloin fought a very fine war indeed. As I said before, the gangs in those days enjoyed fighting for its own sake alone; and when war was declared against Germany, Knucks, with nearly his entire mob behind him, joined up at the first bugle blast. When he stood stripped for his medical examination one of the doctors, noticing the golf links of knife and bullet scars on his body, said: "I see you're a veteran." "Yeah," said Knucks with a grin, "I been through a few campaigns." The Wipers, almost entirely intact in a platoon, fought together in the 27th Division, with Knucks as their sergeant. During the Argonne show the

platoon silenced three German machine-gun nests by the simple ex-
pedient of sneaking around and shooting the gunners in the back, a
maneuver at which they were highly skillful before the World War was
ever thought of. Knucks was wounded and received the D.S.C. for
gallantry under fire. Of course, all the Wipers had enlisted under
phony names.

The war made Knucks McGloin, transformed him from merely an
excellent gorilla and hoodlum into a Man of Vision. The mightiness
of the conflict stirred his imagination and gave him a new set of
values, accustomed him to doing things on a large scale. From tactics
he learned that an offense is the best defense; and that you can't gain
a position without risking the possibility of losing the one you already
hold. He learned how to conserve dash and bravery until the moment
they would be most effective. He learned to store up his resources
and to think ahead for the future. The great value of discipline and
organization also seeped into his skull and stayed there.

When he got back to New York some time in July after the Armi-
stice, he found a different town, a different civilization. There was a
thing called Prohibition, and all the old corner saloons were being
dismantled to make way for soda fountains and chain groceries.
Everybody was wondering what was going to happen and putting
stuff in his cellar to guard against the sandstorm.

It didn't take Knucks long to figure things out. He and Mike, who
was a cousin of his, bought a place in Greenwich Village for almost
nothing at all and started to run it exactly as it had been run before,
only you went in by the side door instead of by the front, and
ladies were welcome at the bar. By 1922 the joint was a radium
mine, and Knucks and Mike owned three more places and a brewery
which supplied every other speako between Fourteenth and Canal
streets.

Now, you know and I know and we all know that you can't deliver
beer in any satchel. Beer comes in barrels, and barrels are hauled
around in trucks, and trucks can't be smuggled up and down the
streets in the tassel of a lady's garter. To run beer you've got to have
protection all up and down the line, and that's where Knucks Mc-
Gloin showed his genius as an organizer. So well did he grease the
wheels of government that by 1930 all competition had been shot,
stabbed, taken for a ride or raided out of business by the authorities.
Don't ask me how. Those things just happened, that's all.

Just as in the days before Prohibition breweries sometimes

owned not only saloons but hotels and cabarets as well, so Knucks McGloin (who soon achieved the title of the Chief and thereafter no more cared to be addressed as Knucks than Mr. Capone cared to be called Scarface to his scar face) found himself at the head of a chain of gaudy hotels, apartment houses and night clubs. The hotels, which were all in the Times Square district, he named after notable American battles in the World War: there was the Chateau Thierry in West Forty-fifth Street, the Belleau Wood on Eighth Avenue, and the Argonne on Broadway just above Forty-seventh. The apartment houses, which were all in the West Seventies, were christened for the attorneys who had successfully defended him at various times: the Fallon Mansions, the Sultsfeldt Arms, Schlotkin Terrace and the Goldsword Towers; while the night clubs had more or less regional names according to the districts in which they were situated. In Harlem were the Club Hotcha and the Club Whambam; three swanky spots just off Park Avenue were known as the Club Delish, the Club Gigolo and the Club Crepe Suzette; in the Broadway belt were the Club Pat and Mike, the Club Whoopee (specializing in the out-of-town-buyer trade) and the Club Heh-heh-heh (named for the gag in Walter Winchell); on the lower East Side was the Roumanian Robot, where Joe Moskowitz performed on the dulcimer; while a place that never went very well which the Chief, for sentimental reasons, insisted on trying was the West Side Riding and Riveting Club over on Tenth Avenue.

In addition, the Chief owned or had a piece of virtually all the fighters, wrestlers, racing dogs and fancy pigeons in the metropolitan area. He was supposed to have been behind Abe (Weasles) Epstein when he fixed the international polo matches the year England, to everyone's vast surprise, took the trophy back to Hurlingham. From a news angle, perhaps the most sensational innovation he made during this period was the killing of an enemy from a helicopter while he sat in his bathtub. The practice is as common now as was murder by machine gun during the 20s; but it was the Chief who first thought it out. Don't ask me how.

IV

Mike, whose full name was John Michael Dumphy, had been born in the same tenement as the Chief and they had been together all their lives. He was a tremendous tall man with thick red curly hair and very pleasant ways about him, although he still retained some of the old West Side Wiper's love of a fight purely for its own sake.

Mike was the front man for the Chief. He handled all his sporting enterprises and looked after the speak-easies and night clubs. One of his duties was supervision of the Central Switchboard. As I said before, the Chief brought a lot of ideas back with him from the Western front that he was able to use in building up his organization, and one was that modern warfare is conducted by platoons. To guard his interests about town he employed the platoon patrol system. The town was divided into districts, and each district was patrolled by a platoon under a sergeant of gorillas. Each gorilla had a beat in which the Chief had a night club or a speako or a big crap game.

The gorilla's job was to patrol the beat and see that everything was O.K. Every hour he would call the sergeant of gorillas, usually stationed in a poolroom in the district, and report. Every hour and fifteen minutes the sergeant of gorillas would call the Central Switchboard at the Argonne, where the Chief's headquarters were situated. Then there were the emergency calls. Say there had been an arrest somewhere. It would be reported to the Central Switchboard within a few minutes after it had occurred, and in five minutes a bondsman or a lawyer or an alderman or a district leader, whichever was required, would be on his way to whatever station house, magistrate or United States commissioner the prisoner was to be taken before. Say there had been a shooting. Within a few minutes there would be either a physician or a reinforcement of gorillas or both on the way to the theater of action.

Mike had the inspiration of dressing the gorillas as mail carriers. A mail carrier is the most innocent-looking person in the world and he can go anywhere he wants to: "Make way for the U. S. mail" stuff. And those leather bags were found to be splendid Mills bomb containers. Both the Chief and Mike had achieved a great fondness for the Mills bomb during the war and were great believers in its efficacy. "One Mills bomb properly threw," Mike often used to say, "can wipe out the toughest truckload of machine-gun choppers that ever come out of Chi any day."

And it proved to be true. A machine gun is an unhandy instrument, even one of the little Thompson subs, and is bound to attract attention under the most favorable circumstances. Whereas, one of the Chief's letter carriers could walk right up unmolested to the desired position, or get in some barricaded place by pretending he had a special delivery for somebody, and then, after fishing around among the property postcards on the top of his bag, pull out a bomb, jerk the pin, throw the lever—and curtains for the opposition.

It got so that the gorillas used postal terms for their various operations. "To drop a card" meant to toss a black powder bomb that wouldn't hurt anybody, merely blow the porch off his house and let him know that if he didn't pay up or lay off it would be just too bad. "Second class matter" was a pineapple loaded with screws and old nails that might cause some pretty serious flesh wounds, but probably wouldn't kill. "Special delivery," however, was one perfectly good Mark III Mills bomb that meant business; while "registered letter" meant a couple. "Air mail" was the works, a regular over-the-top bombardment by prize bombing teams.

Mike had a funny way, just when things were getting really crucial, such, say, as the time to sign the articles for a million-dollar Battle of the Century for the World's Heavyweight Championship, of letting a glaze come over his eyes and a dead look come over his pan and bursting into a sentimental ballad. Some sharpshooter would unlimber a fountain pen and say: "Now, Mr. Dumphy, how about it, let's close right now, huh?" And Mike would look out of the window and sing in a voice that would knock all the pictures crooked on the walls:

"Oh, Ireland must be heaven, for my muthaaaw come from there."

Councilor Sultsfeldt was the best criminal lawyer in New York and a big shot in both the Republican and Democratic parties. He was head of the Chief's legal staff and general officer commanding the bail bondsmen; and he took care of the Chief's enormous business interests, seeing that they were all properly registered and incorporated according to law. He was a great trial lawyer, one of the best in the business; I never saw any attorney who could get a jury weeping faster about the constitutional rights of a mug who was up for shooting somebody in the back. The Councilor's only weaknesses were liquor and ladies; but they were great weaknesses, indeed, for he spent all of his huge takings on them and was always needing a buck to pay for his taxi.

The Chief, Mike and the Councilor were really the whole mob; the rest were like the supers in one of the old Morris Gest productions, say *The Miracle*. If you had drawn up a cast of characters you would have put the three of them, with the Chief at the top and then: headwaiters, members of the floor show, musicians, managers, bookmakers, hostesses, gunmen, etc.

While I am at it, I might as well say a few words about myself. I was press agent for the Chief's stable of fighters and wrestlers. Before I went to work for him, or nominally for Mike, I was a sports writer for three New York papers and before that I worked in San Francisco, Denver and Chicago. I worked for the Chief on straight salary and attended to the ballyhoo that always goes on before a fight or a wrestling match; and at the training camps I took care of the sports writers and saw that they got everything they wanted in the way of information or alcohol.

It was a swell job. Naturally, I saw and heard a lot of things I had to keep under my hat, but it was very fascinating to be on the inside of matters that only a few knew about. I always tried to do what the boys call "keep a clean nose," and I flatter myself that I enjoyed a reputation around town for being on the up and up. If I hadn't I should have been fished out of some ditch a headless torso long ago.

V

Well, the next day was Sunday and I was having some breakfast and trying to find out from the papers who won the game I had watched through the Chief's legs, when the telephone rang. It was the Central Switchboard calling and Miss Hoolihan, the chief operator, told me that I was urgently wanted at No. 1. That meant the Chief had something on his mind, so I got dressed and scrammed right up to the Argonne.

I went up in the elevator we used when we wanted to get to the Chief's suite on the top floor. It was marked: "To the Grand Ballroom Only," and there wasn't any ballroom at the Argonne. Frank, the starter, said: "Hahzit, Mr. Schatz?" and I said: "Hahzit, Frank?"

A benchful of gorillas dressed as bellboys were on guard outside the Chief's door. The sergeant in charge touched his monkey cap. "Hahzit, Mr. Schatz?" "Hahzit, Tommy?" There used to be some funny mistakes at the Argonne when an out-of-town schoolmarm or some W.C.T.U. grandma stopping there through innocence would run into one of the gorilla bellhops in the lobby or a corridor and ask him to fetch ice water or take this canary bird right up to 709. The

management had to exercise great care to keep the gorillas seques-
tered.

Tommy got right on the phone and announced me. There was a
sound of chains dragging and the big door, which looked like oak
and had carvings and a knob and everything but was actually made
of armor plate, started to slide upward like a portcullis. Inside were
more gorillas in the little antechamber like a doctor's waiting room.
I said: "Hahzit?" to the mug in charge and he said: "Hahzit?" and
then the Chief himself, in flame-colored pajamas with black polka
dots, opened. "Hahzit, kid?" "Hahzit, Chief?" There were specks
of talcum powder on the blue beds of scraped whisker on his chin
and in the scar. I walked in.

The Chief's suite took up the whole floor. Mike and the Councilor
shared the floor beneath. The room I walked into was the Chief's
living room. It was full of overstuffed chairs; floor lamps that look
like the kind you win at Coney Island throwing things, but are really
very expensive; onyx ash trays on stands with rounded bottoms;
three gilt statuettes of Italian urchins plopping cast-iron cherries into
their mouths (you see them in the lobbies of all the big talkie
temples); and a huge teak table with mother-of-pearl inlay and
an alabaster top. On the walls were holy pictures; signed photographs of big politicians of both parties and sexes; the Chief's D.S.C.
citation: "Sergeant H. T. Robinson . . . gallantry under fire . . .
Montfaucon," and his discharge papers; heads of moose and elk
he had shot on hunting trips; and eight oil paintings of cows standing
in different positions in puddles. There were many bearskin rugs on
the floor. Four casement windows with bulletproof panes gave on to
Broadway. The Sunday papers and Voine were strewn all over the
bearskin in front of the fireplace.

Voine, the Chief's lady friend, was known by several other names,
by any of which she would have smelled the same. To some of the
boys she was the Princess, while others simply called her Peaches—
all behind her back, of course. Mike, in rare moments of anger, referred to her as Knucksy's Pig. Voine was a big girl. There was a
world of gold in her front teeth and she had that phony blond hair
that always reminded me of the chicken soup they serve in the Jewish
restaurants—you know, that terrible bogus colored stuff.

"Why, Mister Schatz!" she gurgled and started to get up. She was
wearing black lace pajamas with plenty of open work and a pink
ribbon around her waist.

She wound her arm about the Chief's neck and started to play with his ear, that game ear, with her fingers.

"Duzzum wannum baby to weaveum? Divvum ittle tiss, firs', den."

Voine spoke that way most of the time. When she really got going, she broke into what the Holy Rollers call the Gift of Tongues.

"*Scram!*" the Chief roared, and gave her a push that knocked her over and sent her sliding along the floor. She rose, glared at him for a second, and then picked up one of those squiggly dolls and went into the bedroom.

The Chief poured a couple of shots, took the big chair by the fire and motioned me to the one drawn up opposite. I noticed that all the sports sections were scattered over the bearskin. He tossed off his shot and then for a whole minute looked at me with that face of his. I remember thinking that he probably could have peeked through the keyhole of a doll's house with both those terrible eyes at once.

"I suppose you know everything about this here football," he said finally, lighting a cigar.

"Sure."

"Why ain't I been told about it before?"

"Well, I don't know. I, uh, guess I thought you weren't interested in amateur sports."

"Amachers! You ain't setting there telling me them's amachers draws all them gates?"

"Sure."

"Whataya trying to do, kid me or sumpen?"

"No, Chief, I'm leveling. I'm leveling, honest to God."

"The hell you are. Well, go ahead and gimme the payoff on the racket."

"Well, let's see. . . . The game is played on a field 360 feet long including end zones and 160 feet wide, which——"

"Nuts! Forget about them end zones, and all that stuff, and let's have the payoff on the racket."

"Well, there are eleven players on each side——"

"Nuts!"

"Well, football is quite a thing——"

"Aw, *nuts!* Do you figure I'm deaf and dumb or something?"

"Why, of course not, but I'm trying to tell you something about the game, and you keep cutting me off. Well, there are about four-hundred-odd universities and colleges in the United States that play football. The season starts generally on the fourth Saturday in September and is supposed to end on Thanksgiving. Some teams start their seasons earlier and some end later. But eight games, one every Saturday, is the average schedule. Besides the universities, the prep schools and high schools have teams, too."

"Never mind them punks. What about the gates?"

"Well, the gate depends on the attraction. It's just like the fight racket. If two little schools with no class are playing, the crowd is small. But when two traditional rivals—I mean when there are two colleges playing with plenty of class that have it in for each other like two fighters—say like Mickey Walker and Harry Greb, or Dempsey and Tunney, you know, a grudge fight—why, then, they pack 'em in. They fill up the stadium, as you saw yesterday. But that gate was just so-so for two big teams. When the Notre Dame team plays in Chicago, for instance, they always fill Soldier Field, eighty, ninety, maybe even a hundred thousand."

"The hell they do!"

"Honest to God, Chief, I'm leveling. Now you take Harvard and Yale——"

"Them was the Yales we seen yesterday, wasn't it? Geez, what a house! Well, go on, but what I want to know is who does it to who and who pays?"

"Well, Chief, that's kind of hard to explain. First of all——"

"Wait a minute. Do they play this here football in our territory here?"

"Sure. Columbia has a team, and Fordham and N.Y.U. and little Alfred and——"

"Who's this little Alfred?"

"Well, never mind about little Alfred. Over in Jersey, there's Rutgers and——"

"What's the leading stable here in town?"

"Well, I don't know, let's see: I'd say it was N.Y.U. or maybe Fordham. They have the best teams and draw the biggest gates."

"What's this N.Y.U.?"

"It stands for New York University. It's up in the Heights."

"Well, who's the main guy up there?"

"Why, uh, Chancellor Brown."

"Chancellor Brown, eh? Well, anyways, what's to keep me from going up there tomorrow and punching him right in the nose?"

"Punch him in the nose?"

"Sure. Maybe I won't punch him in the nose unless he gets tough. I'll treat him nice and just scare him a little. I don't look for no trouble, though. He can't be very much of a hood or I'd heard of him before and I guess he's heard of *me,* if he's in the racket. Chancellor Brown, eh?"

"Geez, Chief, I don't get you at all."

"You *don't?* Why, I thought you was smart. The gag is this here football. Why, it's the sweetest thing I heard about since Prohibition."

"Yeah, but what's it all got to do with Chancellor Brown?"

"What's it got to do with him? Why, I'm gonna muscle in on his racket, that's what it's got to do with him. He's the main guy at this N.Y.U. jernt, ain't you just told me?"

It would have given me a bellylaugh if I hadn't known the Chief so well, and what he was capable of.

"You've got me all wrong, Chief," I said. "This Chancellor Brown hasn't anything to do with football. He's the head of the university; he looks after the professors and students and the affairs of the university."

"Well, football's part of the affairs of the university, ain't it?"

"It is and it isn't," I said, beginning to realize what a tough spot I was in.

The Chief thought that one over a while.

"Well, who *is* the main guy in football up at this here N.Y.U., then?"

"It's Chick Meehan."

"Chick Meehan, eh? Never heard of him. I heard of Fat Willie Meehan, and plenty of other Meehans, but I never heard of no Chick Meehan. Well, what's his take?"

"He doesn't get any take, he works on a straight salary. I don't know how much it is, but I suppose around ten, twelve, fifteen grand."

"Well, who *does* get all the dough? I see at New Haven last Saturday they was selling hot dogs and programs and feathers and all kinds of stuff. Whose racket is that? *Somebody* must get it, and if I can find out who it is I'm gonna drop around and see him."

"Well, it's kind of a hard thing to explain. There's the college Athletic Association which is sort of the governing body of all the teams the college has——"

"Oh, I see. They cut up the take, eh?"

"Now, wait a minute. At the head of the Athletic Association there is what is called a graduate manager. He's on a salary, just like the coach. Then there's the expenses of the team. It costs about $100 to equip each player and a big college will have thirty or forty or fifty players. Then——"

"How much do they pay the players?"

"Well, they don't pay them anything, but sometimes the players get it made easier for them—they have scholarships or they find jobs for them if they are poor, and——"

"Sure, I get the idea. But where does all this dough go? These here expenses ain't nothing."

"Well, at the end of the year the football team at any big college will have a profit of a couple of hundred thousand—some of them show a profit of a million or more—and this money is turned over to the Athletic Association."

"Ah, now we're getting somewheres."

"And the Athletic Association uses it to pay the expenses of the college's other teams."

"The hell it does!"

"Honest to God, Chief. Football is about the only college sport that shows a profit at the end of the season, and all college athletic associations use the football profits to pay the expenses of the sports that always go in the red, like hockey, baseball, rowing and so on. Anything that's left over is used for intramural athletics, that is, promoting sports among students who aren't good enough to represent the university against other universities, but need to work up a sweat once in a while."

"To hell with all that! What's gonna keep me from muscling into this here football? I muscled into the fight racket and the wrassling racket and the dog racket and plenty other rackets, didn't I? What's gonna keep me from cutting myself a piece of this? We'll find out who this graduate manager up at N.Y.U. is and work out on him. I don't look for no trouble: we'll treat him nice. Mebbe if we drop a card on his steps and jest take the porch off, it will be all we need."

The Chief smiled horribly. I got out my handkerchief and wiped my forehead. I was beginning to sweat.

"Now, listen to me, Chief, and get this straight, for God's sake. *You can't fool with this football racket!* You can kick the head off the Constitution, bust all the laws in the book and run this town to suit yourself, but lay off fooling with college football. It's got too many angles, more'n you ever heard of. You may think you've had headaches in your life, but you won't know what headaches are if you try to muscle in on football. It's the only serious thing in the United States any more—an absolute death or glory proposition. Why, listen, if you try to fool with the football team of any college, no matter which one, you'll have the Army and the Navy and the Marines out hunting you down and they won't quit until the croakers are cutting you up in the morgue and the mob is run down rat holes. If you ever trusted me, trust me now. I've been to college and I know what I'm talking about. Lay off, see, lay off. You're bucking the one racket in the world that can't be bucked."

"But, why?"

"Don't ask me why," I said, realizing that it was hopeless to go into alumni associations. "It's just one of those things, that's all. Just do me and yourself and the mob a favor and lay off. You're doing all right. You've got plenty of dough and less than your share of headaches. Just lay off."

The Chief thought it all over a long time.

"Well, kid," he said, "it's a brand-new gag to me, this here football, and, as you say, I'm doin' all right. But there must be *some* way to cut in. Mebbe you know what it's all about, but I ain't done with it yet."

VI

Well, the Chief didn't have time to think much more about football that Fall, for there was an election coming on and although the wise money was unanimous that it was in the bag, he was worried about it.

And he was right, for when the mugs that make up the body politic went to the polls on the first Tuesday after the first Monday that November, Tammany Hall took an awful tossing around. Every once in about a dozen years it does, you know. The Peepul rise in righteous wrath and sweep 'em out and the reformers get in. The reformers always chew each other to pieces, and at the end of four years there are hardly enough of them left to run again, so Tammany always marches in solidly and gloriously for another dozen years or more.

It's funny that Tammany ever does get licked, even that seldom, considering the wonderful organization it has, working twenty-four hours a day every day in the year. And the opposition has hardly any organization to speak of and kicks up a little dust only before elections. But Tammany does get licked and this was one of the times. Don't ask me how. It just happened, that's all—mayor, district attorney, alderman, all the judges that were running, the whole horse, foot and guns. It wasn't an election; it was more like a census, an anti-Tammany census.

And that anti-Tammany census started what will always be known on Broadway as the Year of the Grand Headache. Old regulars today are just as boring about it ("Let's see, that was back in the Headaches, wasn't it?") as the previous generation was about the blizzard of '88, so I'll just tell how it affected the Chief.

In the first place, he had to make a complete new set of protection arrangements; for, after the first of the year, there was a new police commissioner who blew his whistle and shifted inspectors, captains and even the cops on the beats around until we all got dizzy; and the inspector he put in charge of our district was old Kitty Cochran, a Carrie Nation in a blue coat and brass buttons.

Kitty started off his administration with a regular Olympic Games of raiding. And they weren't just ordinary raids. On these raids they always took axes and crowbars and backed hustle-buggies up to the entrance and moved out all the stock. Poor Mike almost went daffy shagging back and forth between cop houses and the U.S. commissioners' offices and hardly took his hat and coat off for months. And, believe me, it cost plenty before it all got straightened out.

And then fights and wrestling went all to hell. It just seemed that the customers couldn't be bothered, and crowds became so pitifully small that the fighters and wrestlers used to talk to each other for company. It was so scary all alone there in the great big Garden that they would almost whistle to keep up their courage. I got orders to bear down on ballyhoo, but I might as well have been broadcasting household hints over the radio. Here was the Chief's stable of fighters, including the champion or the leading contenders in nearly every division, doing nothing but sitting around on chairs in his front office. And maybe you don't think the fodder for those wrestlers runs into dough! It was terrible.

And then some kind of bug got into the beer. The Chief was always proud of the quality of his wet goods; he never went in for needled stuff (except, of course, in the early days after the war, when he was getting started) and his booze, although all synthetic, was perfectly healthful, no acetone or any of that kind of junk in it. Well, somehow or other, this bacillus found its way into the malt and made it taste as though it was full of old harness buckles and salamanders. That microscopic animalcule was responsible for more than a score of murders, for after old customers began to squawk and walk out, a number of speak-easies started to take beer from the Jersey mob and some discipline had to be enforced.

Then the new district attorney, a young Harvard millionaire from the silk-stocking district on Park Avenue and therefore hard to get at, started to cut up. He traced $5,000,000 worth of hot bonds to Eddie (Fingers) Hogan, a cousin of the Chief's, and then Fingers lost a decision and had to take a five spot up the river, although the Chief did everything in the world to chill the rap for him. And what was even worse, the D.A. opened up that helicopter killing and started an investigation that had the Chief worried plenty.

And then, as if all these headaches weren't enough, Fanny Mc-Gloin, who is the Chief's legally wedded wife, walked into the Crepe Suzette one night when he was there with Voine.

Everybody in the joint scrammed when Fanny began to tear Voine to baby ribbons, and, after that was over, she declared herself to the Chief.

The Chief begged for mercy and took her to the Argonne. It ended in a cash settlement and booking passage for her on a big liner that was making a world tour. For weeks after, the Chief spelled out the ship news in the papers, in the vain hope that unseen icebergs might cross the liner's path in the dead of night.

Well, all that spring and into the summer it continued: raid after raid, flop after flop, headache after headache, until we were all ready for strait jackets. And finally Popchick, the Esthonian Edelweiss, our heavyweight who was scheduled to fight Schmeling for the championship of the world on June 28 in the Yankee Stadium, was killed right in Times Square two days before the battle. A safe he was watching hoisted dropped on the big ape and squashed him flatter than yesterday's *Racing Form*. After that, the headache was to keep all razors and edged tools out of the Chief's reach.

But what a guy! He just locked himself in his suite with a couple of cases of rye (Voine) alone.

And when, on Fourth of July night, Miss Hoolihan called me and said that I was wanted very urgently at No. 1, I knew he was all right and had figured out some more angles, and that it would be no time at all before we were out of the red and into the blue. Don't ask me how. I just knew, that's all.

VII

Mike and the Councilor were there, too, and both of them were looking happy. Mike smiled and nodded his great red head and made a little flip of greeting with an enormous right paw, while the Councilor rubbed his hands together and said: "Hah, Mr. Schatz, a pleasure." They were sitting at the big teak table on which stood a bottle of rye, plenty of glasses and a large pitcher of ice water.

The Chief didn't say a word, but I could tell from his eyes and the way he panthered around that he was all smoked up. I got a glass from the sideboard, poured myself a shot, drew a chair up to the table and sat down.

"You tell him," said the Chief over his shoulder to the Councilor.

"I should tell him, when it's your inspiration," said the Councilor, beginning to wave his arms. "Why——"

"Tell him, tell him!" said the Chief, pacing up and down.

"All right," the Councilor shrugged, "but you shouldn't be so modest." He turned to me. "Before you, Mister Schatz, you see the founders of a great educational institution, the layers of a cornerstone that shall prevail down the corridors of time, that shall——"

"It's a gag to muscle into this here football racket," interrupted the Chief, sitting down on the arm of his big chair. "Since you and me had that talk last year I been figuring angles and now I think I got a way. And with all the headaches this year, we got to try *something*. You say it ain't possible to go up to Columbia or N.Y.U. or Fordham or Harvard or Yale and just muscle right in. I still don't see why, but if you say it means more headaches, why we got plenty right now. Well, see if here ain't a way to do ourself some good."

The Chief slipped into the seat of his chair, put his left elbow on the table and brought his hand gently over the scar. He didn't look straight at me, but out of the corner of his eye. His voice got soft and sleepy.

"What do you say we open a university of our own?" he said, shooting his eyes away and then back at me again. "The Councilor tells me that opening a university ain't much different to opening a speak-easy. All you do is send a couple bucks to Albany and the guy sends your incorporation papers back just like it was a gin mill." (All of the Chief's joints were incorporated as clubs and on all their walls were the framed papers signed and sealed by the Secretary of State.) "Well, we think up some name for our University and get the papers from Albany. Hahzat?"

The terrible eyes crept round to me again.

"That's swell," I said, "but where are you going to get the team?"

"Team!" he said. "Why, the team ain't no trouble at all. It's a wonderful chancet to get some use out of that mob of palooka fighters and wrasslers I got eating their heads off. And it don't make no difference how many of 'em gets killed, because there's more coming up from the amachers every day. Do you think maybe that would work out?"

"Hmmm . . . well, I guess they'd make wonderful material all right. You could use the wrestlers for your line and the fighters for your backfield, although they'd have to be taught to run forward instead of backward. You'll need a coach. But what about a stadium?"

"Well," said the Chief, "we thought the first season we'd play all our games away from home."

"Hmm, that's a good gag. Notre Dame, the place where the best football in the country is played, didn't play a home game for the first forty years. They used to call 'em the Ramblers before they got a stadium of their own—in the early days they traveled around the country with their toothbrushes and spare collars parked in their derby hats. But you'll have to have a place to practice in. It's going to be quite a chore to get these mugs into shape, or rather to teach 'em the game."

"What's all the gyms for?" said Mike just prior to tossing off a shot.

"No, you've got to have dirt. Football players wear cleats in their shoes and Stillman wouldn't like to have his floor scratched up."

"Well, what about one of the cavalry armories? We can have our pick of them."

I thought this over a moment.

"Well, an armory might do in a pinch, but those wrestlers tumbling around would tear such holes in the dirt the horses might fall in and bust their legs. What you've got to have is a field somewhere, and as

I guess we don't want the New York sports writers to nose around too much at first, the field ought to be somewhere they can't get at."

Everybody pondered for a while.

"I got it," said Mike, "that place back of the warehouse in Canarsie. It's out of the way, and nobody to bother us. The ground is kinda swampy, so nobody could hurt theirself if they took a bad fall. Mebbe we could clear out the warehouse and make it a regular training camp."

In case you don't know, Canarsie is a section over on the Long Island waterfront that everybody has heard about but nobody has ever been able to find the way to. Consequently, it makes a wonderful place to land booze, and that's how the Chief happened to have the warehouse over there. It's a terribly lonely place; there is a lunch wagon, and the cop house is a rose-covered white frame cottage. I once fell asleep on a subway train and landed there at the end of the line; but I couldn't do it again in a million years.

The Councilor was smiling up at the ceiling. "You got a wonderful name for the university right there," he said. "Canarsie, Canarsie University. It sounds swell. Good old Canarsie."

Everybody said Canarsie over to himself a couple of times to see how it sounded, and it sounded fine.

"Now, what about games?" said the Chief finally.

"Well, that's going to be tough," I said. "In the first place, most schools have already made their schedules up long ago. And in the second place, nobody ever heard of us, so we can't have our pick of the schools we play. But I'll look around and see what open dates there are and get in touch with anybody I can, and I'll hunt us up a coach, and as soon as I get him lined up he can have a talk with you and let you know how much you'll need for equipment. We won't know what our traveling expenses will be until we get our schedule made up. But this is going to take a lot of my time. What'll I do about the fight and wrestling ballyhoo?"

"Oh, to hell with that," said the Chief. "Get some good guy you know is all right and turn it over to him. I'll pay him whatever you think he ought to have. You bear down on this here football. You'll have to front for us, knowin' the collegiate racket and all. I guess you better be that guy you told me about last fall, you know, the main mug in the racket?"

"The graduate manager of athletics? All right, I'll have to do some traveling around making connections and I'll need some dough."

"How do you want this university incorporated?" the Councilor put in. "You'll be president, of course. What'll I and Mike be?"

The Chief turned to me.

"What monikers would youse give 'em?"

"Well, let's see. Mike can be dean of the College of Liberal Arts and the Councilor, mmm, the Councilor can be—uh—dean of women."

"Why can't *I* be dean of women?" said Mike.

"Shut up," said the Chief. "Okay, kid. Draw on me for whatever dough you'll need. You take care of it so's it's all legitimate, Councilor. You better use the usual monikers, Smith, Jones and Brown, hey?"

"One thing more," I said. "What colors do you want? Every college has got to have its colors. What are old Canarsie's? Most places have two."

"Well, so long as one of 'em's green, I don't care about the other," said the Chief.

There was a long silence.

"I seen some mighty pretty stockings on a little lady at the Suzette the other night," said the Councilor. "They were kind of a, uh, eggplant color and looked fine. I wonder what they call that shade?"

"Puce," I said. My girl friend was the fashion editor of the *Times,* and one Sunday I was reading her stuff and I came across "puce." It struck me as a funny word and when I asked her what it meant she said it meant eggplant color.

"Puce! Geez. Puce, eh? Puce and green. Well, maybe you know what it's all about. Puce!"

The bottle was passed around.

"Gentlemen, I give you old Canarsie," proposed the Councilor. "May the puce and green never falter."

Everybody drank.

"I think this education is gonna be quite a gag," said the Chief. . . . "Puce . . . puce . . . geez . . . !"

VIII

Well, I got Canarsie University a coach and I fixed her up with her first schedule.

The coach was Brick Gilligan, the old Michigan tackle, who turned out some fine teams on the Coast until he got in a little trouble. Poor Brick tried to saw a streetcar in half early one morning with his car. And when the cops came they found a coed with him and some bottles. The whole thing was hushed up, but Brick had to resign "for business reasons." I heard from a sports writer that he was in town and when I tracked him down he was selling typewriter ribbons and accessories from office to office in the financial district. Of course, he was delighted to get the job at ten grand the first year.

I'll never forget that August when the candidates for the Varsity answered the call. Brick and I had spent the last two weeks in July superintending carpenters, painters and plumbers in the conversion of the ramshackle building in Canarsie from a booze drop to a field house with showers, lockers and rubbing tables. We set up a tackling dummy and charging machines and laid out a field that would do to practice on, although it was pretty swampy and full of gulleys, and we never did get the busted bottles and old barrel hoops and dornicks out of it.

It was the strangest array of gridiron material ever assembled: fighters running all the way from world's champions, in the best clothes that Bille Taub turns out, to palookas just graduated from the Golden Gloves with hardly any seats to their pants; heavyweights, light heavies, middleweights, welters, lightweights, feathers, bantams and even little Shrimp Stein, the king of the flies. There were cauliflower ears, squashed noses and swollen cheekbones. Save for the lumbering heavies, they all moved with superb grace.

And the wrestlers! All heavyweights, all around 300, great, fat, good-natured guys, most of them bohunks or grease-balls whose only English was an obliging: "Sure, boss!" There was Nick Tossilitis, world's champion of the week, wearing the gargantuan diamond which unscrewed from his championship belt and could be fitted easily into either ring or stick pin; Hazos, the Horrible Hun, a middle-aged Slav with old-fashioned side whiskers; Baliban, the Neckless Wonder; and dozens of others, panting and sweating. Like faithful domestic animals, they wondered what it was all about, but were eager to perform any task ordered by their masters.

The Chief, Mike and the Councilor stood in the background to see that everything started O.K. Brick, dressed in baseball pants and cap and a sweat shirt, was in command.

Brick had coached teams on the Coast where they produce plenty of Paul Bunyans for football players, but, he told me afterward, he had never seen such material. However, he thought he'd better begin in the usual way by showing them what was what.

"Siddown, everybody, and get the wax outa your ears," he began with a nasty bark. "You've all answered the call to play football for Canarsie, and that's what you're gonna do—play football. Now, in the first place, while you're playin' football for me you're gonna play it the way I want it played, not the way you played it before you come here. And while you're learnin' to play it you're gonna learn it the way I give it to you. Where you come from you may a been the world's champion of this and that and I dunno what all. But now you're gonna start from the bottom. The first thing you gotta do is learn to *use your head!* It don't matter how big you are or how fast you are. If you don't *use your head,* you won't ever be a football player.

"And the first thing about usin' your head you gotta learn is *pay attention to what I say.* Now look at those two men over there. One's pickin' bananas and the other's pickin' his nose while I'm *talking. Hey, you!"*

He was addressing two Hungarian wrestlers, who, not understanding a word of his discourse, had begun amiable conversation with each other in Magyar. As he shouted at them they looked in his direction and smiled like children. Somebody among the boxers let fly a long juicy razzberry, which started the wrestlers laughing, and in a second there was a whole migration of birds in the air. It looked very bad for the general's introduction to his troops until the Chief cuffed a few of the ringleaders, and said a few words, and restored order.

"Get this, you mugs," he shouted, "this here genneman is representing me, see, and anything he tells ya to do, you do it, see, same as if it was me telling ya, see? Go ahead, Mac, and any of 'em gives you any trouble when I ain't here, jest lemme know."

There was a deep silence and a lowering of eyes all around.

"Well, report to Mr. Schatz in the storeroom for your suits," Brick resumed, trying to keep his voice hard, but not quite succeeding, "and leave your names with him. When you get dressed, report to me at the field."

It was quite a chore issuing suits to the squad of sixty-one on account of all the different lengths and contours in it, and we ran short of outsize pants for the wrestlers and shoes for the heavyweight fighters. But when they all assembled on the field there were fifty-two players completely outfitted with headguards ($15 each), jerseys ($10 each), shoulder pads ($14 each), hip and kidney pads ($15 each), pants ($17 each), shoes with screw-on cleats ($16 a pair), and stockings ($4.50 a pair). As it was August I had not issued any blankets ($13.50 each) or side-line shirts with hoods ($12 each).

The first thing that Brick found out was that he had three former college players among the wrestlers on his squad: Switz, of Notre Dame, a fullback; Oolaafsen, of Dartmouth, a tackle; and Schwulkopf, of Nebraska, a guard. After some calisthenics and duck-waddling up and down the field a couple of times by the whole squad, Brick divided his candidates into three groups and set them to falling on the ball.

The boxers took to it right away, being so used to fake fouls, but I wish you could have seen those wrestlers putting the divots in that swampland! It looked like Flanders Field after they were finished. The people that lived out that way must have thought they were blasting for a new subway.

After that they all worked out on the dummy, and Brick had a terrible time explaining to some of the grease-ball wrestlers that they mustn't put the scissors on it. There were more reverberations when they worked out on the charging machines. I don't know if you ever saw a charging machine, but it's a kind of a frame on wheels with a platform in back of it. A bunch of guys stand on the platform and the linemen put their hands on the top bar of the frame and push the whole contraption at a signal from the coach. When they get to the end of their push, they all fall flat at full length—*bam*. Then up, charge and *bam,* all the way up and down the field and over and over again. When you get about half a dozen wrestlers at 300 pounds each all hitting the dirt at once it makes quite a shake.

Well, there was plenty of trouble with that squad. The fighters couldn't be taught at first not to sock instead of using the open hand, and the wrestlers would grab and hold. Brick divided them into Varsity, Second and Third Teams and had them scrimmaging every afternoon with the three collegiate wrestlers helping him as assistants. At first, the boxers wouldn't play on the same teams as the wrestlers, having such a mean opinion of them; and they wanted us to put up another field house for the wrestlers on a kind of Jim Crow system, so that they wouldn't even have to look at them. You know, most fighters are very swell-headed and consider themselves above wrestlers. The wrestlers, however, have no false pride and are willing to take whatever comes their way with no complaints. That is why they all look well fed, while fighters nearly starve to death most of the time.

Although of course he never let them know it, Brick was enthusiastic about the possibilities of the squad.

"I think we can get a great club out of this bunch, Mr. Schatz," he used to say to me after practice. "We'll get a club this year that'll do all right, but just wait till I've had 'em a couple of seasons. There's awful power there, Mr. Schatz, awful power. God, if they could just learn not to use their hands on the offensive! But we'll see, we'll see."

I had terrible trouble and a couple of breaks, but here is the schedule I drew up for old Canarsie for its first year on the gridiron. The Navy game came through one of those severing of relations it has with the Army every once in a while.

Sept. 27.—Alfred University at Alfred, N. Y.
Oct. 4.—Temple University at Philadelphia.
Oct. 11.—Duke University at Durham, N. C.
Oct. 18.—University of Buffalo at Buffalo.
Oct. 25.—University of Detroit at Detroit.
Nov. 1.—Case School of Applied Science at Cleveland.
Nov. 8.—U. S. Naval Academy at Annapolis.
Nov. 15.—St. Mary's College at Oakland, Cal.

"There ain't no harm in trying," said the Chief when I showed him the schedule, "we're all aiming to make a buck, but if we don't do nothing but get off the nut this first year, it's eggs in the coffee."

IX

That was the starting lineup of our first game. We had some debate about whether we should give out fake names for the team, making them all 100% Anglo-Saxon or Celtic, but I pointed out that football players all over the United States have the goofiest names ever heard of anyway, and nobody would think Switz, Radeswicz and Woola anything out of the ordinary. So I sent out the lineup to all the New

York papers, and each of them gave us an inch or two, while three upstate sheets ran as a box a phony interview in which Coach Gilligan said he expected a terrible battle with Alfred. I remember I was kind of ashamed when I sent them out: we averaged 285.8 pounds from tackle to tackle.

CANARSIE		ALFRED
Oolaafsen	L.E.	Angley
Radeswicz	L.T.	Matoon
Hazos	L.G.	Porter
Tossilitis	C.	Schmidt
Baliban	R.G.	Haggerty
Schwulkopf	R.T.	Sessions (c)
Woola	R.E.	Priestley
McGloin	Q.B.	Santorello
Cello	L.H.	Fellowes
Flanahan	R.H.	Stein
Switz (c)	F.B.	Hardell

Switz was our threat man; he could run and pass, and as he had learned football under Rockne you can imagine what his blocking and tackling were like; but he couldn't punt, not more than twenty yards. Nobody on the whole squad could, as a matter of fact. Schwulkopf was a pretty good place kicker and was all right for kickoffs. Oolaafsen, the old Dartmouth tackle, a product of the great Doc Spears, we had to make into an end to catch forward passes and turn in the opposing backfields. Woola, the other end, was a professional basketball player Brick dug up in a moment of desperation when he found so few of his players could catch a ball. Woola could catch anything thrown anywhere in the park, but he was afraid to tackle; so they made big Schwulkopf play defensive end and go down under punts; while Woola, as a defensive half, was great at intercepting passes. The guards, Hazos and Baliban, the center, Chomp Tossilitis, and big Radeswicz, the other tackle, were all wrestlers.

Cello and Flanahan, the halfbacks, were two middleweights, famous for their speed and footwork. McGloin, the quarterback, was a nephew of the Chief's, a little rat-faced guy that used to stand on corners. Brick figured him as the best possibility for a field general.

Signals, early in the team's training, had to be given up as totally unintelligible to the vast majority of the members of the squad. The huddle system of communication was substituted. It used to look very funny from the sidelines with all those wrestlers' cabooses sticking out.

I will say this for Brick Gilligan: he was a smart coach. He realized that with the material he had he couldn't turn out for the first game any N.Y.U. Violets, all doing the Meehan military shift like so many Prussian Guards. What he aimed for was something simple and elemental. Knute Rockne used to say that if every man did his duty perfectly on every play, a touchdown would result. Well, for that first game with Alfred, Brick pointed for an uncomplicated application of that principle. He figured that if those wrestlers could just be made to squat down and push, and then, after they'd waddled forward a few steps, to lean against Alfred's secondary defense and lie on them for a few seconds, somebody in the backfield could carry the ball for a gain. Which wasn't such a bad idea.

Switz won the toss and Schwulkopf kicked off to Santorello, who was downed in his tracks on the thirty-yard line by Flanahan. On the first play Hardell bucked center and gained thirty yards through no fault of his own, for Tossilitis seized him by the waist as soon as he had reached the line, twirled him thrice about his head just as he used to do before he pinned an opponent to the mat, and then slammed him to the ground, knocking him cold. Hardell was removed on a stretcher, Tossilitis, weeping, was banished from the game, and old Canarsie was penalized half the distance to the goal for unnecessary roughness. Tossilitis's place was taken by Nixi, the Finnish champion, a formidable matman, but less showy.

As far as I am concerned there ought to be a law against football games in which one team outweighs the other more than ten pounds to a man, so I hasten to say that we took eighty-four points off Alfred, making three touchdowns each quarter. The Alfred boys were plenty game, but they didn't have a chance, because in every American sport but murder a good big man is always better than a good little man.

What Gilligan knew after the game was that he had the possibilities of an impregnable defense against everything but a forward passing attack. There were possibilities there, too, of a marvelous offense; for if most of your opponents are lying on their backs and looking up at the sky, why you don't need to worry much about losing ground.

The Chief sat on the bench with the squad and was greatly interested in the Alfred cheering section. Outside of the roars of our own squad, we had had no one to cheer us on.

After the game I took him for a walk around the Alfred campus. He was impressed by the buildings.

"Geez, ain't they got a plant here!" he said. "This here is quite a jernt. . . . Say, about them scholars there today with their barks and all . . . we got to have something like that if we're gonna be in this racket. I'll try to figure out some gag this week when I get back to town."

"Oh, don't bother about that, Chief," I told him. "If you get a good team and some decent publicity, you'll have plenty of following. Look at Notre Dame. In the old days they were always playing away from home and couldn't bring their own mob with them; yet whenever they played in New York they always had plenty out there pulling for them to win."

"Well, mebbe so, but we got to have our own mob next week down in Philly. That's Boo Boo Hoff's town, and I wouldn't want him to get the idea we was a bunch of pikers or no class D mob. You leave it to me. I'll figure out some gag. What else do we need beside a mob of scholars to get out there and bark?"

"Well, the big schools usually have a band, too."

"Oh, they have a band, do they? Well, I guess we can pull a connection on a band, all right. A band, eh?"

X

So I was not surprised the next Saturday when a band appeared on the field clad in puce uniforms and green shakoes. It marched out playing "The Maine Stein Song," and playing it surprisingly well for a college band. There was something vaguely familiar about the sways and wiggles of the drum major twirling his baton, but his enormous bearskin busby was so far down over his face that I couldn't make him out. Curious, I went from the press box down to where the Chief was sitting with Mike and the Councilor.

"Swell, but who's the drum major?" I asked. "I've seen him somewhere from the cut of his jib."

"Sure, you have," said the Chief. "It's Ernie Norvelle from the

Suzette, and them's the bands from all the clubs and hotels massed into one. We tried to get Paul Whiteman, but he's playing a date in Chicago. Ernie's been working out on the boys all week."

The Councilor beamed and rubbed his hands together.

"Fine like silk," he purred.

"Get a load of our scholars," said Mike, motioning over his left shoulder.

I looked into the stands behind me. There, row upon row, were fat, bland, blue-chinned faces—each with a set of large, slightly protruding horse-chestnut brown eyeballs. On each head was a soft hat with the brim turned up in front, and overhead floated Canarsie's puce and green pennants on canes. Our student body, all smoking cigars, was mostly inclined to portliness and seemed between thirty-eight and fifty years of age. Presumably many of them were old alumni. Scattered among them were many metallically pretty girls, also waving Canarsie pennants on canes. Our student body looked strangely familiar. I turned inquiringly to Mike.

"The boys wanted to come down and lay a little bet with the Philly mob," he explained, "so I made 'em all go around to Sizzbaum's and get fixed up."

Sizzbaum was the costumer who outfitted all the floor shows of our night clubs.

"I hope everything's O.K.?" Mike continued anxiously.

"And co-heds we got!" purred the Councilor.

"Yeah," said Mike. "I thought it wouldn't do no harm to give the gals the trip down for the day, so I sent them along to Sizzbaum's to get fixed up, too."

Evidently our entire entertainment staff had been enlisted to help out with our appearance in the City of Brotherly Love; for a few minutes later six masters of ceremonies appeared in sweaters and with megaphones and began calling for "a locomotive for Temple and get hot, folks!"

The gamblers removed their cigars and the girls took reefs in their gum, and the cheer was given, given with quite a respectable volume, considering our numbers and lack of practice. Mike nudged me: "Get a load of the little specialty we got between rounds," he said with a wink as the Temple stands roared back a cheer for Canarsie. The band struck up "The Maine Stein Song" again.

Temple had a good club that year, built around McNaboe, their cave-man end. McNaboe weighed 196, was five feet seven inches tall and uglier than a wrestler. He could punt seventy-five or eighty yards, drop or place kick forty-five from any angle, forward pass sixty, and when he tackled, it hurt. They used him as fullback on the offensive, and there wasn't anything he couldn't do in the way of running with the ball.

All right. We kicked off. Their left halfback ran the ball back twenty yards, for we hadn't yet learned to get down under kickoffs as fast as we should. Oolaafsen smeared an end run. On the next play, McNaboe tried an off-tackle buck. They picked him up with both hips dislocated. Don't ask me how. It just happened, that's all. And we won another ball game: 29 to 0. They couldn't stand that terrible pounding our line gave them.

The big feature of the Temple game was what Mike called the between-rounds specialty, which occurred between halves. Ernie Norvelle blew his whistle, spun his baton and the band, playing "The Maine Stein Song" paraded out on to the field and spelled out: "TAKE TEMPLE." After this pretty effect, Ernie again blew his whistle and the band started back toward our stands. Mike, very much excited, nudged me and said: "Let's scram around to the other side so we can catch this right," and led the way, with the Chief and the Councilor and the gorillas following, to a position in front of the Temple bench. I noticed a great shifting and moving among our loyal student body. The band kept pumping out "The Maine Stein Song" softly. Ernie blew his whistle and held his baton, with both hands high above his head, parallel to the ground. The music ceased in the middle of "To the gods, to the fates, to the——"

A double row of coeds, all in white dresses, stood up and formed a very fancy giant C. Ernie blew his whistle. They sat down. He blew his whistle. All the coeds crossed right knees over left and the C turned to puce. Ernie blew his whistle. The C turned to green as the coeds crossed left knees over right. It seemed that each was wearing a puce right stocking and a green left.

Ernie again blew his whistle and the afternoon sun emblazoned a giant C that kaleidoscopically shifted from puce to green to puce to green and back again scores of times, so fast that it dazzled the eyes. The effect was tremendous, and the Temple supporters seemed almost reconciled for the loss of their great McNaboe, so loudly did they cheer.

"A nifty little novelty," was the Chief's comment.

The Duke game, which we won 64 to 0, in spite of the heat, was notable only in that the entire Duke backfield was removed from the game with dislocated hips, and our new anthem, "Dear Old Canarsie o' Mine," was introduced. It was a little thing that Ernie Norvelle had worked out during the week. The tune was a waltz, and, by turns, strongly reminiscent of "When It's Moonlight in Kaluha" and "The Merry Widow." The words were:

> *Alma, Alma, Alma Mater,*
> *Every son of yours and daughter*
> *Far above Canarsie's water*
> *Looks to thee,*
> *Sweet Varsity.*
> *As underneath these stars*
> *We pledge this loyalty of ours*
> *To*
> *Oh, oh say Can-ar-sie,*
> *Old Canarsie o' mine!*

After the student body had finished singing it (and it was a little strange to observe the large number of bald pates among our undergraduates as they stood with their hats off in the Southern sun), Ernie led a double quartette of crooners from the band over in front of the Duke stands where they cooed it through little megaphones, and on the second chorus the tenors rendered it in double time with plenty of "dooden-deepum-boden-eaten" and spasmodic wagglings of the hips. It made a great hit with the Southern crowd, as, of course, did our coeds with their pretty letter effects.

Buffalo is a great sporting town and the Chief had his betting commissioners foraging through the pool parlors as early as Monday, taking all the local dough in sight, and there was plenty. Football was a kind of new gag to the Buffalo boys, at least our team was, and by playing on local pride the commissioners were able to line up plenty of even money. Our club took 112 points off Buffalo without even getting up a sweat, and the local smarten-heimers swore off football for life.

I told Ernie early in the week that every college had not only an alma mater but a special football song as well, so this is the little number he dashed off:

FIGHT-CHA

As the Puce and Green sweeps down the field
To that five-yard line;
Can we make our groaning rivals yield
To a touchdown sure this time?
You will hear Canarsie's rooters yell
For their team to do or die:
"Fight-cha, fight-cha,
They won't hoit nor bite-cha."
[Spoken] "Get in there, you mugs!"
RAH, RAH, RAH!

XI

The University of Detroit was the first tough game on our schedule, and one we had to win. The Chief doubled his flying squadron of
commissioners and sent them ahead with a roll of about 250 grand,
so it looked as though there would be a lot of dead wrestlers if we
came out on the short end. Gus Dorais, the old Notre Dame quarterback who used to throw passes to Rockne, had a big, fast team,
brilliantly coached in the Notre Dame system, seasoned and well
balanced. Brick was worried.

"We'll win if we can get some breaks," was the best he would
predict as he saw me off on the Wolverine early in the week.

It was our first attempt at big-time football, so I bore down on the
advance publicity; and as the town is very proud of the university's
team, the Detroit papers gave me a nice play. Every college football
aggregation that amounts to anything must have a zoological or
meteorological name, such as Bulldogs, Tigers, Panthers, or the
Golden Tornado, the Crimson Tide, the Maroon Monsoon. I christened our boys the Thundering Pachyderms, making rather a neat
combination of both schools, I prided myself.

Brick had scouted the Detroit club thoroughly. Their first-string
backfield, Dugan, Wachtmeister, Nalti and Joyce, was another set of
Four Horsemen; they could do anything and were lightning fast.
What's more, Dorais had two other backfields almost as good as his
first stringers that he could run in there. For fear that he would
recognize Switz as a former Notre Dame player, we changed his

name to Murphy and made him wear a nose guard so big that his own mother would have been doubtful about him.

After Brick had given the squad a long dressing-room harangue on watching out for the Detroit hidden-ball plays, and how to meet their shifts and overhead attack, the Chief, who had been sitting there listening, got up and glared around at the assemblage.

"Which is the five mugs?" he asked Brick.

"Schwulkopf, Hazos, Tossilitis, Radeswicz, Baliban, stand up," barked Brick at the line from tackle to tackle. The five monsters rose abashed.

"Listen, youse," said the Chief, putting the bad eye on them, "I want ten tackles this half from each of youse, and if I don't get 'em . . . well, it'll be just too bad, unnastand, just too bad."

Brick said, "Let's go," and the Thundering Pachyderms rushed out of the locker room, eager to die for the old Puce and Green.

Detroit won the toss and kicked. In about nine seconds they wished they hadn't, because little McGloin caught the ball on our twenty-yard line and made a touchdown. It was the damnedest thing I ever saw, although later on it became famous all over the country as the Canarsie Funnel. It seems that Brick had been working the boys at it all week.

The flying wedge was abolished in 1905, after a disastrous season in which eighteen players were killed; but what Brick uncorked that day on the first play against Detroit was nothing more or less than the old flying wedge, only executed with perfect legality. The idea was simply that as soon as the other side put a boot to the ball, big Tossilitis, our center and world's champion of the week, ran back to a few yards in front of where the ball was to come down and the whole team formed in a wedge behind him. Flanking him to the rear were the guards, Baliban the Neckless, and Hazos the Horrible, with his whiskers tucked into his headguard; back of them the tackles, Radeswicz and Schwulkopf; back of them the ends, Woola and Oolaafsen; and back of them the backs, the whole forming an enormous V, several tons in weight, that moved like a giant tank. Into the mouth of the funnel dashed little McGloin with the ball. None of the ten men touched one another, but so Gibraltar-like was their ability to keep their feet that the Detroit tacklers bounced off like food shot from guns. Oolaafsen kicked goal.

Then we kicked off to them and they ran the ball back to their forty-yard line. Right away they started to hammer the tackles with that marvelous hidden-ball play of theirs, and the first thing we knew it was their first down in mid-field. What a beautiful backfield Detroit had, and how perfectly their line functioned! Signal, shift, snapback, gain; signal, shift, snapback, gain; signal, shift, snapback, gain. Short punches, but the ball kept moving up the field. The shifts were running our wrestlers dizzy.

Brick began biting his nails when the referee signaled to the head linesman and they measured on our five-yard line. The referee blew his whistle, waved toward our goal. First down, goal to gain. Just then the quarter ended, and they started to move the ball to the other end.

As the two teams followed the officials down the field, it was easy to note the difference in morale; the Detroit players bridled and capered, eager for a score; our boys dragged slowly along with bowed heads, unresponsive to the back-slappings and pants-kickings of little McGloin.

Detroit would have had a dozen touchdowns, had it not been for the omnipresent Switz-Murphy. He plugged up holes in the line. He knifed through perfect interference and ended end runs. He dragged down off-tackle bucks, and, on our ten-yard line, he intercepted a short lob, aimed at their left end, when the Detroiter all but had his nails dug into the ball.

By this time, our line was on the ropes, and the Detroit forwards rushed through and hurried poor little McGloin so that his punt went only twenty-five yards.

I looked at Brick inquiringly, wondering why he didn't rush in some subs; but he was still at work on his nails and had got them practically down to the moons. Then the referee blew his whistle. Time out: one of our wrestlers was lying on his back.

Doc Dreen, the Chief's chiropractor and physician to the team, doubled out on the field with his little black bag, the water boy after him. It seemed that Tossilitis was hurt. Our other linemen lay on their backs exhausted. I could see Doc bending over the huge Greek. The water boy was swiftly carrying his bucket from player to player, plying his sponge.

Something queer was happening out there. Our exhausted linemen seemed suddenly electrified with energy. They had leaped up from the ground and were pounding one another on the backs and kicking one another's vast pants; they hopped up and down and several of them began shadow-boxing. When the referee blew his whistle for time in, they lined up in a flash. A miracle had happened. Doc and the water boy doubled off the field. I looked more closely at the water boy and a great light dawned; beneath the cap pulled far down over the ears I saw the long, wicked knife-lash that somebody had given the Chief in his early days. Doubtless, he had been telling the boys it would be just too bad.

And on the next play Dugan was carried off the field with his left leg broken, after a ferocious tackle by Tossilitis.

From then on, bones began snapping like popcorn. Joyce was taken out a few minutes later with a broken wrist, and it was our ball. This time McGloin didn't have to hurry to get his punt off, and the kick sailed thirty-eight yards. The ends got down under it, neck and neck, and when the Detroit safety man came to, a couple of his ribs wouldn't work.

We were out of danger, and when the whistle blew for the end of the half, Baliban, Hazos, and Tossilitis were about to put headlocks on one another in a dispute over who should get credit for the tackle which had just dislocated both of the Detroit quarterback's hips.

We made four more touchdowns the next half, two in each quarter; for the Chief crouched on the side lines in his water-boy make-up the whole time, and whenever a puce and green warrior looked his way, there he was shaking his sponge at him as though it were a pineapple. The leg drive produced by this simple gesture was enormous. Score 33-0.

XII

No sooner were we back home than Brick started to point for the Navy game by spreading anti-Navy propaganda. By the middle of the week, so many sailors, innocently walking along the streets and minding their own business, had been suddenly slugged, that Brick had to declare a three-mile limit around the Navy Yard and put Riverside drive out of bounds to the entire squad.

Tossilitis was particularly bitter, as he claimed his sister had been betrayed in Athens by a sailor during the war. That this sister's betrayer was probably some able-bodied seaman from the Dutch herring fleet, and that the approaching game was to be against American naval cadets made no difference to the world's champion of the week; sailors were sailors, whatever their nationality or rank. His sister had been betrayed and, with his left hand on his heart and his right whipping many times back and forth across his throat in simulation of a shivaree, he swore a great oath that she would be avenged.

That Saturday we went to Cleveland and played the Case School of Applied Science. Case didn't have a particularly strong team, and the Navy had beaten them 47 to 13 in the second game of the season. Well, after a few minutes of play, we marched down the field to their one-yard line and McGloin sent Switz into the heap for the scoring play. The game was such a foregone conclusion that I began to wish I had brought a good book along. There was a pile-up and then the referee's whistle. Switz had fumbled and Case had recovered on their one-yard line. Hawkes, their halfback, tried to punt from back of their goal line, but he was flattened in his tracks by practically everything on the field in a puce and green jersey. We were off to a two-point lead.

And that, to the amazement of the football world, was the score at the end of the game. The Case team fought like tigers, and got to within our ten-yard line four times, once in the second quarter, twice in the third and once in the last. We, on the other hand, seemed to have lost our leg drive after that safety at the start of the game: there were so many fumbles and incomplete forward passes that I got sick counting. McGloin, a remarkably smart field general for (so to speak) a freshman quarterback, seemed to have gone completely daffy. When it was third down on our own ten-yard line he himself tried to buck center. Another time we lost the ball to Case on our twenty-five-yard line after two straight tries at forward passes that went nowhere.

Gilligan sat on the bench chawing his nails, as usual, and making horrible faces; while the Chief, in his water-boy make-up, squatted on the side lines shaking his sponge. The entire squad was sent in the game, but we couldn't score. After the game, the Case team was carried off the field on the shoulders of their rooters, a snake dance was held and their own goal posts were pulled up in celebration of a more than moral victory.

As the game ended I turned to Mike and groaned: "Oh, those poor mugs!"

"What poor mugs?"

"Why, the team. Lake Erie's gonna be strewn with the corpses of murdered wrestlers. Can't you do something with the Chief?"

"Why, what's wrong with the Chief? It all come out like he wanted, didn't it? Two to nothin's the lowest score we could win by. Ain't that O.K.?"

"The lowest score? I don't get you."

Mike looked at me curiously.

"You don't figure angles, do you? Well, the Chief does. We play Navy next Saturday, don't we? Well, the Navy win from these here Cases 47 to 13 early in the season. Here we are, s'posed to be at the top of our form, and we look lucky to take two points off of 'em. What do you s'pose all these here football experts in the papers is gonna say about our chancet of hanging it on the Navy next Saturday?"

It began to glimmer into the old skull.

"They'll say we haven't got a chance, and the Navy will look on us as something soft."

"Sure they will, and it'll blow the odds higher'n a kite. The Chief's got guys in Washington and in the Navy yards and as far as the Pacific fleet, and on Monday as soon as all the sports sections get read, they'll start layin' out our dough. After we finish playin' the Navy next Saturday, the Chief'll have a first mortgage on all the battleships Uncle Sam owns. The Councilor has picked out the submarine fleet to throw parties in, and I got my eye on that *Akron* airship."

"And so the Chief issued orders for the team not to bear down on Case?"

"Sure. That's why he was on the side lines there, threatening to take anybody for a ride that made a touchdown. And the word was passed around to let the Cases have the ball all the time, so's it wouldn't look like we was stalling."

"God," I said, "what a man!"

"Yeah," said Mike, "he sure is. Always in there, figuring angles."

And sure enough, the sports writers doped the game just as Mike predicted. As we had played all of our games on the road with comparatively unimportant teams, none of the New York experts had seen the team play; and as Admiral Byrd himself would have a tough time finding Canarsie, none of the experts had seen us practice. So they all picked Navy.

As I said before, the only reason the Navy had given us a game was because they had had one of their periodic rows with the Army. When they canceled their annual classic with the Kaydets, they shifted Pennsylvania up to the last game of the season and substituted us in the Saturday originally scheduled for Penn. When I thought what swell people the Navy had been to deal with, and then listened to our baboons planning to give them the works, I kind of felt ashamed of myself.

Because the Navy was the classiest team on our schedule, the Chief was anxious to make as good a showing in the stands as on the field, so a chorus call was put in all the want-ad sections of the papers, and Ernie Norvelle worked for two weeks with 300 chorines in puce and green stockings, teaching them to make the giant C.

Then one night the Chief happened to drop into the Newsreel Theater, and there was a shot of the middies' cheering section at one of their games. Each midshipman had a piece of colored cardboard and went through a regular drill with it, so that the whole cheering section made those monster pictures. When the Chief saw that, he decided right away we had to have something like it ourselves.

On the morning of the day of the game four special trains were run out of the Penn Station to Baltimore: the Nick, the Greek and the Gigantic Ginsberg Specials hauled all the gamblers; the Texas Guinan Special hauled all the coeds; while the Puce and Green Special carried the squad and the board of strategy.

I figured we'd win all right, although the Navy had a swell team, big and fast, that had already beaten Princeton, Georgetown and Ohio State, all ace clubs that year; but I was sure they'd be overconfident after that Case game. And in football, when two teams are pretty evenly matched, the one that's out for blood can always hang it on an opponent looking for something soft. And were we out for blood!

However, Brick surprised me with his dressing-room talk. Instead of the usual fifteen minutes of liquid fire, he pulled the old hearts-and-flowers; and in place of that man-eating shark sneer it generally wore, his face looked like a politician's at the tomb of the Unknown Soldier. His voice got all choked up.

"Fellows," he began, and the baboons all looked at each other in amazement, "fellows, we're here on the threshold of our big chance. This is the day we do or die. Today we're fighting for the future of old Canarsie—your future, my future, the future of all of us.

"Now, the first thing I want to insist on is clean play. The Seckatary of the Navy and plenty more Washanun big shots is gonna be out there in the stands looking us over, and I don't want to see any dirty play. And that goes aspesh'ly for you linemen: no toeholds, no head locks, no dislocated hips. Do you get that, Tossilitis? No, never mind about your sister." (For the Greek had risen from his seat and begun to roll his eyes and saw his throat with his imaginary shiv.) "We want to play the Navy again next year, and if we don't show 'em plenty sportsmanship they'll cut us off their schedule. That don't mean, though, that you're not to hit *hard* when you do hit. I wanna see those *guards,* you, Hazos, and you, Baliban, swing out into that interference on those end runs and *take those tackles.* But when a Navy man is knocked cold, the man that did it, get over there and help him up. Pat him on the back and shake hands when he comes to. Remember, this is just a friendly game between two schools. . . . But lemme see lotsa *leg* drive.

"Well, fellows, our future is at stake. All Broadway, your Broadway and mine, is out there in the stands, watching you, praying for you. Your old Prexy here" (the Chief, leaning against a blackboard, glared around him) "is looking to you to win and will be *mighty disapp-oint-ed if you don't.* Mr. Dumphy, Councilor Sultsfeldt and Mr. Schatz here and I have given all our time and money, wearing ourselves to the bone, teaching you every l'il detail, to get you ready for this game. And we'll all be watching you and praying for you.

"But, fellows, never mind about old Canarsie, never mind Broadway, never mind the Prexy, never mind Mr. Dumphy or the Councilor or Mr. Schatz or I. Just listen to this."

He pulled a yellow envelope from his pocket.

"Fellows, I don't mind what Broadway would say, or the great disappointment it would mean to you and me and all of us. But just listen to this telegram I got here. It just now come and it's from my little six-year-ole girl and it says: 'Daddy, bring me back the Navy. Elsie.' 'Daddy . . . bring . . . me . . . back . . . the . . . Navy. . . .' There you see, fellows, the real reason why I don't want you to lose this game. I don't wanna break the heart of a li'l six-year-ole kiddie. Course, we can't bring her back the Navy like she says, but we can bring her back the football we'll take from the Navy, *if we win.* Can you break the heart of a li'l six-year-ole kiddie, fellows? It's for her I'm asking you. Are you gonna disappoint a li'l six-year-ole kiddie? Are you?"

There was a mighty roar of *"No!"* as the squad rose with wet eyes and rushed out of the room. I was the last to leave. I noticed that Brick had left Elsie's telegram lying on the table. I glanced at it.

"Nosegay in the fourth Belmont," was all it said.

XIII

Our band made a great hit before the game with its rendition of "The Maine Stein Song" and "Anchors Aweigh" and the spelling out of "Hahzit, Navy?" complete, with comma and question mark.

It was terrible the way we took the Navy—58 to 0. That score, I guess, is the worst they've ever been licked by since they've had a football team. McGloin caught the kickoff and was funneled over for an immediate touchdown. Not a Navy tackler laid a finger on him; and from then on it was a rout. Our plays—we had only about ten that first season—clicked perfectly almost every time; and our wrestlers tore huge holes in the Navy line and cleaned out their secondary with such regularity that a paralytic could have rolled his wheel chair through for touchdowns behind them. The Navy team seemed in a terrible daze, and the score at the end of the first half was 30 to 0.

When the whistle blew and the two teams went to their dressing rooms, the midshipmen in the stands got out their colored cardboard rectangles and started to make pictures. First they made the Stars and Stripes fluttering in the breeze. We gave them a great hand on that, and our band favored with a quick refrain of "The Maine Stein Song." Then they made a gigantic anchor. More applause and "Anchors Aweigh" from our band. Then the left half of their cheering section made an enormous puce elephant which got up on its hind legs and waved its green trunk. Our stands went crazy. Then the right half of their cheering section made a field gun out of which spurted a cloud of smoke.

As the score was then 30 to 0 in our favor, the stunt that Ernie Norvelle had worked out for our cardboard wielders seemed all the more appropriate. He blew his whistle. There was a frantic shifting and stirring. And then our rooters spelled out in colossal puce and green letters very rapidly: "NUTS, NAVY! NUTS, NAVY! NUTS, NAVY!"

An ominous growl came rumbling out of the Navy stands, but the spirit of good feeling was restored a few seconds later when our co-eds made the old puce and green C.

As usual, I was sitting next to Mike on the bench.

"I thought we'd win all right," I told him some time in the third quarter as our apes were rushing up and down the field almost unimpeded, "but I didn't figure on anything like this. I've been watching Army and Navy teams play football for years, but I never saw one that looked like that one out there. The service teams are famous for their wonderful shape, and when they hit they hit like a million dornicks. They've always got all the leg drive in the world. But those boys out there are stale, they're sluggish, and they haven't got any more leg drive than a plate of oysters. I can't figure it out."

Mike took a comb from his pocket and ran it through his curls.

"When Irish eyees are smileeeing," he sang under his breath.

"No, sir," I said, "it's a mystery to me. I don't see how that club out there ever hung it on Princeton and Georgetown."

Mike put his comb back in his pocket and winked at me.

Later, I found out that two weeks before the game a little spade waiter at the Club Whambam turned up at the Naval Academy and got a job as scullion or something in the kitchen that prepared the steaks for the football squad. Whether he did anything to that food, I don't know. All I do know is that the Navy was incredibly sluggish that afternoon against us. I got the story from the Councilor at the Club Whambam one night when he was pretty cockeyed. I know, also, that the little spade had been made headwaiter. And it was a Broadway proverb the way the Chief always took every precaution to insure his wagers.

We made four more touchdowns the next half. The way our mugs picked up the Navy boys and dusted them off after they had been knocked cold made a fine impression in the stands, and nearly all the sports writers commented on it the next day. We got a fine play, by the way, in all the New York papers; and in his Monday column in the *Sun* Grantland Rice said our line would recall to old followers of the sport the 1901-1905 point-a-minute juggernaut teams that Michigan put on the field.

After the game there was a big tea dance at the Belvedere Hotel in Baltimore, and eighteen of our coeds became engaged to midshipmen. What the Councilor did when he got full of that Maryland rye was plenty, too.

Brick pulled a fast one in the St. Mary's game. St. Mary's had a corking team which had come to New York earlier in the season and licked a fine Fordham eleven 28 to 12; but Brick figured he could beat them if all the odds were even. When an Eastern team goes out to the Coast for a game it has not only got a rival to lick but the change of climate as well.

So when the squad got back to town that night from Baltimore they were rushed right off the train to the hot room of the Turkish bath at the Argonne. The bath was cleared of customers, and the squad was put right to bed. The next day they were made to run through signals there; the day after that, all bundled up in sweaters and blankets, they were taxied in limousines to the Grand Central Terminal, where three specially heated Pullmans on the Twentieth Century were ready for the word. Every member of the squad had an electric hot water bottle and extra blankets in his berth. Did those mugs sweat!

But when the train reached San Francisco, and they got out in the air, they were shivering. And sore! They took it out on St. Mary's. Bones snapped like garters on a Coney Island Saturday night, and there seemed a never ending procession of stretcher bearers interrupting the game. We won 46 to 0. It was the worst any Coast outfit had ever been beaten by an Eastern team since the war. All the New York papers sent staff men to cover the game, and there were play-by-play accounts in the late editions the same afternoon.

As a special treat for our undefeated, unscored-upon gladiators, the Chief threw a banquet at the St. Francis Hotel that night at which everybody down to the lowest sub made a speech. Brick talked of next year and spring training; Mike sang "Mother Machree"; while the Councilor brought tears to all eyes by his disquisition on "Football as a Character Builder." After the banquet he spent the rest of the night hunting for the Barbary Coast.

Altogether, it was a wonderful season for a first year. We had beaten the pants off three major teams and scored 426 points. Nobody had been able to cross our goal line or even score a safety against us. To be sure, 426 points weren't as many as those Michigan juggernaut teams used to run up. For five consecutive years they averaged 526 points a season. But they used to play ten- and eleven-game schedules, while we had played only eight.

Of course, blocking is the quintessence of winning football. And our wrestlers, with their tremendous strength and specialized knowledge of how to throw an opponent off his balance or on his back and even dislocate or break his bones, made probably the best linemen that ever played football. And the boxers, with their speed and wonderful sense of co-ordination, became excellent ball carriers. Of course, their defensive play, especially against a forward passing attack, was crude that first season. But whenever an opponent successfully executed a forward pass, the successful executants—the back who passed and the end who caught the ball—would be out of the game after the next play with dislocated hips, and there would be no more of *that* nonsense for a while.

But the actual end of the season was not yet. One night two weeks after the St. Mary's game I was at the Chief's suite when Mike and the Councilor came in. The Councilor was carrying a brief case.

"O.K.," said the Chief, glancing at the brief case.

He led the way into an adjoining room. The Councilor opened the brief case. And there on the bed before my goggling eyes were counted out one million, one hundred dollars in $5,000, $1,000 and $100 bills, and the whole was cut up 50-25-25.

The Chief counted his cut once more, opened a little wall safe behind an oil painting, tossed the hippo-choking roll in, twirled the knob, and carefully set the picture straight.

"This here education is gonna be all right," he said. His face was very serious.

XIV

As soon as spring came Brick had the whole squad out plus about twenty young fighters who had turned pro that winter and a couple of dozen young wrestlers. The new arrivals he herded off into a freshman squad and began to break them in on fundamentals. Last season's players were drilled in kicking and passing.

Brick realized he'd have to teach his team something to vary the bone-crushing, slaughter-house game that came to them so naturally. If he could develop a skillful, spectacular forward passing attack, it would be a better draw at the gate, and something had to be done to cut down the terrible casualty lists we had left in our wake the first season, or the sports writers and the Rules Committee and the various college athletic authorities might get suspicious and mark us for lousy, as the boys say; that is, refuse to give us a game, and then we'd have to play the barber colleges or the Alexander Hamilton Institute.

So all that spring and summer, Brick had the squad catching and throwing passes. He taught the boys to grab the ball with their arms relaxed from the elbows down and their fingers limp; and he taught the passers to throw a few yards ahead of the receivers away to hell and gone down the field. Brick didn't believe in short, flat passes: what he liked were the ones that looked as though they came out of the Boche 70-mile gun and flew right over the heads of the secondary defense into the paws of some galloping end or half.

Those were the plays that made the turnstiles click, so we concentrated on them. By the time fall came around every member of the squad, even Tossilitis, could collar a forty- or fifty-yard pass almost behind his back.

Then he concentrated on kicking. In the spring the Chief sent over to France and imported three *savate* fighters, Cocluche, Plon and Moustiquaire, figuring they ought to make great kickers. You know, the *savate* fighters do all their boxing with their feet. Well, the Chief's hunch was O.K.: they turned into swell kickers right off, averaging sixty and seventy yards each and Moustiquaire could sometimes stretch his punts to eighty, but they were all such little guys that they were broken to pieces before the first week's scrimmaging was over and had to be shipped back to Paris. Anyway, they weren't needed, as Brick had developed both Switz and Flanahan, a left-footer, into a pair of fine punters by the time the season started.

Then the Chief decided that this season our opponents should be allowed to do some scoring, as it would make the games more exciting and benefit the gate. So it was agreed that every time one of the opponents threw a pass of fifteen yards or more he should be allowed to complete it (providing, of course, that it was not muffed or grounded) and we were ahead far enough so that a touchdown wouldn't matter.

This system led to almost uniform results. The Thundering Pachyderms would go to work and run up about four touchdowns in the first half. We still used the Canarsie Funnel, as it was a sure-fire gag to bring the customers to their feet; but after a while rival coaches warned their captains not to kick off to us if they won the toss, so we couldn't start the game with it unless the coin spun our way. (If we had made our four touchdowns in the first half, we didn't use it if it was our turn to receive.) Then, in the second quarter, we'd let our opponents run the ball up to mid-field, if we had kicked to them, or purposely fumble the ball, if it were ours, and let them recover.

On or about the fifty-yard line, however, we'd turn into a stone wall, so that they'd be forced to open up and start passing. Then we'd let them make about three touchdowns and all the customers went home with a warm glow, each satisfied that he'd got his money's worth.

I'd done a lot of traveling that winter and we had a fine schedule. Whenever a school didn't have a stadium of its own or wasn't in a big city where a good gate would be assured, we used the nearest big-league ball park. That New Year's Day we played Southern California in the Rose Bowl at Pasadena before 80,000, beat them 28 to 21 and won the Erskine trophy, emblematic of the National Intercollegiate Football Championship.

These were the scores of that second season:

Canarsie 28—Washington and Jefferson 21 (Polo Grounds)
Canarsie 28—Pittsburgh 21 (Forbes Field)
Canarsie 28—Colgate 20 (Yankee Stadium)
Canarsie 28—Michigan 26 (Ann Arbor)
Canarsie 28—Ohio State 18 (Columbus, O.)
Canarsie 28—Missouri 21 (Columbus, Mo.)
Canarsie 28—Navy 21 (Baltimore)
Canarsie 28—Army 21 (Polo Grounds)
Canarsie 28—Southern California 21 (Pasadena)

Some time in the middle of January we gathered around the Chief's bed, and on this occasion the roll they cut totaled $1,900,000, including gambling returns, or as the Chief put it: "With tips and all."

That winter and spring passed pretty uneventfully. There were the usual murders, but nothing outside the routine killings that always come along. Legs Diamond was shot for the eleventh time as thousands yawned. Professional boxing and wrestling were virtually nonexistent; but nobody seemed to notice. The only fights of any account that year were the finals in Paul Gallico's Golden Gloves Tournament, which were postponed until the summer and moved out to the Yankee Stadium and substituted for the usual Milk Fund Heavyweight Battle of the Century. Everyone was more pleased, including the Milk Fund.

The Councilor was doing a good deal of lushing. Most of his days were spent in his rooms, snoring off hangovers; at night he teetered about more or less in the gauze. It was certainly a break that there were no big cases up just then that required his personal attention, cases that couldn't be taken care of by his assistants—say the trial of some important member of the mob for murder—because there was no telling what might have happened. The guy was so irresistible to any dozen mugs he ever faced in a jury box. If he'd had a case, he probably would have pleaded with them to send his client to the electric chair. And it would have been curtains for the client, all right, if the Councilor had asked for it.

A funny thing happened that summer. The Chief had opened up a new joint, the 'Varsity Inn, on part of the take from that second season. It was decorated with more college seals than there are in the gents' only at the Paramount Theater and became a great hangout for gamblers and hustlers of all kinds. One day a big strapping apple-knocker with a straw suitcase came in and asked the bartender if he could direct him to Canarsie University. He said he was from some high school out in the sticks and wanted to enroll as a student. Mike, who happened to be there at the time, gave the bartender the office, and the apple-knocker was told to take the subway. All summer long kids kept coming to the joint, wanting to know how to get to Canarsie. They'd looked in the telephone books and asked the Travelers' Aid, but although everyone had heard of the place, nobody had actually *been* there. We just told them to take the subway. Nothing was ever heard of them again. They're probably still wandering around, lost in that vast labyrinth.

I had arranged a great schedule for the coming season. Not only did we have games with the Army and Navy again and Notre Dame and Leland Stanford, but we were taking on Princeton, Yale and Harvard in the order named, merely for tune-ups at the start. We weren't going to wind up the season on the Coast again, but instead we were to finish off at Soldier Field in Chicago with Lake Shore Tech, a new school that had had a fine first season the year before. They were so anxious to get a game with us that they guaranteed us seven-tenths of the gate. Obviously they wanted to play us for the prestige.

The Chief jumped at the chance, as our troupe had never played Chicago; and ever since that Tunney-Dempsey fight back in '27 it had been his ambition to count the house there some day. The stadium was then still the largest in the country. So I wrote the Lake Shore graduate manager that we should be delighted.

The Councilor kept right on lushing. I was stopped one night at Forty-first Street and Seventh Avenue by a letter carrier who told me I'd better come along with him. We went over to the other side of Eighth, and he led the way up some stairs to a door and rang a bell. A peephole opened and he said: "O.K., Jerry."

It was one of those little neighborhood joints that smelled of yesterday's beer and had a bowl of cole slaw on the free-lunch counter. The cole slaw changed three colors if you forked it around a little. A knot of taxi drivers and laborers in shirt sleeves was gathered at one end of the bar. At the other was the Councilor. He was shaking his finger at his reflection in the mirror. It made your flesh creep as he began trying to break the reflection down, just as though it were a prosecution witness in a trial. Every now and then he would turn to the terrified bartender and speak to him as though he were the judge.

"You'll be open with me, won't you?" he said to himself with a horrible sneer on those thick lips. "Now, what do you do for a living, Mr. Julheim? Oh, a tailor, eh? A tailor. You don't mean a pants-presser, do you? No, never mind that, answer yes or no. Yes, you're just a pants-presser, aren't you? Not a tailor at all, are you? Isn't it a fact, Mr. Julheim, that you couldn't sew a button on, and as for a lapel—you'd be *lost, wouldn't you?* Answer yes or no. You would, wouldn't you? Yes, you're really not a tailor at all, are you—just a pants-presser."

"Geez, Mac, take it easy," pleaded the bartender.

"All right, Your Honor, I'm just attacking the credibility of the witness. Very well, Your Honor, we respectfully except. . . . Now, Mr. Julheim, you say the defendant's face was white when you saw him come out of the room. You testified before Magistrate Wilson that his face was as white as a collar, didn't you? Well, did you or didn't you? Yes, you did. Well, was it *this white?*"

And the Councilor ripped off his starched collar and shook it at his reflection in the mirror. His big brown eyeballs rolled. *"Here's a collar! Was it this white? Was his face as white as this?"*

The postman and I led him out brandishing the ripped-off collar and jabbering about subornation of perjury. We finally got him back to the Argonne and in bed. The house physician gave him a stab.

It seemed the Councilor was cracking up.

XV

The Chief, after looking over the team at the end of the summer workout and seeing what superb form it was in, decided on a new plan of strategy for the third season.

As I said before, during our second season we allowed our opponents to score three touchdowns in the last half after we had scored four in the first.

For the third season, the Chief thought it would improve showmanship if we allowed the other teams to score four touchdowns in the first half; and then we'd get in there and score five in the second. It is always more thrilling when a team comes from behind and wins out, especially if it is from 24 to 28 points behind. And it turned out to be a great gag. In addition, the system had wonderful gambling possibilities: between halves, with the score four touchdowns to nothing against us, the betting commissioners could get wonderful odds.

We opened the season with Princeton at the Palmer Memorial Stadium and took them 35 to 27, coming from behind in the last thirty seconds on a long pass, Switz to Woola. The following Saturday we beat the Elis in the Bowl 35 to 28. The next week Harvard fell 28 to 19. The score was lower than usual because the Crimson suffered from a bad epidemic of fumbling in the first half and couldn't score four touchdowns, no matter how hard we tried. Then we cleaned the Army (35 to 27) and the Navy (35 to 26).

Brick was taking no chances with Notre Dame, however, and we opened up with the old Canarsie Funnel right at the kickoff and ran up five touchdowns in the first half. Hunk Anderson had an unusually weak team that year, and they were able to score only a field goal. But what a field goal: a tremendous long boot from the sixty-one-yard line and worthy of the immortal Gipp! Switz did not make the trip to South Bend.

On the next three Saturdays we restored the virility of the effete East by toying with Leland Stanford (35 to 0), Southern California (35 to 0) and Oregon (35 to 0) before vast crowds in the Yankee Stadium. The Chief figured that plenty of Eastern fans would be willing to pay dough to see some of those Coast teams take a good shellacking, for a change. And he was right.

The Sunday after we hung it on Oregon, Brick and I were at the

Chief's waiting for Mike, who had gone to Chicago to scout the Lake Shore-Nebraska game. The Chief was in his big chair. Voine, black-lace-pajamaed, was sitting on the arm. One of those goofy dolls with the squiggly legs she held snuggled up to her. Every now and then she would make a pass at the Chief, and he would duck and spar her off as though she were some kind of fly. He was discussing the future.

"I been figuring," he was saying, "if there ain't some way to make a buck out of these other college sports. It strikes me there ought to be something in this here basketball for us. I figure there is if we could get a big enough house, say if we could fill up the Garden oncet a week. They tell me basketball ain't made a dime since the rules was drawed up. Maybe, if we put on a swell floor show in between halves, or had a dance afterwards with plenty of our dames mixing in the crowd."

"Oo naughty sing," purred Voine, trying to muss his hair. "Oo wet dose dirls awone. Don't be finkin' about 'em so muts."

The Chief gave her a look and parried with his left. He pulled out his watch.

"What's keeping Mike?" he said. "He ought to show any minute now. It's ten after eight. The big loogan musta stopped somewheres to grab a few shots. Well, anyways, I'm trying to figure some new angles on this education racket. Basketball maybe, if the public will go for a side show. Hockey's all sewed up by the pros, and ain't no good anyways. College baseball's a laugh. There might be something to this foot racing, if you didn't have to cut the gate with so many people. When one school runs another, there ain't anybody there but the towel-holders. When there's a big meet you got to cut the gate fifty ways. Now this rowing, maybe if you could fence off a couple miles of the Hudson on both sides——"

The ring of the door buzzer by the gorilla outside cut into this discourse. Voine got up and got a cigarette off the ebony table.

"There's Mike now," said the Chief. "Let him in, Kid."

Without bothering to ask over the phone who it was I opened the door.

On the threshold, swaying slightly, stood the Councilor. He was stiff as a plank. There was a wide smile on his face. On his arm, Fanny McGloin, presumably just back from her world tour.

"S'prise, s'prise!" the Councilor muttered.

Fanny took four steps into the room and then paused, unable to make up her mind whether to go to work on the Chief or Voine. Finally, she chose Voine, but during that brief pause Brick and I rushed and held her.

"I knew it'd be like this," she screamed, struggling fiercely. "I knew I'd find that trollop here! Lemme at her till I pull that yeller mop offen her ugly head! Lemme at her!"

Voine had backed up against the table, frozen.

"Willya listen, Fanny," pleaded the Chief, "willya listen!"

Then she tractored her fingernails down my cheek as she tried to get at *him*.

"And as for *you,* you doidy bum, you," she squalled, "wait till I get my hands on you! You doidy bum, you! You come outa the gutter and that's where you belong, you doidy bum, you! I'll give you night goils, you doidy beast!"

She stopped her struggling for a little to catch her breath. Then she tried to spit on Voine. Women are lousy spitters. Suddenly Mike was in the room.

"Why, hahzit, Fanneee!" he roared, coming over to her and forcibly taking her hand and pumping it up and down. "Hahzit, bebee! Geez, it's great to see you. Whenja get in? How ya doin' in there, palleee?"

"You get outa my way, Mike Dumphy," Fanny yelled. "Lemme at that doidy bum. Him and that thing of his. I'll give 'em a honeymoon. Lemme at 'em!"

Mike was pumping her hand up and down and patting her shoulder.

"Why, there ain't nothin' wrong, is there, bebee?" he bellowed. "You ain't sore at the tomato here, are ya? Why, this here's Voine, my gal. I'm just after comin' up here to fetch her. I been outa town, same as you have, and she got lonesome and come upstairs here to wait for me, didn'ya, bebee?"

He shot a tremendous burlesque-show wink at Voine, who rallied and managed to nod her head up and down, like a counting horse.

"Nobody got a girl frien' for me?" the Councilor put in thickly.

Mike went right on roaring.

"Did you think Voine was Frankie's tomato, Fanny? Geez, that's a laugh, ain't it, Voine? Why, Voine's my little gal, ain't you, bebee? You got Voine all wrong, Fanny. Why, say, if I caught a mug like Frankie McGloin foolin' with Voine I'd punch him right in the nose, wouldn't I, Voine? I'm levelin', Fanny, honest to God. Ain't that the truth, boys? Well, Fanny, it's great to see you again. I know you got plenty to talk over with Frankie about your wonderful trip and all, so I'll say good night. We better scram, boys, and let the happy pair get together."

He walked over to Voine, grabbed a couple of arms and hands full of her, and gave her a long noisy kiss that ended with a bang.

"Glad to see me, bebee? Was you a good gal while I was out in Chi?"

Brick and I had let go of Fanny. She was looking at Mike and Voine with everything she had. Mike went into his act harder than ever, and used everything but a knife and fork on his partner.

"How'd you make out in Chicago?" asked Brick.

"O.K.," said Mike, pausing a moment. "Come on downstairs, bebee," he said to Voine, "I brought you a present."

He started for the door with her under his arm. She was afraid to look back at the Chief, for fear Fanny would see.

"What's the payoff on Lake Shore?" Brick yelled to him.

He stopped on the threshold and turned around.

"Geez, that's a pip," he said, and went into a loud laugh. The Councilor started to laugh, and we were all in such a state that we laughed, too. The Chief laughed and even Fanny smiled. It sounded crazy as hell.

"Yes, sir, that's a pip," said Mike. *The jernt belongs to Capone! Well, good night, all.*"

He dragged Voine out with him.

It was like a quick first-act curtain.

XVI

There was a large solid block of gray-blue almost exactly in the middle of the Capone stands which I was trying to determine the cause of. Mike, beside me in our box on the fifty-yard line, had brought a pair of binoculars, the kind the bookies carry at the tracks.

"Take a squint through your glasses, Mike, at those people over there. It looks like a bunch of French soldiers."

With great gravity Mike raised the binoculars to his eyes and adjusted the micrometer screw. He chuckled softly.

"It looks from here like they was mail carriers," he said. "Must

be the boys from the Postal Workers' Union givin' their dogs a holiday."

"Aha, mail carriers!"

"Yeah, that's what it looks like from here they was. Must be havin'
a convention or sumpen. And the little Doctor heard about it and
sent 'em all to the ball game. That guy always did have a yen for the
U.S. mail."

He passed me the glasses.

"Yeah, they're mail carriers, all right. But it doesn't look as though
they were here on any outing. They all seem to have brought their
leather bags along, and the bags look full."

"Mebbe they got sumpen for somebody. Get a load of the little
Doctor."

The Chief was standing on his iron chair, carefully counting the
house of 110,000, trying on his fingers to deduct the nonpaying
customers from the paying.

There was a roar from the Capone side of the field as a long
stream of black-helmeted, black-jerseyed, black-panted, black-hosed,
black-booted players, most of them of swarthy complexion, flowed
out onto the field from a tunnel under the stands, divided up into four
teams and began running through signals. Their band struck up "Gio-
vanezza, Primavera." But a moment later there were four puce and
green teams on the field and our band was blaring the buttons off its
instruments in a counterrendition of "Old Canarsie o' Mine."

You could smell the stink of trouble beginning to spread as soon
as those bands started to out-umpah each other. And matters weren't
helped when the Lake Shore band spelled out: "Kill Kanarsie" in
the middle of the field a few minutes later. Immediately after they
had finished, Ernie Norvelle blew his whistle and our band came
back with a bit of clever repartee: "Louse Up Lake Shore."

Our rivals had worked out a novel variation of the old skyrocket:
instead of giving the long whistle rising to a crescendo and the conventional *Boom!—aaaaah!,* their rooters, teeth clenched and eyeballs
wild, would slowly swell from their seats with horrible cries—half
hiss, half growl—saw their necks with imaginary stilettos, à la Tossilitis, and then point to our stands with wild yells of: "Canarsie, Canarsie, *tutti, tutti, tutti!*"

Such black curses would have jelled our blood had not the ingeni-
ous Ernie devised a sure means of passing them off lightly by pluck-
ing from the band half a dozen double bass tuba players and forming

them into a battery which greeted every massed Sicilian imprecation with prehistoric birds.

The two captains were in the center of the field. The referee spun a coin. Switz won the toss and chose to kick with the wind. Oolaafsen teed the ball; the team ranged itself on either side of him along our thirty-five-yard line; a whistle beeped; there was a dull thump. The ball flew in a beautiful high parabola straight to the arms of the Lake Shore quarterback.

Imagine our dismay when he ran ninety-five yards for a touchdown behind a perfectly executed Canarsie Funnel!

They kicked goal.

But then we received, and little McGloin was funneled a hundred yards just as perfectly for a touchdown in return, and Oolaafsen tied the score by putting the ball straight between the posts.

This time, after a huddle in which apparently Oolaafsen was instructed not to kick to the Capone backs, the ball went to their left tackle on their thirty-yard line and he was down before he had run three steps.

Lake Shore opened with a wide end run around Oolaafsen, which he smeared; but before the next play began Tossilitis, world's champion of the week three years ago, was removed from the game with a pair of dislocated hips. A little later, Hazos the Horrible was similarly afflicted and had to be hauled off.

Mike whistled.

"The Capone mob always was famous for stealin' the other guys' stuff, but I never expected nothin' like this. Well, I ain't surprised. They got the whole Pacific Coast troupe of wrasslers on their club, and all the fighters around this here section. It's a laugh on the little Doctor, at that. He give Gilligan orders before the game, to hell with the customers, but give them Capones the woiks. You know, plenty of that old slugaroo, like we done the foist season. It's all on account the way he hates Capone. Capone ain't a bad guy, but the little Doctor's been after him ever since he got outa Levingwoith. He clipped the Doc in a deal. So he orders the woiks from Gilligan, and here they are lettin' us have it. Ain't that a laugh?"

But just then Lake Shore punted, and on the next play we put their left tackle out of the game with a broken instep. Two plays after that the casualty list was neck and neck. The Chief leaned over to Mike. His eyes were on fire:

"Mike!" he yelled, cupping his mouth with a hand, for the Canarsie cheering section was roaring delightedly as the body of our enemy was borne from the field, "scram down to Gilligan and tell him to take all them fighters outa that game and put nothin' but wrasslers in there 'til I tell him to stop. And tell him to make them wrasslers plenty big and tough. And tell him to tell them mugs to get in there and give them Capone guinzos the woiks or I'll be down and cut their heads off. Tell 'em no holds barred. Now, scram."

"O.K., Frankie," and Mike had disappeared.

So that was why, when the half ended, twenty-nine of our baboons and thirty of theirs (we put two out on the last play) had been dragged wounded from the field. Stretcher bearers on both sides certainly earned their pay that day. And that was why the football that first half, after what the Chief ordered, was not very interesting to watch. For with 300-pound wrestlers carrying the ball and directing the field generalship (Lake Shore had quickly followed our lead in bringing out the mastodons) the ball remained almost stationary in the middle of the field. At the whistle the score was still 7 to 7.

We all went down to the dressing room between halves, so I don't know what unpleasantnesses took place in the stadium or how the cops kept the rival factions from climbing out of the stands and going to work on each other.

There was enough unpleasantness in our dressing room, filled as it was with stretchers of the groaning. Doc Dreen and a corps of trainers, rubbers and towel-swingers were rushing about ministering to the patients. It was like a base hospital after a heavy bombardment at the Western front.

"Get all these mugs outa here and on the train," was the Chief's first command.

Brick was standing in a corner, pale and shaky.

"How we fixed?" The Chief looked him over with a hard eye.

"God, Chief, I, uh, we're running outa wrasslers. That's hell on 'em out there."

"Nuts!"

It was the old Wiper war cry. You could feel the voltage in the voice.

"All youse mugs 'at's in shape, c'mere."

He swept the quick and the able with those terrible eyes as he began panthering up and down, his hands folded behind him.

"Now listen, youse. Foist of all, the fighters goes back in this half.

Switz! Flanahan! Cello! McGloin! And you Oolaaf, you big screwy Swede, and you, Woola! We're gonna pass 'em to death, see, pass 'em to death, right from the bell, see? And youse mugs inna line, give 'em plenty protection, see, or *it'll be jest too bad.* And 'at goes for youse ends and backs, too, see. The mug 'at muffs a pass or heaves one wild—well, *it'll be jest too—*"

The Chief broke off, scrambled to the top of a locker and clawed at a tiny wire cleated to the wall. There was a ripping and a banging of metal against metal, and then, up over the locker's top, he reeled in a little japanned box that looked like the bottom part of an electric bell.

"A dictygraph, hey, the doity, double-crossin' grease-ball rats! Well, let 'em get a load of it."

He began screaming frantically into the little box.

"Nuts! Nuts! Nuts! And 'at goes for you, too, Capone, you big guinzo grease-ball! This here's McGloin speakin'. Yeah, Knucks Mc-Gloin, you big Bohunk, you! And get this——"

Mike touched him on the arm and pointed to the broken-off end of the dictograph wire lying on the floor.

Brick looked at his stop watch and said in a weak voice that it was time to return to the field.

They kicked off to us, but a Canarsie Funnel failed to put the ball back farther than the middle of the field. We just didn't have the wrestlers for it. On the first play Switz whipped a short pass to Mc-Gloin which gained eight yards. Another to Woola brought us six more and first down. A long heave to Flanahan was batted down by a Lake Shore halfback. Then McGloin tossed a short one to Cello that was good for nine. By way of variation, Switz went off tackle for three, and it was first down again. Switz lobbed another to McGloin for seven.

Half a dozen consecutive plays without a single casualty! Evidently, they, too, were running out of wrestlers.

Switz cocked his arm and threw one a mile down the field to Oolaafsen, who caught it and had started for a touchdown with a clear field when two Lake Shore backs hit him at once—and he fumbled.

Up in the box we had to hold the Chief to keep him from climbing right out onto the field and cutting that Swede's head off.

Lake Shore got off a beautiful punt to our twenty-yard line, and their ends nailed McGloin as soon as he touched the ball. The kick had come down near a side line, so on the first play McGloin ran himself straight across to the center of the field.

Switz was back with his arms outstretched, the ball was snapped, he cocked his arm, and there, clear, away down the field was Woola, good old basketball Woola, who could catch anything that stayed in the park. A sure touchdown!

And then, suddenly, like a wild goose shot in mid-flight, the ball stopped dead in its arc and dropped straight to the ground, right smack on the fifty-yard line. It was as though it had struck an invisible wire. But when it hit the ground it neither bounced nor bobbed, just parked where it landed, like a coffee cake.

White-knickered officials and players had run up to it. There was much arm-waving. Mike was gazing through his binoculars.

"It's Switz," he said. "Switz has got it in his hands. He's stickin' his fingers right through it."

"Through what, you muzzler?"

"Right through the ball. They's a hole in it big enough to jump through."

The Chief's curses could be heard clearly above the roar of the crowd.

"We been jobbed!" he roared, ripping off his hat and tearing his hair. "Them lousy wops shot it down. They put it onna spot. It was inna bag for a touchdown and they put it onna spot. Oh, them lousy wop grease-balls!"

Down on the field the white-knickered puppets were fluttering rule books. Evidently they found no provision for assassinated footballs; for, after a great deal of argument they procured another from the side lines and the referee marched with it back to our twenty-yard line. "Second down. Ten yards to gain. Incompleted forward pass," announced the scoreboard.

Lake Shore cheers were equaled by our boos.

"Maxim silencer?" I asked Mike, remembering there had been no report when the ball pancaked.

"Sure," he said. He was sweeping the Capone stands with the binoculars.

"Lookit! There's the mug done it. There, see? Right where I'm pointing at."

He handed me the glasses and, sure enough, in the top row about the center of the stands I saw a tall, slender man, dark and mustached, with a rifle to his shoulder at the ready. The rifle had a tele-scopic sight, I noticed. The dark sharpshooter turned to make some remark to a man beside him and when he smiled I noticed he had beautiful even teeth. Over the muzzle of the rifle was a pear-shaped silencer.

Three consecutive short passes brought the ball from our twenty-yard line to the middle of the field. Switz tossed a beauty to Oolaaf-sen for twenty more.

Then the dark sharpshooter spoiled another sure touchdown when he murdered a long pass just before it reached Flanahan standing well over the goal line. It was a beautiful heave and a beautiful shot. After a terrific squabble, the referee ruled that the ball had grounded over the goal line, and therefore it was a touchback and Lake Shore's ball on their twenty-five-yard line.

The Chief was fit to be tied, and I remember wondering why blue flames were not pouring from his palpitating noseholes.

"Mike," he bellowed, "go over there to that mob and tell them Capones, them bohunk so-and-so's, that if they don't lay off they get the woiks, see, the woiks!"

Mike looked at him curiously for a second, patted the armpit hol-ster under his breast pocket, laughed, handed me the binoculars and departed, singing softly:

" 'Tis the most distressful country that I have ever seen."

Lake Shore punted immediately, long and high, and little McGloin was again flattened by their ends on our twenty-yard line.

Once more three short flat passes brought us to the middle of the field.

I trained the glasses on the dark sharpshooter and caught him in the act of changing the rifle with a telescopic sight for what appeared to be a double-barreled shotgun.

Switz had cocked his arm. There was Woola loose again and run-ning as though all the fiends of hell were chasing him. And there went the ball after him as though all the fiends of hell were in its leather casing.

I saw the dark sharpshooter aim, and I saw the fingers of his right hand contract as though he were slowly squeezing a sponge.

The ball in mid-flight had suddenly vanished. He had scored a direct hit with both barrels!

I turned in horror to look at the Chief. He had disappeared.

After much puzzled gazing up into the sky, followed by a molten debate between the rival captains, the officials decided to penalize us for unsportsmanlike conduct in having concealed the ball.

Our winded warriors lay on their backs panting, while the referee with the new pigskin under his arm began pacing off the fifteen-yard penalty. The Lake Shore team was drawn up in a huddle.

Suddenly, a dumpy figure in an old black sweater and battered cap darted out from our bench onto the field with a water bucket. Instead, however, of making for the spent forces of old Canarsie he hared straight for the huddle. A few paces from it, he groped in his bucket for his sponge, found it, seemed to give it a squeeze and then tossed it straight in the hub of the human wheel.

There was a flash, and a terrific explosion went echoing through the stadium. The little water carrier was tearing back toward our bench. It was the Chief.

"Scraaaam! Scraaaam!" he screamed, waving the bucket he was still holding by the handle. "Scraaaam!"

The field was strewn with black-helmeted heads, black-jerseyed torsos, black-hosed legs.

Another moment and the Capone machine guns had opened on the puce and green figures on the field which had suddenly sat up when the bomb went off. One after another they all lay down again.

Then the block of blue figures in the middle of the Lake Shore stands rose as one man and began to bomb all points of the compass.

The crowd stampeded.

XVII

Don't ask me how I ever got out of that thing alive. Somehow I did, but just how I couldn't tell you. I remember being carried all the way out of the stands to the ground without once putting a foot down. I remember the dames screaming and the yells of the wounded and I remember the furious ringing of ambulance bells and the bombs roaring and the machine guns rattling away like riveting hammers. I remember the cops losing their heads and starting to club anybody they could reach. One big bull reached over and caught me one on the head with his billy and I went out like a light.

When I came to I was standing outside the stadium, wondering how I got there and supposing I had been sardined out in the crowd.

The Chief was standing in front of me. He was drenched with sweat and dirt, and most of the old sweater and shirt were torn off, and the peak of his cap was around 'way to one side. He was helping two letter carriers load some big canvas sacks into a black car with the curtains up. The Councilor was parked in the back seat.

"Hahzit, Kid?" he said. "You O.K.? We're just after kicking in the main box office. This here's the gate. I'm taking it on the lam to Dee-troit 'til this blows over. Tell the boys I'm O.K. and I'll be back in about a month."

He opened a back door of the car and put a foot on the running board.

"Listen," he said, "it looks like Canarsie University was all washed up for a while. Did you know they got Mike, them lousy Bohunks?"

"They did? God, that's terrible."

"We'll see 'em for it. Tell the mob I'm O.K."

"Sure, Chief. Geez, I'm sorry about poor old Mike."

"Yeah, 'at was tough. Tell Voine I'll drop her a card. All set, boys?"

"O.K., Chief," said one of the gorillas as the last of the day's gross proceeds were swung into the tonneau over the Councilor's feet. "You wanna drive?"

"Yeah, I'll drive," said the Chief, climbing in behind the steering wheel. "We ain't got room for you, Kid. Tell you what you do. Ed Grogan is just leaving over there, look, by that ambulance. See where I'm pointing at? Scram over there, now, and he'll give you a lift. So long, Kid. Hurry up, now."

I started to run over to where the Grogan car was just starting, waving over my shoulder to the Chief.

He stepped on the starter. There was a flash and a terrible explosion. Some of the heavy metal work of the car came down, but they never found a button of the Chief or the Councilor or the letter carriers. The Capones had fastened an extra-special bomb on the starting mechanism of the car. An old gag, but effective. So that's why Canarsie University hasn't had a team in the field for the last couple of seasons.

THE HAUNTED MAJOR

---

by ROBERT MARSHALL

(1902)

The Haunted Major *is one of those unpresuming books which pilgrims visiting St. Andrews and other Scottish golf towns find slumbering on the shelves of small bookstores and stationers' shops along with other locally produced books and pamphlets on such subjects as clan tartans, the outstanding ruins of the area, and how to prepare and cook haggis. It is what the movie people call a "sleeper"—an unheralded piece of work of markedly superior quality: the very funny story of Major Jacky Gore, self-admittedly "the finest sportsman living."* Completely unknown in the United States, The Haunted Major *apparently has been discovered by decade after decade of British readers, for inside our copy the date of each previous edition is listed and it bespeaks a really remarkable vitality: 1902; 1912; 1932; 1937; 1940; 1951.*

I: ABOUT MYSELF

I AM a popular man and withal I am not vain.

To the people who know me I am an acquaintance of importance. This is due to a combination of circumstances.

First of all, I am a youthful (aged thirty-five) major in that smart cavalry regiment, the 1st Royal Light Hussars, commonly called the "Chestnuts."

Secondly, I am an excellent polo player, standing practically at the top of that particular tree of sport; and again, I am a quite unusually brilliant cricketer. That I do not play in first-class cricket is due to long service abroad with my regiment; but now that we are at last quartered in England, I daily expect to be approached by the committee of my county eleven.

I consider myself, not before taking the opinion of my warmest friends, the best racket player of my day in India; and I have rarely played football (Rugby) without knowing by a strange instinct (born, I feel sure, of truth) that I was the best man on the ground.

In the hunting field I am well known as one of the hardest riders across country living; and this statement, so far from being my own, emanates from my father's land agent, a poor relative of ours, and himself a fair performer in the saddle. As a shot, I will refer you to my own game book; and if, after examining the records contained therein, you can show me an equally proficient man in that special line, well—I'll take off my hat to him.

The trophies of head, horn, and skin at Castle Goresby, our family's country seat, are sufficient guarantees of my prowess with big game in all parts of the world; and when I mention that I have been one of an Arctic Expedition, have climbed to the highest mountain peaks explored by man, voyaged for days in a balloon, dived to a wreck in the complete modern outfit of a professional diver, am as useful on a yacht as any man of my acquaintance, think nothing of scoring a hundred break at billiards, and rarely meet my match at whist, piquet, or poker, it will be admitted that I have not confined my talents, such as they are, to any one particular branch of sport.

In fact, I am "Jacky Gore," and although the War Office addresses me officially as "Major the Honorable John William Wentworth Gore, 1st Royal Light Hussars," nothing is sweeter to my ear than to hear, as I often do, a passing remark such as "There goes good old Jacky Gore, the finest sportsman living!"

I take it for granted that the reader will accept this candor as to my performances in the spirit which inspires it, and not as a stupid form of self-conceit. I desire to be absolutely confidential and unreserved with those who peruse these pages, and a false modesty would be as misleading as it would be untrue to my nature.

For true modesty, as I conceive it, consists in an accurate valuation of one's own worth; an estimate of one's self that is conceived, not for purposes of advertisement, but rather to foster one's own self-respect. Thus, were these pages designed only for the eyes of sportsmen, there would appear no other description of myself than the laconic intimation, "I am Jacky Gore."

That, I know, would be sufficient to arrest electrically the ears of the sporting world. But as I desire my singular story to interest the whole range of human beings, from the Psychical Research Society down to the merest schoolboy who vaguely wonders if he will ever see a ghost, I must perforce be explicit, even to the extent of expounding my personal character as well as enumerating my achievements.

First, then, I am not a snob; I have no occasion to be one. I am the younger son of one of England's oldest earls, Lord Goresby, and my mother is the daughter of one of our newest marquises, Lord Dundrum. My friends are all of the very best, socially and otherwise. Indeed, I have established myself on a plane from which all acquaintances who have been financially unfortunate, or have otherwise become socially undesirable, must inevitably drop. For I hold that true friends are those whose position, affluence, and affection for one may be of material assistance in the race toward the goal of one's personal ambition.

If there is one thing that jars on me more than another, it is when a person of lower social status than my own presumes to associate with me in a style and with a manner that imply equality. I can readily, and I believe gracefully, meet people of higher rank than mine on their own platform, but the converse is, at least to me, odious.

Lest, from these candid statements, the reader might be inclined to consider me a trifle exclusive, I will frankly own that I often shoot, fish, or yacht with those *nouveaux riches* whose lacquer of gold so ineffectually conceals the real underlying metal. Still, a breadth of view of life, which has always been one of my characteristics, inspires me with the hope that the association of such people with one of my own type may in the process of time tend to the refining of the class from which they spring. Besides, one need not know people all one's life.

A keen eye for the artistic, a considerable talent for painting, a delicate and highly trained ear for music, and a quick perception as to what is of value in literature, have led me to frequent at times the houses where one meets the best class of so-called Bohemians. They are interesting people whom one may cultivate or drop according to social convenience, and useful as living dictionaries of the intellectual fashions of the moment. Sometimes I have thought that their interest in my experiences (as related in conversation by myself) has been strangely apathetic, not to say inattentive, due perhaps (as indeed I have been told) to their admiration of my physical points. In explanation I may point out that I have been modeled in marble as Hercules. It was a birthday gift I devised for my second cousin (by marriage) the Duke of Haredale, and I gave the commission to that admirable French sculptor, Moreau.

My means, viewed in proportion to those of my friends, are at least sufficient. For, although my allowance is nominally but £2,000 a year, my father has such a morbid sense of the family honor that he is always ready to pay up the casual debts that spring from daily intercourse with the best of everything. And as he enjoys an income of quite £150,000 a year, mainly derived from coal mines in Wales, there really seems no reason why I should not occasionally, indeed frequently, furnish him with an opportunity for indulging in his harmless hobby of keeping the family escutcheon clean.

I endeavor to keep in touch with society journalism and frequently entertain the editors of the more responsible sporting and smart papers. The Press being one of the glories of the age, I am ever ready to foster it; and though I care not one straw for the personal puffs of which I myself am so often the subject, still I know that they give pleasure to my friends, both at home and abroad.

As regards the literary style of these pages, I desire to point out that its agreeable flavor has been purveyed by a friend of mine, an eminent critic who writes for all the best daily and weekly papers both in London and the provinces. I have merely supplied the facts with such reflections and embroideries thereon as seemed to me both necessary and graceful. He has done the rest. Thus, if any adverse criticisms of my book should appear—an idea which I do not seriously entertain—the reader will understand that they are prompted either by professional jealousy or unfair rivalry, motives which, I am happy to think, have no place in the advanced and altruistic journalism of today.

And now, my reader, just before we plunge *in medias res,* I approach a subject which, if treated with candor, must also be handled with delicacy.

I desire to marry.

I desire to marry Katherine Clavering Gunter.

She is an American and a widow.

She is an enthusiastic golfer.

She is quite beautiful, especially in her photographs.

Since the day Carmody said, in the billiard room at White's, that she reminded him of a blush rose whose outer petals were becoming touched with the tint of biscuits, I have cut him dead. Her beauty is to me full of freshness, especially at night.

She has a fortune of £2,000,000 sterling, and I love her with a very true and real love. That is to say, I love her with a perfectly balanced affection; an affection based impartially on an estimate of her personal worth, an admiration for her physical charms, and an appreciation of her comfortable circumstances. I perceive that our union would further our respective interests in providing each of us with certain extensions of our present modes of living. I have long desired a place of my own in the country; and Katherine, I know, wishes to move freely in smart circles without having to employ the services of impoverished dowagers. In many other ways I could be of assistance to Katherine. I could tell her how to wear her diamonds, for instance, a difficult art she has not yet acquired. She is inclined on the slightest provocation to decorate herself in exuberant imitation of a cut-crystal chandelier.

There are, however, difficulties.

Prominent among these is the fact, already mentioned, that she is an ardent golfer. Except during the season in town, she spends her year in golfing, either at St. Magnus or Pau, for, like all good Americans, she has long since abjured her native soil.

Now golf is a game that presents no attractions to me. I have never tried it, nor even held a golf stick in my hand. A really good game, to my mind, must have an element, however slight, of physical danger to the player. This is the great whet to skilled performance. It is the condition that fosters pluck and self-reliance and develops our perception of the value of scientific play. It breeds a certain fearlessness that stimulates us not merely during the actual progress of the game, but unconsciously in the greater world where we play at Life with alert and daring opponents.

Now golf presents no such condition, and I despise it.

Once, by means of jocular query (a useful method of extracting such information as may not always be asked for bluntly), I gathered from Katherine that marriage with a keen golfer would probably be her future state; and this admission, I confess, was extremely galling to me, the more so as I had just been entertaining her with a long summary of my own achievements in other games.

I little thought at the time that before many weeks had passed I should be playing golf as heaven knows it was never played before. And this is how it happened.

II: I DINE AT LOWCHESTER HOUSE

One warm, delicious evening late in July I was dining at Lowchester House. It was almost my last dinner engagement for the season, as all the world and his wife had suddenly got sick of the baking pavements and dusty trees of the great city and were making in shoals for green fields or briny sea.

The ladies had just left us, and we men were preparing to enjoy the heavenly hour that brings cigarettes, coffee, and liqueurs in its wake. Through the wide-open French windows of the dining room (which look out over St. James's Park) came softened sounds of busy traffic; a ravishing odor of sweet peas stole in from the garden, and the moon gave to the trees and shrubs without those strange, grave tints that are her wonderful gifts to the night.

As a rule such an environment impresses and invigorates me pleasurably. I enjoy the journeys of the eye as it travels lightly over polished mahogany, glittering silver, and gleaming glass, noting here the deep red of the wine and roses, there the sunsetlike effulgence of the hanging lamps, the vague outlines of the pictured oak walls, and the clearer groups of well-groomed men that sit in easy comfort under a blue canopy of lazily curling smoke. Or, as the glance passes to the scented garden without, noting the blue-green and silver wonderlands that the moon creates in the most commonplace and probably grimy of trees, and the quiver that the soft July wind gives to branch, leaf, and flower.

But tonight, somehow, such things had no charm for me.

And yet Lady Lowchester's dinner had been good. The cutlets, perhaps, a trifle uninteresting and the wine somewhat overiced; but, on the whole, distinctly good.

How, then, account for my mood?

Katherine was of the party, but at the other end of the table from mine. A tall, well-built, massive man, good-looking, and possessed of an attractive smile, had taken her in to dinner, and I have rarely seen two people so completely absorbed in each other.

Therein lay the sting of the evening.

I had eaten and drunk mechanically with eyes riveted, as far as good breeding would permit, on Katherine and her neighbor.

Who was he?

I know everybody that one meets in London, either personally or by sight, yet I had never before come across this good-looking Hercules. I must find out.

He was talking to Lowchester as, leaving my chair, I carelessly joined the group at the other end of the table.

"Yes, I first held the open championship five years ago," I heard him say.

I pricked my ears. Of what championship was he speaking?

"And again last year, I think?" asked Lowchester.

"Yes," replied Hercules.

I quickly inquired of my neighbor as to what championship was under discussion.

"Why golf, of course," was the response. "That's Jim Lindsay, the finest player living."

So that was it. No wonder Katherine was so deeply absorbed during dinner.

I hated the man at once. I lost not a moment. I darted my eyes across the table, caught his, and stabbed him with one of those withering knifelike glances that only the descendants of the great can inflict.

Then I discovered that he wasn't looking at me at all, but at one of my shirt studs which had escaped from its buttonhole. He drew my attention to it. I grunted out an ungrateful "Thanks!" and hated him the more.

Now, as a rule, after dinner—wherever I may be—I manage to hold the conversation. So much a habit has this become with me, that I can scarcely endure to hear another man similarly exploiting himself. Not, I am bound to say, that Lindsay was belauding his own prowess. But, what was worse, he appeared a center of enormous interest to the men around him. They drew him out. They hung on his words. They gaped at him with reverential admiration. Truly golf must have made many converts during the last three years I had been in India. Bah! And I knew it to be such a childish game.

"I've taken a house close to the links at St. Magnus for the summer, Lindsay," Lowchester presently observed. "And as you tell me you're going there next month, you must let me put you up. There's lots of room, and Mrs. Gunter will be with us during August and September."

"I shall be delighted; it will suit me exactly," replied Lindsay.

So Lowchester too had become a golfer! Lowchester—who used to live for hunting and cricket! Lowchester—the President of the Board of Education! Good heavens!

Presently we were all in the hideous gilded and damasked drawing room; for Lowchester House is a sort of museum of the tawdry vulgarities of the early fifties.

The rooms were hot. That no doubt was the reason why presently Mrs. Gunter and the champion were to be seen hanging over the railing of a flower-laden balcony; but the heat could in no way account for their gazing into each other's eyes so frequently, or so raptly.

I seized on a slip of a girl in pink, led her close to the window, and in tones that I knew must be overheard by the occupants of the balcony, began to relate how I won the Lahore Polo Cup for my team in '92.

I was well under way and just reaching a stirring description of the magnificent goal I scored by taking the ball the whole length of the ground, on a pony that had suddenly gone lame, when Katherine and the champion pointedly left the window and proceeded to another and more distant one.

So! My reminiscences bored them! Polo was nothing if golf were in the air!

It was enough. I could stand no more. I peevishly bade my hostess good night and passed through the rooms.

As I entered the great hall, which was but dimly lit, my eyes encountered a portrait of the famous (or infamous) Cardinal Smeaton, one of Lowchester's proudest pictorial possessions. The great Scotch prelate, I could have sworn, winked at me.

I was moving on, when suddenly, close to my shoulder, I heard the words, "I will meet ye at St. Magnus!"

I started and turned. There was no one near. I gazed fixedly at the portrait, but never was marble more immovable. I was about to investigate a recess and some pillars, near me, when I observed a footman at the hall door eying me with mild but interested scrutiny. He came forward with my coat and hat, and putting them on I passed listlessly into the courtyard and thence to St. James's Street, where I mechanically entered the doors of the Racing Club.

I rang the bell and ordered a brandy-and-soda.

III: THE CHALLENGE

The Racing Club, as the reader knows, is the smartest sporting club in London, and the Inner Temple of the popular game of bridge. But tonight cards held no temptation for me; and I sat alone in the reading room, chewing the cud of a humiliation that was quite novel to my experience.

The incident of the Cardinal's wink and the unknown voice had already escaped my memory, and I was rapt in rankling memories of the unsatisfactory evening I had spent.

To me, it was inconceivable that even the finest exponent of a wretched game like golf could oust an all-round sportsman like myself from the circle of interest at a dinner table. It was not so much that I had not been afforded an opportunity to talk, as that when I did I was listened to with a wandering and simulated attention, suggesting that the listeners were only waiting for me to stop. The moment I paused between two anecdotes, someone precipitately led the conversation away to a channel that had no possible interest for me.

Then Katherine had indubitably avoided and ignored me.

It has always been understood between us that if I am in a room with her, mine is the first claim on her attention. Yet, tonight, there was, if not an open rebellion, at least a new departure.

It was extremely galling, and I ordered a second brandy-and-soda.

Must I, then, take to golf in self-defense?

Of course I could pick it up easily. There is no minor game that I have not mastered with ease, after about a week's hard application; and to acquire the art of striking a ball from a certain distance into a hole presents no alarming difficulties to the adroit cricketer and practiced polo player. Still, to go over, as it were, to the camp of the enemy, to apply myself to a game that I have openly and avowedly sneered at, was not altogether a pleasing prospect.

How it would tickle my pals at Hurlingham, Ranelagh, the Oval, and Lord's!

I took from the bookshelves the Badminton volume on golf and with a third brandy-and-soda applied myself to a rapid study of its contents. I admit that I was somewhat dismayed at the mass of printed matter and numerous diagrams that confronted me, but reflecting that I had often seen voluminous books on such trivial games

as croquet or tennis, I concluded that the principle of sporting journalism is to make the maximum of bricks out of the minimum of
straw.

I had not read more than three chapters when half a dozen men,
including Lowchester and Lindsay, entered the room.

"My dear Jacky," said the former, "you left us very early tonight."

"Yes," I replied. "I found the atmosphere indoors a bit oppressive;
and I'm not as yet a convert to golf, your sole topic of discussion during the evening."

"You ought to try the game," said Lindsay. "There's more in it
than outsiders imagine."

" 'Outsiders' in what sense?" I inquired, with an obvious courtship
of a wordy wrangle.

"Oh! only as regards golf, of course. For aught I know you may be
a celebrity in many other branches of sport."

"I am," was on the tip of my tongue, but I repressed it.

I felt strangely antagonistic toward this man. A sort of magnetic
antipathy (if I may be allowed such a seeming contradiction in
terms) warned me that we should influence each other's lives in the
future, and that to the detriment of one, if not both of us. In fact, I
felt myself being drawn irresistibly toward the vulgar vortex of a
"row" with him.

"Golf," I suddenly found myself asserting after one of those deadly
pauses that give an altogether exaggerated significance to any casual
remark that may break the silence, "golf is a game for one's dotage."

"A period that sets in quite early in the lives of many of us," retorted Lindsay.

There was another pause. Lowchester was chuckling quietly. A
club waiter with thin lips was grinning faintly.

"Which means?" I asked, with an affectation of bored inattention.

"Well, it means," was the reply, "that to stigmatize as only suitable
for one's dotage a fine, healthy, outdoor sport, that employs skill and
science, and exercises one's patience and temper as few other games
do, suggests to my mind incipient dotage in common perception."

I did not understand this at first, so merely remarked, "Really," an
ambiguous and useful word, which commits one to nothing.

But as I reflected on Lindsay's words, I perceived a deadly stab at
my authority as a judge of sport. My blood tingled. I seized a fourth
brandy-and-soda and drank it. It was Lowchester's, but I was only
aware of this when the glass was empty. My lips compressed them-

selves. I recalled Katherine and the champion hanging over the balcony. The thin-lipped club waiter was loitering with an evident desire to overhear what else was to be said. Lowchester looked at me with gently humorous inquiry in his eyes. The others regarded me with the sphinxlike calm that is the ordinary expression of the average Englishman when he is thinking hard but not lucidly. I had, in fact, an audience, always to me an overpowering temptation.

"I'll tell you what I'll do," I said, in the calm, deep tones born of a great determination. "After one week's practice on the St. Magnus links I'll play you a match on even terms, and I dare to hope lick your head off at your own game."

There was a pause of a moment. Then, as if to clear the oppressive air, a chorus of "Bravo, Old Jacky!" broke out from the bystanders.

Only Lindsay was silent, barring, of course, the waiters.

"Well?" I asked him.

"I accept, of course," said he; "you leave me no alternative. But the whole scheme is absolutely childish, and, as I fear you will find, quite futile."

"I'll take my chance of that," I replied. "I can reach St. Magnus by August eighth, and on the fifteenth I'll play you."

"It's a match," cried Lowchester, and proceeded to enter it in a notebook. "Any stakes?"

"I will privately suggest to Mr. Lindsay the stakes to be played for," I answered. "May I ask you to come with me for a moment?"

Lindsay assented, and I led him to an adjoining room that was empty.

"The stake I suggest—and it must be known to none but ourselves —is this. The winner of the match shall have the first right to propose matrimony to a certain lady. I mention no names. It is enough if we agree that neither of us shall propose to any lady whatsoever on or before August fifteenth, and that the loser shall further abstain from any such proposal till August twenty-second. This will give the winner a clear week's start, which really constitutes the stake. The subject is a delicate one," I hastily added, as I saw his surprise and evident desire to go further into the matter, "and I shall be obliged if you merely signify your assent or dissent, as the case may be."

With a certain bewildered yet half-amused air he replied, "I assent, of course, but——"

"There is nothing more that need be said," I hurriedly interrupted, "except that I shall be glad if you will join me at supper."

For at one of my own clubs, when a stranger is introduced, even by another member, I trust I can ever play the host with tact and grace. I asked Lowchester and Grimsby to join us, and during supper I was able to recount the chief exploits of my life to the attentive audience that a host can always rely on.

IV: ST. MAGNUS

I left London on August 6th, traveling by night to Edinburgh, and leaving the latter city at 9 A.M., on the 7th, reached St. Magnus a few minutes before noon. I had been recommended to try the Metropole Hotel, and accordingly took up my quarters there. It is quite near the St. Magnus Golf Club (for which I was put up at once as a temporary member) and is equally convenient to the links. Lord and Lady Lowchester were in their house, a stone's throw from the hotel, and amongst their guests were Mr. Lindsay and Mrs. Gunter.

St. Magnus, as the golfing world knows, is situated on the east coast of Scotland, and is second only in importance as a golfing center to St. Andrews, which, indeed, it closely resembles. It is a grim, gray old town, standing on bleak, precipitous cliffs that court every passing hurricane, and possessed in addition of a respectable perennial gale of its own. It is always blowing there. Indeed, I think a fair description of normal weather of St. Magnus would be "Wind with gales."

The ancient town boasts many ruins of once noble buildings. Cathedrals, castles, monasteries, colleges, and priories, that formed strongholds of Roman Catholicism before the Reformation, are now outlined only by picturesque and crumbling walls, held in a green embrace by the ever sympathetic ivy, and preserved mainly to please the antiquarian or artistic eye.

And many the tales that are told of the ghostly occupants of these dead strongholds.

The hotel was tolerably comfortable, although under any conditions hotel life is, to me, a hateful business. The constant traversing of passages that lead chiefly to other people's rooms; the garrulous noisiness of the guests, the forced yet blasé alacrity of the waiters, the commercial suavity and professional geniality of the proprietor, the absolute lack of originality in the cook, the fact that one becomes merely an easily forgotten number, these and a thousand other trivial humiliations combine to render residence in a hotel a source of irritation to the nerves.

The clubhouse, however, was airy and comfortably managed; and the older frequenters appeared to me to be good types of Scotch county gentlemen, or courteous members of the learned professions. Some of the younger men I met I did not quite understand. They had, to begin with, quite extraordinary accents. If you can imagine a native and strong Scotch accent asserting itself in defiance of a recently acquired cockney twang, you have some idea of the strange sounds these youths emitted. They were, however, quite harmless; and there really seemed no reason why, if it pleased them, they should not garnish their Caledonian and somewhat bucolic dialogue with misplaced "Don't-you-knows," or denude it, in accordance with a long defunct phonetic fashion, of the letter "g." They were quite charmed with my prefix "Honorable" and duly acquainted me of such people of title as they had either seen at a distance or once spoken to at a railway station.

The general society of the place was considered "mixed" by the younger bloods of the town; though, to my mind, these latter formed the most unpalatable part of the mixture. It numbered, to my surprise, half a dozen socially well-known people whom I frequently met in London. True, they kept pretty much to themselves and were not to be seen at the numerous tea parties, female putting tournaments, badly cooked but pretentious dinners, and other social barbarities that were—heaven help us!—considered *de rigueur* in this fresh seaside country town.

I, too, avoided all such festivities; though from the moment I set foot in the club, with name and condition advertised on the notice board, I was inundated with invitations; one of the many penalties, I suppose, of being more or less of a sporting celebrity. I felt, indeed, much as a great actor must when he goes "starring" in the provinces.

There is, however, one charming section of society in the gray old town, comprising mainly those learned and cultured people who own the city as their home. Mingling with these, some modern *littérateurs* in search of bracing health give a vivacity to the free exchange of ideas; whilst one or two staid but intelligent clergymen form a sort of moral anchor that holds cultured thought to the needs of the world rather than let it drift to the summer seas of imagination.

In such society I should have been, of course, a welcome recruit; but I was in St. Magnus for one purpose only, and that was golf.

I have been writing calmly, but during the days that followed my challenge to Lindsay, my brain was in a fever. I had stipulated for but one week's practice, and, consequently, though dying to handle the sticks (or "clubs" as I find I ought to call them), I had been debarred from more than a study of the game, as set forth in the various published works on the subject.

I had taken a suite of four rooms in the hotel. One was my sitting room, another my bedroom, a third my servant's room, and the fourth I had fitted up as a golf studio. The latter is entirely my own invention, and I make no doubt that, after the publication of this volume, similar studios will become quite common institutions.

By arrangement with the proprietor, I had the room denuded of all furniture; and it was understood between us that during my residence no one, not even a housemaid, should be permitted to enter the chamber, with, of course, the exception of myself and my servant. I had no desire that St. Magnus should know the extent to which I was laying myself out to defeat my opponent.

A strip of coconut matting, lightly strewn with sand, represented a teeing ground, whilst a number of padded targets, designed to receive the balls as I drove them, almost entirely covered the walls. A fourth of the floor was boarded in with sand, eighteen inches deep, to represent a bunker. The remainder I turfed to represent a putting green. I constructed a small movable grassy hillock which could be placed in the center of the room for practice in "hanging" or "uphill" lies, and I imported whin bushes, sods of long grass, etc., to represent the assorted difficulties that beset the golfer. By day, and until I was finished with the studio for the night, the windows were removed in case of accidents; and altogether nothing was left undone that would conduce to complete and unobserved practice of the game.

In addition to this indoor preparation, I decided to do at least two rounds daily, starting at daybreak. Allowing two hours for each round, this could easily be accomplished before 9 A.M., and St. Magnus would be little the wiser. Then, if my progress should prove unsatisfactory, starting out about 5 P.M., I could edge in a third almost unnoticed round.

I had six volumes by different writers on the game, and from these I gathered that instruction from a first-class professional was practically indispensable to the beginner. By dint of offering extremely liberal terms, I secured the services of the well-known professional Kirkintulloch, it being understood that he was to coach me more or less *sub rosa,* and that in any case he was not to talk promiscuously of the extent to which I practiced. I exhorted him to spare no expense—an arrangement he accepted with evident and spontaneous alacrity, selling me a number of his own unrivaled clubs at what I have since learned were exorbitant prices. He also made a selection of other implements of the game from the best makers, that included fifteen beautifully balanced and polished clubs, four dozen balls, and several minor appliances, such as artificial tees, sponges, etc., to say nothing of a seven-and-sixpenny and pagodalike umbrella. All these preparations were completed on the day of my arrival, and it was arranged that I should begin practice in deadly earnest at 4:30 on the following morning.

V: I BEGIN TO GOLF

The morning of the 8th dawned with a warm flush of saffron, rose, and gold, behind which the faint purple of the night that was gone died into the mists of early morning. The pure, sweet air was delicious as the sparkling vapor that rises from a newly opened bottle of invigorating wine. The incoming tide plashed on the beach with lazy and musical kisses, and a soft, melodious wind was stirring the bending grasses that crowned the sand dunes on the outskirts of the links.

I inhaled the glorious air with the rapture of the warrior who sniffs the battle from afar.

[The literary grace of my esteemed journalistic colleague will be observed in the foregoing lines. "It was a ripping morning" was all I actually said to him.—J. W. W. G.]

Kirkintulloch was waiting for me at the first putting green.

I may say at once that during my entire stay in St. Magnus I never quite mastered this man's name. It became confused in my mind with other curious-sounding names of Scotch towns, and I addressed him promiscuously as Tullochgorum, Tillicoutry, Auchtermuchty, and the like. To his credit, be it said that after one or two attempts to put me right, he suppressed any claim to nominal individuality and adapted himself philosophically to my weakness; answering cheerfully to any name that greeted his surprised but resigned ears.

He was the brawny son of honest fisher folk. Of middle height, he was sturdily yet flexibly built. His hands were large and horny; his feet, I have no doubt, the same. At all events his boots were of ample proportions. He had blue eyes, with that alert, steady, and farseeing gaze that is the birthright of folk born to look out over the sea; sandy hair and mustache, and a ruddy color that suggested equally sunshine, salt winds, and whisky. His natural expression was inclined to be sour, but on occasion this was dissipated by a quite genial smile. His manner and address had the odd deferential familiarity that belongs exclusively to the old-fashioned Scotch peasantry. His face I soon found to be a sort of barometer of my progress, for every time I struck a ball I could see exactly the value of the stroke recorded in the grim lines of his weather-beaten features. In movement he was clumsy, except, indeed, when golfing, for then his body and limbs became possessed of that faultless grace which only proficiency in a given line can impart.

"It's a fine moarn fur goalf," was his greeting.

"So I suppose," said I. "Where do we go?"

"We'll gang ower here," he replied, as, tucking my clubs under his arm, he led me in the direction of a comparatively remote part of the links.

As we went I thought it advisable to let him know that, although not yet a golfer, I could more than hold my own in far higher branches of sport. I told him that I was one of the best-known polo players of the day.

There was a considerable pause, but we tramped steadily on.

"Whaat's polo?" said he, at length.

I gave him a brief description of the game.

"Aweel, ye'll no hae a hoarse to help ye at goalf."

"But, don't you see, Tullochgorum——"

"Kirkintulloch, sir."

"Kirkintulloch, that the fact of playing a game on ponies makes it much more difficult?"

"Then whaat fur d'ye hae them?"

"Well, it's the game, that's all."

"M'hm" was his sphinxlike response.

I felt that I had not convinced him.

I next hinted that I was a prominent cricketer, and, as a rule, went in first wicket down when playing for my regiment.

"Ay, it's a fine ploy fur laddies."

"It's a game that can only properly be played by men," I replied, with indignant warmth.

"Is't?"

"Yes, is't—I mean it is." He had certain phrases that I often unconsciously and involuntarily repeated, generally with ludicrous effect.

The reader, of course, understands that I was not in any sense guilty of such gross taste as to imitate the man to his own ears. I simply could not help pronouncing certain words as he did.

"Aweel, in goalf ye'll no hae a man to birstle the ba' to yer bat; ye'll just hae to play it as it lies."

"But, man alive," I cried, "don't you see that to hit a moving object must be infinitely more difficult than to strike a ball that is stationary?"

"Ye've no bunkers at cricket," he replied, with irrelevant but disconcerting conviction, adding, with an indescribable and prophetic relish, "No, nor yet whins."

I could make no impression on this man, and it worried me.

"I take it," I resumed presently, "that what is mainly of importance at golf is a good eye."

"That's ae thing."

"What's ae thing?"

"Yer e'e. The thing is, can ye keep it on the ba'?"

"Of course I can keep it on the ba'—ball."

"We'll see in a meenit," he answered, and stopped. We had reached a large field enclosed by a wall, and here Kirkintulloch dropped the clubs and proceeded to arrange a little heap of damp sand, on which he eventually poised a golf ball.

"Noo, tak' yer driver. Here," and he handed me a beautifully varnished implement decorated with sunk lead, inlaid bone, and resined cord. "Try a swing" (he said "swung") "like this," and, standing in position before the ball, he proceeded to wave a club of his own in semicircular sweeps as if defying the world in general and myself in particular, till suddenly and rapidly descending on the ball, he struck it with such force and accuracy that it shot out into the faint morning mist and disappeared. It was really a remarkably fine shot. I began to feel quite keen.

"Noo it's your turn," said he, as he teed a second ball, "but hae a wheen practice at the swung first."

So I began "addressing" an imaginary ball.

We wrestled with the peculiar flourishes that are technically known as "addressing the ball" for some minutes, at the end of which my movements resembled those of a man who, having been given a club, was undecided in his mind as to whether he should keep hold of it or throw it away. I wiggled first in one direction, then in another. I described eights and threes, double circles, triangles, and parallelograms in the air, only to be assailed with—

"Na, na!" from Kirkintulloch.

"See here, dea it like this," he cried; and again he flourished his driver with the easy grace of a lifetime's practice.

"I'll tell you what, Kirkcudbright——"

"Kirkintulloch, sir."

"Kirkintulloch, just you let me have a smack at the ball."

"Gang on then, sir. Hae a smack."

I took up position. I got my eye on the ball. I wiggled for all I was worth, I swung a mighty swing, I swooped with terrific force down on the ball, and behold, when all was over, there it was still poised on the tee, insolently unmoved, and Kirkintulloch sniffing in the direction of the sea.

"Ye've missed the globe," was his comment. "An' it's a black disgrace to a gowfer."

I settled to the ball again—and with a running accompaniment from Kirkintulloch of "Keep yer eye on the ba'; up wi' yer richt fut; tak' plenty time; dinna swee ower fast"—I let drive a second time, with the result that the ball took a series of trifling hops and skips like a startled hare, and deposited itself in rough ground some thirty yards off, at an angle of forty-five degrees from the line I had anxiously hoped to take.

"Ye topped it, sir," was Kirkintulloch's view of the performance.

"I moved it, anyhow," I muttered moodily.

"Ay, ye did that," was the response; "and ye'll never move that ba' again, fur it's doon a rabbit hole and oot o' sicht."

Nevertheless, I went steadily on, ball after ball. They took many and devious routes, and entirely different methods of reaching their destinations. Some leaped into the air with halfhearted and affrighted purpose; others shot along the ground with strange irregularity of direction and distance; a number went off at right or left angles with the pleasing uncertainty that only a beginner can command; whilst not a few merely trickled off the tee in sickly obedience to my misdirected energy. At length I struck one magnificent shot. The ball soared straight and sure from the club just as Kirkintulloch's had, and I felt for the first time the delicious thrill that tingles through the arms right to the very brain, as the clean-struck ball leaves the driver's head. I looked at Kirkintulloch with a proud and gleaming eye.

"No bad," said he, "but ye'll no do that again in a hurry. It was guy like an accident."

"Look here, Kirkincoutry," I said, nettled at last, "it's your business to encourage me, not to throw cold water; and you ought to know it."

"Ma name's Kirkintulloch," he answered phlegmatically; "but it doesna' maitter." (And this was the last time he corrected my errors as to his name.) "An' I can tell ye this, that cauld watter keeps the heed cool at goalf, and praise is a snare and a deloosion." Then with the ghost of a smile he added, "Gang on, ye're daein' fine."

The field was now dotted with some fifteen balls at such alarmingly varied distances and angles from the tee that they formed an irregular semicircle in front of us (one ball had even succeeded in traveling backward); and as I reflected that my original and sustained purpose had been to strike them all in one particular line, I began to perceive undreamed-of difficulties in this royal and ancient game.

But I struggled on, and Kirkintulloch himself admitted that I showed signs of distinct, if spasmodic, improvement. At seven o'clock the driver was temporarily laid aside, and I was introduced in turn to the brassie, the iron, the cleek, the putter, and the niblick, the latter a curious implement not unlike a dentist's reflector of magnified proportions. The brassie much resembled the driver, but the iron opened out quite a new field of practice; and my first attempts with it were rather in the nature of sod-cutting with a spade, varied at intervals by deadly strokes that left deep incisions on the ball.

As the clock of the parish church tolled the hour of 8:30, I returned to the hotel with an enormous appetite and a thoughtful mind.

VI: I CONTINUE TO PRACTICE

My practice in the studio was not attended with that measure of success I had anticipated. The turf got dry and lumpy, and when, by my instructions, my servant watered it liberally, an old lady occupying the room immediately below intimated to the proprietor that her ceiling had unaccountably begun to drip, and that strange noises from the floor above deprived her of that tranquil rest for which she had sought the salubrious breezes of St. Magnus. A gouty dean, whose room adjoined the studio, also complained that sudden bangs and rattles on the walls, intermittent and varied but on the whole continuous, had so completely got on his nerves that residence in that quarter of the hotel had become an impossibility; whilst a number of other guests pointed out that to walk beneath my window was an extremely dangerous proceeding, as golf balls and even broken clubs flew out on them with alarming frequency and exciting results. I admit that I had a thoughtless habit of throwing offending clubs from the window in moments of extreme exasperation, but I exonerate myself of any intentional bombarding of my fellow lodgers.

I myself suffered from this indoor zeal, for if a ball failed to strike one of the padded targets and came in contact with the wall (as often happened), it would fly back boomeranglike to where I stood, not infrequently striking me so hard as to raise grisly lumps on various parts of my body. Once I invited Wetherby, my servant, to witness my progress, and during the few minutes of his incarceration with me he was driven to execute a series of leaps and springs to avoid the rapidly traveling and seemingly malignant ball. It struck him, I believe, three times, which somewhat militated against his evident desire to pay me encouraging compliments, for these latter he condensed into a meager and breathless "Wonderful, sir!" as he dashed from the studio with an alacrity that was by no means constitutional with him.

The miniature bunker also gave rise to a certain amount of speculation on the part of inmates of the hotel, for as I generally practiced on it facing the window, casual loiterers below experienced brief but disconcerting sandstorms, and the porters and hall boys were kept busily occupied in sweeping the unaccountably sanded pavement.

I will not weary the reader with a description of my progress on the links from day to day. Suffice it to say that whilst I really made wonderful strides, it became borne in upon me, after five days' practice, that under no possible conditions could I hope to win the match I had set myself to play. For although I made many excellent, and even brilliant, strokes, I would constantly "foozle" others, with the result that I never got round the links under 100, whereas Lindsay, I knew, seldom if ever exceeded 90 and averaged, I suppose, something like 86.

What, then, was I to do? Give in?

No.

I would play the match and be beaten like a man. There was a remote chance that fortune might favor me. Lindsay might be seedy—I knew he suffered at times from the effects of malarial fever—or I might by some unlooked-for providence suddenly develop a slashing game.

At all events I felt I must confide in Kirkintulloch's ears the task I had set myself.

Accordingly, on the morning of Saturday the 13th, I intimated to him, as we started on our first round, that I had to play my first match on the Monday.

"Ay," said he quite imperturbably.

"Yes," I resumed, "and rather an important one."

"Weel, I'll cairry for ye. Whaat time?"

"Eleven o'clock," I replied; and then, plunging *in medias res,* I added, "I'm playing a single against Mr. Lindsay, Mr. James Lindsay."

Kirkintulloch stopped dead and gazed at me with blue-eyed and unceremonious incredulity.

"Jim Lindsay!" he cried.

"Yes," I growled doggedly.

We proceeded to walk on, but, despite his impenetrable expression, I knew that Kirkintulloch was charged with violent emotion of some sort.

"What's he giein' ye?" he asked presently.

"What?"

"What's yer hondicop?"

"None. I'm playing him level."

"Weel, of a' the pairfect noansense——"

"Eh?" I interrupted, with a certain dignity that was not lost on

Kirkintulloch. But he again stopped dead, and for once in a way betrayed signs of some excitement.

"See here whaat I'm tellin' ye. He'll lay ye oot like a corp! D'ye ken thaat? Forbye ye'll be the laughin'-stock o' the links. Ay, and *me* cairryin' for ye! I've pit up wi' a' the names ye've ca'd me—Tullochgorum, Tillicoutry, ay, and Auchtermuchty tae—but I'd hae ye mind I'm Wully Kirkintulloch, the professional. I've been in the mileeshy, an' I've done ma fowerteen days in the clink, but I'm no for ony black disgrace like cairryin' in a maatch the tail end o' which'll be Jim Lindsay scorin' nineteen up an' seventeen tae play."

I am not vain, but I confess that this speech, the longest oratorical effort that I remember Kirkintulloch to have indulged in, wounded my *amour propre*.

"If you don't wish to cairry—I mean carry—for me on Monday," I said, "there is no occasion for you to do so. I can easily get another caddie, and whoever does undertake the job will be paid one guinea."

I watched his features keenly as I said this, and though he in no wise betrayed himself by look or gesture, there was an alteration in his tone when next he addressed me.

"It's like this, ye see," said he. "I ken ma business fine, and I ken a reel gentleman when I see yin, even when he's no whaat ye might ca' profeecient as a goalfer, an' I'm no sayin' I'll no cairry fur ye; a' I say is that ye're no tae blame me if Jim Lindsay wuns by three or fower holes."

With this change of professional attitude we proceeded on our way and were soon absorbed in the intricacies of the game.

That morning—how well I remember it!—I was pounding away in one of the deepest bunkers, filling my eyes, ears, hair, and clothes with sand, exhausting my vocabulary of language, and yet not appreciably moving the ball. I had played seven strokes with ever increasing frenzy. With the eighth, to my momentary relief, the ball soared from the sand to the grassy slope above, only—oh, maddening game!—to trickle slowly back and nest itself in one of my deepest heel marks. Under the impression that I was alone, I was engaging in a one-sided, but ornate, conversation with the ball—for it is quite extraordinary how illogically angry one gets with inanimate objects—when, suddenly, from behind me came the clear ring of a woman's laughter.

I turned and beheld Mrs. Gunter.

She was dressed in a tailor-made coat and skirt of butcher blue, and wore a tam o' shanter of the same color. A white collar and bright red sailor knot, adorable white spats, and a white waistcoat completed the costume. Over her shoulder she carried a cleek, and by her side was a caddie bearing her other clubs. Her eyes were sparkling with humor and enjoyment of life, her cheeks glowed with the bright fresh red that comes of sea air and healthy exercise. Her enemies used to say she was an adept at suitable complexions, but, personally, I give credit to the salubrious breezes of St. Magnus.

"Well?" she cried lustily (and she did *not* pronounce it "wal"). "How goes it?"

"Tolerably," I replied, as I mopped my perspiring brow. "You see me at present at my worst."

"Anna Lowchester is going to ask you to dinner on Monday to celebrate the great match. Mind you come. Say now, what are the stakes? You know it's all over the town you're playing for something colossal. You'll have quite a crowd at your heels. And tell me why you avoid us all?"

"I am here simply and solely to golf," I replied, with as much dignity as is possible to the occupant of a bunker that the merest novice could have avoided.

"Ye're keepin' the green waitin', sir," cried Kirkintulloch, as he appeared on the grassy slope in front of me.

"Then will you excuse me?" I asked Mrs. Gunter, and settling down again I proceeded patiently to maneuver under and round my ball. As I played the "eleven more," it rose in the air, and I left the bunker with a dignified bow to Katherine.

She passed on with a merry laugh and a wave of the hand, crying out as she watched the destination of my gutta-percha, "You poor soul! You're bang into another."

And so I was. For a passing moment I almost hated Katherine.

It was quite true that I had avoided the Lowchesters. I was in no mood for society, still less did I care to meet Mr. Lindsay. True, I stumbled across him frequently in the club, but we instinctively limited our intercourse to a distant "Good morning," or a perfunctory "Good night."

Moreover, I was becoming extremely depressed.

Katherine's flippant and unsympathetic bearing during my vicissitudes in the bunker; the certainty that for the first time in my life I was about to be made a fool of; the extraordinary difficulty I experienced in attaining to anything like an even sample of play; and the half-pitiful, half-fearful regard in which I was held by the guests at the hotel, combined to rob life of the exhilaration that I had hitherto never failed to enjoy.

VII: I MEET THE CARDINAL

The morning of Sunday the 14th broke with a dark and stormy scowl. The sea was lashed to a foaming lather by frantic gusts of easterly wind, and great black masses of clouds sped landward and piled themselves in ominous canopy over the gray and bleak-looking city. A seething and swirling mist all but enveloped the links, and the bending grasses of the dunes swayed and swished with every scourge of the salt-laden gale. Hard-driven and drenching rain swept in furious torrents across land and sea. The ground was as a swamp; the wet rocks, cold and streaming, stood as black targets for the fury of the mighty and resounding breakers that, spent in impotent attack, rose in vast clouds of spray.

Not a soul was to be seen out of doors. The church bells, faintly and fitfully heard, clanged their invitation to an irresponsive town; indoors, fires were already crackling, pipes were lighted, magazines unearthed, and soon St. Magnus was courting the drowsy comfort that snug shelter from a raging storm ever induces.

I passed the time till luncheon in the golf studio, but, out of consideration for such Sabbatarian scruples as might possibly be entertained by the adjoining dean, I merely trifled with a putter, and indeed I had little heart even for that. The clamor of the gong for the midday meal was a welcome break to the black monotony of the morning, and, descending to the dining room, I partook freely of such northern delicacies as haggis (a really excellent if stodgy dish), crab pies, and oat cakes.

I then devoted a couple of hours to the perusal of my books on golf and copied out, on a scale sufficiently small to be easily carried in the pocket, a map of the St. Magnus links for use on the morrow. A glance at this before each stroke would show me all the concealed hazards with which this admirably-laid-out course abounds. The idea is, I believe, a new one, and I present it gratuitously to all golfers who peruse this veracious history.

Dinner at the Metropole on Sundays is a more pretentious meal than on weekdays. Game, cooked to a rag, figures on the menu, as also a profuse dessert of the cheaper and not quite ripe fruits of the season. Why this should be is not quite clear, as the golfer is robbed of his wonted exercise on a Sunday and therefore should be lightly fed. It may be that in view of the spiritual rations dealt out to the immortal part of man that day, the hotel proprietor, in the spirit of competition which becomes his second nature, feels it incumbent on him to provide for the mortal interior with a prodigality that will bear comparison. Be that as it may, I did full justice to my host's catering, seeing it out to the bitter end, and banishing my depression with a bottle of the "Boy" and a few glasses of a port which was officially dated '64. It may have been that this wine had reached the sober age claimed for it, but to my palate, at least, it seemed to retain all the juvenile vigor and rough precocity of a wine still in its infancy.

About 10 P.M. I proceeded to the smoking room and stretched myself luxuriously on a couch in front of a blazing fire, only to find that rest was not possible, and that I was the victim of what Scotch folk so aptly term the "fidgets." First, it appeared that I had been wrong to cross the right leg over the left, and I accordingly reversed the position. The momentary ease secured by this change was succeeded by a numbness in the right elbow which demanded that I should turn over on my left side. But this movement led to a stiffening of the neck, unaccountable yet unmistakable, and I turned for relief to the broad of my back, only to start a sudden and most irritating tickling in the sole of my right foot. I endured these tortures in silence for a time, attributing them, rightly, I imagine, to the fact that I had had no exercise during the day. The culminating point, however, was reached when the tickling sensation incontinently transferred itself to the back, suggesting to my now maddened imagination two prickly-footed scorpions golfing between my shoulder blades. I scraped myself, after the manner of cattle, against the wooden arms of the couch without obtaining appreciable relief, and finally sprang to my feet with a bound that startled a number of somnolent old gentlemen into wide-awake and indignant observation.

I must have exercise.

I drew aside one of the curtains and looked out on the night. The storm had somewhat abated, and the moon sailed brilliantly at intervals through the black and scudding clouds.

I decided on a walk, despite the weather and the lateness of the hour. I made for my room, arrayed myself, with Wetherby's assistance, in top boots, mackintosh, and sou'-wester, and thus armored against the elements I sallied forth into the wild and eerie night.

As I left the doors of the hotel eleven solemn clangs from the parish church warned me of the approaching "witching hour of night."

The town, despite the fact that most of the town councilors are interested in the local gas company, is extremely badly lighted; and by the time I had passed the hospitable and inviting rays that streamed from the doors and lamps of the clubhouse, I was practically in the dark.

I took the road that extends along the cliffs to the harbor, at times compelled to probe for and feel my way, at times guided by fitful splashes of moonlight. And the scene when the moon chose to break through her pall-like veil was superb. Before me, in cold and inky outline, stood the ruined towers and windows of cathedral and castle; to the left the sea, in a riot of black and white, still hurled itself with unabated fury against the adamant rocks and along the unresisting beach. The sky was an ever changing canopy of black and sullen gray, sparsely streaked with rifts of gleaming silver. Great trees bent and creaked on my right, flinging, as in a perspiration of midnight fear, great drops on the roadway below, sighing and screaming as if the horrid winds were whispering ghastly tales to their sobbing and tearstained leaves, tales not to be breathed in the light of day.

A profound sense of awe stole over me as, riveted by the scene each passing glimpse of the moon revealed, I stood my ground from time to time and held my breath in a frame of mind quite foreign to my experience.

[Here again will be observed the literary elegance of my gifted colleague. The preceding paragraphs have been evolved from my simple statement, "It was a beastly wet night."—J. W. W. G.]

So slow had been my progress that almost an hour must have passed before I reached the gates of the ruined castle. As I stood gazing up at the weather-beaten heights, faintly limned against the flying clouds, I became conscious of a sudden and strange atmospheric change. The gale inexplicably died; the trees hushed themselves into a startling silence; the moon crept behind an enormous overhanging mountain of clouds; and warm, humid, and oppressive air replaced the sea-blown easterly winds. A great and portentous stillness prevailed around me, broken only by a dull moaning—as of a soul in agony—from the sea.

The effect was awful.

I strained eyes and ears in an ecstasy of anxiety. I knew not what was awaiting me, and yet knew of a certainty that I was about to face some strange revelation of the night.

Above all a great and overpowering horror of the dead was in me.

I tried to retrace my steps and found myself immovable, a living and breathing statue clutching the iron bars of the castle gate, waiting—waiting for what?

Could it be that I, this quivering, powerless, quaking creature, was indeed John William Wentworth G——

Crash!—Crash! !

Within, as it seemed to me, a few feet of where I stood, a mighty blue and blinding flame shot out from the massive pile of clouds, firing sea and land with livid and fearsome light. Crash upon crash, roar upon roar of such thunder as I pray I may never hear again, struck up into the heights of the heavens and down again to the resounding rocks and ruins that fronted me. They broke in deafening awful blows upon my ear and stunned me. In a moment of utter collapse I fell through the gate and lay with closed eyes on the soaking turf within. But closed eyes had no power to keep out such burning fire, and each blue flash came piercing through the eyelids.

Gasping, and with a supreme and almost superhuman effort, I staggered to my feet and opened my eyes in bewildered and fearful expectation.

And what was the wild, weird thing I saw?

At the entrance to the castle, just beyond the drawbridge, holding aloft a wrought-iron lamp of ecclesiastical design that burned with a sputtering and spectral flame, stood the red-robed figure of a ghostly cardinal!

With a wildly beating heart I recognized at a glance the face of the long-dead Cardinal Smeaton, the cardinal whose portrait had arrested my eyes at Lowchester House!

VIII: THE CARDINAL'S CHAMBER

I shivered in every limb, and a cold beady dew sprang out on my temples as I stood with eyes riveted on the spectral figure before me. The light from the lamp fell on the left side of the Cardinal's head with a weird and Rembrandt-like effect, revealing a face with the tightly stretched gray-blue skin of the dead, and a fiercely flashing eye that seemed to divine the fear and horror that possessed me. Never to my dying day shall I forget that awful burning eye, glowing in what seemed to be the face of a corpse. I saw in its depths a grim triumph, a sardonic rapture, and a hideous relish of the blind horror betrayed in my blanched and streaming face.

The faded *vieux-rose* robes of the Cardinal (through which, as it seemed to me, I could faintly see the gray walls of the castle) only served to heighten the unearthly pallor of the face.

I swayed to and fro in the weakness of a sudden fever. My dry lips bit the air. I raised a hand to my eyes to shut out the appalling sight; but of strength I had none, and my arm dropped nervelessly to my side. Presently—and I almost shrieked aloud as I saw it—his thin but redly gleaming lips moved, displaying a set of yellow and wolfish teeth.

"Come," he said, in hollow yet imperious tones; "it's a sair nicht, and there is shelter within."

"No! no!" I cried, in an agony of fearful apprehension. But even as I spoke I moved mechanically toward him, and no words can convey the horror with which I realized my unconscious advance.

The wind shrieked out anew, and a deluge of sudden rain beat down from the clouds above.

Nearer and nearer I drew, with staring eyes and parted lips, until, as I found myself within a few feet of the ghastly thing, I stretched out my hands toward it in mute and awe-stricken appeal.

In a moment the Cardinal's right hand shot out and fixed an icy grasp on my left wrist. I shivered violently to the very marrow, stricken powerless as a little child. The calm of despair came to me. I moved as in a dream. I was conscious that I was absolutely in the power of a spirit of the dead.

A flash of lightning and a crash of thunder heralded our entrance beneath the portcullis gate of the ruins.

I dared not look at the Cardinal's face. My eyes I kept on the ground, and I noted in a dreamily unconscious way the yellow pointed shoes of my ghostly guide as they slipped noiselessly from beneath the flowing draperies. At times, through his robes, I seemed to see glimpses of a white skeleton, and my teeth chattered loudly at the fearsome sight.

We had passed into the shelter of the archway that leads to the open courtyard of the castle, and on our right was a doorway that opened into a dark and damp recess.

Into this I was dragged, the bony fingers of His Eminence still eating into my throbbing wrist. At the distant end of the recess the Cardinal pressed with the open palm of his disengaged hand (for he had set down the lamp) a keystone that stood out an inch or so from the dripping and moss-grown wall. In immediate answer to the pressure a great block in the wall moved slowly inward, revealing a faintly lit staircase with a spiral descent, evidently cut through solid rock. This we descended, I half slipping, half dragged, until at length we reached a chamber lighted almost brilliantly with flickering tapers, and furnished in what had once no doubt been sumptuous fashion.

Here the Cardinal closed the old oak and iron-studded door with a clang that resounded eerily behind me and, releasing my almost frozen wrist, seated himself with grave dignity in a carved chair of ancient and pontifical design.

I looked around me.

The chamber, some sixteen feet square, was vaulted in the manner of a crypt, and the roofing stones were painted in frescoes, each panel representing the coat of arms of some old Catholic family. The walls were hung with faded and moth-eaten tapestry, depicting scenes of wild carousal, wherein nymphs, satyrs, and bacchantes disported themselves with cup and vine leaf to the piping of a figure that closely resembled his satanic majesty. In one corner of the room stood a *prie-dieu,* and above it a broken and almost shapeless crucifix, overgrown with a dry, lichenlike moss, and shrouded in cobwebs. In front of this, depending from the roof, swung an incense burner that emitted a faint green light and an overpowering and sickly aromatic vapor.

The floor was of plain, dull granite in smooth slabs, from which a cold sweat seemed to exude. The four chairs were of carved oak, with the high pointed backs of the cathedral stall, and on either side of each tall candles burned with sepulchral flames of yellow and purple.

In the center was a small square table of oak, the legs of which were carved to represent hideous and snakelike monsters, and on it stood a skull, a book, and an hour glass.

A sense of disconcerting creepiness was diffused throughout the chamber by the fact that it was overrun by numerous immense spiders, some red, some yellow, and others black. Indeed, so ubiquitous were these horrid creatures that once or twice I fancied I saw them running up and down the faint white lines of His Eminence's skeleton. But as the Cardinal himself evinced no signs of inconvenience from these intimate and presumably tickling recreations, I concluded that they were the fevered creations of my own heated imagination.

Another strange thing was that through the apparently material appointments of the chamber, I could dimly, yet undoubtedly, see the rough, dripping walls of the solid rock; and when, by the Cardinal's invitation, I seated myself on one of the chairs facing him, I was conscious that I passed, as it were, through it, and actually sat on a wet stone, to which the chair was seemingly but a ghostly and ineffective covering.

There was a certain sense of relief in this, for I argued that if my surroundings had no substance, no more probably had the Cardinal or the spiders. And yet a glance at my wrist showed me the livid imprints of His Eminence's bony fingers.

Presently I ventured to let my gaze fall on the Cardinal and was somewhat relieved to note in his otherwise inscrutable face a distinct twinkle of amusement. The corners of his lips suggested an appreciation of humor; and his eyes betrayed an ill-concealed merriment as, from time to time, I shifted uneasily on my seat in an endeavor to find the driest part of it.

I was reflecting on the strange calm that was gradually coming to me—for, oddly enough, I began to lose the overwhelming sense of terror that a few minutes before had possessed me—when my ghostly companion broke the silence, speaking in profound and dignified tones.

"When the moon is at the full, gude sir, and eke the tide is low, a body that spiers within the castle gates maun e'en be guest o' mine."

I did not quite understand this, but feeling it to be an announcement that demanded a response of some sort, I replied respectfully, if somewhat feebly, "Quite so."

That my answer did not altogether satisfy His Eminence seemed apparent, for after regarding me in contemplative silence for a moment he uttered the portentous words, "I'm tellin' ye!"

I quite felt that it was my turn to say something, but for the life of me I could not focus my ideas. At length, with much diffidence, and with a distinct tremor in my voice, I murmured, "I fear I'm inconveniencing Your Eminence by calling at so late an hour."

At this the Cardinal lay back in his chair and laughed consumedly for the space of at least a minute.

"Gude sake!" cried he at last. "The Sassenach is glib eneuch tae jest; wi' deeficulty nae doot, as indeed befits the occasion!"

It will be observed that my ghostly prelate spoke in broad Scotch, much as Kirkintulloch did, with, however, the difference that is lent to speech by cultured cadences and a comparatively exhaustive vocabulary. From the unexpected laughter with which my diffident remark had been received, I instinctively derived a cue. It seemed to me that the Cardinal appreciated the subdued effrontery that I now perceived in my words, though at the moment of their utterance, heaven knows, I only intended to convey extreme humility and deference. So I hazarded a question.

"May I ask," I ventured, with deferential gravity, "what keeps Your Eminence up so late?"

"Hech! sir," was the reply. "That's what liteegious folk would ca' a leadin' question. Forbye, I'm no just at leeberty tae tell ye. Ye see, folk maun work oot their ain salvation, and it's no permitted to the likes o' me, a wanderer in the speerit, to acquaint mortal man wi' information as to the existence of heaven, hell, purgatory, or—or otherwise."

"Then," I timidly pursued, with a good deal of hesitation, and beating about the bush to find appropriate terms, "I presume I have the—the—honor of addressing a—a spirit?"

"Jist that," responded the Cardinal, with a sort of jocose cordiality that was very reassuring and comforting.

His whole manner had incredibly changed and was now calculated to set one at ease, at least as far as might be between one representative of the quick and another of the dead. So conspicuously was this the case that I soon found the fear and horror that at first had so completely overwhelmed me replaced by an absorbing and inquisitive interest.

IX: HIS EMINENCE AND I

"From the exalted ecclesiastical position held in life by Your Emi- nence," I presently found myself saying, "I feel justified in assuming that you are now enjoying the well-merited reward of residence in heaven."

The Cardinal eyed me shrewdly for a moment and eventually replied in diplomatic but evasive terms—

"I'm obleeged for the coampliment, be it merited or otherwise; but I'm na' disposed tae enter into ony personal exposeetion of my speeritual career. This, however, I'm constrained to tell ye, that nine tenths o' the clergy and pious laity of a' creeds, at present in the enjoyment o' life, will be fair dumfounded when they shuffle off this moartal coil and tak' possession of the immortal lodgin' provided for them—lodgin's that hae scant resemblance to the tangible Canaans of their quasi-releegious but businesslike imaginations. Catholic and Protestant alike, they're a' under the impression that releegion is a profession for the lips and no' for the lives. As for Presbyterians, aweel! they'll find oot in guid time the value o' their dour pride in hard and heartless piety. They ken fine hoo tae mak' a bargain in siller wi' their neebors, but the same perspicacity 'll no' avail them when it comes tae——but Hoots! It's nae business o' mine." Then, as if to change the subject, he added, "I suppose ye've read a' aboot me in the Histories of Scotland?"

"Well," I replied, "I've read a good deal about Your Eminence. I've often pictured you sitting at a window of the castle, watching with grim enjoyment young Dishart burning at the stake."

It was an unwise remark to make, and I saw the Cardinal's eye flash balefully.

"Yer speech," he answered slowly and with dignity, "is no' in the best of taste, but it affords me an opportunity of explaining that misrepresented circumstance. Ye see, from a lad upward, I was aye fond of a bonfire, and what for was I no' to watch the bonny red flames loupin' up forenenst the curlin' smoke? Was that pleasure tae be denied me, a' because a dwaibly manbody ca'd Dishart was frizzlin' on the toap? Na, na, guid sir, I was glowering at the bonny flames, no' at Dishart. I saw Dishart, nae doot; still, and there had no' been a fire, I wouldna hae lookit."

During this speech my attention had been somewhat distracted by the creepy spectacle of two spiders, one red, one black, fighting viciously on one of His Eminence's white ribs. The sight affected me so disagreeably that I felt constrained to inform the Cardinal of the unpleasant incident.

"Your Eminence will excuse me," I said respectfully, "but I see two poisonous-looking spiders diverting themselves on one of your ribs, the lowest but one on the left side."

The Cardinal smiled, but made no movement. "I'm much obleeged," he responded, with grave amusement. "Nae doot ye're ruminatin' that sich internal gambols are no' compatible wi' the residence in heaven ye were guid eneuch to credit me wi'." Then, with a certain air of resigned weariness, he added, "Dinna mind them, they're daein' nae herm; ye canna kittle a speerit, ye ken."

My seat was so extremely wet, and the damp was now penetrating my clothes in such an uncomfortable manner, that I resolved to assume an erect position at any cost. I may mention that we have rheumatism in our family. I cast about in my mind for a suitable reason for rising, and after some hesitation rose, remarking—

"Your Eminence will excuse me, but I feel it fitting that I should stand whilst a prelate of your exalted rank and undying celebrity" (this last, I thought, under the circumstances, a particularly happy inspiration) "is good enough to condescend to hold intercourse with me."

"Ay! Ye're guy wet," replied the undying celebrity, with a grasp of the situation that I had not looked for.

I stood shifting about on my feet, conscious of a rather painful stiffness in my joints, and wondering when and how this extraordinary séance would draw to a close, when the Cardinal, who had been lost for a time in the silence of a brown study, suddenly leaned forward in his chair and addressed me with an eager intensity that he had not displayed before.

"I'm gaun tae tell 'ee," said he, "what for I summoned ye here this nicht. Here!" he exclaimed, and rising he indicated the vaulted chamber with an imposing sweep of his gaunt arms and bony fingers. "Here! In this ma *sanctum sanctorum*."

He paused and eyed me steadily.

"I'm delighted, Your Eminence," I murmured feebly.

"Ye'll be mair than delighted, I'm thinkin'," he continued, "when ye ken ma purpose; the whilk is this. The moarn's moarn ye're playin', an I'm no mistaken, a match at goalf agin a callant ca'd Jim Lindsay?"

"That is so," I answered, in vague bewilderment at this sudden reference to a standing engagement in real life. For a moment a wild doubt swept over me. Was I living or dead? The dampness of my trousers gave a silent answer in favor of the former condition.

"Aweel!" resumed the Cardinal, "I'd have 'ee ken that he's a descendant in the straight line o' ane o' my maist determined foes—ye'll understand I'm referrin' tae sich time as I was Cardinal Airchbishop o' St. Magnus in the flesh—and ony blow that I can deal tae ane o' his kith is a solace to ma hameless and disjasket speerit. Noo, in ma day, I was unrivaled as a gowfer; there wasna ma equal in the land. Nane o' the coortiers frae Holyrood were fit tae tee a ba' tae me. It's a fac'. And here—here ma gentleman!" (and the Cardinal sank his voice to the low tremulous wail of a sepulchral but operatic specter, and his eyes gleamed with the sudden and baleful light that had first so riveted my gaze), "ahint the arras in this verra chamber is concealed ma ain bonny set of clubs!"

He paused and scrutinized my face to observe the effect of this announcement. I accordingly assumed an expression of intense interest.

"Noo," he continued, his eyes blazing with vindictive triumph, "I'm gaun tae lend ye this verra set o' clubs, an' I guarantee that an ye play wi' them ye'll win the day. D'ye hear that?"

"It is extremely good of you," I murmured hurriedly.

"Hoots! It's mair for ma ain gratification than for yours. In addeetion I'll be wi' ye on the links, but veesible to nane but yersel. Ye'll wun the day, and fair humeeliate the varmint spawn o' my ancient foe; and, eh! guid sir, but these auld bones will fair rattle wi' the pleasure o't! Will 'ee dae't?"

"I will," I solemnly replied. What else could I have said?

"Then hud yer wheest whiles I fetch the clubs."

With this His Eminence turned to the tapestry behind him, and, drawing it aside, disclosed a deep and narrow cavity in the rock. From this he extracted, one by one, a set of seven such extraordinarily unwieldy-looking golf clubs that I felt it in me to laugh aloud. Needless to say I indulged in no such folly. I examined them one by one with apparent interest and simulated appreciation, as, fondling them lovingly, my companion expatiated on their obviously obsolete beauties. A strange and almost pathetic enthusiasm shone in his eyes.

"Nane o' yer newfangled clubs for me," cried the Cardinal; "they auld things canna be bate. Tak' them wi' ye back tae whaur ye bide; bring them to the links the moarn's moarn, and as sure as we stand here this nicht—or moarn, fur the brak o' day is close at haun'—I'll be wi' ye at the first tee, tae witness sic a game o' gowf as never mortal played before. But eh! guid sir, as ye'd conserve yer body and soul frae destruction and damnation, breathe nae word o' this queer compact tae man, wumman, or bairn. Sweer it, man, sweer it on this skull!"

His bloodless hands extended the grinning skull toward me, and I, repressing an involuntary shudder, stooped and kissed it.

A gleam of malignant triumph again lit up his face as I took the oath. Then he seized the weird-looking clubs and, caressing them with loving care, muttered to himself reminiscences of bygone years.

"Ay, fine I mind it," he cried, "when young Ruthven came gallivantin' tae St. Magnus and thocht his match was naewhere tae be foond. We had but five holes in thae days, ye ken, and ilka yin a mile in length. Hech, sir! what a match was that! I dinged him doon wi' three up and twa tae play. Ye'll no be disposed to gie me credence, but it's a fact that I did yin hole in seventeen!"

"That was unfortunate," I replied, mistaking his meaning.

"Ay, for Ruthven," was his quick and peevish rejoinder. "For he took thirty-seven and lost the hole."

I had not grasped that he considered his own score extremely good.

"Of course I meant for Ruthven," I stammered, with the vague and silly smile of clumsy apology.

"Ye didna," replied His Eminence; "but I'm no mindin'. Ruthven, wi' a' his roughness, was an affectit callant in thae days, and rode his horse atween ilka shot. He moonted and dismoonted seeventy-fower times in three holes that day." And the Cardinal chuckled loud and long.

He related many other tales of his prowess with great gusto and enjoyment. We were now on such unaccountably familiar terms that

I ventured to tell him of the marvelous goal I had won, playing for the Lahore Polo Cup in '62, when, of a sudden, he interrupted me, crying out—

"The oor is late! Ye maun hae a sleep. Awa! man, awa! For ony sake, tak' the set and awa!"

And indeed I needed no second invitation; so, seizing the seven weird clubs, I made a low obeisance to His Eminence, and turning, found the door behind me open. I fled up the stone-cut staircase, passed like a flash through the recess to the archway, and, with a cry of such delight as surely never greeted mortal ears, I hailed the faintly dawning day. With the joy of a captive set free, or the rapture of one who has returned from a living tomb to bustling life, I inhaled the precious air in deep lung-filling draughts.

The storm had passed, the sea was calm, birds twittered in the gently whispering trees, the world was waking, and I was on its broad earth again.

But my thoughts were chaos. My brain refused to work. I had but one desire, and that was to sleep. In wretched plight I reached the doors of the hotel, where the astounded night porter eyed me, and more particularly the hockey-stick-like clubs, with a questioning surprise and bated breath.

I made him bring me a stiff glass of hot whisky and water. This revived me somewhat, and telling him to warn my servant not to call me before 10 A.M., I staggered to my room, flung the clubs with a sudden, if scarcely surprising, abhorrence into a wardrobe, got out of my dripping clothes into welcome pajamas, and, pulling the bedclothes up to my chin, was soon at rest in a dreamless sleep.

X: THE FATEFUL MORNING

I woke to find sunshine streaming in at the windows, a cloudless sky without, and my servant Wetherby busily occupied over his customary matutinal duties.

With a sudden flash of memory I recalled the weird scene of the night that was gone, only, however, to dismiss it as an unusually vivid dream. For a time I felt quite sure it was nothing more. But presently, as my eye fell on the empty glass that had held the hot whisky and water, I began to experience an uneasy doubt.

Ah! Now I remembered!

If it were a dream, there would be no clubs in the wardrobe.

I lit a cigarette, and asked Wetherby the time.

"Ten o'clock, sir," was the reply; "and you've no time to lose, sir. The match is at eleven."

I sprang from bed and casually opened the wardrobe.

Good heavens! It was no dream! There they were! Seven of the queerest clubs that antiquarian imagination could conceive.

So it had actually happened! I had been the guest of Cardinal Smeaton's ghost, and had entered into a compact with him to use his ridiculous clubs in order that he might revel in a trumpery revenge on the house of Lindsay.

Be hanged if I would! I remembered vaguely that in law an oath extracted from a party by threat or terror was not held to be binding, and I determined to ignore my unholy bond with the shadowy prelate. I would play with my own clubs and be defeated like a man.

I jumped into my bath. The pure morning air swept through the open window, the sunlight streamed in on the carpet and danced in circles of glancing gold in the clear cold water of the bath, and a glow of health and vigor (despite the late hours I had kept) sent the blood tingling through my veins. Indeed, what with the ordinary routine of dressing, my servant's presence, the hum of life that came from the links, the footsteps of housemaid and boots hurrying past my door, and generally my accustomed surroundings, I found it all but impossible to believe that I had really gone through the strange experiences of a few hours ago.

Yet, undoubtedly, there stood the clubs. Curious and perplexing ideas flashed through my mind as I dressed, ideas that clashed against or displaced each other with kaleidoscopic rapidity.

Was such an oath binding? Was the whole incident a dream, and the presence of the clubs an unexplainable mystery? Was there mental eccentricity on either side of my family? Had my father, the son of a hundred earls (or, more correctly, of as many as can be conveniently crowded into a period of a hundred years), transmitted to me some disconcerting strain in the blue blood that filled my veins; or, had my mother, with her less important but more richly gilt lineage, dowered me with a plebeian taint of which absurd superstition was the outcome? Or had the combination of both produced in myself a decadent creature abashed at his first introduction to the supernatural? How could I tell? Was there really a spectral world, and I its victim? Was I reaping the harvest of years of cynical unbelief? Was I myself? And, if not, who was I?

I gave it up.

I determined to ignore and if possible to forget entirely my creepy adventure in the vaults of the ruined castle. In this endeavor I was assisted by the pangs of healthy hunger. There is something so homely, so accustomed, so matter-of-fact in a good appetite, that I felt less awed by the unwilling oath I had taken, when Wetherby announced that an omelette and a broiled sole were awaiting me in the next room.

I was endeavoring to force into my tie and collar one of those aggravating pins that bend but never break, and alternately wounding my neck and my forefinger in the process, when, through the open window, my eye fell on a dense and apparently increasing crowd that surged on the links behind the first teeing ground. A dozen men held a rope that must have measured close on a hundred yards, and behind it the entire population of the town seemed to be gathering.

What could it be? Possibly a popular excursion, a public holiday, or a big professional match.

I asked Wetherby.

"I understand, sir," replied that phlegmatic youth, "the crowd is gatherin' in anticipation of your match with Mr. Lindsay, sir."

"Oh! Is it?" I murmured vaguely.

"It's been talked about considerable, sir."

"Has it?" was all the comment I could muster.

I was appalled at the sight. There was a horribly expectant air in the crowd. Their faces had that deadly going-to-be-amused expression that I have seen in the spectators at a bullfight in Spain. Many eager faces were turned in the direction of my windows, and I shrank instinctively into the seclusion that a muslin curtain affords.

That dim recollection of the bullfight I had seen in Cadiz haunted me.

Was I to be a golfing bull?

Or was Lindsay?

Was I to be the golfing equivalent of the wretched horse that eventually is gored to death, to the huge delight of thousands of butcher-souled brutes?

Well, if so, they would see a bold front. I'd show no craven spirit.

I began to wonder if the seven queer clubs had the properties that the Cardinal claimed for them. And then an idea seized me. I would have them near me on the links, and if the game went desperately against me I'd put them to the test.

"Wetherby," I said, as I put the finishing twist to my mustache, "I should like you to carry these odd-looking clubs round the links in case I want them. I don't propose to use them, but it is just possible that I might."

"Yes, sir."

I handed him a capacious canvas bag. I had purchased three similar bags from Kirkintulloch by his advice, one for fine weather, a second for wet, and the third (which I now gave Wetherby) an immense one for traveling. Kirkintulloch had informed me that without these my equipment as a golfer was incomplete.

"I don't wish them to be seen, unless it happens that I decide to use them, so you needn't follow me too closely," I added.

"I understand, sir."

"But you'll be at hand should occasion arise."

"Certainly, sir."

And shouldering the seven unwieldy weapons, Wetherby left the room with a twinkle in his eye that I had never remarked before.

I took another furtive glance at the crowd, and my heart gave a leap as I saw way being made for a party that included Mrs. Gunter and Lord and Lady Lowchester.

I passed mechanically to my sitting room and sat down to breakfast.

I began to eat.

Thanks to the discipline of daily habit, my hands and jaws performed their accustomed tasks, but my mind was in a condition alternately comatose and chaotic, so much so that it was a matter of surprise to me when I found my eyes resting on the bones of my sole and the sloppery trail of a departed omelette.

I drained my coffee to the dregs and lit a cigarette.

I began to feel a sense of importance. The knowledge that one's personality is of interest to a crowd is always stimulating, but I was haunted with the uncomfortable reflection that sometimes a crowd is bent on jeering, not to say jostling. Ah! if only I could manage that those who came to laugh remained to—well to laugh at the other man.

Presently the door opened and Wetherby presented himself, with the smug deference for which I paid wages at the rate of sixty pounds a year.

"Mr. Lindsay's compliments, sir, and if you are ready, sir, he is."

"I am coming," I replied, as, passing a napkin across my lips, I pulled myself together for the impending ordeal.

As I walked through the hall of the hotel I saw that the entire domestic staff had gathered together to witness my exit. There was an uncomfortable sort of suppressed merriment in their faces that was not encouraging. The waiter who attended me at meals had the refined impertinence to blush as I passed. The boots seized his lips with two blacking-black hands, as if to deny his face the satisfaction of an insubordinate smile. A beast of a boy in buttons winked, and the general manager bowed to me with a deference so absurdly overdone as to be extremely unconvincing.

I passed through the folding doors and stood on the steps of the hotel facing the crowd.

A tremendous cheer greeted me. When I say "cheer," possibly I don't quite convey what I mean. It was more of a roar. It was a blend of delight, expectation, amusement, derision, and exhilaration. Every face was smiling, every mouth open, every eye glistening. As the first hoarse echoes died a sound of gratified mumbling succeeded, as when the lions of the zoo, having bellowed at the first glimpse of their food, merely pant and lick their lips till the raw meat is flung to them.

Kirkintulloch was waiting for me at the foot of the steps. He looked a trifle shamefaced, I thought, and I fancied I heard him say to a bystander as I went toward him, "Aweel, it's nae business o' mine!"

Presently it pleased the mob to adopt a facetious tone, and as Kirkintulloch elbowed a passage for me through the crowd, I heard on all sides cries of "Here comes the champion!" "He's guy jauntylike!" "Eh! but he looks awfy fierce!" "Gude luck ti ye, ma man!" "He's a born gowfer!" "Gude sakes! He's a braw opeenion o' himsel'!" "The puir lamb's awa tae the slaughter!" "It's an ill day this for Jim Lindsay!" (this with a blatant laugh intended to convey irony) "Ay! His pride'll hae a fa', nae doot!" and the like.

XI: AN EXPECTANT CROWD

Of a sudden my heart stood still, and for a moment I stopped dead. There in front of me, and approaching by a series of jinks and dives amid the crowd, was the ghostly figure of the Cardinal. Faint and ill-defined as the apparition seemed in the brilliant sunshine, there was no mistaking the cadaverous features or the flowing robes. In less time than it takes to tell he had reached my side and was whispering into my ear.

"Dinna mind thae folk," he said, "they'll sing anither tune afore the day's dune. And dinna mind me. I'm no veesible to livin' soul but yerself, and nane but yer ain ears can hear what I'm sayin'. But if ye've a mind tae speak tae me, a' ye've got tae dae is to *thenk;* tae speak in tae yersel, as it were; for I can thole the jist o' yer thochts, wi' no sae muckle as a soond frae yer lips."

I was flabbergasted.

"Sic a clanjamfray o' vermin!" he added, as he swept a contemptuous glance over the noisy mob.

But his presence exasperated me beyond endurance. My nerves were strung to all but the breaking strain, and I found a relief in venting my spleen on this self-appointed colleague of mine.

"Look here," I said, and I was at no pains to conceal my illhumor, "I'm fed up with you! You understand, I'm sick of you and your devilish wiles. I'm no longer in your power, and I snap my fingers at you. Get out!"

I had neglected His Eminence's instructions only to *think* when I addressed him, and the crowd naturally regarded my words as a sally in reply to its own ponderous wit.

The result was a babel of words, furious, jocular, jeering.

"Did ye ever hear the like?" "Ay! Did ye hear him say 'deevilish wiles'? An' this a Presbyterian toon forbye!" "Mercy on us! An' ma man an elder in Doctor MacBide's kirk!" "Awa wi' the bairns; a'll no hae their ears contaminated," and so on.

"Hoots toots!" was the Cardinal's response, "and you a gentleman! I'm fair ashamed o' ye. But ye canna win awa' frae yer oath, ye ken. It wad mean perdeetion to yer soul an ye did, though I'm far frae assertin' that ye'll no receive that guerdon as it is."

I stopped again, with the intention of arguing out the point once and for all, when I realized that if I went on addressing this invisible specter, I might possibly be mistaken for a madman. I therefore contented myself with a withering glance of abhorrence at the prelate, and a few unspoken words to the effect that nothing in heaven or earth would induce me to have further truck with him. I then walked calmly on, but I was conscious of the ghostly presence dogging my steps with grim persistence, and several times I heard the never-to-be-forgotten voice mutter, "Ay! We'll jist see," or "M'hm! Is he daft, I wonder?"

At last I reached the inner circle of the crowd, and at the teeing ground Lindsay came forward, looking, I am bound to admit, the picture of manly health and vigor.

He held out his hand.

I accepted it with dignity, then looked about me, bowing here and there as I recognized acquaintances. This section of the crowd showed signs of better breeding. There was neither vulgar laughter nor insolent jeering. On the contrary, its demeanor was so extremely grave as to suggest to my sensitive imagination a suspicion of covert irony. I recognized many celebrities of the golfing world. There was Grayson, who wept if he missed a putt and spent his evenings in chewing the cud of his daily strokes to the ears of his depressed but resigned family. There too was Twinkle, the founder of the Oxbridge Golf Club, whose "style" was as remarkable as his mastery of the technical "language" of the game. Near him was General Simpkins, who, having had a vast experience of fighting on the sandy plains of the Sahara, now employed his old age in exploring the sandy tracts of the St. Magnus bunkers so assiduously that he seldom, if ever, played a stroke on the grass. He was one of the many golfers who find a difficulty in getting up a "foursome." Not far off was Sir William Wilkins, another notable enthusiast, whose scores when playing alone are remarkably low, though he seldom does a hole in less than eight strokes if playing in a game or under the scrutiny of a casual onlooker. I nodded to Mr. Henry Grove, the celebrated actor-manager, and a keen golfer. I didn't know that he was celebrated when first I met him, but I gathered it from the few minutes' conversation that passed between us.

Standing near the Lowchesters was Mrs. Gunter, in a heavenly confection of shell pink and daffodil yellow, a sort of holiday frock, delicate in tint, and diaphanous as a sufficiently modest spider's web. She greeted me with the brightest of smiles and laughingly kissed her finger tips to me. Certainly she was the most charming woman present. Her bright color and gleaming hair seemed to defy the wind and sunshine, though I fancy that rain might have proved a trifle inconvenient. There was no manner of doubt that I loved her. She represented to me a sort of allegorical figurehead symbolizing affluence, luxury, and independence. That is, assuming that she would consent to occupy the central niche in my own ambitious temple of matrimony.

Even the University of St. Magnus was represented in the gathering by a group of its professors, rusty-looking gentlemen who betrayed no indication of anything so trivial as a bygone youth; but, on the contrary, closely resembled a number of chief mourners at the funeral of their own intellects. A notable figure was the genial and cultured Doctor MacBide, one of the ablest and most popular divines that Scotland has given to the world, one in whom is to be found the rare combination of an æsthetic soul allied to a fearless character, a man who, keeping one eye on heaven and the other on earth, has used both to the benefit of the world in general and St. Magnus in particular.

Mr. Monktown, the more or less distinguished politician, was also in the crowd. His eyes had the faraway look of a minor celebrity on whom has been forced the conviction that due recognition of his talents will never be found this side of the grave. On the other hand, his charming and brilliant wife conveys the impression that she will continue to lustily insist on the aforesaid recognition until a peerage or some such badge of notoriety is administered as a narcotic by a peace-at-any-price premier.

But to enumerate all the interesting people in the dense crowd is an impossible task. Suffice it to say that such a constellation of golfing stars could be seen only on the links of St. Magnus, with perhaps the single exception of those of St. Andrews.

How little did the crowd guess that, unruffled and confident as I seemed, I yet knew that I was destined to a humiliating defeat; and how much less did I know what a bitter thing is defeat to a man of my sanguine temperament and former achievements!

XII: THE MATCH BEGINS

I was startled from a brief brown study by the sound of Lindsay's voice.

"Shall we toss for the honor?"

"As you please," I replied.

He spun a coin.

"Head or tail?"

I chose the head.

"It's a tail," he said, as, pocketing the coin, he took the driver that his caddie handed.

Then he drove. It was a magnificent shot, straight and sure, and the ball landed halfway between the public road and the stream that bounds the first putting green. A murmur of approval rose from the crowd.

Then I took up position.

Again a murmur arose from the crowd, but not a reassuring one.

Kirkintulloch endeavored to inspire me with confidence as he handed me my driver by whispering in a hoarse, spirituous undertone that must have been audible to everyone near, "Dinna mind the crowd, sir. Just pretend that ye *caan* goalf."

I was about to address the ball when my eye caught sight of the Cardinal. His face was livid with rage, and I could barely repress a chuckle as he shrieked in a voice that apparently only reached my ears (for the crowd never budged), "Tak' the auld clubs, I tell 'ee!"

Afraid of betraying myself by vacant look or startled mien, I ignored His Eminence's fury and precipitately drove the ball.

I topped it.

It shot along the ground, hurling itself against casual stones, as if under the impression that I was a billiard player desirous of making a break in cannons.

Then we moved on.

As we walked over the hundred yards that my ball had traveled, the Cardinal sidled up to me, and thrusting his face (through which I could clearly see a view of beach and sea) close to mine, exclaimed, "Ye're a fule!"

I took no notice. I was beginning to enjoy the discomfiture of one who had caused me such acute sufferings a few hours before.

"D'ye hear?" he persisted. "Wi' yer ain clubs ye're no match for a callant like Lindsay! For ony sake, tak' mine. Are ye feared the folk'll laugh at sic antediluvian implements? Ye needna mind the mob, I assure ye. If ye win hole after hole, ye'll turn the laugh on Lindsay, nae maitter what the clubs be like. Forbye, there's yer oath."

I still ignored him, and I saw the yellow teeth grind in silent fury.

Meantime, behind us plodded the crowd, the dull thud of their steps on the spongy grass almost drowned by their voluble and exasperating chatter.

There are no words in my vocabulary to express the humiliation that I felt as I played. I was at my worst. My second shot landed me about a hundred yards further; Lindsay dropped his onto the putting green. With my third the ball traveled to the burn and stopped there, embedding itself in the soft black mud. This incident afforded unbounded delight to the mob, and I fancied that I heard Mrs. Gunter's silvery laugh. The only satisfaction that I experienced was in the uncontrollable rage of the Cardinal. He danced and leaped about me, gesticulating wildly, alternately pouring sixteenth-century vituperation into my ears and imploring me to use his accursed clubs. He even indulged in weeping on the off-chance of softening my heart, but I saw no pathos in the tears that flowed down his spectral cheek from eyes that never lost their vindictive glare.

Lindsay behaved extremely well. He showed no sign of triumph as he won hole after hole, and several times he turned upon the crowd and upbraided them roundly for the howls of laughter with which they received my miserable efforts. Kirkintulloch became gradually more and more depressed and eventually took the line of a Job's comforter.

"It's jist as I tell't ye. He's layin' ye oot like a corp," said he.

"Well, let him," I growled.

"It's mesel' I'm thinkin' o'. Ye see I've a poseetion tae keep up. They a' ken I've been learnin' ye the game, forbye I'm the professional champion. I'll be fair howled at when I gang in tae the public hoose the nicht."

"Then the simple remedy is not to go there," I argued.

"Whaat? No gang tae the public hoose?"

I had apparently propounded a quite unheard-of course of action, but I stuck to it, and said, "No."

"Aweel," he resumed, "a' I can say is ye dinna ken oor faimily" (which was true). "Ma faither never missed a nicht but what he was

half-seas over in the 'Gowfer's Arms,' an' it's no in my blood to forget
the words, 'Honor yer faither and mither,' an' a' the rest o' it. So I
just dae the same, and it's a grand tribute to the memory o' my kith
and kin. Forbye—I like it. I canna sleep if I'm ower sober."

I leave the reader to imagine my feelings as Kirkintulloch thus un-
folded the hereditary tendencies of his family to one ear, and the
Cardinal poured violent anathemas into the other. The crowd was
convulsed in spasms of derisive delight at each of my futile strokes,
and certainly Mrs. Gunter seemed furtively amused when I ventured
to glance in her direction. Only Wetherby was unmoved. Bearing the
Cardinal's clubs, he followed me at a discreet distance, with an inscrutable expression that would have done credit to a priest of the
Delphic Oracle.

I got into every possible bunker, to the noisy gratification of the
mob which, despite the frequent remonstrances of the better class of
people present, had now abandoned itself to the wildest hilarity. The
match was, in fact, a harlequinade, with Lindsay as the clever clown
and myself as the idiotic pantaloon.

I seemed to tread on air, with only a vague idea of what was
going on.

By a lucky fluke I won the short hole, albeit in a rather undignified
manner. Mr. Lindsay's caddie, though some distance off, was nevertheless slightly in front of me as I drove, and my ball (which I topped
so that it shot away at right angles) struck his boot, on which Kirkintulloch loudly claimed the hole.

At the "turn" (*i.e.,* the end of the first nine holes) I was seven
down; and at the end of the eighteen—let me confess it at once—
Lindsay was sixteen up.

The first round over, the garrulous crowd dispersed in various
directions, gabbling, cackling, laughing, and howling with an absence of breeding truly astounding.

Even the "society" section no longer concealed its amusement.
I have never understood the limitations of that word "society." It
seems to me such an elastic term nowadays, that if a person says he is
in it, then *ipso facto* he is. Formerly it applied exclusively to my own
class, *i.e.,* the aristocracy; but since we latter have taken to emulating
the peculiarities and tendencies of the criminal classes we are
possibly excluded.

An interval of an hour and a half was allowed for luncheon, and
it was arranged that we should meet for the final round at 2:30.

I refused all invitations to lunch at the club or at private houses, and retired to a solitary meal in my own room.

But it was only solitary in a sense.

I had just begun to tackle a mutton cutlet and tomato sauce when, raising my eyes for a moment to look for the salt, I beheld my ubiquitous Cardinal seated opposite me.

This was a little too much, and seizing a decanter of claret I hurled it in his face. His shadowy features offered so little resistance that the wine eventually distributed itself over Wetherby, who seemed for once mildly surprised.

I muttered an apology to that irreproachable domestic, explaining that the liquor was corked, and then I desired him to leave the room.

I was alone with my tormentor, and I determined to have it out with him. But His Eminence anticipated me, for whilst I was framing in my mind a declamatory and indignant exordium, he leaned across the table, and with a singularly suave voice and subdued manner addressed me as follows:—

"I apologize, young sir, if I have caused you ony inconvenience on this momentous occasion. I was ower keen, an' I tak a' the blame o' yer ill fortune on ma ain shoulders. Just eat your denner like a man, and dinna fash yersel' wi' me; but when ye've feenished, an ye'll be sae gude as to hear me for the space of five meenits, I'll be obleeged. Mair than that, I'll undertake that ye'll no' be worrit by me again."

This was an important offer, and a certain unexpected charm in my unbidden guest's suavity turned the balance in his favor.

"Do you mean," I asked, "that if I grant you a short interview when I have finished luncheon, you will undertake to cease annoying me by your enervating companionship and intemperate language?"

"That's it," replied the prelate.

"Very good," said I; "I agree."

I continued the meal. Wetherby returned with a fresh bottle of wine and a custard pudding, brought me cigarettes, coffee, and cognac in due course, and though in the discharge of his duties he frequently walked through the dim anatomy of my ecclesiastical patron, his doing so seemed to afford no inconvenience whatever to that perplexing prelate.

As I ate and drank in silence my red-robed friend paced the room with bent head and thoughtful mien, in the manner adopted by every Richelieu that I have seen on the stage. I fancied that I detected a wistful glance in his eyes as from time to time I raised a glass of wine to my lips, but I may have been mistaken.

It must seem odd to the matter-of-fact reader that I could golf, talk, eat, drink, and generally comport myself as an ordinary mortal whilst haunted by this remarkable specter; but the fact is, I had no choice in the matter. Suppose I had drawn the attention of my neighbors to the fact that I was pursued by a shadowy Cardinal! It was abundantly clear that none but I could see him, and I should only have been laughed at. And, after all, a man of my varied experiences and quick intelligence adapts himself, through sheer force of habit, to any situation, though at the time he may utterly fail to comprehend its *raison d'être* or significance.

At one period of the meal I was on the point of asking Wetherby if he saw no faintly defined figure, robed in red and standing near him. But just as I was about to speak to him he advanced with the coffee, and in setting down the tray actually stood within the same cubic space that the Cardinal occupied. That is to say, I distinctly saw them mixed up with each other, Wetherby passing in and out of the prelate's robes quite unconsciously. Nor did His Eminence seem to mind, for not only did the coffee and cognac pass through the region of his stomach, but also the tray, cups, saucers, and cigarettes.

XIII: I TEST THE CLUBS

My luncheon over, I pushed back the plates, drank a glass of cognac, poured out a cup of coffee, and lit a cigarette.

The combined effects of the fresh air of the links and the moderately good wine I had drunk during lunch had braced me up, and as the first puff of pale blue smoke left my lips, I leaned back in my chair and contemplated my guest. "Well, old man," said I, with perhaps undue familiarity, "out with it!"

He turned and swept me such a graceful bow that I felt a sheepish shame at the flippant and vulgar tone I had adopted.

"I will noo mak' ye a final proposal, young sir," he said. "Ahint the hotel is a secluded field, and if ye'll tak' ma clubs there and try a shot or two, I ask nae mair. If so be ye find a speecial virtue in them, gude and weel; if no', then a' thing is ower atween us, and the even tenor o' yer way'll no be interfered wi' by me."

I saw what he meant. I was to try the clubs and test the marvelous qualities that he insisted on.

Well, there was no harm in that.

I rang the bell and told Wetherby to carry the clubs to the field indicated by my ghostly counselor.

It was a good grass meadow of some ten acres, and not a soul was near, with, of course, the exception of the Cardinal.

I teed a ball, and selecting a club that most resembled a driver (though it was more like a gigantic putter than anything else), I began to address the ball.

As I did so I experienced a curious sensation.

I suddenly felt as if I had been a golfer all my life. There was no longer any hesitation as to where my hands or feet should be. Instinctively I fell into the right attitude.

I was no longer self-conscious. I found myself addressing the ball with the same easy grace I had observed in Kirkintulloch. A sense of extraordinary power came over me. My legs and arms tingled as if some strong stimulant were flowing in my veins. The club had taken a mastery over me. I swung it almost involuntarily, and the first shot was by far the finest drive I had ever made. I tried again and yet again, six shots in all, and each was as straight and sure as the very best of Lindsay's.

I was amazed and dumfounded.

"Weel! Did I no' tell ye?" cried the Cardinal, as he hopped about in a grotesque and undignified ecstasy. "Try the putter noo!"

I took the putter. It was something like a flat-headed croquet mallet, and very heavy. Then I threw a silver matchbox on the ground to represent a hole and began to putt.

I simply couldn't miss it. A sense of awe came over me.

No matter from what distance I played, nor how rough the ground was, the ball went straight to the box, as a needle to a magnet. I even tried to miss it and failed in the attempt.

I looked at His Eminence, and words fail me to describe the childish yet passionate exultation that shone in his face.

"I can dae nae mair!" he cried. "Ye see what they're like. Play wi' them, and ye'll win as sure as my name's Alexander Smeaton! It's a fact. Ay! And ye've time to wander into the clubhoose and lay yer wagers, if ye're minded to mak' a wheen siller. For the love o' ma auld bones, dae as I tell ye, man!"

I didn't at all love his old bones, but my mind was made up.

"I'll play with the clubs," I said, and the old man staggered in an intensity of delight.

"Hech! sir," he cried, "this'll be a grand day for Sandy Smeaton! When the match is ower I'll be there to compliment ye, and then— aweel, then I'll no fash ye till ye 'shuffle off yer mortal coil,' as auld Bacon has it. When ye're like myself—a speerit, ye ken—ye may be glad tae hae a freend at court, an' I'll dae what I can for ye. I can introduce ye to a' the canonized saints. They're a wheen ponderous in conversation and awfy orthodox in doctrine, but on the whole verra respectable. Hooever, that'll no' be for a while. Meantime, young sir, win yer match and humeeliate this varmint spawn o' the hoose o' Lindsay. So—'Buon giorno'—as we used to say in the auld Vatican days—'A rivederci!'"

With these valedictory remarks the Cardinal left me, and returning the clubs to Wetherby, who had been standing some hundred yards off, I returned to the hotel.

It was two o'clock.

How shall I describe what I felt? I could win this match—of that I felt absolutely sure. I cannot explain this curious sense of certainty as to the issue of the game, but I knew by a sort of prophetic inspiration that I could not lose.

The Cardinal had hinted at wagers. Well, why not?

I could turn the tables on some of the crowd who had smiled in pity at my efforts of the morning, and there is no revenge so sweet as that of scoring off men who have laughed at one. I decided to get a little money on the event, if possible.

I strolled leisurely over to the club and entered the smoking room, an immense room with bay windows that open onto the links. It was crowded. The members had finished luncheon and were discussing coffee, liqueurs, cigars, and cigarettes, amid a noisy jingle of laughter, talk, clinking of glasses, tinkling of cups, hurrying footsteps of waiters, and general hubbub.

My entrance had something of the effect that oil has on troubled waters. Everybody near me ceased laughing. No doubt I had been the bull's-eye for their hilarious shafts of wit. They hemmed and hawed as if I had detected them in some nefarious plot. A few bowed to me, and one or two invited me to have a drink. But I was bent on business, so, joining a group in which I saw a few acquaintances, I asked casually if any bets had been made on the match.

"Not one, don't you know!" replied O'Hagan, a Scotch youth of Irish name, who cultivated a highly ornate English accent with intermittent success.

"Anybody want a bet?" I asked, adding, "Of course I should want very heavy odds."

There was a general movement on this. Members gathered round me, some laughing, some chaffing, some whispering. Lowchester came up to me and growled in an undertone, "Don't make a fool of yourself, my dear chap; you can't possibly win."

"Still, I don't mind making a bet or two," I persisted. "Will anyone lay me fifty to one?"

"I'll lay you forty to one in fivers," said Mr. Grove, the actor, no doubt considering the publicity of the offer as a good advertisement.

"Done!" I replied, and took a note of it.

"So will I!" "And I!" "Put me down for the same." "In sovereigns?" "Yes." "Tenners if you like!" "Done!"

These and other cries now sounded all round the room till the babel reminded me of the Stock Exchange, and I think quite two thirds of the men present laid me the odds at forty to one in sovereigns, fivers, or tenners.

I suppose they considered me a madman, or at least an intolerably vain and eccentric person who deserved a "dressing down." A hurried adding up of my bets showed me that I stood to lose about £250, or win £10,000.

It was now past two o'clock, and we moved off to the links. The crowd was not quite so dense. Evidently many people considered the match as good as over, and the interest of those who remained was almost apathetic. The heavy midday meal that is eaten in St. Magnus may account to some extent for this lethargy.

I found the faithful Wetherby waiting for me, at a discreetly remote distance, and telling him that I meant to play with the clubs he was carrying, I walked up to Kirkintulloch. The latter had all the air of a martyr. His head was thrown back, as if in the act of challenging the world in general to laugh at him. He glared suspiciously at everyone near him and with difficulty brought himself to touch his hat at my approach.

I chuckled inwardly.

"Whaat's this I hear, sir?" he said. "Ye've been wagerin', they tell me."

"I've made a few bets, if that's what you mean," I answered.

"Weel, sir, as man tae man, if ye'll excuse the leeberty, ye're fair demented. It's no' possible to win. A'body kens that. As for mesel', I'm the laughin'stock o' the toon. I huvna had sae muckle as time for ma denner——"

"Why not?" I asked.

"I've been busy blackin' the een and spleetin' the nebs o' yer traducers. I've been fechtin' seeven men. It's a caddie's beesiness to stand up for his maister, nae maitter what kind o' a gowfer he is."

"Ah, well!" I answered, "you'll make them sing to another tune tonight. I am going to play with these."

And uncovering the canvas flap that concealed them, I exposed the weird-looking clubs to his gaze.

I think he thought I was joking. He looked first at the clubs, and then at me, with a half-questioning, half-stupid twinkle in his hard, blue eyes. Then he spat.

I apologize to the reader for mentioning anything so unpleasant, but it is an uncomfortable habit that certain classes indulge in when they desire to punctuate or emphasize their views. Amongst themselves, I believe, it is considered highly expressive, if employed at the true psychological moment.

"What kin' o' things are they?" he asked, after a portentous pause.

"The clubs I mean to play with," I replied.

"Aweel!" he answered, "that concludes a' relations atween us. I may be daft, but I'm no' a fule, an' I'm seek of the hale stramach. Ye mun get another caddie, I'll no cairry the likes o' thae things."

"My servant is going to carry them," I answered quickly; and I fancied Kirkintulloch looked a trifle crestfallen at such an unexpected exhibition of independence.

"I'll be glad, however," I added, "if you'll accompany me round the links, and I promise you the pleasing sensation of astonishment if you do."

With this I left him, but I could hear fragments of a voluble explanation that he apparently deemed it necessary to make to the bystanders.

"There are leemits, ye ken—it's no' for the likes o' me to say— I've been a caddie twenty-fower year—the man's no' richt in the heed—no' but what he's free with his siller an' a born gentleman—

I wouldna say he wasna—but ma name's Kirkintulloch, an' I've a poseetion tae keep up."

The clock of the parish church boomed out the half-hour, and I advanced to the teeing ground, with Wetherby at my heels. The flap had been replaced over the heads of the clubs, and the bag looked ordinary enough, though my new "caddie" was so faultlessly attired in his well-cut gray suit as to be a target for the derision of a number of Kirkintulloch's professional friends.

XIV: THE SECOND ROUND

The "honor" being Lindsay's, the first drive was his. It was a clean-hit ball, but a wind had arisen that carried it a trifle out of the course.

Then I took my stand and received from Wetherby the Cardinal's driver.

Of all hearty laughter that my ears have ever listened to, none could equal that of the bystanders who were near enough to see the club. If I had made the most witty joke that mind can conceive, it could not have elicited more spontaneous, prolonged, or uproarious appreciation. Mrs. Gunter's mezzo-soprano rang out in a paroxysm of musical hysterics. Even Lindsay edged behind me that I might not see the smile he found it impossible to repress. Members of the club and their friends, who had behaved with decorous gravity during the morning, now abandoned themselves frankly to unrestrained laughter. The infection spread to the masses of the crowd who were not near enough to see my curious club, and they gradually pressed closer and closer, anxious to share and enjoy any new source of merriment, so that it took the men with the rope all their time to maintain the semicircle that divided the spectators from the players.

Under ordinary circumstances I should have resented such behavior, but somehow it didn't seem to affect me. I even felt inclined to join in the general hilarity. I certainly felt the humor of the situation. As it was, I approached the ball with perfect composure and the ghost of a sardonic smile.

And then I drove it.

Away it winged, hard-hit and fast, traveling straight in the line of the hole. I had never, of course, played such a magnificent shot, and the effect on the crowd was electrical. Laughter died of a sudden, as if choked in a thousand throats. Broad grins seemed frozen on the upraised faces round me. Mouths opened unconsciously, eyes stared vacantly at the flying ball. For the moment I was surrounded by so many living statues, transfixed in mute amazement.

I think it was Lowchester who first spoke. "A fine shot," I fancied I heard him say mechanically.

We moved on, and the act of walking loosened the tongues around me. A confused murmuring ensued, gradually increasing in volume till everybody seemed to be talking and arguing, agreeing with or contradicting each other at the pitch of the voice.

I caught stray phrases from time to time.

"I never seed the likes o' that." "Man, it was a braw drive!" "He'll no' dae it again, I'm thinkin'." "By Jove! that was a flyer—but what an extraordinary club!" and so on.

I had outdriven Lindsay by about sixty yards—no small feat when one bears in mind that he has the reputation of being the longest driver living.

His second shot was a good one, landing him some thirty yards short of the burn. As we reached my ball, I selected the Cardinal's ponderous and much-corroded cleek. There were faint indications of amusement at the sight of it, but a nervous curiosity as to my next shot was the predominating note.

I played the shot quite easily. As before, the ball flew straight as a bird in the line of the hole, crossed the burn and dropped dead within a few feet of the flag. An unwilling murmur of admiration rose from the crowd, and Lindsay, no longer smiling, said very frankly that he had never seen two finer strokes in his life.

I think it only right to admit that he is a sensible, manly, and modest fellow.

He took his lofting iron and with a very neat wrist shot dropped the ball dead, within a foot of the hole.

A hearty cheer greeted the stroke. It was quite evident that he was the popular favorite. Well, I could wait, and I meant to.

Arrived on the putting green, I advanced with the odd-looking putter. One or two of the spectators indulged in a cynical, though somewhat half-hearted, snigger at its curious lines, but for the most part the crowd was quite silent, and one could almost feel in the air the nervous tension of the onlookers. My ball was about seven feet from the hole. With complete self-possession I went up to it and glanced almost carelessly at the ground.

There was a dead silence.

I played, and the ball dropped lightly into the hole. I was one up on the second round. I had holed out in three.

I half expected a murmur of applause for the putt, but a bewildered stupor was the actual effect produced. In all that concourse of people only two appeared to be quite calm and collected, namely, Wetherby and myself. I caught a glimpse of Kirkintulloch's face. The features were there, but all expression had departed.

For myself, I walked on air. The outward calm of my demeanor gave no index to the wild exultation that I felt. Truly there is no more satisfying or stimulating anticipation than that of a coming revenge. The sentiment, I am aware, is not a Christian one, but at least it is eminently human. I felt no desire to be revenged on Lindsay. Any hostile feeling that I had entertained toward him had passed away. But I did desire to score off the crowd. More, I desired to humiliate Mrs. Gunter. Her callous treatment of me, her silvery but malicious laughter, her avowed admiration of Lindsay, had galled me to an extent the expression of which I have carefully kept from these pages. *Noblesse oblige!* One cannot be rude. But I wanted to annoy her—a very common phase of love.

As the match proceeded I won hole after hole, often in the most astonishing manner. Twice I landed in bunkers close to the greens (the result of exceptionally long shots), and in each case the Cardinal's iron lifted the ball from the sand and deposited it in the hole. I cannot take credit to myself for such prodigious feats; they were undoubtedly the work of the clubs.

At the eighth hole, however, I experienced an important reverse. It is, as everybody who knows the St. Magnus links is aware, the short hole. I took the iron and dropped the ball within a yard of the hole. Lindsay followed and landed some twenty yards off; and then, by a splendid putt; he holed out in two. I, of course, had no difficulty in doing likewise, and we halved the hole; but the awkward fact remained that I must now gain every hole to win the match, for my opponent's score was nine up, and there only remained ten holes to play.

If the match was intensely exciting—and to me it was more than that—the demeanor of the crowd was no less psychologically interesting. The tag-rag and bobtail, with the fickleness that has ever characterized the emotions of the unwashed, and even of the occasionally clean, now began to acclaim me as their chosen champion, and each brilliant shot I made was hailed with a vociferous delight that might have turned a less steadily balanced head than my own. The reason of this is, of course, more or less obvious. There is more pleasurable excitement to be derived from making a god of the man whose star is in the ascendant than in continuing allegiance with falling crest to one whom we have placed on a pinnacle by an error of judgment, to which we are loath to attract attention.

But if the crowd was a source of ever increasing interest, what shall I say of the demeanor of the men who had made heavy bets with me?

It is not strictly true that Scotchmen are mean in money matters, any more than it is to say that they can't see a joke. As regards the latter point, it is my experience that a Scot won't laugh at the average jest that amuses an Englishman, simply because it isn't good enough. And since he doesn't laugh he is supposed to have missed the point. In support of my theory is the fact that there is an established vein of Scotch wit and humor, but I have yet to learn that England has evolved anything of the sort. True, England has many comic papers, and Scotland has none. But it must be borne in mind that the statements announcing such periodicals to be "comic" emanate solely from the proprietors.

There is, however, a substratum—or rather a perversion—of truth in the aphorism that deals with the Scotch and their money. And I take it the real truth is that a Scot cannot bear to part with money for which he gets no return of any sort—a very natural and proper feeling. Again, he dislikes any extra or unusual call on his purse. For the rest he is generous, hospitable, and public-spirited to a degree. It may be argued that if this be the case the Scot ought never to make a bet; the answer to which is that as a rule he doesn't, unless something almost in the nature of a certainty presents itself. Then he forgets his nationality and becomes merely human. And that is precisely what happened to my Caledonian friends in the smoking room of the club. An apparently unprecedented opportunity of making a little money had presented itself, and they had accepted its conditions with a noisy humor intended to lacquer their inbred acquisitive propensities.

And now, as I casually watched their faces, I saw an interesting awakening. Their faces were as those of infants who, having been roused from a long and profound sleep, gaze about with inquiring but stupefied wonder. They were quite silent for the most part, as with every shot I played they seemed to feel the sovereigns melting in their pockets. Ah! this unhappy craze for gold! I have seen the same set faces at Monte Carlo, when, as the croupier cries out, "Rouge, Pair et Passe!" the bulk of the money is staked on "Noir, Impair et Manque." How deplorable it all is! And I stood to win £10,000— a most exhilarating prospect.

XV: IN THE THROES

As the match progressed I continued playing an absolutely fault-less game, and there was no manner of doubt that Lindsay had become more or less demoralized. At the end of the fifteenth hole his score was reduced to two up, with three more holes to play. That is to say, so far I had won every hole of the second round, with the exception of the short one which we had halved. I had only to win the last three holes to gain the match, nay more, to break the record score of the links!

A curious change in the crowd's bearing was now apparent. They preserved a complete silence. Each shot, whether my own or Lindsay's, was played in a profound stillness. An intense suppressed excitement seemed to consume every soul present. Even during the marches from shot to shot scarcely a word was spoken; only the dull thud of thousands of feet gave audible token of their presence.

The news of the sudden and extraordinary change in the fortunes of the game had evidently traveled backward to St. Magnus, for as we worked homeward the mob was increased at every hole by such vast numbers that it seemed impossible for the men with the rope to control so great a concourse.

Once or twice I glanced in Mrs. Gunter's direction, and I should have thought her face was pale but for two vivid splashes of a most exquisite carmine that glowed, or at all events dwelt, on her cheeks. Her jet-black eyebrows formed two thoughtful lines below the golden cloud of her beautiful hair. How resplendent she was! I have never seen a complexion at all like hers except on the stage. What wonder that Lindsay should be demoralized, with the prospect of being fore-stalled hanging over him like the sword of Damocles?

Only once did I catch sight of the shadowy Cardinal, and that was at the end of the sixteenth hole, which I had won easily. As we walked toward the teeing ground of the seventeenth I chanced to let my eyes fall on the railway shed built against the wall bounding the links, and there—executing the most extraordinary and grotesque fandango of delight—was His Eminence. He was evidently in a rapture of delirious intoxication, for, in the passing glimpse I had, I saw him standing on his head, so that the ghostly robes fell downward to the roof of the shed, leaving his white skeleton immodestly bare and feet upward in the air. It was not a pleasing exhibition, and very nearly unnerved me; but the mere handling of my marvelous driver seemed to steady me in a moment. And fortunately none but I could see the antics of my ecclesiastical patron.

Reader, do you know what it is to be outwardly as calm as a blasé policeman, and all the time quivering with inward excitement? If I could have yelled once or twice it would have been an immense relief, but I had a part to play, and I meant to play it. As it was, I puffed carelessly at a cigarette, professed to admire the view, glanced carelessly at my watch, and generally indulged in such little bits of byplay as were calculated to indicate extreme *sang-froid*. [I ought to mention that I am a very capable amateur actor, and at our annual Thespian Club theatricals always take the leading part. I founded the club and manage it.]

That I played my new role of champion golfer with credit was evident. The seething crowd had originally assembled to jeer, but it remained to accept me at my own valuation—always a pleasing change to find registered in the barometer of public opinion.

My drive at the seventeenth hole (the last but one to be played) was a perfect shot, whilst Lindsay's was comparatively feeble. He was now but one up, and at the end of the hole we ought to be "all square and one to play." But the strain on my nerves was beginning to tell. I felt like Hood's Eugene Aram—

> "Merrily rose the lark, and shook
> The dewdrop from its wing;
> But I never marked its morning flight,
> I never heard it sing;
> For I was stooping once again
> Beneath the horrid thing!"

I was conscious in a vague somnambulistic fashion of the green links, the blue sky, the purple crowd, splashed here and there with the bright colors of frock and parasol. My eyes took in mechanically the onward movement of the people, the rosy light that caught the spires of the old gray town, the shrieking railway train, the red blaze of the sun in the windows of St. Magnus, and a hundred other ocular impressions. Yet all these things seemed unreal; the dream background in a land whereof the Cardinal, Lindsay, and I formed the sole population.

Moreover, pressing as it seemed on my very brain, came the humiliating conviction that I was nothing short of a fraud, a charlatan, a ghostly conjurer's accomplice.

Was it an honorable game that I was playing? Would I be justified in taking the money I stood to win? Was it fair to usurp the throne of champion by the aid of a supernatural agency, whose purpose I could not even pretend to fathom? Could I look Mrs. Gunter in the face if, crowned with a stolen golfing halo, I asked her to be my wife? And if I couldn't, what more deplorable type of lover was possible? Ought I to burden myself with a secret that I should have to carry with me in silence to the grave? Was the nominal prefix "Honorable," with which my parents had dowered me without either warrant on my part or inquiry on their own, to be a prefix only? These and many other thoughts flashed through my mind as we played the seventeenth hole.

I got on the green in three, Lindsay in four. He then played the "two more," and by a remarkably good putt holed out in five.

I took the putter, and in a profound and most impressive silence holed out in four. A stifled gasp rose from the crowd.

The score was now "All square, and one to play."

I stood on the teeing ground of the eighteenth hole. The landscape in front of me was blurred and blotted; the dense crowds on either side of me were as mere inky blotches. The ground at my feet seemed miles away. Only the teed ball was in focus. That I saw clearly.

It was a test moment in my life. I could lose the match if I chose, and keep a clean conscience.

I could play the last hole with my own clubs!

And if I did—well, I'd lose; but, by heaven! I'd still be an honorable gentleman.

I caught sight of Lindsay's face. It was white and set, but he looked a manly fellow for all that. It was a cowardly trick to tear the laurels from his brow as I was doing. He had won them after a life-time's devotion to the game.

And I——?

Faugh! I would not touch the accursed clubs again. For aught I knew, to win was to sell my soul, and become a servile creature doomed to the tender mercies of a phantom's patronage.

"Ye fushiomless eediot!" I suddenly heard the words ring in my ears, and at the same moment I saw the Cardinal's deadly face peering into my eyes as if to read my very soul. "What's come ower ye? Are ye daft? Nane o' yer pauky humor at this time o' day. Tak' ma driver an' catch the ba' the bonniest skite of a'! Whaat?"—and his voice rose in indescribable fury—"Ye'll no do sic a thing? Ye lily-livered loon, if ye dinna dae as I tell ye I'll hae ye back in the castle vaults and wring the neck o' yer soul wi' ma ain bony fingers! Ay, an' haunt ye till the day ye're deid!" (What good purpose could be served by haunting me till the day of death, after wringing the neck of my soul, was not quite clear.) "Mind that!" he continued. "I'm no' to be trifled wi'!"

I turned on him and answered deliberately, "You fiend!"

"Beg pardon, sir?" said Wetherby. I had forgotten for the moment and spoken aloud.

"Give me the driver from Kirkintulloch's bag," I replied.

Kirkintulloch heard me and elbowed his way to my side. He was shaking with excitement. I feel certain he had never been so sober for years.

"Will 'ee no jist gang on wi' the one ye've been playin' wi'?" he urged. "Ye're daein' fine!"

"Give me the driver with which I played the first round this morning," I persisted.

During all this the Cardinal was moving and shrieking round me in a whirlwind of red draperies and white corroded bones.

Reluctantly Kirkintulloch drew the driver from his bag and handed it to me.

"I think ye're wrong, sir," he whispered very earnestly in my ear, mixing himself up with the demented prelate in doing so.

"For heaven's sake let no one speak to me!" I cried. "Get out of my way!" I added fiercely—really to the Cardinal, though Kirkintulloch, Wetherby, and everyone near seemed to take it to themselves, and drew back hastily. Then I gave a vicious kick at His Eminence's shins. Lowchester has since told me the action appeared most inexplicable and uncalled for, inasmuch as I apparently kicked at space.

I addressed the ball.

His Eminence promptly sat on it. Then, stretching his arms in front of me, he cursed me wildly and volubly in Latin. What the exact words were I cannot tell, and could not have translated had I known, but the general effect was awful.

Crash through his bones—not that such a trifle could inconveaience my intangible enemy—went the club.

The ball, feebly struck on the top, shot along the grass and dropped into the burn!

The match was as good as lost.

A shriek, whether of delight, dismay, relief, or anxiety, I know not, rose from the mob. I believe everyone in that crowd was suffering from the same nervous strain that affected me.

Then Lindsay stepped to the front.

He drove a magnificent ball, and, strange as it may seem, the mere sight wrought a complete upheaval of the altruistic pedestal on which I had perched myself. I was suddenly conscious of a wild exasperation at having thrown my chances to the winds. For, after all, my objections to winning had been purely sentimental, not to say childish. It is marvelous how the realization of our best intentions very frequently betrays the insincerity of the moral mood that inspired them. It is easy to be magnanimous if we don't foresee the unhappy but common result of poignant regret.

The vision of a heavenly and luxurious life with Mrs. Gunter seemed to fade. I turned and looked at her. She was as white as a sheet, save for the faithful discs of carmine. Ah, what a fool I had been!

But the game was not yet over; and even as the thought flashed across me, Lindsay made his first serious mistake. It was a mistake of judgment.

"Thank heaven," he exclaimed, with an ill-bred grunt of relief, "I've cooked your goose for you at last!"

I have no doubt this thoughtless and ill-timed speech was the result of the strain he had been put to. Perhaps I ought to have made allowance for it. In point of fact, it reawakened in me the most consuming desire to win, and I cursed my extravagant magnanimity.

Meantime a rapt and beautiful change had come over the faces of the men with whom I had made bets. Frowns were dissipated as by a ray of beatific sunshine, and lively smiles and chuckles were the order of the moment. There was even a touch of insolence in their sidelong glances. They began to chatter volubly. I could hear the drift of their sudden recall to speech.

"I knew he was bound to break down in the long run," said somebody.

"Undoubtedly; still he's played a remarkable game." "I win ten pounds"—"And I a fiver," and so forth. My miserable drive had acted on their tongues as the first round of champagne does at dinner.

We were walking toward the burn as Lindsay spoke, and I was about to answer when—springing apparently from nowhere—the Cardinal again appeared, or rather shot up before me, in a state of incontinent frenzy. None the less, he seemed to divine the thoughts that were chasing each other through my mind, for, bending toward me, he whispered in hoarse, trembling tones, and with the utmost intensity—

"Tak' ma club! Tak' ma club!! Tak' ma club—ye eediot!!! He's dealt ye a black affront; but, by a' the buried bones o' the Smeatons he hasna yet won the day!"

"You think I still may win?" I silently asked him, albeit in a state of incredulous stupefaction.

"Try, man—try!" he shrieked in reply; "I'll see what I can dae!"

And with that he caught up his skirts and flew off in a series of amazing leaps and bounds in the direction of the last hole. What this change in his tactics meant I was at a loss to conjecture.

I wish I could adequately describe the extraordinary flight of the prelate across the green turf of the links. He seemed to be borne on the wings of the wind, and each leap he took must have covered at least twenty yards. He gave me the impression of a grotesque competitor in an unearthly game of "Hop, skip, and leap." At length, after an elapse of perhaps fifteen seconds, I saw him halt in the distance about twenty yards from the red flag of the hole. Then he turned and faced us, as if patiently awaiting the next shot. I little guessed what his purpose was. His figure was clearly outlined against a distant crowd of some two or three hundred assembled behind the final hole to witness the end of this unprecedented struggle.

XVI: AN EXCITING FINISH

My ball was duly fished out of the burn and dropped behind my shoulder. I returned my own faithless driver to Kirkintulloch and once again took hold of the Cardinal's. As I did so a telepathic throb of excitement passed through the bystanders.

I played the shot.

It eclipsed all my former efforts. I never have seen, nor shall I ever see again, such a hard-hit ball. With a trajectory scarcely higher than that of a rifle bullet at a medium range, it winged its way straight to the hole, dropping eventually within a yard or so of His Eminence. And then, straining my eyes, I saw a sight that startled me into a sudden realization of the latter's purpose. He had, so to speak, fielded the ball—that is to say, he had dashed toward it as it fell; and now, by a series of nervous but skillful kicks, he was directing its course straight to the hole! The red skirts were held high in his hands, and the white bony legs flashed to and fro as he sped in the wake of the running globe. I could not, of course, actually see the ball, but, by an intuition that admitted of no doubt whatever, I knew what he was up to. I held my breath in an agony of suspense as nearer and nearer to the red flag flew the gaunt figure of the Cardinal. I swear my heart stopped beating, and the paralyzed crowd seemed similarly affected, though the sight that I saw was mercifully denied to its eyes. There was no doubt about it. The Cardinal had so manipulated the ball that I had holed out in three.

But the match was not yet over.

What Lindsay's feelings at the moment were I know not, but he managed to play a clever second stroke that landed him on the green, some seven feet from the hole.

And now came the supreme moment.

If Lindsay holed his putt we halved the match, if he failed I won the day.

Such was the pressure of the excited crowd that only the most strenuous efforts enabled the rope holders to maintain a clear circular space round the hole. It measured about fifteen yards in diameter, and within this charmed circle stood Lindsay and his caddie, Wetherby and Kirkintulloch, old Jock Johnson (the keeper of the green), Hanbury-Smith (the captain of the golf club), and myself. All other spectators were without the pale, with the important exception of the Cardinal.

I looked about me. My part in the game was over. I had but to watch and wait. I was thankful the final shot was Lindsay's and not mine.

The faces of my betting friends had changed again in expression and become drawn and strained. The unfortunate gentlemen no longer chattered and chuckled. The magnet of luck was again slowly but surely attracting golden coins from the depths of their purses, and such pangs could only be borne with dumb fortitude.

The crowd were so terribly congested that two women fainted. I looked anxiously at Mrs. Gunter, but—thank Heaven!—the rich carmine still glowed on her cheeks.

At length, putter in hand, Lindsay approached his ball, and even the breathing of the crowd seemed to be suspended.

I moved to a spot some six feet from the hole, on the opposite side to Lindsay. As I did so my eyes fell on the ground, and I saw a startling and curious sight.

My terrible ally, the Cardinal, had stretched himself at full length, face downward, on the turf, so that his ghastly head was directly over the hole and his shadowy feet close to mine.

A sense of faintness crept over me.

As in a red mist I saw Lindsay strike the ball. I saw it traveling straight and sure to the hole!

And then—heavens above us!—I saw the Cardinal take a quick and gulping breath, and blow with might and main against the skillfully directed ball! It reached the edge of the hole, trembled a moment on the brink, and then ran off at an angle and lay still on the turf a couple of inches from the hole!

I had won the match.

A tumult sounded in my ears, the sky turned a blazing scarlet, the crowd swam before my eyes, and of a sudden I fell prone on the turf with my nose plunged in the fateful hole!

When I came to myself I found kind friends grouped about me, and my head resting luxuriously in Mrs. Gunter's lap. I think I should have been perfectly happy and content with this state of things, had I not unfortunately just at that moment caught a glimpse of the ubiquitous Cardinal standing ridiculously on his head and kicking his heels in mid-air in an ecstasy of frenzied glee.

The sight so upset me that I went off a second time into a dead faint.

XVII: AND LAST

Again I was myself, and this time I felt revived and strong. I rose to my feet. Immediately the crowd closed round me and acclaimed me with cheers and yells. Presently I found myself being carried shoulder-high by a dozen lusty caddies, Kirkintulloch heading their progress with proud bearing and gleaming eye.

A thousand voices were howling "See, the conquering hero comes!" A thousand hats and handkerchiefs were waving in the air. A thousand smiling faces beamed up into mine.

Mrs. Gunter cried out to me, as I passed her in triumphal procession, "You'll dine with the Lowchesters tonight, won't you?"

And turning a smiling and radiant face to her, I answered, "I will."

I was the idol of the hour, not—I may add—an altogether new experience.

At length, after what seemed an eternity of acclamation and adulation, I was set down in the great bay window of the club and immediately surrounded by all members who had *not* made bets with me. Fulsome flattery, genuine congratulation, and general admiration were showered on me. At writing tables in distant corners of the room I saw my betting friends busily writing out checks. They did not seem inclined to participate in the enthusiastic ovation. But what did I care?

Surfeited with the overwhelming tributes to my achievement (and, I fancy, to my personality), I broke away from my friends, only to be seized again by my escort of caddies and carried shoulder-high in the direction of the Metropole. The sturdy fellows finally deposited me on the top step of the main entrance to the hotel, and I stood facing the seething crowd.

Here a fresh outburst of applause greeted me from my fellow guests and the domestic staff.

I bowed incessantly right and left.

"Speech! Speech!" now rang out on every side from a thousand throats, and I felt that if only to get rid of them, I must say something. So holding aloft my right hand as a token that I accepted the invitation, and in the profound silence instantly produced by my action, I said—

"My friends, I thank you. I have excelled in all other games, and why not in golf? Again I thank you."

The simple words completely captivated them, and I retired indoors to a volley of tumultuous and long-continued cheers.

As an example of how trivial things often imprint themselves on our dazed memories during crises in our lives, I remember noting, as I passed through the hall to my suite of rooms, an immense pile of luggage, evidently just arrived, and labeled "The Prince Vladimir Demidoff." I had not heard of his intention to visit St. Magnus. In fact, I don't think I'd ever heard of the man at all.

Reaching my room, I stretched myself on a couch, lit a cigarette, and got Wetherby to bring me a stiff brandy-and-soda. At last, thought I, I had breathing space. Imagine, then, my consternation and irritation when, on opening my eyes—I had closed them for a moment as I reveled in the first deep draught of my "peg"—I beheld, seated opposite me, His Eminence!

"Upon my soul!" I cried, "this is too bad. You swore——"

"Hud yer wheesht!" interrupted the Cardinal. "I'm here to thank ye and bid ye gude-bye."

"I'm glad to hear it," I muttered, sulkily.

"Ye've focht a grand fecht," he proceeded, "an' I'm much obleeged tae ye. But, man, there's ae thing that worrits me extraordinar'. Ye ken, I had tae cheat! I aye played fair in the auld days, and it gaed agin' the grain tae blaw on Lindsay's ba' at the last putt, but what could I dae? Hooever, it canna be helpit. The queer thing is that noo that my revenge is complete, it doesna seem to gratify me muckle. Hech, sir!—life moartal or speeritual's guy disappintin'. For a' that I'm much obleeged, an' ye'll never see me mair. Gude-bye!"

And with that he faded into space, and, truth to tell, he has honorably abstained from haunting me since.

Sheer physical fatigue precluded the possibility of anything in the nature of psychical research, or even of attempting to think out the weird supernatural experiences I had gone through.

I was dozing off into a gentle sleep when Wetherby opened the door and informed me that Kirkintulloch was waiting below and would be proud if I could grant him a short interview.

I consented, and presently Kirkintulloch appeared.

"It's no' for the guinea I've come, sir," he began (I've no doubt, by way of a gentle reminder); "I thocht ye'd be glad o' a card wi' yer score, an' I've had it made oot."

He handed me a card, and on it I read the score:—

$$\begin{array}{lccccccccc}
\text{Out,} & 3 & 3 & 4 & 3 & 4 & 5 & 3 & 2 & 3 & \bullet & 30 \\
\text{In,} & 3 & 2 & 3 & 4 & 5 & 3 & 3 & 4 & 3 & \bullet & 30 \\
\end{array}$$

Total • • • $\overline{60}$

"Ye're a credit to my teachin', sir," he continued, "an' I'm real prood o' ye. The record for thae links is seventy-twa, and ye're jist a clean dozen below that. The likes o' it was never seen. It's a fact. Ay! an' long after a'body here's dead ye'll still hud the record. I little thocht I had pit ma ain style sae coampletely into ye! Ye're a pairfect marvel!"

"Thank you," I muttered wearily.

"I see ye're tired, sir, an' I'll no keep ye, but jist afore I gang, wad ye mind showin' me thae queer-like clubs ye played wi'?"

"By all means," said I. "Wetherby, where are the clubs?"

"Ain't you got 'em, sir?" asked the latter, with some surprise.

"Not I!" I answered. "You had them."

"Well, sir, I can't quite tell 'ow it is, but in the crowd I suddenly felt 'em slip out from under my arm, and look as I would I couldn't lay eyes on 'em after that. I supposed some friend of yours had taken them out of curiosity and meant to bring 'em to you, sir."

"Dinna fash yersel'," broke in Kirkintulloch; "if they're in St. Magnus I'll lay hands on them, never fear. Gude nicht, sir!"

And so that admirable caddie passed out of my life. I tipped him well (and I've since been told he paid me the high—if deplorable— compliment of a week's continuous intoxication), but from that day to this no mortal eye has seen the bewitched clubs of the ghostly Cardinal Archbishop of St. Magnus.

Much revived by two hours' sound and dreamless sleep, I dressed at half past seven, and a few minutes before eight I started for the Lowchesters' house.

It had somehow got abroad that I was dining there, and a large crowd had assembled in front of the hotel. I was again received with an outburst of cheers and subsequently escorted to my destination to a lustily sung chorus of "For he's a jolly good fellow!"

Arrived at the Lowchesters' gates, I bade the kindly crowd good night and retired from their sight to a final volley of echoing cheers.

I need not describe the welcome I received from my host and hostess, Mrs. Gunter, and the other guests. Even Lindsay spoke to me tactfully on the subject of our match, expressing genuine admiration of my performance, though I was slightly startled when he said, "In fact, I consider your play today nothing short of supernatural."

So did I, but I didn't venture to say so.

The dinner was delightful. Excellent food, perfect wine, charming people, and myself the center of interest. I ask no more at such a function.

I took my hostess in to dinner of course but on my other side was Mrs. Gunter, exquisitely dressed in a Parisian triumph of eau-de-Nil velvet with groups of mauve and purple pansies. Her wonderful complexion was more ravishing than ever in the soft lamplight. Indeed it seemed to have specially adapted itself to the requirements of her delicately tinted gown. Her hands and arms had the bloom of peaches, and her luxuriant hair, dark underneath, was a mist of ever changing gold on the top.

Several times during dinner I saw the jet-black lashes raised and felt her glorious eyes regarding me with the rapt gaze of hero worship.

Well, tonight I should know, for weal or woe, what fortune the Fates held in store for me.

When the ladies had left us I drew Lindsay aside on the pretense of examining some engravings in the hall, and as soon as we were alone I touched on the subject uppermost in my mind.

"I think it only right to tell you, my dear Lindsay," I began, "that tonight I shall propose to Mrs. Gunter, and if by any chance she should dismiss me, then I leave the field clear for you. I have to thank you for all the courtesy you have shown during my visit to St. Magnus, and I sincerely trust that whatever may happen we shall always remain friends."

"As far as I'm concerned you may be sure of that," replied Lindsay. "But it does seem to me that you've been laboring under a delusion. I've never desired to propose to Mrs. Gunter. And even if I wanted to, I couldn't. I'm a married man, with three of a family. More than that, I'm very deeply in love with my wife, and not at all with Mrs. Gunter."

"But—good heavens!" I exclaimed, "surely we agreed——"

"If you remember," he interrupted, "that night in the Racing Club, I wanted to explain these things, and you simply wouldn't hear me."

"Then," I continued blankly, as in a sudden flash of memory I recalled the fact he alluded to, "we've been fighting for nothing?"

"Exactly," he replied.

In silence we shook hands, and the matter dropped.

Presently we joined the ladies in the drawing room, and after a decent interval I drew Mrs. Gunter aside. We sat by each other on a couch concealed from view by a group of palms. A pretty girl in white was playing the "Moonlight Sonata."

I admit it at once—my heart was beating. I wished I had rehearsed the role I was about to play. Then I reflected that I had often witnessed proposals on the stage, so taking a leaf from that reliable book I cleared my throat.

"Mrs. Gunter," I began, "may I say Katherine?"

"Ah! So it has come to this!" she murmured, lowering her eyes with the most captivating grace.

"Yes, this," I whispered passionately. "This, that I love you and only you! This, that I am here to ask you to be my wife!"

"It can never be!" she murmured conventionally, and a low cry, half sob, half sigh, escaped her.

"Katherine!" I cried. "Why not?"

"Because," she answered slowly, and as if the words were dragged from her, "I have lost every penny of my fortune. And a penniless woman I cannot, will not come to you. Unless——" and her voice trembled into silence.

She was wearing several thousand pounds' worth of diamonds at the time, but somehow I didn't grasp the sparkling contradiction.

Now I am a man of quick resolution. I can grasp a situation in a moment. In a flash I realized that I alone could never afford to keep this beautiful creature in surroundings worthy of her, at least not without such personal sacrifice as at my time of life would be extremely inconvenient. I am but a younger son. To force her then to marry me under such circumstances would be a cruelty to her and an injustice to myself.

Afraid, therefore, that the murmured word "Unless——" was about to open up possibilities not altogether desirable, I broke the silence with—

"And so you dismiss me?"

She looked at me for a moment in blank surprise.

Then the ghost of a faint smile flickered over her face, as she answered—

"Yes, *so I dismiss you!*"

I gave a suitable sigh.

The "Moonlight Sonata" was over, and poor Katherine rose.

I followed her to a group of guests in the center of the room, and as I did so she turned and said—

"I was going to say, '*Unless* you can induce my future husband to give me up,' when you interrupted me."

"Your future husband!" I exclaimed aghast.

"Yes," she answered serenely; "let me introduce you to him."

And touching the sleeve of the good-looking foreigner who had taken her in to dinner, she said—

"Vladimir, let me present Major Gore," adding to me, "Prince Vladimir Demidoff. Didn't you know that we are to be married next week?"

I murmured confused words of congratulation and escaped to Lady Lowchester's side.

"Are they really going to be married?" I asked her.

"Of course they are!" replied my hostess. "Why shouldn't they?"

"But—but," I stammered, "she's lost every penny of her fortune!"

"Not she!" replied Lady Lowchester, with a merry ringing laugh. "That's what she tells every man who proposes to her. She says she finds it an excellent gauge of devotion."

"I see," I answered.

I stood still for a moment. Then I walked over to Lowchester and asked him which was the best morning train from St. Magnus to London.

I did not feel justified in keeping for my own use the £10,000 I had won, but it may interest the reader to know that with it I founded the now flourishing and largely patronized Home for Inebriate Caddies.

LISHEEN RACES,
SECOND-HAND

---

by *SOMERVILLE & ROSS*

(1897)

In the late 1880s Edith OEnone Somerville and Violet Florence Martin, two young cousins raised in Ireland's southwest country and saturated from childhood in its horse and hunting traditions, began to collaborate on stories and novels. Their first efforts were well received, but it was the publication in 1899 of Some Reminiscences of an Irish R.M. *(R.M. standing for Resident Magistrate) that ushered in their first exultant popular and critical acclaim. Since Miss Somerville used only her initials along with her last name and Miss Martin used a literary pseudonym (the Ross coming from the name of her family's seat), the fact that the authors were women was generally unknown and unsuspected for many years, which was the authors' intention, since they felt that the public might jump to the conclusion that women could not be expected to know the subjects which they usually wrote about. They went on from their first great success to write other wonderful stories and books, among them* Further Experiences of an Irish R.M., *published in 1908. Their first R.M. collection, however, is regarded as their classic performance.* Lisheen Races, Second-Hand *and* A Misdeal *come from that volume of stories, and in them you will meet Major Yeates (the R.M.), his wife, Philippa, Flurry Knox (the local master of the foxhounds), Slipper, and many of the other celebrated characters who appear in the stories.*

I T MAY or may not be agreeable to have attained the age of thirty-eight, but, judging from old photographs, the privilege of being

132

nineteen has also its drawbacks. I turned over page after page of an ancient book in which were enshrined portraits of the friends of my youth, singly, in David and Jonathan couples, and in groups in which I, as it seemed to my mature and possibly jaundiced perception, always contrived to look the most immeasurable young bounder of the lot. Our faces were fat, and yet I cannot remember ever having been considered fat in my life; we indulged in low-necked shirts, in "Jemima" ties with diagonal stripes; we wore coats that seemed three sizes too small, and trousers that were three sizes too big; we also wore small whiskers.

I stopped at last at one of the David and Jonathan memorial portraits. Yes, here was the object of my researches; this stout and earnestly romantic youth was Leigh Kelway, and that fatuous and chubby young person seated on the arm of his chair was myself. Leigh Kelway was a young man ardently believed in by a large circle of admirers, headed by himself and seconded by me, and for some time after I had left Magdalen for Sandhurst, I maintained a correspondence with him on large and abstract subjects. This phase of our friendship did not survive; I went soldiering to India, and Leigh Kelway took honors and moved suitably on into politics, as is the duty of an earnest young Radical with useful family connections and an independent income. Since then I had at intervals seen in the papers the name of the Honorable Basil Leigh Kelway mentioned as a speaker at elections, as a writer of thoughtful articles in the reviews, but we had never met, and nothing could have been less expected by me than the letter, written from Mrs. Raverty's Hotel, Skebawn, in which he told me he was making a tour in Ireland with Lord Waterbury, to whom he was private secretary. Lord Waterbury was at present having a few days' fishing near Killarney, and he himself, not being a fisherman, was collecting statistics for his chief on various points connected with the liquor question in Ireland. He had heard that I was in the neighborhood, and was kind enough to add that it would give him much pleasure to meet me again.

With a stir of the old enthusiasm I wrote begging him to be my guest for as long as it suited him, and the following afternoon he arrived at Shreelane. The stout young friend of my youth had changed considerably. His important nose and slightly prominent teeth remained, but his wavy hair had withdrawn intellectually from his temples; his eyes had acquired a statesmanlike absence of expression, and his neck had grown long and birdlike. It was his first visit to

Ireland, as he lost no time in telling me, and he and his chief had already collected much valuable information on the subject to which they had dedicated the Easter recess. He further informed me that he thought of popularizing the subject in a novel, and therefore intended to, as he put it, "master the brogue" before his return.

During the next few days I did my best for Leigh Kelway. I turned him loose on Father Scanlan; I showed him Mohona, our champion village, that boasts fifteen public houses out of twenty buildings of sorts and a railway station; I took him to hear the prosecution of a publican for selling drink on a Sunday, which gave him an opportunity of studying perjury as a fine art, and of hearing a lady, on whom police suspicion justly rested, profoundly summed up by the sergeant as "a woman who had th' appairance of having knocked at a back door."

The net result of these experiences has not yet been given to the world by Leigh Kelway. For my own part, I had at the end of three days arrived at the conclusion that his society, when combined with a notebook and a thirst for statistics, was not what I used to find it at Oxford. I therefore welcomed a suggestion from Mr. Flurry Knox that we should accompany him to some typical country races, got up by the farmers at a place called Lisheen, some twelve miles away. It was the worst road in the district, the races of the most grossly unorthodox character; in fact, it was the very place for Leigh Kelway to collect impressions of Irish life, and in any case it was a blessed opportunity of disposing of him for the day.

In my guest's attire next morning I discerned an unbending from the role of Cabinet minister toward that of sportsman; the outlines of the notebook might be traced in his breast pocket, but traversing it was the strap of a pair of field glasses, and his light gray suit was smart enough for Goodwood.

Flurry was to drive us to the races at one o'clock, and we walked to Tory Cottage by the short cut over the hill, in the sunny beauty of an April morning. Up to the present the weather had kept me in a more or less apologetic condition; anyone who has entertained a guest in the country knows the unjust weight of responsibility that rests on the shoulders of the host in the matter of climate, and Leigh Kelway, after two drenchings, had become sarcastically resigned to what I felt he regarded as my mismanagement.

Flurry took us into the house for a drink and a biscuit, to keep us going, as he said, till "we lifted some luncheon out of the Castle Knox people at the races," and it was while we were thus engaged that the first disaster of the day occurred. The dining-room door was open, so also the window of the little staircase just outside it, and through the window traveled sounds that told of the close proximity of the stable-yard; the clattering of hoofs on cobblestones, and voices uplifted in loud conversation. Suddenly from this region there arose a screech of the laughter peculiar to kitchen flirtation, followed by the clank of a bucket, the plunging of a horse, and then an uproar of wheels and galloping hoofs. An instant afterward Flurry's chestnut cob, in a dog-cart, dashed at full gallop into view, with the reins streaming behind him, and two men in hot pursuit. Almost before I had time to realize what had happened, Flurry jumped through the half-opened window of the dining room like a clown at a pantomime, and joined in the chase, but the cob was resolved to make the most of his chance, and went away down the drive and out of sight at a pace that distanced everyone save the kennel terrier, who sped in shrieking ecstasy be-side him.

"Oh, merciful hour!" exclaimed a female voice behind me. Leigh Kelway and I were by this time watching the progress of events from the gravel, in company with the remainder of Flurry's household. "The horse is desthroyed! Wasn't that the quare start he took! And all in the world I done was to shlap a bucket of wather at Michael out of the windy, and 'twas himself got it in place of Michael!"

"Ye'll never ate another bit, Bridgie Dunnigan," replied the cook, with the exulting pessimism of her kind. "The master'll have your life!"

Both speakers shouted at the top of their voices, probably because in spirit they still followed afar the flight of the cob.

Leigh Kelway looked serious as we walked on down the drive. I almost dared to hope that a note on the degrading oppression of Irish retainers was shaping itself. Before we reached the bend of the drive the rescue party was returning with the fugitive, all, with the exception of the kennel terrier, looking extremely gloomy. The cob had been confronted by a wooden gate, which he had unhesitatingly taken in his stride, landing on his head on the farther side with the gate and the cart on top of him, and had risen with a lame foreleg, a cut on his nose, and several other minor wounds.

"You'd think the brute had been fighting the cats, with all the scratches and scrapes he has on him!" said Flurry, casting a vengeful eye at Michael, "and one shaft's broken and so is the dashboard. I haven't another horse in the place; they're all out at grass, and so there's an end of the races!"

We all three stood blankly on the hall-door steps and watched the wreck of the trap being trundled up the avenue.

"I'm very sorry you're done out of your sport," said Flurry to Leigh Kelway, in tones of deplorable sincerity; "perhaps, as there's nothing else to do, you'd like to see the hounds——?"

I felt for Flurry, but of the two I felt more for Leigh Kelway as he accepted this alleviation. He disliked dogs, and held the newest views on sanitation, and I knew what Flurry's kennels could smell like. I was lighting a precautionary cigarette, when we caught sight of an old man riding up the drive. Flurry stopped short.

"Hold on a minute," he said; "here's an old chap that often brings me horses for the kennels; I must see what he wants."

The man dismounted and approached Mr. Knox, hat in hand, towing after him a gaunt and ancient black mare with a big knee.

"Well, Barrett," began Flurry, surveying the mare with his hands in his pockets, "I'm not giving the hounds meat this month, or only very little."

"Ah, Master Flurry," answered Barrett, "it's you that's pleasant! Is it give the like o' this one for the dogs to ate! She's a vallyble strong young mare, no more than shixteen years of age, and ye'd sooner be lookin' at her goin' under a sidecar than eatin' your dinner."

"There isn't as much meat on her as'd fatten a jackdaw," said Flurry, clinking the silver in his pockets as he searched for a match-box. "What are you asking for her?"

The old man drew cautiously up to him.

"Master Flurry," he said solemnly, "I'll sell her to *your* honor for five pounds, and she'll be worth ten after you give her a month's grass."

Flurry lit his cigarette; then he said imperturbably: "I'll give you seven shillings for her."

Old Barrett put on his hat in silence, and in silence buttoned his coat and took hold of the stirrup leather. Flurry remained immovable.

"Master Flurry," said old Barrett suddenly, with tears in his voice, "you must make it eight, sir!"

"Michael!" called out Flurry with apparent irrelevance, "run up to your father's and ask him would he lend me a loan of his sidecar."

Half an hour later we were, improbable as it may seem, on our

way to Lisheen races. We were seated upon an outside car of im-
memorial age, whose joints seemed to open and close again as it
swung in and out of the ruts, whose tattered cushions stank of rats
and mildew, whose wheels staggered and rocked like the legs of a
drunken man. Between the shafts jogged the latest addition to the
kennel larder, the eight-shilling mare. Flurry sat on one side, and
kept her going at a rate of not less than four miles an hour; Leigh
Kelway and I held on to the other.

"She'll get us as far as Lynch's anyway," said Flurry, abandoning
his first contention that she could do the whole distance, as he pulled
her onto her legs after her fifteenth stumble, "and he'll lend us some
sort of a horse, if it was only a mule."

"Do you notice that these cushions are very damp?" said Leigh
Kelway to me, in a hollow undertone.

"Small blame to them if they are!" replied Flurry. "I've no doubt
but they were out under the rain all day yesterday at Mrs. Hurly's
funeral."

Leigh Kelway made no reply, but he took his notebook out of his
pocket and sat on it.

We arrived at Lynch's at a little past three, and were there confronted by the next disappointment of this disastrous day. The door of
Lynch's farmhouse was locked, and nothing replied to our knocking
except a puppy, who barked hysterically from within.

"All gone to the races," said Flurry philosophically, picking his way
round the manure heap. "No matter, here's the filly in the shed here.
I know he's had her under a car."

An agitating ten minutes ensued, during which Leigh Kelway
and I got the eight-shilling mare out of the shafts and the harness,
and Flurry, with our inefficient help, crammed the young mare into
them. As Flurry had stated that she had been driven before, I was
bound to believe him, but the difficulty of getting the bit into her
mouth was remarkable, and so also was the crablike manner in which
she sidled out of the yard, with Flurry and myself at her head, and
Leigh Kelway hanging on to the back of the car to keep it from jam-
ming in the gateway.

"Sit up on the car now," said Flurry when we got out onto the
road; "I'll lead her on a bit. She's been plowed anyway; one side of
her mouth's as tough as a gad!"

Leigh Kelway threw away the wisp of grass with which he had
been cleaning his hands, and mopped his intellectual forehead; he

was very silent. We both mounted the car, and Flurry, with the reins in his hand, walked beside the filly, who, with her tail clasped in, moved onward in a succession of short jerks.

"Oh, she's all right!" said Flurry, beginning to run, and dragging the filly into a trot; "once she gets started——" Here the filly spied a pig in a neighboring field, and despite the fact that she had probably eaten out of the same trough with it, she gave a violent side spring, and broke into a gallop.

"Now we're off!" shouted Flurry, making a jump at the car and clambering on; "if the traces hold we'll do!"

The English language is powerless to suggest the view-halloo with which Mr. Knox ended his speech, or to do more than indicate the rigid anxiety of Leigh Kelway's face as he regained his balance after the preliminary jerk, and clutched the back rail. It must be said for Lynch's filly that she did not kick; she merely fled, like a dog with a kettle tied to its tail, from the pursuing rattle and jingle behind her, with the shafts buffeting her dusty sides as the car swung to and fro. Whenever she showed any signs of slackening, Flurry loosed another yell at her that renewed her panic, and thus we precariously covered another two or three miles of our journey.

Had it not been for a large stone lying on the road, and had the filly not chosen to swerve so as to bring the wheel on top of it, I dare say we might have got to the races; but by an unfortunate coincidence both these things occurred, and when we recovered from the consequent shock, the tire of one of the wheels had come off, and was trundling with cumbrous gaiety into the ditch. Flurry stopped the filly and began to laugh; Leigh Kelway said something startlingly unparliamentary under his breath.

"Well, it might be worse," Flurry said consolingly as he lifted the tire onto the car; "we're not half a mile from a forge."

We walked that half-mile in funereal procession behind the car; the glory had departed from the weather, and an ugly wall of cloud was rising up out of the west to meet the sun; the hills had darkened and lost color, and the white bog cotton shivered in a cold wind that smelt of rain.

By a miracle the smith was not at the races, owing, as he explained, to his having "the toothaches," the two facts combined producing in him a morosity only equaled by that of Leigh Kelway. The smith's sole comment on the situation was to unharness the filly, and drag her into the forge, where he tied her up. He then proceeded to whistle viciously on his fingers in the direction of a cottage, and to command, in tones of thunder, some unseen creature to bring over a couple of baskets of turf. The turf arrived in process of time, on a woman's back, and was arranged in a circle in a yard at the back of the forge. The tire was bedded in it, and the turf was with difficulty kindled at different points.

"Ye'll not get to the races this day," said the smith, yielding to a sardonic satisfaction; "the turf's wet, and I haven't one to do a hand's turn for me." He laid the wheel on the ground and lit his pipe.

Leigh Kelway looked pallidly about him over the spacious empty landscape of brown mountain slopes patched with golden furze and seamed with gray walls; I wondered if he were as hungry as I. We sat on stones opposite the smoldering ring of turf and smoked, and Flurry beguiled the smith into grim and calumnious confidences about every horse in the country. After about an hour, during which the turf went out three times, and the weather became more and more threatening, a girl with a red petticoat over her head appeared at the gate of the yard, and said to the smith:

"The horse is gone away from ye."

"Where?" exclaimed Flurry, springing to his feet.

"I met him walking wesht the road there below, and when I thought to turn him he commenced to gallop."

"Pulled her head out of the headstall," said Flurry, after a rapid survey of the forge. "She's near home by now."

It was at this moment that the rain began; the situation could scarcely have been better stage-managed. After reviewing the position, Flurry and I decided that the only thing to do was to walk to a public house a couple of miles farther on, feed there if possible, hire a car, and go home.

It was an uphill walk, with mild, generous raindrops striking thicker and thicker on our faces; no one talked, and the gray clouds crowded up from behind the hills like billows of steam. Leigh Kelway bore it all with egregious resignation. I cannot pretend that I was at heart sympathetic, but by virtue of being his host I felt responsible for the breakdown, for his light suit, for everything, and divined his sentiment of horror at the first sight of the public house.

It was a long, low cottage, with a line of dripping elm trees overshadowing it; empty cars and carts round its door, and a babel from within made it evident that the race-goers were pursuing a gradual homeward route. The shop was crammed with steaming countrymen, whose loud brawling voices, all talking together, roused my English friend to his first remark since we had left the forge.

"Surely, Yeates, we are not going into that place?" he said severely; "those men are all drunk."

"Ah, nothing to signify!" said Flurry, plunging in and driving his way through the throng like a plow. "Here, Mary Kate!" he called to the girl behind the counter, "tell your mother we want some tea and bread and butter in the room inside."

The smell of bad tobacco and spilled porter was choking; we worked our way through it after him toward the end of the shop, intersecting at every hand discussions about the races.

"Tom was very nice. He spared his horse all along, and then he put into him———" "Well, at Goggin's corner the third horse was before the second, but he was goin' wake in himself." "I tell ye the mare had the hind leg fasht in the fore." "Clancy was dipping in the saddle." " 'Twas a dam nice race whatever———"

We gained the inner room at last, a cheerless apartment, adorned with sacred pictures, a sewing machine, and an array of supplementary tumblers and wineglasses; but, at all events, we had it so far to ourselves. At intervals during the next half hour Mary Kate burst in with cups and plates, cast them on the table, and disappeared, but of food there was no sign. After a further period of starvation and of listening to the noise in the shop, Flurry made a sortie, and, after lengthy and unknown adventures, reappeared carrying a huge brown teapot, and driving before him Mary Kate with the remainder of the repast. The bread tasted of mice, the butter of turf smoke, the tea of brown paper, but we had got past the critical stage. I had entered upon my third round of bread and butter when the door was flung open, and my valued acquaintance, Slipper, slightly advanced in liquor, presented himself to our gaze. His bandy legs sprawled consequentially, his nose was redder than a coal of fire, his prominent eyes rolled crookedly upon us, and his left hand swept behind him the attempt of Mary Kate to frustrate his entrance.

"Good evening to my vinerable friend, Mr. Flurry Knox!" he began, in the voice of a town crier, "and to the Honorable Major Yeates, and the English gintleman!"

This impressive opening immediately attracted an audience from the shop, and the doorway filled with grinning faces as Slipper advanced farther into the room.

"Why weren't ye at the races, Mr. Flurry?" he went on, his roving eye taking a grip of us all at the same time; "sure the Miss Bennetts and all the ladies was asking where were ye."

"It'd take some time to tell them that," said Flurry, with his mouth full; "but what about the races, Slipper? Had you good sport?"

"Sport is it? Divil so pleasant an afternoon ever you seen," replied Slipper. He leaned against a side table, and all the glasses on it jingled. "Does your honor know Driscoll?" he went on irrelevantly. "Sure you do. He was in your honor's stable. It's what we were all sayin'; it was a great pity your honor was not there, for the likin' you had to Driscoll."

"That's thrue," said a voice at the door.

"There wasn't one in the barony but was gethered in it, through and fro," continued Slipper, with a quelling glance at the interrupter; "and there was tints for sellin' porther, and whisky as pliable as new milk, and boys goin' round the tints outside, feeling for heads with the big ends of their blackthorns, and all kinds of recreations, and the Sons of Liberty's piffler and dhrum band from Skebawn; though faith! there was more of thim runnin' to look at the races than what was playin' in it; not to mintion different occasions that the band-masther was atin' his lunch within in the whisky tint."

"But what about Driscoll?" said Flurry.

"Sure it's about him I'm tellin' ye," replied Slipper, with the practiced orator's watchful eye on his growing audience. " 'Twas within in the same whisky tint meself was, with the bandmasther and a few of the lads, an' we buyin' a ha'porth o' crackers, when I seen me brave Driscoll landin' into the tint, and a pair o' thim long boots on him; him that hadn't a shoe nor a stocking to his foot when your honor had him picking grass out o' the stones behind in your yard. 'Well,' says I to meself, 'we'll knock some spoort out of Driscoll!'

" 'Come here to me, acushla!' says I to him; 'I suppose it's some way wake in the legs y' are,' says I, 'an' the docther put them on ye the way the people wouldn't thrample ye!'

" 'May the divil choke ye!' says he, pleasant enough, but I knew by the blush he had he was vexed.

" 'Then I suppose 'tis a left-tenant colonel y' are,' says I; 'yer mother must be proud out o' ye!' says I, 'an' maybe ye'll lend her a loan o' thim waders when she's rinsin' yer bauneen in the river!' says I.

" 'There'll be work out o' this!' says he, lookin' at me both sour and bitther.

" 'Well indeed, I was thinkin' you were blue-molded for want of a batin',' says I. He was for fightin' us then, but afther we had him pacificated with about a quarther of a naggin o' sperrits, he told us he was goin' ridin' in a race.

" 'An' what'll ye ride?' says I.

" 'Owld Bocock's mare,' says he.

" 'Knipes!' says I, sayin' a great curse; 'is it that little staggeen from the mountains; sure she's somethin' about the one age with meself,' says I. 'Many's the time Jamesy Geoghegan and meself used to be dhrivin' her to Macroom with pigs an' all soorts,' says I; 'an' is it leppin' stone walls ye want her to go now?'

" 'Faith, there's walls and every vari'ty of obstackle in it,' says he.

" 'It'll be the best o' your play, so,' says I, 'to leg it away home out o' this.'

" 'An' who'll ride her, so?' says he.

" 'Let the divil ride her,' says I."

Leigh Kelway, who had been leaning back seemingly half asleep, obeyed the hypnotism of Slipper's gaze, and opened his eyes.

"That was now all the conversation that passed between himself and meself," resumed Slipper, "and there was no great delay afther that till they said there was a race startin' and the dickens a one at all was goin' to ride only two, Driscoll, and one Clancy. With that then I seen Mr. Kinahane, the Petty Sessions clerk, goin' round clearin' the coorse an' I gethered a few o' the neighbors, an' we walked the fields hither and over till we seen the most of th' obstackles.

" 'Stand aisy now by the plantation,' says I; 'if they get to come as far as this, believe me ye'll see spoort,' says I, 'an' 'twill be a convanient spot to encourage the mare if she's anyway wake in herself,' says I, cuttin' somethin' about five foot of an ash sapling out o' the plantation.

" 'That's yer sort!' says Owld Bocock, that was thravelin' the racecoorse, peggin' a bit o' paper down with a thorn in front of every lep, the way Driscoll'd know the handiest place to face her at it.

"Well, I hadn't barely thrimmed the ash plant——"

"Have you any jam, Mary Kate?" interrupted Flurry, whose meal had been in no way interfered with by either the story or the highly scented crowd who had come to listen to it.

"We have no jam, only thraycle, sir," replied the invisible Mary Kate.

"I hadn't the switch barely thrimmed," repeated Slipper firmly, "when I heard the people screechin', an' I seen Driscoll an' Clancy comin' on, leppin' all before them, an' owld Bocock's mare bellusin' an' powdherin' along, an' bedad! whatever obstackle wouldn't throw *her* down, faith, she'd throw *it* down, an' there's the thraffic they had in it.

" 'I declare to me sowl,' says I, 'if they continue on this way there's a great chance some one o' thim'll win," says I.

" 'Ye lie!' says the bandmasther, bein' a thrifle fulsome after his luncheon.

" 'I do not,' says I, 'in regard of seein' how soople them two boys is. Ye might observe,' says I, 'that if they have no convanient way to sit on the saddle, they'll ride the neck o' the horse till such time as they gets an occasion to lave it,' says I.

" 'Arrah, shut yer mouth!' says the bandmasther; 'they're puckin' out this way now, an' may the divil admire me!' says he, 'but Clancy has the other bet out, and the divil such leatherin' and beltin' of owld Bocock's mare ever you seen as what's in it!' says he.

"Well, when I seen them comin' to me, and Driscoll about the length of the plantation behind Clancy, I let a couple of bawls.

" 'Skelp her, ye big brute!' says I. 'What good's in ye that ye aren't able to skelp her?' "

The yell and the histrionic flourish of his stick with which Slipper delivered this incident brought down the house. Leigh Kelway was sufficiently moved to ask me in an undertone if "skelp" was a local term.

"Well, Mr. Flurry, and gintlemen," recommenced Slipper, "I declare to ye when owld Bocock's mare heard thim roars she shtretched out her neck like a gandher, and when she passed me out she give a couple of grunts, and looked at me as ugly as a Christian.

" 'Hah!' says I, givin' her a couple o' dhraws o' th' ash plant across the butt o' the tail, the way I wouldn't blind her; 'I'll make ye grunt!' says I, 'I'll nourish ye!'

"I knew well she was very frightful of th' ash plant since the winter Tommeen Sullivan had her under a sidecar. But now, in place of havin' any obligations to me, ye'd be surprised if ye heard the blaspheemious expressions of that young boy that was ridin' her; and whether it was overanxious he was, turnin' around the way I'd hear him cursin', or whether it was some slither or slide came to owld Bocock's mare, I dunno, but she was bet up agin the last obstackle

but two, and before ye could say 'Shnipes,' she was standin' on her
two ears beyond in th' other field! I declare to ye, on the vartue of me
oath, she stood that way till she reconnoithered what side would
Driscoll fall, an' she turned about then and rolled on him as cozy as if
he was meadow grass!"

Slipper stopped short; the people in the doorway groaned appreci-
atively; Mary Kate murmured: "The Lord save us!"

"The blood was dhruv out through his nose and ears," continued
Slipper, with a voice that indicated the cream of the narration, "and
you'd hear his bones crackin' on the gound! You'd have pitied the
poor boy."

"Good heavens!" said Leigh Kelway, sitting up very straight in his
chair.

"Was he hurt, Slipper?" asked Flurry casually.

"Hurt is it?" echoed Slipper in high scorn; "killed on the spot!" He
paused to relish the *dénouement* on Leigh Kelway. "Oh, divil so
pleasant an afthernoon ever you seen; and indeed, Mr. Flurry, it's what
we were all sayin', it was a great pity your honor was not there for
the likin' you had for Driscoll."

As he spoke the last word there was an outburst of singing and
cheering from a carload of people who had just pulled up at the door.
Flurry listened, leaned back in his chair, and began to laugh.

"It scarcely strikes one as a comic incident," said Leigh Kelway,
very coldly to me; "in fact, it seems to me that the police ought——"

"Show me Slipper!" bawled a voice in the shop; "show me that
dirty little undherlooper till I have his blood! Hadn't I the race won
only for he souring the mare on me! What's that you say? I tell ye he
did! He left seven slaps on her with the handle of a hay-rake——"

There was in the room in which we were sitting a second door,
leading to the back yard, a door consecrated to the unobtrusive visits
of so-called "Sunday travelers." Through it Slipper faded away like a
dream, and, simultaneously, a tall young man, with a face like a red-
hot potato tied up in a bandage, squeezed his way from the shop into
the room.

"Well, Driscoll," said Flurry, "since it wasn't the teeth of the rake
he left on the mare, you needn't be talking!"

Leigh Kelway looked from one to the other with a wilder expression in his eye than I had thought it capable of. I read in it a re-
solve to abandon Ireland to her fate.

At eight o'clock we were still waiting for the car that we had been

assured should be ours directly it returned from the races. At half past
eight we had adopted the only possible course that remained, and had
accepted the offers on the laden cars that were returning to Skebawn,
and I presently was gratified by the spectacle of my friend Leigh Kelway wedged between a roulette table and its proprietor on one side of
a car, with Driscoll and Slipper, mysteriously reconciled and excessively drunk, seated, locked in each other's arms, on the other. Flurry
and I, somewhat similarly placed, followed on two other cars. I was
scarcely surprised when I was informed that the melancholy white
animal in the shafts of the leading car was Owld Bocock's much-
enduring steeplechaser.

The night was very dark and stormy, and it is almost superfluous
to say that no one carried lamps; the rain poured upon us, and
through wind and wet Owld Bocock's mare set the pace at a rate that
showed she knew from bitter experience what was expected from her
by gentlemen who had spent the evening in a public house; behind her
the other two tired horses followed closely, incited to emulation by
shouting, singing, and a liberal allowance of whip. We were a good
ten miles from Skebawn, and never had the road seemed so long. For
mile after mile the half-seen low walls slid past us, with occasional
plunges into caverns of darkness under trees. Sometimes from a way-
side cabin a dog would dash out to bark at us as we rattled by;
sometimes our cavalcade swung aside to pass, with yells and counter-
yells, crawling carts filled with other belated race-goers.

I was nearly wet through, even though I received considerable
shelter from a Skebawn publican, who slept heavily and irrepressibly
on my shoulder. Driscoll, on the leading car, had struck up an ap-
proximation to "The Wearing of the Green," when a wavering star
appeared on the road ahead of us. It grew momently larger; it came
toward us apace. Flurry, on the car behind me, shouted suddenly:

"That's the mail car, with one of the lamps out! Tell those fellows
ahead to look out!"

But the warning fell on deaf ears.

> *"When laws can change the blades of grass*
> *From growing as they grow——"*

howled five discordant voices, oblivious of the towering proximity of
the star.

A Bianconi mail car is nearly three times the size of an ordinary outside car, and when on a dark night it advances, Cyclops-like, with but one eye, it is difficult for even a sober driver to calculate its bulk. Above the sounds of melody there arose the thunder of heavy wheels, the splashing trample of three big horses, then a crash and a turmoil of shouts. Our cars pulled up just in time, and I tore myself from the embrace of my publican to go to Leigh Kelway's assistance.

The wing of the Bianconi had caught the wing of the smaller car, flinging Owld Bocock's mare on her side, and throwing her freight headlong on top of her, the heap being surmounted by the roulette table. The driver of the mail car unshipped his solitary lamp and turned it on the disaster. I saw that Flurry had already got hold of Leigh Kelway by the heels, and was dragging him from under the others. He struggled up hatless, muddy, and gasping, with Driscoll hanging on by his neck, still singing "The Wearing of the Green."

A voice from the mail car said incredulously: *"Leigh Kelway!"* A spectacled face glared down upon him from under the dripping spikes of an umbrella.

It was the Right Honorable the Earl of Waterbury, Leigh Kelway's chief, returning from his fishing excursion.

Meanwhile Slipper, in the ditch, did not cease to announce that "Divil so pleasant an afthernoon ever ye seen as what was in it!"

A MISDEAL

---

by *SOMERVILLE & ROSS*

(1897)

See Editors' Introduction on page 132.

T HE WAGONETTE slewed and slackened mysteriously on the top of
the long hill above Drumcurran. So many remarkable things had
happened since we had entrusted ourselves to the guidance of Mr.
Bernard Shute that I rose in my place and possessed myself of the
brake, and in so doing saw the horses with their heads hard in against
their chests, and their quarters jammed crookedly against the splash-
board, being apparently tied into knots by some inexplicable power.

"Someone's pulling the reins out of my hand!" exclaimed Mr.
Shute.

The horses and pole were by this time making an acute angle with
the wagonette, and the groom plunged from the box to their heads.
Miss Sally Knox, who was sitting beside me, looked over the edge.

"Put on the brake! The reins are twisted round the axle!" she cried,
and fell into a fit of laughter.

We all—that is to say, Philippa, Miss Shute, Miss Knox, and I—
got out as speedily as might be; but, I think, without panic; Mr. Shute
alone stuck to the ship, with the horses struggling and rearing below
him. The groom and I contrived to back them, and by so doing
caused the reins to unwind themselves from the axle.

"It was my fault," said Mr. Shute, hauling them in as fast as we could give them to him; "I broke the reins yesterday, and these are the phaeton ones, and about six fathoms long at that, and I forgot and let the slack go overboard. It's all right, I won't do it again."

With this reassurance we confided ourselves once more to the wagonette.

As we neared the town of Drumcurran the fact that we were on our way to a horse fair became alarmingly apparent. It is impossible to imagine how we pursued an uninjured course through the companies of horsemen, the crowded carts, the squealing colts, the irresponsible led horses, and, most immutable of all obstacles, the groups of countrywomen, with the hoods of their heavy blue cloaks over their heads. They looked like nuns of some obscure order; they were deaf and blind as ramparts of sandbags; nothing less callous to human life than a Parisian cabdriver could have burst a way through them. Many times during that drive I had cause to be thankful for the sterling qualities of Mr. Shute's brake; with its aid he dragged his overfed bays into a crawl that finally, and not without injury to the varnish, took the wagonette to the Royal Hotel. Every available stall in the yard was by that time filled, and it was only by virtue of the fact that the kitchenmaid was nearly related to my cook that the indignant groom was permitted to stable the bays in a den known as the calf house.

That I should have lent myself to such an expedition was wholly due to my wife. Since Philippa had taken up her residence in Ireland she had discovered a taste for horses that was not to be extinguished, even by an occasional afternoon on the Quaker, whose paces had become harder than rock in his many journeys to Petty Sessions; she had also discovered the Shutes, newcomers on the outer edge of our vast visiting district, and between them this party to Drumcurran Horse Fair had been devised. Philippa proposed to buy herself a hunter. Bernard Shute wished to do the same, possibly two hunters, money being no difficulty with this fortunate young man. Miss Sally Knox was of the company, and I also had been kindly invited, as to a missionary meeting, to come, and bring my checkbook. The only saving clause in the affair was the fact that Mr. Flurry Knox was to meet us at the scene of action.

The fair was held in a couple of large fields outside the town, and on the farther bank of the Curranhilty River. Across a wide and glittering ford, horses of all sizes and sorts were splashing, and a long row of steppingstones was hopped, and staggered, and scrambled over by a ceaseless variety of foot passengers. A man with a cart plied as a ferryboat, doing a heavy trade among the apple women and vendors of "crubeens," alias pigs' feet, a grisly delicacy peculiar to Irish open-air holiday-making, and the July sun blazed on a scene that even Miss Cecilia Shute found to be almost repayment enough for the alarms of the drive.

"As a rule, I am so bored by driving that I find it reviving to be frightened," she said to me, as we climbed to safety on a heathery ridge above the fields dedicated to galloping the horses; "but when my brother scraped all those people off one side of that car, and ran the pole into the cart of lemonade bottles, I began to wish for courage to tell him I was going to get out and walk home."

"Well, if you only knew it," said Bernard, who was spreading rugs over the low furze bushes in the touching belief that the prickles would not come through, "the time you came nearest to walking home was when the lash of the whip got twisted round Nancy's tail. Miss Knox, you're an authority on these things—don't you think it would be a good scheme to have a light anchor in the trap, and when the horses began to play the fool, you'd heave the anchor over the fence and bring them up all standing?"

"They wouldn't stand very long," remarked Miss Sally.

"Oh, that's all right," returned the inventor; "I'd have a dodge to cast them loose, with the pole and the splinter-bar."

"You'd never see them again," responded Miss Knox demurely, "if you thought that mattered."

"It would be the brightest feature of the case," said Miss Shute.

She was surveying Miss Sally through her pince-nez as she spoke, and was, I have reason to believe, deciding that by the end of the day her brother would be well on in the first stages of his fifteenth love affair.

It has possibly been suspected that Mr. Bernard Shute was a sailor, had been a sailor, rather, until within the last year, when he had tumbled into a fortune and a property, and out of the Navy, in the shortest time on record. His enthusiasm for horses had been nourished by the hirelings of Malta, and other resorts of Her Majesty's ships, and his knowledge of them was, so far, bounded by the fact that it was more usual to come off over their heads than their tails. For the rest, he was a clean-shaven and personable youth, with a laugh which I may, without offensive intention, define as possessing a whatcheeriness special to his profession, and a habit, engendered no doubt by long sojourns at the Antipodes, of getting his clothes in large hideous consignments from a naval outfitter.

It was eleven o'clock, and the fair was in full swing. Its vortex was in the center of the field below us, where a low bank of sods and earth had been erected as a trial jump, with a yelling crowd of men and boys at either end, acting instead of the usual wings to prevent a swerve. Strings of reluctant horses were scourged over the bank by dozens of willing hands, while exhortation, cheers, and criticism were freely showered upon each performance.

"Give the knees to the saddle, boy, and leave the heels slack." "That's a nice horse. He'd keep a jock on his back where another 'd throw him!" "Well jumped, begor! She fled that fairly!" as an ungainly three-year-old flounced over the bank without putting a hoof on it. Then her owner, unloosing his pride in simile after the manner of his race:

"Ah ha! when she give a lep, man, she's that free, she's like a hare for it!"

A giggling group of country girls elbowed their way past us out of the crowd of spectators, one of the number inciting her fellows to hurry on to the other field "until they'd see the lads galloping the horses," to which another responding that she'd "be skinned alive for the horses," the party sped on their way. We—*i.e.,* my wife, Miss Knox, Bernard Shute, and myself—followed in their wake, a matter by no means as easy as it looked. Miss Shute had exhibited her wonted intelligence by remaining on the hilltop with the *Spectator;* she had not reached the happy point of possessing a mind ten years older than her age, and a face ten years younger, without also developing the gift of scenting boredom from afar. We squeezed past the noses and heels of fidgety horses, and circumnavigated their attendant groups of critics, while half-trained brutes in snaffles bolted to nowhere and back again, and whinnying foals ran to and fro in search of their mothers.

A moderate bank divided the upper from the lower fields, and as every feasible spot in it was commanded by a refusing horse, the choice of a place and moment for crossing it required judgment. I got Philippa across it in safety; Miss Knox, though as capable as any young woman in Ireland of getting over a bank, either on horseback or on her own legs, had to submit to the assistance of Mr. Shute, and the laws of dynamics decreed that a force sufficient to raise a bower anchor should hoist her seven stone odd to the top of the bank with such speed that she landed half on her knees and half in the arms of her pioneer. A group of portentously quiet men stood near, their eyes on the ground, their hands in their pockets; they were all dressed so much alike that I did not at first notice that Flurry Knox was among them; when I did, I perceived that his eyes, instead of being on the ground, were surveying Mr. Shute with that measure of disapproval that he habitually bestowed upon strange men.

"You're later than I thought you'd be," he said. "I have a horse half-bought for Mrs. Yeates. It's that old mare of Bobby Bennett's; she makes a little noise, but she's a good mare, and you couldn't throw her down if you tried. Bobby wants thirty pounds for her, but I think you might get her for less. She's in the hotel stables, and you can see her when you go to lunch."

We moved on toward the rushy bank of the river, and Philippa and Sally Knox seated themselves on a low rock, looking, in their white frocks, as incongruous in that dingy preoccupied assemblage as the dreamy meadowsweet and purple spires of loosestrife that thronged the riverbanks. Bernard Shute had been lost in the shifting maze of men and horses, who were, for the most part, galloping with the blind fury of charging bulls; but presently, among a party who seemed to be riding the finish of a race, we descried our friend, and a second or two later he hauled a brown mare to a standstill in front of us.

"The fellow's asking forty pounds for her," he said to Miss Sally; "she's a nailer to gallop. I don't think it's too much."

"Her grandsire was the Mountain Hare," said the owner of the mare, hurrying up to continue her family history, "and he was the grandest horse in the four baronies. He was forty-two years of age when he died, and they waked him the same as ye'd wake a Christian. They had whisky and porther—and bread—and a piper in it."

"Thim Mountain Hare colts is no great things," interrupted Mr. Shute's groom contemptuously. "I seen a colt once that was one of his stock, and if there was forty men and their wives, and they after him with sticks, he wouldn't lep a sod of turf."

"Lep, is it!" ejaculated the owner in a voice shrill with outrage. "You may lead that mare out through the counthry, and there isn't a fence in it that she wouldn't go up to it as indepindent as if she was going to her bed, and your honor's ladyship knows that dam well, Miss Knox."

"You want too much money for her, McCarthy," returned Miss Sally, with her little air of preternatural wisdom.

"God pardon you, Miss Knox! Sure a lady like you knows well that forty-five pounds is no money for that mare. Forty-five pounds!" He laughed. "It'd be as good for me to make her a present to the gentleman all out as take three farthings less for her! She's too grand entirely for a poor farmer like me, and if it wasn't for the long weak family I have, I wouldn't part with her under twice the money."

"Three fine lumps of daughters in America paying his rent for him," commented Flurry in the background. "That's the long weak family!"

Bernard dismounted and slapped the mare's ribs approvingly.

"I haven't had such a gallop since I was at Rio," he said. "What do you think of her, Miss Knox?" Then, without waiting for an answer, "I like her. I think I may as well give him the forty-five and have done with it!"

At these ingenuous words I saw a spasm of anguish cross the countenance of McCarthy, easily interpreted as the first pang of a lifelong regret that he had not asked twice the money. Flurry Knox put up an eyebrow and winked at me; Mr. Shute's groom turned away for very shame. Sally Knox laughed with the deplorable levity of nineteen.

Thus, with a brevity absolutely scandalous in the eyes of all beholders, the bargain was concluded.

Flurry strolled up to Philippa, observing an elaborate remoteness from Miss Sally and Mr. Shute.

"I believe I'm selling a horse here myself today," he said; "would you like to have a look at him, Mrs. Yeates?"

"Oh, are you selling, Knox?" struck in Bernard, to whose brain the glory of buying a horse had obviously mounted like new wine; "I want another, and I know yours are the right sort."

"Well, as you seem fond of galloping," said Flurry sardonically, "this one might suit you."

"You don't mean the Moonlighter?" said Miss Knox, looking fixedly at him.

"Supposing I did, have you anything to say against him?" replied Flurry.

Decidedly he was in a very bad temper. Miss Sally shrugged her shoulders, and gave a little shred of a laugh, but said no more.

In a comparatively secluded corner of the field we came upon Moonlighter, sidling and fussing, with flickering ears, his tail tightly tucked in and his strong back humped in a manner that boded little good. Even to my untutored eye, he appeared to be an uncommonly good-looking animal, a well-bred gray, with shoulders that raked back as far as the eye could wish, the true Irish jumping hindquarters, and a showy head and neck; it was obvious that nothing except Michael Hallahane's adroit chucks at his bridle kept him from displaying his jumping powers free of charge. Bernard stared at him in silence; not the pregnant and intimidating silence of the connoisseur, but the tongue-tied muteness of helpless ignorance. His eye for horses had most probably been formed on circus posters, and the advertisements of a well-known embrocation, and Moonlighter approximated in color and conduct to these models.

"I can see he's a ripping fine horse," he said at length; "I think I should like to try him."

Miss Knox changed countenance perceptibly, and gave a perturbed glance at Flurry. Flurry remained impenetrably unamiable.

"I don't pretend to be a judge of horses," went on Mr. Shute. "I dare say I needn't tell *you* that!" with a very engaging smile at Miss Sally; "but I like this one awfully."

As even Philippa said afterward, she would not have given herself away like that over buying a reel of cotton.

"Are you quite sure that he's really the sort of horse you want?" said Miss Knox, with rather more color in her face than usual; "he's only four years old, and he's hardly a finished hunter."

The object of her philanthropy looked rather puzzled. "What! can't he jump?" he said.

"Is it jump?" exclaimed Michael Hallahane, unable any longer to contain himself; "is it the horse that jumped five foot of a clothesline in Heffernan's yard, and not a one on his back but himself, and didn't leave so much as the thrack of his hoof on the quilt that was hanging on it!"

"That's about good enough," said Mr. Shute, with his large friendly laugh; "what's your price, Knox? I must have the horse that jumped the quilt! I'd like to try him, if you don't mind. There are some jolly-looking banks over there."

"My price is a hundred sovereigns," said Flurry; "you can try him, if you like."

"Oh, don't!" cried Sally impulsively; but Bernard's foot was already in the stirrup. "I call it disgraceful!" I heard her say in a low voice to her kinsman—"you know he can't ride."

The kinsman permitted himself a malign smile. "That's his lookout," he said.

Perhaps the unexpected docility with which Moonlighter allowed himself to be maneuvered through the crowd was due to Bernard's thirteen stone; at all events, his progress through a gate into the next field was unexceptionable. Bernard, however, had no idea of encouraging this tranquillity. He had come out to gallop, and without further ceremony he drove his heels into Moonlighter's sides, and took the consequences in the shape of a very fine and able buck. How he remained within even visiting distance of the saddle it is impossible to explain; perhaps his early experience in the rigging stood him in good stead in the matter of hanging on by his hands; but, however preserved, he did remain, and went away down the field at what he himself subsequently described as "the rate of knots."

Flurry flung away his cigarette and ran to a point of better observation. We all ran, including Michael Hallahane and various onlookers, and were in time to see Mr. Shute charging the least advantageous spot in a hollow-faced furzy bank. Nothing but the gray horse's extreme activity got the pair safely over; he jumped it on a slant, changed feet in the heart of a furze bush, and was lost to view. In what relative positions Bernard and his steed alighted was to us a matter of conjecture; when we caught sight of them again, Moonlighter was running away, with his rider still on his back, while the slope of the ground lent wings to his flight.

"That young gentleman will be apt to be killed," said Michael Hallahane with composure, not to say enjoyment.

"He'll be into the long bog with him pretty soon," said Flurry, his keen eye tracking the fugitive.

"Oh!—I thought he was off that time!" exclaimed Miss Sally, with a gasp in which consternation and amusement were blended. "There! He *is* into the bog!"

It did not take us long to arrive at the scene of disaster, to which, as to a dogfight, other foot runners were already hurrying, and on our arrival we found things looking remarkably unpleasant for Mr. Shute and Moonlighter. The latter was sunk to his withers in the sheet of black slime into which he had stampeded; the former, submerged to the waist three yards farther away in the bog, was trying to drag himself toward firm ground by the aid of tussocks of wiry grass.

"Hit him!" shouted Flurry. "Hit him! he'll sink if he stops there!"

Mr. Shute turned on his adviser a face streaming with black mud, out of which his brown eyes and white teeth gleamed with undaunted cheerfulness.

"All jolly fine," he called back; "if I let go this grass I'll sink too!"

A shout of laughter from the male portion of the spectators sympathetically greeted this announcement, and a dozen equally futile methods of escape were suggested. Among those who had joined us was, fortunately, one of the many boys who pervaded the fair selling halters, and by means of several of these knotted together, a line of communication was established. Moonlighter, who had fallen into the state of inane stupor in which horses in his plight so often indulge, was roused to activity by showers of stones and imprecations but faintly chastened by the presence of ladies. Bernard, hanging on to his tail, belabored him with a cane, and, finally, the reins proving good, the task of towing the victims ashore was achieved.

"He's mine, Knox, you know," were Mr. Shute's first words as he scrambled to his feet; "he's the best horse I ever got across—worth twice the money!"

"Faith, he's aisy plased!" remarked a bystander.

"Oh, do go and borrow some dry clothes," interposed Philippa practically; "surely there must be someone——"

"There's a shop in the town where he can strip a peg for 13s. 9d.," said Flurry grimly; "I wouldn't care myself about the clothes you'd borrow here!"

The morning sun shone jovially upon Moonlighter and his rider, caking momently the black bog stuff with which both were coated, and as the group disintegrated, and we turned to go back, every man present was pleasurably aware that the buttons of Mr. Shute's riding breeches had burst at the knee, causing a large triangular hiatus above his gaiter.

"Well," said Flurry conclusively to me as we retraced our steps, "I always thought the fellow was a fool, but I never thought he was such a damned fool."

It seemed an interminable time since breakfast when our party, somewhat shattered by the stirring events of the morning, found itself gathered in an upstairs room at the Royal Hotel, waiting for a meal that had been ordained some two hours before. The air was charged with the mingled odors of boiling cabbage and frying mutton; we affected to speak of them with disgust, but our souls yearned to them. Female ministrants, with rustling skirts and pounding feet, raced along the passages with trays that were never for us, and opening doors released roaring gusts of conversation, blended with the clatter of knives and forks, and still we starved. Even the ginger-colored check suit, lately labeled "The Sandringham. Wonderful value, 16s. 9d." in the window of Drumcurran's leading mart, and now displayed upon Mr. Shute's all too lengthy limbs, had lost its power to charm.

"Oh, don't tear that bell quite out by the roots, Bernard," said his sister, from the heart of a lamentable yawn. "I dare say it only amuses them when we ring, but it may remind them that we are still alive. Major Yeates, do you or do you not regret the pigs' feet?"

"More than I can express," I said, turning from the window, where I had been looking down at the endless succession of horses' backs and men's hats, moving in two opposing currents in the street below. "I dare say if we talk about them for a little we shall feel ill, and that will be better than nothing."

At this juncture, however, a heavy-laden tray thumped against the door, and our repast was borne into the room by a hot young woman in creaking boots, who hoarsely explained that what kept her was waiting on the potatoes, and that the ould pan that was in it was playing Puck with the beefsteaks.

"Well," said Miss Shute, as she began to try conclusions between a blunt knife and a bulletproof mutton chop, "I have never lived in the country before, but I have always been given to understand that the village inn was one of its chief attractions." She delicately moved the potato dish so as to cover the traces of a bygone egg, and her glance lingered on the flies that dragged their way across a melting mound of salt butter. "I like local color, but I don't care about it on the tablecloth."

"Well, I'm feeling quite anxious about Irish country hotels now," said Bernard, "they're getting so civilized and respectable. After all, when you go back to England no one cares a pin to hear that you've been done up to the knocker. That don't amuse them a bit. But all my friends are as pleased as anything when I tell them of the pothouse where I slept in my clothes rather than face the sheets, or how, when I complained to the landlady next day, she said, 'Cock ye up! Wasn't it his Reverence the Dean of Kilcoe had them last!'"

We smiled wanly; what I chiefly felt was respect for any hungry man who could jest in presence of such a meal.

"All this time my hunter hasn't been bought," said Philippa presently, leaning back in her chair, and abandoning the unequal contest with her beefsteak. "Who is Bobby Bennett? Will his horse carry a lady?"

Sally Knox looked at me and began to laugh.

"You should ask Major Yeates about Bobby Bennett," she said.

Confound Miss Sally! It had never seemed worth while to tell Philippa all that story about my doing up Miss Bobby Bennett's hair, and I sank my face in my tumbler of stagnant whisky-and-soda to conceal the color that suddenly adorned it. Any intelligent man will understand that it was a situation calculated to amuse the ungodly, but without any real fun in it. I explained Miss Bennett as briefly as possible, and at all the more critical points Miss Sally's hazel-green eyes roamed slowly and mercilessly toward me.

"You haven't told Mrs. Yeates that she's one of the greatest horse-copers in the country," she said, when I had got through somehow; "she can sell you a very good horse sometimes, and a very bad one too, if she gets the chance."

"No one will ever explain to me," said Miss Shute, scanning us all with her dark, half-amused, and wholly sophisticated eyes, "why horse-coping is more respectable than cheating at cards. I rather respect people who are able to cheat at cards; if everyone did, it would make whist so much more cheerful; but there is no forgiveness for dealing yourself the right card, and there is no condemnation for dealing your neighbor a very wrong horse!"

"Your neighbor is supposed to be able to take care of himself," said Bernard.

"Well, why doesn't that apply to cardplayers?" returned his sister; "are they all in a state of helpless innocence?"

"I'm helplessly innocent," announced Philippa, "so I hope Miss Bennett won't deal me a wrong horse."

"Oh, her mare is one of the right ones," said Miss Sally; "she's a lovely jumper, and her manners are the very best."

The door opened, and Flurry Knox put in his head. "Bobby Bennett's downstairs," he said to me mysteriously.

I got up, not without consciousness of Miss Sally's eye, and prepared to follow him. "You'd better come too, Mrs. Yeates, to keep an eye on him. Don't let him give her more than thirty, and if he gives that she should return him two sovereigns." This last injunction was bestowed in a whisper as we descended the stairs.

Miss Bennett was in the crowded yard of the hotel, looking handsome and overdressed, and she greeted me with just that touch of Auld Lang Syne in her manner that I could best have dispensed with. I turned to the business in hand without delay. The brown mare was led forth from the stable and paraded for our benefit; she was one of those inconspicuous, meritorious animals about whom there seems nothing particular to say, and I felt her legs and looked hard at her hocks, and was not much the wiser.

"It's no use my saying she doesn't make a noise," said Miss Bobby, "because everyone in the country will tell you she does. You can have a vet if you like, and that's the only fault he can find with her. But if Mrs. Yeates hasn't hunted before now, I'll guarantee Cruiskeen as just the thing for her. She's really safe and confidential. My little brother Georgie has hunted her—*you* remember Georgie, Major Yeates?—the night of the ball, you know—and he's only eleven. Mr. Knox can tell you what sort she is."

"Oh, she's a grand mare," said Mr. Knox, thus appealed to; "you'd hear her coming three fields off like a German band!"

"And well for you if you could keep within three fields of her!" retorted Miss Bennett. "At all events, she's not like the hunter you sold Uncle, that used to kick the stars as soon as I put my foot in the stirrup!"

" 'Twas the size of the foot frightened him," said Flurry.

"Do you know how Uncle cured him?" said Miss Bennett, turning her back on her adversary; "he had him tied head and tail across the yard gate, and every man that came in had to get over his back!"

"That's no bad one!" said Flurry.

Philippa looked from one to the other in bewilderment, while the badinage continued, swift and unsmiling, as became two hierarchs of horse-dealing; it went on at intervals for the next ten minutes, and at the end of that time I had bought the mare for thirty pounds. As Miss Bennett said nothing about giving me back two of them, I had not the nerve to suggest it.

After this Flurry and Miss Bennett went away, and were swallowed up in the fair; we returned to our friends upstairs, and began to arrange about getting home. This, among other difficulties, involved the tracking and capture of the Shutes' groom, and took so long that it necessitated tea. Bernard and I had settled to ride our new purchases home, and the groom was to drive the wagonette—an alteration ardently furthered by Miss Shute. The afternoon was well advanced when Bernard and I struggled through the turmoil of the hotel yard in search of our horses, and, the hotel hostler being nowhere to be found, the Shutes' man saddled our animals for us, and then withdrew, to grapple singlehanded with the bays in the calf house.

"Good business for me, that Knox is sending the gray horse home for me," remarked Bernard, as his new mare followed him tractably out of the stall. "He'd have been rather a handful in this hole of a place."

He shoved his way out of the yard in front of me, seemingly quite comfortable and at home upon the descendant of the Mountain Hare, and I followed as closely as drunken carmen and shafts of erratic carts would permit. Cruiskeen evinced a decided tendency to turn to the right on leaving the yard, but she took my leftward tug in good part, and we moved on through the streets of Drumcurran with a dignity that was only impaired by the irrepressible determination of Mr. Shute's new trousers to run up his leg. It was a trifle disappointing that Cruiskeen should carry her nose in the air like a camel, but I set it down to my own bad hands, and to that cause I also imputed her frequent desire to stop, a desire that appeared to coincide with every fourth or fifth public house on the line of march. Indeed, at the last corner before we left the town, Miss Bennett's mare and I had a serious difference of opinion, in the course of which she mounted the pavement and remained planted in front of a very disreputable public house, whose owner had been before me several times for various infringements of the Licensing Acts. Bernard and the corner boys were, of course, much pleased; I inwardly resolved to let Miss Bennett know how her groom occupied his time in Drumcurran.

We got out into the calm of the country roads without further incident, and I there discovered that Cruiskeen was possessed of a dromedary swiftness in trotting, that the action was about as comfortable as the dromedary's, and that it was extremely difficult to moderate the pace.

"I say! This is something like going!" said Bernard, cantering hard beside me with slack rein and every appearance of happiness. "Do you mean to keep it up all the way?"

"You'd better ask this devil," I replied, hauling on the futile ring snaffle. "Miss Bennett must have an arm like a prize fighter. If this is what she calls confidential, I don't want her confidences."

After another half mile, during which I cursed Flurry Knox, and registered a vow that Philippa should ride Cruiskeen in a cavalry bit, we reached the crossroads at which Bernard's way parted from mine. Another difference of opinion between my wife's hunter and me here took place, this time on the subject of parting from our companion, and I experienced that peculiar inward sinking that accompanies the birth of the conviction one has been stuck. There were still some eight miles between me and home, but I had at least the consolation of knowing that the brown mare would easily cover it in forty minutes. But in this also disappointment awaited me. Dropping her head to about the level of her knees, the mare subsided into a walk as slow as that of the slowest cow, and very similar in general style. In this manner I progressed for a further mile, breathing forth, like St. Paul, threatenings and slaughters against Bobby Bennett and all her confederates; and then the idea occurred to me that many really first-class hunters were very poor hacks. I consoled myself with this for a further period, and presently an opportunity for testing it presented itself. The road made a long loop round the flank of a hill, and it was possible to save half a mile or so by getting into the fields. It was a short cut I had often taken on the Quaker, and it involved nothing more serious than a couple of low stone "gaps" and an infantine bank. I turned Cruiskeen at the first of these. She was evidently surprised. Being in an excessively bad temper, I beat her in a way that surprised her even more, and she jumped the stones precipitately and with an ease that showed she knew quite well what she was about. I vented some further emotion upon her by the convenient medium of my cane, and galloped her across the field and over the bank, which, as they say in these parts, she "fled" without putting an iron on it. It was not the right way to jump it, but it was inspiriting, and when she had disposed of the next gap without hesitation my waning confidence in Miss Bennett began to revive. I cantered over the ridge of the hill, and down it toward the cottage near which I was accustomed to get out onto the road again. As I neared my wonted opening in the fence, I saw that it had been filled by a stout pole, well fixed into the bank at each end, but not more than three feet high. Cruiskeen pricked her ears at it with intelligence; I trotted her at it, and gave her a whack.

Ages afterward there was someone speaking on the blurred edge of a dream that I was dreaming about nothing in particular. I went on dreaming, and was impressed by the shape of a fat jug, mottled white and blue, that intruded itself painfully, and I again heard voices, very urgent and full of effort, but quite outside any concern of mine.

I also made an effort of some kind; I was doing my very best to be good and polite, but I was dreaming in a place that whirred, and was engrossing, and daylight was cold and let in some unknown unpleasantness. For that time the dream got the better of the daylight, and then, apropos of nothing, I was standing up in a house with someone's arm round me; the mottled jug was there, so was the unpleasantness, and I was talking with most careful, old-world politeness.

"Sit down now, you're all right," said Miss Bobby Bennett, who was mopping my face with a handkerchief dipped in the jug.

I perceived that I was asking what had happened.

"She fell over the stick with you," said Miss Bennett; "the dirty brute!"

With another effort I hooked myself onto the march of events, as a truck is dragged out of a siding and hooked to a train.

"Oh, the Lord save us!" said a gray-haired woman who held the jug, "ye're desthroyed entirely, asthore! Oh, glory be to the merciful will of God, me heart lepped across me shesht when I seen him undher the horse!"

"Go out and see if the trap's coming," said Miss Bennett; "he should have found the doctor by this." She stared very closely at my face, and seemed to find it easier to talk in short sentences.

"We must get those cuts looking better before Mrs. Yeates comes."

After an interval, during which unexpected places in my head ached from the cold water, the desire to be polite and coherent again came upon me.

"I am sure it was not your mare's fault," I said.

Miss Bennett laughed a very little. I was glad to see her laugh; it had struck me her face was strangely haggard and frightened.

"Well, of course, it wasn't poor Cruiskeen's fault," she said. "She's nearly home with Mr. Shute by now. That's why I came after you!"

"Mr. Shute!" I said; "wasn't he at the fair that day?"

"He was," answered Miss Bobby, looking at me with very compassionate eyes; "you and he got on each other's horses by mistake at the hotel, and you got the worst of the exchange!"

"Oh!" I said, without even trying to understand.

"He's here within, your honor's ladyship, Mrs. Yeates, ma'am," shouted the gray-haired woman at the door; "don't be unaisy, achudth; he's doing grand. Sure, I'm telling Miss Binnitt if she was his wife itself, she couldn't give him betther care!"

The gray-haired woman laughed.

ALIBI IKE

———◆———

by *RING LARDNER*

(1915)

There are two types of enthusiasts for the works of Ring Lardner: those who rate him as a masterly satirist who wrote with one of the most savage pens since Jonathan Swift; those who read him to laugh. Lardner's first fiction was his baseball series about "the busher," Jack Keefe, which was eventually collected in book form under the title You Know Me, Al. *That was out-and-out humor. *Alibi Ike, *written a few years later, continues in that strain and has comparatively little of the bitterness of other Lardner stories of a later period, such as* Champion *and* Haircut. *Lardner, it seems, always reserved large measures of compassion and affection for his erratic baseball heroes even when he was writing pessimistically about the rest of the human race. For all of its lack of social sting and import, serious critics rate* Alibi Ike *one of his great stories. Humor lovers and baseball fans call it his greatest.*

H IS RIGHT NAME was Frank X. Farrell, and I guess the X stood for "Excuse me." Because he never pulled a play, good or bad, on or off the field, without apologizin' for it.

"Alibi Ike" was the name Carey wished on him the first day he reported down South. O' course we all cut out the "Alibi" part of it right away for the fear he would overhear it and bust somebody. But we called him "Ike" right to his face and the rest of it was understood by everybody on the club except Ike himself.

He ast me one time, he says:

163

"What do you all call me Ike for? I ain't no Yid."

"Carey give you the name," I says. "It's his nickname for everybody he takes a likin' to."

"He mustn't have only a few friends then," says Ike. "I never heard him say 'Ike' to nobody else."

But I was goin' to tell you about Carey namin' him. We'd been workin' out two weeks and the pitchers was showin' somethin' when this bird joined us. His first day out he stood up there so good and took such a reef at the old pill that he had everyone lookin'. Then him and Carey was together in left field, catchin' fungoes, and it was after we was through for the day that Carey told me about him.

"What do you think of Alibi Ike?" ast Carey.

"Who's that?" I says.

"This here Farrell in the outfield," says Carey.

"He looks like he could hit," I says.

"Yes," says Carey, "but he can't hit near as good as he can apologize."

Then Carey went on to tell me what Ike had been pullin' out there. He'd dropped the first fly ball that was hit to him and told Carey his glove wasn't broke in good yet, and Carey says the glove could easy of been Kid Gleason's gran'father. He made a whale of a catch out o' the next one and Carey says "Nice work!" or somethin' like that, but Ike says he could of caught the ball with his back turned only he slipped when he started after it and, besides that, the air currents fooled him.

"I thought you done well to get to the ball," says Carey.

"I ought to been settin' under it," says Ike.

"What did you hit last year?" Carey ast him.

"I had malaria most o' the season," says Ike. "I wound up with .356."

"Where would I have to go to get malaria?" says Carey, but Ike didn't wise up.

I and Carey and him set at the same table together for supper. It took him half an hour longer'n us to eat because he had to excuse himself every time he lifted his fork.

"Doctor told me I needed starch," he'd say, and then toss a shovelful o' potatoes into him. Or, "They ain't much meat on one o' these chops," he'd tell us, and grab another one. Or he'd say: "Nothin' like onions for a cold," and then he'd dip into the perfumery.

"Better try that apple sauce," says Carey. "It'll help your malaria."

"Whose malaria?" says Ike. He'd forgot already why he didn't only hit .356 last year.

I and Carey begin to lead him on.

"Whereabouts did you say your home was?" I ast him.

"I live with my folks," he says. "We live in Kansas City—not right down in the business part—outside a ways."

"How's that come?" says Carey. "I should think you'd get rooms in the post office."

But Ike was too busy curin' his cold to get that one.

"Are you married?" I ast him.

"No," he says. "I never run round much with girls, except to shows onct in a wile and parties and dances and roller skatin'."

"Never take 'em to the prize fights, eh?" says Carey.

"We don't have no real good bouts," says Ike. "Just bush stuff. And I never figured a boxin' match was a place for the ladies."

Well, after supper he pulled a cigar out and lit it. I was just goin' to ask him what he done it for, but he beat me to it.

"Kind o' rests a man to smoke after a good workout," he says. "Kind o' settles a man's supper, too."

"Looks like a pretty good cigar," says Carey.

"Yes," says Ike. "A friend o' mine give it to me—a fella in Kansas City that runs a billiard room."

"Do you play billiards?" I ast him.

"I used to play a fair game," he says. "I'm all out o' practice now —can't hardly make a shot."

We coaxed him into a four-handed battle, him and Carey against Jack Mack and I. Say, he couldn't play billiards as good as Willie Hoppe; not quite. But to hear him tell it, he didn't make a good shot all evenin'. I'd leave him an awful-lookin' layout and he'd gather 'em up in one try and then run a couple o' hundred, and between every carom he'd say he put too much stuff on the ball, or the English didn't take, or the table wasn't true, or his stick was crooked, or somethin'. And all the time he had the balls actin' like they was Dutch soldiers and him Kaiser William. We started out to play fifty points, but we had to make it a thousand so as I and Jack and Carey could try the table.

The four of us set round the lobby a wile after we was through

playin', and when it got along toward bedtime Carey whispered to me
and says:

"Ike'd like to go to bed, but he can't think up no excuse."

Carey hadn't hardly finished whisperin' when Ike got up and pulled
it.

"Well, good night, boys," he says. "I ain't sleepy, but I got some
gravel in my shoes and it's killin' my feet."

We knowed he hadn't never left the hotel since we'd came in from
the grounds and changed our clo'es. So Carey says:

"I should think they'd take them gravel pits out o' the billiard
room."

But Ike was already on his way to the elevator, limpin'.

"He's got the world beat," says Carey to Jack and I. "I've knew
lots o' guys that had an alibi for every mistake they made; I've heard
pitchers say that the ball slipped when somebody cracked one off'n
'em; I've heard infielders complain of a sore arm after heavin' one
into the stand, and I've saw outfielders tooken sick with a dizzy spell
when they've misjudged a fly ball. But this baby can't even go to bed
without apologizin', and I bet he excuses himself to the razor when he
gets ready to shave."

"And at that," says Jack, "he's goin' to make us a good man."

"Yes," says Carey. "Unless rheumatism keeps his battin' average
down to .400."

Well, sir, Ike kept whalin' away at the ball all through the trip till
everybody knowed he'd won a job. Cap had him in there regular the
last few exhibition games and told the newspaper boys a week before the season opened that he was goin' to start him in Kane's place.

"You're there, kid," says Carey to Ike, the night Cap made the
'nnouncement. "They ain't many boys that wins a big league berth
their third year out."

"I'd of been up here a year ago," says Ike, "only I was bent over
all season with lumbago."

II

It rained down in Cincinnati one day and somebody organized a
little game o' cards. They was shy two men to make six and ast I and
Carey to play.

"I'm with you if you get Ike and make it seven-handed," says
Carey.

So they got a hold of Ike and we went up to Smitty's room.

"I pretty near forgot how many you deal," says Ike. "It's been a long wile since I played."

I and Carey give each other the wink, and sure enough, he was just as ig'orant about poker as billiards. About the second hand, the pot was opened two or three ahead of him, and they was three in when it come his turn. It cost a buck, and he throwed in two.

"It's raised, boys," somebody says.

"Gosh, that's right, I did raise it," says Ike.

"Take out a buck if you didn't mean to tilt her," says Carey.

"No," says Ike, "I'll leave it go."

Well, it was raised back at him, and then he made another mistake and raised again. They was only three left in when the draw come. Smitty'd opened with a pair o' kings and he didn't help 'em. Ike stood pat. The guy that'd raised him back was flushin' and he didn't fill. So Smitty checked and Ike bet and didn't get no call. He tossed his hand away, but I grabbed it and give it a look. He had king, queen, jack and two tens. Alibi Ike he must have seen me peekin', for he leaned over and whispered to me.

"I overlooked my hand," he says. "I thought all the wile it was a straight."

"Yes," I says, "that's why you raised twice by mistake."

They was another pot that he come into with tens and fours. It was tilted a couple o' times and two o' the strong fellas drawed ahead of Ike. They each drawed one. So Ike throwed away his little pair and come out with four tens. And they was four treys against him. Carey'd looked at Ike's discards and then he says:

"This lucky bum busted two pair."

"No, no, I didn't," says Ike.

"Yes, yes, you did," says Carey, and showed us the two fours.

"What do you know about that?" says Ike. "I'd of swore one was a five spot."

Well, we hadn't had no pay day yet, and after a wile everybody except Ike was goin' shy. I could see him gettin' restless and I was wonderin' how he'd make the getaway. He tried two or three times. "I got to buy some collars before supper," he says.

"No hurry," says Smitty. "The stores here keeps open all night in April."

After a minute he opened up again.

"My uncle out in Nebraska ain't expected to live," he says. "I ought to send a telegram."

"Would that save him?" says Carey.

"No, it sure wouldn't," says Ike, "but I ought to leave my old man know where I'm at."

"When did you hear about your uncle?" says Carey.

"Just this mornin'," says Ike.

"Who told you?" ast Carey.

"I got a wire from my old man," says Ike.

"Well," says Carey, "your old man knows you're still here yet this afternoon if you was here this mornin'. Trains leavin' Cincinnati in the middle o' the day don't carry no ball clubs."

"Yes," says Ike, "that's true. But he don't know where I'm goin' to be next week."

"Ain't he got no schedule?" ast Carey.

"I sent him one openin' day," says Ike, "but it takes mail a long time to get to Idaho."

"I thought your old man lived in Kansas City," says Carey.

"He does when he's home," says Ike.

"But now," says Carey, "I s'pose he's went to Idaho so as he can be near your sick uncle in Nebraska."

"He's visitin' my other uncle in Idaho."

"Then how does he keep posted about your sick uncle?" ast Carey.

"He don't," says Ike. "He don't even know my other uncle's sick. That's why I ought to wire and tell him."

"Good night!" says Carey.

"What town in Idaho is your old man at?" I says.

Ike thought it over.

"No town at all," he says. "But he's near a town."

"Near what town?" I says.

"Yuma," says Ike.

Well, by this time he'd lost two or three pots and he was desperate. We was playin' just as fast as we could, because we seen we couldn't hold him much longer. But he was tryin' so hard to frame an escape that he couldn't pay no attention to the cards, and it looked like we'd get his whole pile away from him if we could make him stick.

The telephone saved him. The minute it begun to ring, five of us jumped for it. But Ike was there first.

"Yes," he says, answerin' it. "This is him. I'll come right down."

And he slammed up the receiver and beat it out o' the door without even sayin' good-by.

"Smitty'd ought to locked the door," says Carey.

"What did he win?" ast Carey.

We figured it up—sixty-odd bucks.

"And the next time we ask him to play," says Carey, "his fingers will be so stiff he can't hold the cards."

Well, we set round a wile talkin' it over, and pretty soon the telephone rung again. Smitty answered it. It was a friend of his'n from Hamilton and he wanted to know why Smitty didn't hurry down. He was the one that had called before and Ike had told him he was Smitty.

"Ike'd ought to split with Smitty's friend," says Carey.

"No," I says, "he'll need all he won. It costs money to buy collars and to send telegrams from Cincinnati to your old man in Texas and keep him posted on the health o' your uncle in Cedar Rapids, D.C."

III

And you ought to heard him out there on that field! They wasn't a day when he didn't pull six or seven, and it didn't make no difference whether he was goin' good or bad. If he popped up in the pinch he should of made a base hit and the reason he didn't was so-and-so. And if he cracked one for three bases he ought to had a home run, only the ball wasn't lively, or the wind brought it back, or he tripped on a lump o' dirt, roundin' first base.

They was one afternoon in New York when he beat all records. Big Marquard was workin' against us and he was good.

In the first innin' Ike hit one clear over that right field stand, but it was a few feet foul. Then he got another foul and then the count come to two and two. Then Rube slipped one acrost on him and he was called out.

"What do you know about that!" he says afterward on the bench. "I lost count. I thought it was three and one, and I took a strike."

"You took a strike all right," says Carey. "Even the umps knowed it was a strike."

"Yes," says Ike, "but you can bet I wouldn't of took it if I'd knew it was the third one. The scoreboard had it wrong."

"That scoreboard ain't for you to look at," says Cap. "It's for you to hit that old pill against."

"Well," says Ike, "I could of hit that one over the scoreboard if I'd knew it was the third."

"Was it a good ball?" I says.

"Well, no, it wasn't," says Ike. "It was inside."

"How far inside?" says Carey.

"Oh, two or three inches or half a foot," says Ike.

"I guess you wouldn't of threatened the scoreboard with it then," says Cap.

"I'd of pulled it down the right foul line if I hadn't thought he'd call it a ball," says Ike.

Well, in New York's part o' the innin' Doyle cracked one and Ike run back a mile and a half and caught it with one hand. We was all sayin' what a whale of a play it was, but he had to apologize just the same as for gettin' struck out.

"That stand's so high," he says, "that a man don't never see a ball till it's right on top o' you."

"Didn't you see that one?" ast Cap.

"Not at first," says Ike; "not till it raised up above the roof o' the stand."

"Then why did you start back as soon as the ball was hit?" says Cap.

"I knowed by the sound that he'd got a good hold of it," says Ike.

"Yes," says Cap, "but how'd you know what direction to run in?"

"Doyle usually hits 'em that way, the way I run," says Ike.

"Why don't you play blindfolded?" says Carey.

"Might as well, with that big high stand to bother a man," says Ike. "If I could of saw the ball all the time I'd of got it in my hip pocket."

Along in the fifth we was one run to the bad and Ike got on with one out. On the first ball throwed to Smitty, Ike went down. The ball was outside and Meyers throwed Ike out by ten feet.

You could see Ike's lips movin' all the way to the bench and when he got there he had his piece learned.

"Why didn't he swing?" he says.

"Why didn't you wait for his sign?" says Cap.

"He give me his sign," says Ike.

"What's his sign with you?" says Cap.

"Pickin' up some dirt with his right hand," says Ike.

"Well, I didn't see him do it," Cap says.

"He done it all right," says Ike.

Well, Smitty went out and they wasn't no more argument till they come in for the next innin'. Then Cap opened it up.

"You fellas better get your signs straight," he says.

"Do you mean me?" says Smitty.

"Yes," Cap says. "What's your sign with Ike?"

"Slidin' my left hand up to the end o' the bat and back," says Smitty.

"Do you hear that, Ike?" ast Cap.

"What of it?" says Ike.

"You says his sign was pickin' up dirt and he says it's slidin' his hand. Which is right?"

"I'm right," says Smitty. "But if you're arguin' about him goin' last innin', I didn't give him no sign."

"You pulled your cap down with your right hand, didn't you?" ast Ike.

"Well, s'pose I did," says Smitty. "That don't mean nothin'. I never told you to take that for a sign, did I?"

"I thought maybe you meant to tell me and forgot," says Ike.

They couldn't none of us answer that and they wouldn't of been no more said if Ike had of shut up. But wile we was settin' there Carey got on with two out and stole second clean.

"There!" says Ike. "That's what I was tryin' to do and I'd of got away with it if Smitty'd swang and bothered the Indian."

"Oh!" says Smitty. "You was tryin' to steal then, was you? I thought you claimed I give you the hit and run."

"I didn't claim no such a thing," says Ike. "I thought maybe you might of gave me a sign, but I was goin' anyway because I thought I had a good start."

Cap prob'ly would of hit him with a bat, only just about that time Doyle booted one on Hayes and Carey come acrost with the run that tied.

Well, we go into the ninth finally, one and one, and Marquard walks McDonald with nobody out.

"Lay it down," says Cap to Ike.

And Ike goes up there with orders to bunt and cracks the first ball into that right-field stand! It was fair this time, and we're two ahead, but I didn't think about that at the time. I was too busy watchin' Cap's face. First he turned pale and then he got red as fire and then he got blue and purple, and finally he just laid back and busted out laughin'. So we wasn't afraid to laugh ourselfs when we seen him doin' it, and when Ike come in everybody on the bench was in hysterics.

But instead o' takin' advantage, Ike had to try and excuse himself. His play was to shut up and he didn't know how to make it.

"Well," he says, "if I hadn't hit quite so quick at that one I bet it'd of cleared the center-field fence."

Cap stopped laughin'.

"It'll cost you plain fifty," he says.

"What for?" says Ike.

"When I say 'bunt' I mean 'bunt,' " says Cap.

"You didn't say 'bunt,' " says Ike.

"I says 'Lay it down,' " says Cap. "If that don't mean 'bunt,' what does it mean?"

" 'Lay it down' means 'bunt' all right," says Ike, "but I understood you to say 'Lay on it.' "

"All right," says Cap, "and the little misunderstandin' will cost you fifty."

Ike didn't say nothin' for a few minutes. Then he had another bright idear.

"I was just kiddin' about misunderstandin' you," he says. "I knowed you wanted me to bunt."

"Well, then, why didn't you bunt?" ast Cap.

"I was goin' to on the next ball," says Ike. "But I thought if I took a good wallop I'd have 'em all fooled. So I walloped at the first one to fool 'em, and I didn't have no intention o' hittin' it."

"You tried to miss it, did you?" says Cap.

"Yes," says Ike.

"How'd you happen to hit it?" ast Cap.

"Well," Ike says, "I was lookin' for him to throw me a fast one and I was goin' to swing under it. But he come with a hook and I met it right square where I was swingin' to go under the fast one."

"Great!" says Cap. "Boys," he says, "Ike's learned how to hit Marquard's curve. Pretend a fast one's comin' and then try to miss it. It's a good thing to know and Ike'd ought to be willin' to pay for the lesson. So I'm goin' to make it a hundred instead o' fifty."

The game wound up 3 to 1. The fine didn't go, because Ike hit like a wild man all through that trip and we made pretty near a clean-up. The night we went to Philly I got him cornered in the car and I says to him:

"Forget them alibis for a wile and tell me somethin'. What'd you do that for, swing that time against Marquard when you was told to bunt?"

"I'll tell you," he says. "That ball he throwed me looked just like the one I struck out on in the first innin' and I wanted to show Cap what I could of done to that other one if I'd knew it was the third strike."

"But," I says, "the one you struck out on in the first innin' was a fast ball."

"So was the one I cracked in the ninth," says Ike.

IV

You've saw Cap's wife, o' course. Well, her sister's about twict as good-lookin' as her, and that's goin' some.

Cap took his missus down to St. Louis the second trip and the other one come down from St. Joe to visit her. Her name is Dolly, and some doll is right.

Well, Cap was goin' to take the two sisters to a show and he wanted a beau for Dolly. He left it to her and she picked Ike. He'd hit three on the nose that afternoon—of'n Sallee, too.

They fell for each other that first evenin'. Cap told us how it come off. She begin flatterin' Ike for the star game he'd played and o' course he begin excusin' himself for not doin' better. So she thought he was modest and it went strong with her. And she believed everything he said and that made her solid with him—that and her make-up. They was together every mornin' and evenin' for the five days we was there. In the afternoons Ike played the grandest ball you ever see, hittin' and runnin' the bases like a fool and catchin' everything that stayed in the park.

I told Cap, I says: "You'd ought to keep the doll with us and he'd make Cobb's figures look sick."

But Dolly had to go back to St. Joe and we come home for a long serious.

Well, for the next three weeks Ike had a letter to read every day and he'd set in the clubhouse readin' it till mornin' practice was half over. Cap didn't say nothin' to him, because he was goin' so good. But I and Carey wasted a lot of our time tryin' to get him to own up who the letters was from. Fine chanct!

"What are you readin'?" Carey'd say. "A bill?"

"No," Ike'd say, "not exactly a bill. It's a letter from a fella I used to go to school with."

"High school or college?" I'd ask him.

"College," he'd say.

"What college?" I'd say.

Then he'd stall a wile and then he'd say:

"I didn't go to the college myself, but my friend went there."

"How did it happen you didn't go?" Carey'd ask him.

"Well," he'd say, "they wasn't no colleges near where I lived."

"Didn't you live in Kansas City?" I'd say to him.

One time he'd say he did and another time he didn't. One time he says he lived in Michigan.

"Where at?" says Carey.

"Near Detroit," he says.

"Well," I says, "Detroit's near Ann Arbor and that's where they got the university."

"Yes," says Ike, "they got it there now, but they didn't have it there then."

"I come pretty near goin' to Syracuse," I says, "only they wasn't no railroads runnin' through there in them days."

"Where'd this friend o' yours go to college?" says Carey.

"I forget now," says Ike.

"Was it Carlisle?" ast Carey.

"No," says Ike, "his folks wasn't very well off."

"That's what barred me from Smith," I says.

"I was goin' to tackle Cornell's," says Carey, "but the doctor told me I'd have hay fever if I didn't stay up North."

"Your friend writes long letters," I says.

"Yes," says Ike; "he's tellin' me about a ballplayer."

"Where does he play?" ast Carey.

"Down in the Texas League—Fort Wayne," says Ike.

"It looks like a girl's writin'," Carey says.

"A girl wrote it," says Ike. "That's my friend's sister, writin' for him."

"Didn't they teach writin' at this here college where he went?" says Carey.

"Sure," Ike says, "they taught writin', but he got his hand cut off in a railroad wreck."

"How long ago?" I says.

"Right after he got out o' college," says Ike.

"Well," I says, "I should think he'd of learned to write with his left hand by this time."

"It's his left hand that was cut off," says Ike; "and he was left-handed."

"You get a letter every day," says Carey. "They're all the same writin'. Is he tellin' you about a different ballplayer every time he writes?"

"No," Ike says. "It's the same ballplayer. He just tells me what he does every day."

"From the size o' the letters, they don't play nothin' but double-headers down there," says Carey.

We figured that Ike spent most of his evenins answerin' the letters from his "friend's sister," so we kept tryin' to date him up for shows and parties to see how he'd duck out of 'em. He was bugs over spaghetti, so we told him one day that they was goin' to be a big feed of it over to Joe's that night and he was invited.

"How long'll it last?" he says.

"Well," we says, "we're goin' right over there after the game and stay till they close up."

"I can't go," he says, "unless they leave me come home at eight bells."

"Nothin' doin'," says Carey. "Joe'd get sore."

"I can't go then," says Ike.

"Why not?" I ast him.

"Well," he says, "my landlady locks up the house at eight and I left my key home."

"You can come and stay with me," says Carey.

"No," he says, "I can't sleep in a strange bed."

"How do you get along when we're on the road?" says I.

"I don't never sleep the first night anywheres," he says. "After that I'm all right."

"You'll have time to chase home and get your key right after the game," I told him.

"The key ain't home," says Ike. "I lent it to one o' the other fellas and he's went out o' town and took it with him."

"Couldn't you borry another key off'n the landlady?" Carey ast him.

"No," he says, "that's the only one they is."

Well, the day before we started East again, Ike come into the club-house all smiles.

"Your birthday?" I ast him.

"No," he says.

"What do you feel so good about?" I says.

"Got a letter from my old man," he says. "My uncle's goin' to get well."

"Is that the one in Nebraska?" says I.

"Not right in Nebraska," says Ike. "Near there."

But afterwards we got the right dope from Cap. Dolly'd blew in from Missouri and was going to make the trip with her sister.

V

Well, I want to alibi Carey and I for what come off in Boston. If we'd of had any idear what we was doin', we'd never did it. They wasn't nobody outside o' maybe Ike and the dame that felt worse over it than I and Carey.

The first two days we didn't see nothin' of Ike and her except out to the park. The rest o' the time they was sight-seein' over to Cambridge and down to Revere and out to Brook-a-line and all the other places where the rubes go.

But when we come into the beanery after the third game Cap's wife called us over.

"If you want to see somethin' pretty," she says, "look at the third finger on Sis's left hand."

Well, o' course we knowed before we looked that it wasn't goin' to be no hangnail. Nobody was su'prised when Dolly blew into the dinin' room with it—a rock that Ike'd bought off'n Diamond Joe the first trip to New York. Only o' course it'd been set into a lady's-size ring instead o' the automobile tire he'd been wearin'.

Cap and his missus and Ike and Dolly ett supper together, only Ike didn't eat nothin', but just set there blushin' and spillin' things on the tablecloth. I heard him excusin' himself for not havin' no appetite. He says he couldn't never eat when he was clost to the ocean. He'd forgot about them sixty-five oysters he destroyed the first night o' the trip before.

He was goin' to take her to a show, so after supper he went upstairs to change his collar. She had to doll up, too, and o' course Ike was through long before her.

If you remember the hotel in Boston, they's a little parlor where the piano's at and then they's another little parlor openin' off o' that. Well, when Ike come down Smitty was playin' a few chords and I and Carey was harmonizin'. We seen Ike go up to the desk to leave his key and we called him in. He tried to duck away, but we wouldn't stand for it.

We ast him what he was all duded up for and he says he was goin' to the theayter.

"Goin' alone?" says Carey.

"No," he says, "a friend o' mine's goin' with me."

"What do you say if we go along?" says Carey.

"I ain't only got two tickets," he says.

"Well," says Carey, "we can go down there with you and buy our own seats; maybe we can all get together."

"No," says Ike. "They ain't no more seats. They're all sold out."

"We can buy some off'n the scalpers," says Carey.

"I wouldn't if I was you," says Ike. "They say the show's rotten."

"What are you goin' for, then?" I ast.

"I didn't hear about it bein' rotten till I got the tickets," he says.

"Well," I says, "if you don't want to go I'll buy the tickets from you."

"No," says Ike, "I wouldn't want to cheat you. I'm stung and I'll just have to stand for it."

"What are you goin' to do with the girl, leave her here at the hotel?" I says.

"What girl?" says Ike.

"The girl you ett supper with," I says.

"Oh," he says, "we just happened to go into the dinin' room together, that's all. Cap wanted I should set down with 'em."

"I noticed," says Carey, "that she happened to be wearin' that rock you bought off'n Diamond Joe."

"Yes," says Ike. "I lent it to her for a wile."

"Did you lend her the new ring that goes with it?" I says.

"She had that already," says Ike. "She lost the set out of it."

"I wouldn't trust no strange girl with a rock o' mine," says Carey.

"Oh, I guess she's all right," Ike says. "Besides, I was tired o' the stone. When a girl asks you for somethin', what are you goin' to do?"

He started out toward the desk, but we flagged him.

"Wait a minute!" Carey says. "I got a bet with Sam here, and it's up to you to settle it."

"Well," says Ike, "make it snappy. My friend'll be here any minute."

"I bet," says Carey, "that you and that girl was engaged to be married."

"Nothin' to it," says Ike.

"Now look here," says Carey, "this is goin' to cost me real money if I lose. Cut out the alibi stuff and give it to us straight. Cap's wife just as good as told us you was roped."

Ike blushed like a kid.

"Well, boys," he says, "I may as well own up. You win, Carey."

"Yatta boy!" says Carey. "Congratulations!"

"You got a swell girl, Ike," I says.

"She's a peach," says Smitty.

"Well, I guess she's O. K.," says Ike. "I don't know much about girls."

"Didn't you never run round with 'em?" I says.

"Oh, yes, plenty of 'em," says Ike. "But I never seen none I'd fall for."

"That is, till you seen this one," says Carey.

"Well," says Ike, "this one's O. K., but I wasn't thinkin' about gettin' married yet a wile."

"Who done the askin', her?" says Carey.

"Oh, no," says Ike, "but sometimes a man don't know what he's gettin' into. Take a good-lookin' girl, and a man gen'ally almost always does about what she wants him to."

"They couldn't no girl lasso me unless I wanted to be lassoed," says Smitty.

"Oh, I don't know," says Ike. "When a fella gets to feelin' sorry for one of 'em it's all off."

Well, we left him go after shakin' hands all round. But he didn't take Dolly to no show that night. Sometime wile we was talkin' she'd came into that other parlor and she'd stood there and heard us. I don't know how much she heard. But it was enough. Dolly and Cap's missus took the midnight train for New York. And from there Cap's wife sent her on her way back to Missouri.

She'd left the ring and note for Ike with the clerk. But we didn't ask Ike if the note was from his friend in Fort Wayne, Texas.

VI

When we'd came to Boston Ike was hittin' plain .397. When we got back home he'd fell off to pretty near nothin'. He hadn't drove one out o' the infield in any o' them other Eastern parks, and he didn't even give no excuse for it.

To show you how bad he was, he struck out three times in Brooklyn one day and never opened his trap when Cap ast him what was the matter. Before, if he'd whiffed oncet in a game he'd of wrote a book tellin' why.

Well, we dropped from first place to fifth in four weeks and we was still goin' down. I and Carey was about the only ones in the club that spoke to each other, and all as we did was to remind ourself o' what a boner we'd pulled.

"It's goin' to beat us out o' the big money," says Carey.

"Yes," I says. "I don't want to knock my own ball club, but it looks like a one-man team, and when that one man's dauber's down we couldn't trim our whiskers."

"We ought to knew better," says Carey.

"Yes," I says, "but why should a man pull an alibi for bein' engaged to such a bearcat as she was?"

"He shouldn't," says Carey. "But I and you knowed he would or we'd never started talkin' to him about it. He wasn't no more ashamed o' the girl than I am of a regular base hit. But he just can't come clean on no subjec'."

Cap had the whole story, and I and Carey was as pop'lar with him as an umpire.

"What do you want me to do, Cap?" Carey'd say to him before goin' up to hit.

"Use your own judgment," Cap'd tell him. "We want to lose another game."

But finally, one night in Pittsburgh, Cap had a letter from his missus and he come to us with it.

"You fellas," he says, "is the ones that put us on the bum, and if you're sorry I think they's a chancet for you to make good. The old lady's out to St. Joe and she's been tryin' her hardest to fix things up. She's explained that Ike don't mean nothin' with his talk; I've wrote and explained that to Dolly, too. But the old lady says that Dolly says that she can't believe it. But Dolly's still stuck on this baby, and she's pinin' away just the same as Ike. And the old lady says she thinks if you two fellas would write to the girl and explain how you was always kiddin' with Ike and leadin' him on, and how the ball club was all shot to pieces since Ike quit hittin', and how he acted like he was goin' to kill himself, and this and that, she'd fall for it and maybe soften down. Dolly, the old lady says, would believe you before she'd believe I and the old lady, because she thinks it's her we're sorry for, and not him."

Well, I and Carey was only too glad to try and see what we could do. But it wasn't no snap. We wrote about eight letters before we got one that looked good. Then we give it to the stenographer and had it wrote out on a typewriter and both of us signed it.

It was Carey's idear that made the letter good. He stuck in some-thin' about the world's serious money that our wives wasn't goin' to spend unless she took pity on a "boy who was so shy and modest that he was afraid to come right out and say that he had asked such a beautiful and handsome girl to become his bride."

That's prob'ly what got her, or maybe she couldn't of held out much longer anyway. It was four days after we sent the letter that Cap heard from his missus again. We was in Cincinnati.

"We've won," he says to us. "The old lady says that Dolly says she'll give him another chance. But the old lady says it won't do no good for Ike to write a letter. He'll have to go out there."

"Send him tonight," says Carey.

"I'll pay half his fare," I says.

"I'll pay the other half," says Carey.

"No," says Cap, "the club'll pay his expenses. I'll send him scoutin'."

"Are you goin' to send him tonight?"

"Sure," says Cap. "But I'm goin' to break the news to him right now. It's time we win a ball game."

So in the clubhouse, just before the game, Cap told him. And I certainly felt sorry for Rube Benton and Red Ames that afternoon! I and Carey was standin' in front o' the hotel that night when Ike come out with his suitcase.

"Sent home?" I says to him.

"No," he says, "I'm goin' scoutin'."

"Where to?" I says. "Fort Wayne?"

"No, not exactly," he says.

"Well," says Carey, "have a good time."

"I ain't lookin' for no good time," says Ike. "I says I was goin' scoutin'."

"Well, then," says Carey, "I hope you see somebody you like."

"And you better have a drink before you go," I says.

"Well," says Ike, "they claim it helps a cold."

TENNIS

by ROGER ANGELL

(1950)

Possessing an adeptness for a certain sport is a matter of almost outlandish pride with many men. As they grow older they may philosophically accept gray hair and stronger optical prescriptions, and bow gracefully to the inevitable encroachments of the years. But the once good tennis player (or golfer or participant in other man-to-man sports) frequently cannot tolerate a lowering of the standard of proficiency he once possessed. The effect that this type of vanity can have on the relationship of a father and son and the corollary reaction of the son lie at the heart of Roger Angell's story.

THE THING you ought to know about my father is that he plays a lovely game of tennis. Or rather, he used to, up to last year, when all of a sudden he had to give the game up for good. But even last summer, when he was fifty-five years of age, his game was something to see. He wasn't playing any of your middle-aged tennis, even then. None of that cute stuff, with lots of cuts and drop shots and getting everything back, that most older men play when they're beginning to carry a little fat and don't like to run so much. That wasn't for him. He still played all or nothing—the big game with a hard serve and coming right in behind it to the net. Lots of running in that kind of game, but he could still do it. Of course, he'd begun to make more errors in the last few years and that would annoy the hell out of him. But still he wouldn't change—not him. At that, his game was something to see when he was on. Everybody talked about it. There was always quite a little crowd around his court on the weekends, and when he and the other men would come off the court after a set of doubles, the wives would see their husbands all red and puffing. And then they'd look at my old man and see him grinning and not even breathing hard after *he'd* been doing all the running back after the lobs and putting away those overheads, and they'd say to him, "Honestly, Hugh, I just don't see how you do it, not at your age. It's *amaz*ing! I'm going to take my Steve [or Bill or Tom] off cigarettes and put him on a diet. He's ten years younger and just look at him." Then my old man would light up a cigarette and smile and shake his head and say, "Well, you know how it is. I just play a lot." And then a minute later he'd look around at everybody lying on the lawn there in the sun and pick out me or one of the other younger fellows and say, "Feel like a set of singles?"

If you know north Jersey at all, chances are you know my father. He's Hugh Minot—the Montclair one, not the fellow out in New Brunswick. Just about the biggest realty man in the whole section, I guess. He and my mother have this place in Montclair, thirty-five acres, with a swimming pool and a big vegetable garden and this En-Tout-Cas court. A lovely home. My father got a little name for himself playing football at Rutgers, and that helped him when he went into business, I guess. He never played tennis in college, but after getting out he wanted something to sort of fill in for the football—something he could do well, or do better than the next man. You know how people are. So he took the game up. Of course, I was too little to remember his tennis game when he was still young, but friends of his have told me that it was really hot. He picked the game up like nothing at all, and a couple of pros told him if he'd only started earlier he might have gotten up there in the big time—maybe even with a national ranking, like No. 18 or so. Anyhow, he kept playing and I guess in the last twenty years there hasn't been a season where he missed more than a couple of weekends of tennis in the summertime. A few years back, he even joined one of these fancy clubs in New York with indoor courts, and he'd take a couple of days off from work and go in there just so that he could play in the wintertime. Once, I remember, he played doubles in there with Alice Marble and I think Sidney Wood. He told my mother about that game lots of times, but it didn't mean much to her. She used to play tennis years ago, just for fun, but she wasn't too good and gave it up. Now the garden is the big thing with her, and she hardly ever comes out to their court, even to watch.

I play a game of tennis just like my father's. Oh, not as good. Not nearly as good, because I haven't had the experience. But it's the same game, really. I've had people tell me that when they saw us playing together—that we both made the same shot the same way. Maybe my backhand was a little better (when it was on), and I used to think that my old man didn't get down low enough on a soft return to his forehand. But mostly we played the same game. Which isn't surprising, seeing that he taught me the game. He started way back when I was about nine or ten. He used to spend whole mornings with me, teaching me a single shot. I guess it was good for me and he did teach me a good, all-round game, but even now I can remember that those morning lessons would somehow discourage both of us. I couldn't seem to learn fast enough to suit him, and he'd get upset and shout across at me, "Straight arm! Straight arm!" and then *I'd* get jumpy and do the shot even worse. We'd both be glad when the lesson ended.

I don't mean to say that he was so *much* better than I was. We got so we played pretty close a lot of the time. I can still remember the day I first beat him at singles. It was in June of 1937. I'd been playing quite a lot at school and this was my first weekend home after school ended. We went out in the morning, no one else there, and, as usual, he walked right through me the first set—about 6-1 or so. I played much worse than my regular game then, just like I always did against him for some reason. But the next set I aced him in the second game and that set me up and I went on and took him, 7-5. It was a wonderful set of tennis and I was right on top of the world when it ended. I remember running all the way back to the house to tell Mother about it. The old man came in and sort of smiled at her and said something like "Well, I guess I'm old now, Amy."

But don't get the idea I started beating him then. That was the whole trouble. There I was, fifteen, sixteen years old and getting my size, and I began to think, Well, it's about time you took him. He wasn't a young man any more. But he went right on beating me. Somehow I never played well against him and I knew it, and I'd start pressing and getting sore and of course my game would go blooey.

I remember one weekend when I was in college, a whole bunch of us drove down to Montclair in May for a weekend—my two roommates and three girls we knew. It was going to be a lot of fun. But then we went out for some tennis and of course my father was there. We all played some mixed doubles, just fooling around, and then he asked me if I wanted some singles. In that casual way of his. And of course it was 6-2, 6-3, or some such thing. The second set we were really hitting out against each other and the kids watching got real quiet, just as if it was Forest Hills. And then when we came off, Alice, my date, said something to me. About him, I mean. "I think your father is a remarkable man," she said. "Simply remarkable. Don't you think so?" Maybe she wanted to make me feel better about losing, but it was a dumb question. What could I say except yes?

It was while I was in college that I began to play golf a little. I liked the game and I even bought clubs and took a couple of lessons. I broke ninety one day and wrote home to my father about it. He'd never played golf and he wrote back with some little gag about its being an old man's game. Just kidding, you know, and I guess I should have expected it, but I was embarrassed to talk about golf at home after that. I wasn't really very good at it, anyway.

I played some squash in college, too, and even made the B team, but I didn't try out for the tennis team. That disappointed my father, I think, because I wasn't any good at football, and I think he wanted to see me make some team. So he could come and see me play and tell his friends about it, I guess. Still, we did play squash a few times and I could beat him, though I saw that with time he probably would have caught up with me.

I don't want you to get the idea from this that I didn't have a good time playing tennis with him. I can remember the good days very well —lots of days where we'd played some doubles with friends or even a set of singles where my game was holding up or maybe even where I'd taken one set. Afterward we'd walk back together through the orchard, with my father knocking the green apples off the path with his racket the way he always did and the two of us hot and sweaty while we smoked cigarettes and talked about lots of things. Then we'd sit on the veranda and drink a can of beer before taking a dip in the pool. We'd be very close then, I felt.

And I keep remembering a funny thing that happened years ago— oh, away back when I was thirteen or fourteen. We'd gone away, the three of us, for a month in New Hampshire in the summer. We played a lot of tennis that month and my game was coming along pretty fast, but of course my father would beat me every single time

we played. Then he and I both entered the little town championship
there the last week in August. Of course, I was put out in the first
round (I was only a kid), but my old man went on into the finals.
There was quite a big crowd that came to watch that day, and they had
a referee and everything. My father was playing a young fellow—
about twenty or twenty-one, I guess he was. I remember that I sat by
myself, right down beside the court, to watch, and while they were
warming up I looked at this man playing my father and whispered to
myself, but almost out loud, "Take him! Take him!" I don't know why,
but I just wanted him to beat my father in those finals, and it sort of
scared me when I found that out. I wanted him to give him a real
shellacking. Then they began to play and it was a very close match
for a few games. But this young fellow was good, really good. He
played a very controlled game, waiting for errors and only hitting out
for winners when it was a sure thing. And he went on and won the first
set, and in the next my father began to hit into the net and it was
pretty plain that it wasn't even going to be close in the second set. I
kept watching and pretty soon I felt very funny sitting there. Then
the man won a love game off my father and I began to shake. I
jumped up and ran all the way up the road to our cabin and into my
room and lay down on my bed and cried hard. I kept thinking how
I'd wanted to have the man win, and I knew it was about the first time
I'd ever seen my father lose a love game. I never felt so ashamed. Of
course, that was years and years ago.

I don't think any of this would have bothered me except for one
thing—I've always *liked* my father. Except for this game, we've always gotten along fine. He's never wanted a junior-partner son, either
in his office or at home. No Judge Hardy stuff or "Let me light your
cigar, sir." And no backslapping, either. There have been times where
I didn't see much of him for a year or so, but when we got together (at
a ball game, say, or during a long trip in a car), we've always found
we could talk and argue and have a lot of laughs, too. When I came
back on my last furlough before I went overseas during the war, I
found that he'd chartered a sloop. The two of us went off for a week's
cruise along the Maine coast, and it was swell. Early-morning swims
and trying to cook over charcoal and the wonderful quiet that comes
over those little coves after you've anchored for the night and the
wind has dropped and perhaps you're getting ready to shake up some
cocktails. One night there, when we were sitting on deck and smoking cigarettes in the dark, he told me something that he never even

told my mother—that he'd tried to get into the Army and had been turned down. He just said it and we let it drop, but I've always been glad he told me. Somehow it made me feel better about going overseas.

Naturally, during the war I didn't play any tennis at all. And when I came back I got married and all, and I was older, so of course the game didn't mean as much to me. But still, the first weekend we played at my father's—the very first time I'd played him in four years —it was the same as ever. And I'd have sworn I had outgrown the damn thing. But Janet, my wife, had never seen me play the old man before and *she* spotted something. She came up to our room when I was changing afterward. "What's the matter with you?" she asked me. "Why does it mean so much to you? It's just a game, isn't it? I can see that it's a big thing for your father. That's why he plays so much and that's why he's so good at it. But why you?" She was half kidding, but I could see that it upset her. "This isn't a contest," she said. "We're not voting for Best Athlete in the County, are we?" I took her up on that and tried to explain the thing a little, but she wouldn't try to understand. "I just don't like a sorehead," she told me as she went out of the room.

I guess that brings me down to last summer and what happened. It was late in September, one of those wonderful weekends where it begins to get a little cool and the air is so bright. Father had played maybe six or seven sets of doubles Saturday, and then Sunday I came out with Janet, and he had his regular tennis gang there—Eddie Earnshaw and Mark O'Connor and that Mr. Lacy. I guess we men had played three sets of doubles, changing around, and we were sitting there catching our breath. I was waiting for Father to ask me for our singles. But he'd told me earlier that he hadn't been able to get much sleep the night before, so I'd decided that he was too tired for singles. Of course, I didn't even mention that out loud in front of the others—it would have embarrassed him. Then I looked around and noticed that my father was sitting in one of those canvas chairs instead of standing up, the way he usually did between sets. He looked awfully pale, even under his tan, and while I was looking at him he suddenly leaned over and grabbed his stomach and was sick on the grass. We all knew it was pretty bad, and we laid him down and put his cap over his eyes, and I ran back to the house to tell Mother and phone up the doctor. Father didn't say a word when we carried him into the house in the chair, and then Dr. Stockton came and said it was a heart attack and that Father had played his last game of tennis.

You would have thought after that and after all those months in bed that my father would just give up his tennis court—have it plowed over or let it go to grass. But Janet and I went out there for the week-end just last month and I was surprised to find that the court was in good shape, and Father said that he had asked the gang to come over, just so I could have some good men's doubles. He'd even had a chair set up in the orchard, halfway out to the court, so he could walk out there by himself. He walked out slow, the way he has to, and then sat down in the chair and rested for a couple of minutes, and then made it the rest of the way.

I haven't been playing much tennis this year, but I was really on my game there that day at my father's. I don't think I've ever played better on that court. I hardly made an error and I was relaxed and I felt good about my game. The others even spoke about how well I played.

But somehow it wasn't much fun. It just didn't seem like a real contest to me, and I didn't really care that I was holding my serve right along and winning my sets no matter who my partner was. Maybe for the first time in my life, I guess, I found out that it was only a game we were playing—only that and no more. And I began to realize what my old man and I had done to that game. All that time, all those years, I had only been trying to grow up and he had been trying to keep young, and we'd both done it on the tennis court. And now our struggle was over. I found that out that day, and when I did I suddenly wanted to tell my father about it. But then I looked over at him, sitting in a chair with a straw hat on his head, and I decided not to. I noticed that he didn't seem to be watching us at all. I had the feeling, instead, that he was *listening* to us play tennis and perhaps imagining a game to himself or remembering how he would play the point—the big, high-bouncing serve and the rush to the net for the volley, and then going back for the lob and looking up at it and the wonderful feeling as you uncoil on the smash and put the ball away.

SEE HOW THEY RUN

by GEORGE HARMON COXE

(1941)

Track and field is the great international sport, the feature of the Olympic Games. Times, distances and measurements are understood and can be compared in sports-loving nations all over the world, even if the mathematicians have to be called in now and then to convert meters into yards and kilograms into pounds. Americans and Britishers are primarily Mile-minded, but for a great many of the competing nations the big track event of the Olympics is not the 1,500-meter run (which is the closest metric equivalent race to the mile) but it is rather the 26-mile, 385-yard run known as the Marathon. In the United States there is one important Marathon held annually, the Boston Marathon, which has steadily built up a tradition of its own. George Harmon Coxe's intimate picture of the people who build their lives around this comparatively unheralded sport is one of the best behind-the-scenes glimpses in this book.

THE BUS stopped at the side of the road opposite the country lane, and as he waited for the door to open, Johnny Burke could see the farmhouse and the sea of parked cars in the yard beyond.

"It's going to be hot out there today," the driver said. "And, brother, I sure don't envy you any. When I go twenty-six miles I want to do it sitting down."

Johnny swung to the ground, leather carryall in hand. The smell of the countryside was fresh and fragrant in his nostrils, but he knew the driver was right. It would be hot. In the seventies now by the feel of it. He was right about the twenty-six miles too. Why anyone should want to run that distance had always been a mystery that not even his father could satisfactorily explain.

Going up the lane he remembered the farmhouse from that other trip, years ago, but he did not remember the yard. Like a picnic ground or gypsy carnival, with the relatives of the contestants milling around and laughing and eating basket lunches. Already there were some who stood about in track suits and sweaters, and Johnny Burke smiled a little scornfully. Coming here that other time with his father he had been thrilled and excited, but that, he realized now, was because he had been so young.

On the porch of the rambling farmhouse which had for this one day been turned into the marathon headquarters of the world, the hubbub of voices lay thick about him. Inside there would be places to change, for his father had told him how the furniture would be carted to the barn beforehand. Somehow this seemed as fantastic as the crowd outside or the race itself. Why should the owner turn her house inside out for a couple hundred maniacs? A Mrs. Tebeau, the papers had said. And although she was seventy-three years old she had, with the help of her daughter, served as hostess to the marathoners for sixteen years, furnishing sandwiches and milk for all who wanted them.

He noticed the girl as he climbed the steps. She was standing a few feet away, talking to some man; a slim, straight, pleasant-faced girl, looking strangely out of place here with her trim, heather-colored suit. She glanced toward him as he stopped, and smiled, and it was such a friendly smile that he smiled back and felt a sudden tingling ripple through him.

"Aren't you Johnny Burke?" The man, moving forward now, was a lank, lazy-looking individual, all but his eyes, which were blue and quizzical and direct. "I thought so," he said when Johnny nodded. "I saw you at the Intercollegiates last year. That was a nice mile you ran. I'm Dave Shedden, of the *Standard*."

Johnny shook hands and thanked him. Shedden glanced at a list in his hand.

"So you're the John Burke that entered this year? We thought it was your dad. This would have been his twentieth."

"He couldn't make it," Johnny said, and then, because he could not explain: "So I thought I'd come up and take his place."

"It'll take some running to do that."

"So I understand."

"And what about the invitation mile in New York tomorrow?"

"I'm passing it up."

"Oh? I thought that was supposed to be your dish."

Johnny began to dislike Shedden. There was an undertone of sarcasm in his words, a skepticism that Johnny found annoying.

"I'd rather win this," he said.

"Just like that?"

"Don't you think I can?"

"Could be." Shedden shrugged. "Only you're stepping out of your class, aren't you? You won't be running against a select little group of college boys today."

Johnny gave him back his sardonic grin. "Select, maybe; but they all know how to run or they couldn't get entered."

"They've got reputations, you mean," Shedden said. "Well, out here a guy needs more than that. It's pretty tough on prima donnas."

Johnny let it go and would have moved on had it not been for a sturdy, bronzed man of forty-five or so who bustled up to take the reporter's arm.

"Hey, Dave, where's Burke? You seen Burke anywhere?"

"This is Burke," said Shedden, and Johnny saw the man's wide-eyed glance and then his grin.

"Johnny Burke!" He was pumping Johnny's hand now and slapping his shoulder. "Young Johnny, huh? I'm Tom Reynolds. I've run with your old man for nineteen years. Did he ever tell you? Where is he? Is he quittin'? Old age getting him? . . . Oh, Kay."

And then, miraculously, the girl Johnny had been watching was standing in front of him. Her hand was firm and warm in his and he saw that there were auburn lights in her dark hair, that her nose was cute and lightly freckled.

"I saw you in the meet at the Garden two years ago," she said. "And I think it's grand, your running in place of your father today. He wanted to make it twenty races in a row, didn't he? And I heard what you said to Mr. Shedden about the race in New York. Will you mind so awfully?"

Johnny Burke said he wouldn't. He was used to the idea now, but two weeks ago it had been different. He had not known until then that his father would never run again, and he remembered too vividly coming down the stairs with the doctor that evening and going out on the porch where, with the darkness masking their faces, they had talked of Johnny, senior, and the verdict had been given. No more than six months, the doctor said. Probably not that.

It had been a bad night for Johnny, and before he fell asleep at dawn he knew what he wanted to do. His father, not yet aware how sick he was, had entered the marathon months before, and so, the next afternoon, Johnny told him he was going to use that entry and run this year's race by proxy and make the record an even twenty.

Even now he could see the thin wan face brighten as his father lay there in bed with the pillows propping him up.

"You will? You'll take my place?" he'd said. "Honest, Johnny?" And then, thinking, the doubt had come. "But that race in New York you've been talking about? That's the next day."

"The invitation mile?" Johnny had said. "What's that? I've beaten all those guys before, one time or another."

"You could win that race, though."

"I'll win the marathon too."

His father had laughed at that. "You're crazy! I only won twice in nineteen years and I was better than most."

"Ah, you were never anything but a fair country runner."

"I could outrun you the best day you ever saw," his father had cracked, and Johnny had jeered at him past the hardness in his throat because he saw how good it made his father feel.

There had been but two weeks in which to train, and he had worked diligently, following the schedule his father mapped out, wanting to cry sometimes when he saw how thrilled and proud his father seemed when he listened to the nightly reports. Johnny had worked up to twenty miles the day before yesterday, and when his father heard the time he admitted that Johnny might have a chance.

"Only don't try to win it, Johnny," he said. "This is no mile. You've been running races where only the first three places count. In this one the first thirty-five get listed in the papers."

Johnny hadn't argued then, nor had he told anyone the truth.

He knew how the newspapers would pounce on the sentimental elements of the story if they knew his father had run his last race. Not even his father must know that. And there was no sacrifice involved anyway. He had looked forward to that New York race, but he was glad to run this race instead, for he loved his father and knew how much this day meant to him each year.

He saw that Shedden and Tom Reynolds had moved on and realized the girl was waiting for him to speak. "No, I don't mind," he said again. "I've been arguing with Dad for years about this race and now I want to find out for myself."

"Arguing?"

"I can't figure it out. Dad has won twice, but in the past ten years he hasn't even been in the first five."

"My father hasn't been in the first five lately either."

"That's what I mean. Twenty-six miles, three hundred and eighty-five yards is an awful grind. If a guy feels he can't win——"

"You think no one should enter unless he feels he can win?"

"Not unless he's young and on the way up. There's maybe a dozen runners in the bunch. The rest of it's a farce." She looked at him strangely, but he did not notice and waved his hand to include the yard and farmhouse. "Look at them," he said, and in his laugh there was something superior, unconscious perhaps, but noticeable, for his was the viewpoint of one who has been at the top. "Anybody can get in that mails an entry. Anybody."

"Yes," Kay Reynolds said. "It's a poor man's race. You don't have to go to college or belong to any club, and there's nothing in it but a medal and a cup if you win. And yet they've been running this race for over forty years. There have been marathons ever since the Greeks defeated the Persians."

"Sure," Johnny said. "But why do they let all the clowns in? I read in the paper about some of them that even smoke——"

"Benny 'Cigars' Kelly and Jim 'Tobacco' Lane."

"Yes," Johnny said. "And the papers say they flatfoot the whole distance, puffing cigars and making faces at the crowd."

"Yes," Kay Reynolds said, "there are clowns. There always are in any event that's truly open. And there is Clarence De Mar, who is fifty-two and has won seven times. And Kennedy. He's fifty-seven. He's run twenty-eight times and finished twenty-seven races. And Semple, who's been running for twenty-four years. And your father and mine. That's why the papers call this race the biggest and freest sport spectacle on earth. Did you ever run before a half-million people?"

Johnny looked at her then. Her eyes were steady now and she wasn't smiling. "That's a lot of people," he said, and grinned. "Let's settle for a spectacle."

"But still a little beneath you."

Johnny's grin went away and his cheeks got hot. Who did she think she was, bawling him out? "What difference does it make? If a couple hundred fellows want to come out and run twenty-six miles, that's their business. I didn't come up here to make a spectacle; I came to win a race."

"Yes," the girl said, not looking at him now, and distance in her voice. "And I can see why you think you will. You've had every advantage, haven't you? The best coaches, and trainers and special food and privileges and expense money. These others have nothing but enthusiasm and determination. They are self-taught and trained and what food they get they work for six days a week."

"Okay," said Johnny, "I'm a snob. I came up to run this race, but I don't have to like it." He turned away, stopped to say stiffly: "It's nice to know you'll be rooting for me."

"I will," Kay Reynolds said, "because I'll be remembering your father, like thousands of others. I only hope you can do as well today as he would if he were here."

Johnny went inside, red-faced and angry, and the sight that met his eyes served only to heighten the irritation and bear out his argument. Like a side show at the circus. Skins of every shade from skim milk to chocolate. Fuzzy-chinned kids, gray-thatched and bald-topped oldsters; fat boys with pillow stomachs and skinny ones with pipestem legs.

He made his way into a side room that smelled of wintergreen oil and stale perspiration and old shoes. He found a place to sit down and began to change, not listening to the babble about him until someone addressed him.

"Your first race?" The thin Yankee drawl came from a blond, shaggy-haired fellow beside him. "It's my fifth. My name's Bronson."

Johnny had to take the outthrust hand. "Burke," he said.

"Not Johnny Burke's boy?" Bronson's face lit up. "Hey, fellows! What do you think? This is Johnny Burke's boy."

They flocked about him then, fifteen or twenty of them, shaking hands and asking questions and wanting to know about his father and wishing him luck. And though he was proud of his father when he heard their tributes, he was scornful, too, because, of the group, only a few made mention of his own achievements; even then the others did not seem impressed, cataloguing him not as Johnny Burke who'd done a 4:10 mile but only as Johnny Burke's boy.

"I'll never forget him," Bronson said as they went out on the porch. "Hadn't been for your dad I'd never finished my first race. I was down around Lake Street, running about twentieth when your dad

came up. You know they got official cars that have paper cups of water and lemon halves and things like that to hand out when you need
'em, but they're caterin' to the leaders mostly. And I think I'm about
done when a car comes past and your dad hollers and they pull alongside to give him a cup of water and he douses it on my head." Bronson
grinned. "I finished. Twenty-third."

Johnny looked at him. "Did you ever win?"

"Oh, no. Finished ninth once, though. Got me a medal for it. I figure to be in the first ten this year too. Look, I'd like you to meet my
wife. She's heard me talk about your dad——" He turned and was
waving to someone, and Johnny Burke saw the sturdy apple-cheeked
girl on the running board of a five-year-old sedan. She had a child on
her knee and waved back. Johnny drew away, confused and a little
embarrassed.

"Thanks," he said, "but hadn't we better get along to the starting
line? Where you from?" he asked, to change the subject.

"Over Pittsfield way. Got a farm there."

"That's quite a jaunt, isn't it?"

"Oh, no. Lots come from Canada, even. We make a day of it. Start
early, you know, and stop for a bite somewhere."

"And drive back afterwards?"

"You bet. Alice now, that's my wife, will ride along after we start
and find some spot down around Brookline to watch the fellows go
by; then she'll pick me up at Exeter Street after I finish. The official
car'll have our bags all there waiting for us; and say——" He smiled
with some embarrassment. "I guess you know a lot more about running than I do, but if this is your first marathon—well, I don't want to
try and tell you, but don't let these front runners bother you. It's an
awful long haul and——"

Johnny sighed. "I guess I can make out," he said, and then Tom
Reynolds was there, looking bronzed and sturdy and fit, Johnny
thought, like his father before that illness came.

"Been looking for you." He took Johnny's arm and drew him
aside. "Don't let any of those fancy Dans fool you after we start.
They'll dance away from the rest of us for three or four miles and
then they'll get a stitch and get picked up by the Red Cross car and
watch the rest of the race over a tailboard. They're like some of the
other phonies."

"I'll remember," Johnny said, but Reynolds wasn't through.

"Your old man and I've been doing this for nineteen years. This

was to be our last—we're no Clarence De Mars or Bill Kennedys—
and we're old enough to quit. But now you've got to take old Johnny's
place. Stick with me. I know the pace."

Johnny nodded his thanks. "We'll see," he said. "I never ran the
course, but I think I can go the distance all right." Funny. To hear
them talk you'd think he wasn't even going to finish without everybody helping him. "I'll make out."

"Sure you will. And say, Coolidge Corner in Brookline was always
a bad spot for Johnny and me. That's gettin' near the end, you know,
with lots of autos around, and not bein' front runners we couldn't always count on an official car bein' near. So Kay's always been there
since she was a little girl, with lemon halves in case we needed 'em.
She'll have one for you today." He paused and Johnny's glance fal-
tered before the steady eyes because it seemed as though Reynolds
had read his thoughts. "But maybe you won't need anything," he
said abruptly. "Anyway, good luck."

The starter got them away promptly at the stroke of twelve and
down the lane they went, stretched clear across its width and fifteen
or twenty deep. To Johnny, it was nothing but a mob and he moved
out briskly to get away from the dust and jostling.

By the time he reached the main highway he was running fifth and
satisfied with his position, and for a while then he did not think about
the race, but only how he felt. He felt good. Loose, with lots of juice
in his flat-muscled body and an easy animal grace that brought the
road back under him in long effortless strides. He didn't think about
his pace until he heard someone pounding up beside him and then a
voice in his ear.

"Easy, son." It was Tom Reynolds and he looked worried. "This
is no mile."

Johnny nodded, a little irritated that this man should tell him how
to run. He shortened his stride slightly and fell off the pace. Two
chunky individuals went by him, one young and one old, flat-footed
runners, making it tough for themselves already. Another came alongside, a string bean with pasty skin and a handkerchief, knotted at
the corners, on his head, to keep the sun off.

He saw that Tom Reynolds was at his shoulder and thought about
his advice. He thought of other things Tom Reynolds did not know
about. He'd grown up knowing of this hobby of his father's, and how
he trained, and hearing over and over the details of all these B.A.A.

marathons. As a boy the race had seemed a colorful and exciting climax that he might sometime reach himself, but later, as he grew older and there were no more victories for his father, the idea of this annual contest had become an object of secret ridicule. Even his mother had sometimes acted ashamed in those last few years before her death. It wasn't dignified for a man of his age, she said. And what did he get out of it? It was probably the other women in her bridge club, Johnny thought, who asked her questions that she could not answer because she herself did not know why her husband ran on, year after year.

His own training had started while he was a junior in high school, and he could remember his father making him jog along with him sometimes, short distances at first, and working up in easy stages until he could do three or four loping miles without too much uneasiness. He had never lost a race in high school, and in college, though he was the son of a machinist and had to earn part of his expenses, he had become a figure of some importance on the campus solely because of the training his father had given him. That's why he was running today: to pay back a little of what he owed while it would do some good.

He saw now that they were running through a town and knew it must be Framingham. About five miles, he guessed, and he still felt good and there was no tightness in his lungs. There were crowds along the curbing now and he could hear them yelling encouragement up ahead of him. Then he was going by the checking station and from somewhere at the side he heard a roar that made him smile.

"Yeah, Burke," they said, and he waved back, thinking of the times he'd heard that same cry in the Stadium and Franklin Field and in the Garden.

He thought then of Tom Reynolds and glanced over his shoulder. Runners were strung out behind him as far as he could see, but Reynolds was not among them and he knew he must have stepped up his pace while he had been thinking.

Well, that was all right. There were other things Reynolds did not know. He and Bronson and those runners who had shaken hands. Some had probably never heard of him because they had no racing interest but the marathon distance; the others who knew of his reputation—Shedden, the reporter, and Kay Reynolds included—did not give him a chance. To them he was just another miler, and a cocky one at that.

Perhaps he was. And this race was as he'd always maintained in good-natured arguments with his father: a bunch of screwballs out to make an exhibition of themselves for the most part, with a dozen or so real runners in the pack. Well, he was running this one race and he was going to win it and that would be that. What the others did not know was that even while he was in college he had often trained with his father during vacations, sometimes driving the car slowly behind him to protect him from the other cars along the road, and sometimes jogging alongside him, mile after mile. He knew what it was to go twenty miles—he'd once gone twenty-five. Today he was going to do twenty-six miles and three hundred and eighty-five yards.

He brought the race back into the focus of his thoughts and found himself approaching the center of Natick with perhaps ten miles behind him. Across the square some enthusiasts had stretched a banner as a token of encouragement for a local contestant and as Johnny drew near he heard his name called from the edges of the road and found the tribute a cheerful sound, warmly stimulating. But the race was already taking its toll of impudent front runners. Of the dozen or more who had been in front of him, seven had dropped out. Approaching Wellesley he saw the pasty fellow with the handkerchief on his head sitting at the roadside waiting for a lift.

"Blisters," he said as Johnny went by. "Terrible blisters," he said, and waved cheerfully.

Along by the college the girls were out in force. Bright-faced, smiling girls in sweaters and gay skirts and saddle-strapped shoes. There would be girls like that in New York tomorrow night, and though he would not run he would be there for the meet and the parties and dancing afterward. He'd get the four o'clock down this afternoon, and Stan Tarleton would meet him, and with no racing tomorrow he could step out.

"Halfway," he said as he passed the checking station and took stock of himself and the race.

He was breathing pretty well, but he could feel his legs and the pounding of the pavement now, realizing that the roadbed was a lot harder on his feet than a cinder track. He lengthened his stride for a hundred yards to get a kink out of his right thigh and it went away all right and he dropped back to his former pace.

Between Wellesley and Auburndale two runners passed him and he let them go. Like the third quarter in a mile run, he thought, when it's still a long way to the end, but you have to keep the pace up. He was conscious of the heat now and it was harder to breathe. The pain was coming slowly, not real bad yet, but frightening when he counted the miles. Eighteen behind him. The hills of Newton and eight more to go.

The first hill seemed endless, slowing him down until he was practically walking at the top. Then, not sure how much longer he could go, he gained the downslope and his strength came back and he was struggling upward again. Gradually, as he fought that rise, a curious giddiness he had never experienced before came upon him and he did not know he was walking until he heard someone speak his name.

"Come on, young Johnny," the voice said. "Only a couple more hills to go."

It was an effort for Johnny to put the voice and the tanned blond face together and then, through the curtain of his giddiness, he knew it was Bronson, and picked up his stride again to match the other. The car, coming up from behind, meant nothing to him until there came a sudden icy shock upon his head and the feel of water trickling through his hair and down his neck. Then, abruptly, his giddiness had gone and he saw Bronson grinning at him, an empty paper cup in his hand as the official car moved on ahead.

"Thanks," Johnny Burke said. "I guess it was the heat." And he was both grateful and angry with himself for not remembering that in this race there were accompanying cars and refreshments for those lucky enough to get them.

"Sure," Bronson said. "Let's go now."

He started out in front, grinning over his shoulder, and Johnny went after him, seeing the other draw ahead until he realized that a country boy from Pittsfield was showing him his heels; then he pulled his shoulders back a little and sardonic resentment at his near collapse kept him dogging Bronson's footsteps all the way up the College hill and down the long slope to Cleveland Circle.

Here it was flat and he knew there were only five miles to go. The pain was coming again and a numbness crept along his legs and he thought, *It's like the last lap,* and then a new and horrible awareness came to him and he forgot the man up ahead. This last-lap pain for him had never lasted longer than a minute or so; now it must go on for five more miles.

"You went out a little fast, boy. You got anything left?"

Tom Reynolds was at his shoulder, though he seemed a block

away. His face was twisted and set, too, but he was breathing all right and his stride was firm and solid.

"Sure I've got something left." Johnny got the words out one at a time, laboriously, angrily.

"Show me. Come on. Match me for a hundred strides. Your old man could do it if he was here."

Anger drove Johnny Burke along for quite a while. He matched Tom Reynolds' pace, forgetting the torture in his lungs and the aching numbness in his legs. He wanted to talk back to this man who drove him on, but he knew he could not speak, and kept pounding on, not counting the strides any longer but always matching them until, somewhere down along the misty row of faces on the curbstone, Reynolds spoke again.

"This is the place," he said heavily. "This is where your dad and I always find out who's the better man each year. You're on your own now, Johnny Burke."

He moved out in front then, Reynolds did, an inch at a time, and Johnny saw the number on his back pull away and dissolve into soft focus. Somewhere, dim and thin and faraway, he could hear the voice of the crowd. "Come on, Burke," it said.

And he kept on, holding his own as a new nausea began to fasten about his stomach. Not cramps, but a simple sickness he could not understand until he realized that over the past few miles the poisonous smell of automobile exhausts had become much stronger as traffic increased. The thought that a contest must be run under such conditions infuriated him, and yet, even as he raged, he knew that this was but another hazard in the race to be shared by all who dared to try it.

For a step or two he ran bent over to see if this would help. There were more people here, he knew, and he could see some kind of square with shops and store fronts and streetcar tracks down the middle of the street. He staggered finally, fighting the nausea rather than his weariness. He looked about for an official car and found none near him. Then, his stride breaking now, he saw something loom out from the edge of the crowd. A hand found his and a girl's voice was in his ear.

"Suck on this," it said. "It's not far now. You can do it."

There was something in his hand and he put it to his lips and there was a tart strong taste of lemon in his mouth, laving his throat and starting the saliva again. He felt it going down his throat, the quick contraction of his stomach. He sucked greedily, breathing around the lemon, and gradually his head cleared and the nausea fled and there was nothing left but the pain and torment that come near the end for every runner who goes all out.

Someone drew alongside him. He could hear the slap of shoes against the asphalt pavement. The sound angered him and he pulled away, finding the strength somehow and knowing then that he was running better.

Up ahead he saw a bobbing figure and focused on it, watching it come nearer, drawing even and then hearing Bronson's voice as he went past: "Give it to 'em, Burke! Give 'em hell for me!"

Vaguely he remembered passing someone else, for the sound of labored breathing was not his own, and as he came into the approach of Kenmore Square he saw a familiar number just ahead and then he was matching strides with Tom Reynolds.

"Go on," the older man called, though it must have been an effort now. "What're you waitin' for? It's only a mile and you've got two ahead of you."

He saw them out in front as he pulled away from Reynolds. They were running shoulder to shoulder, raggedly, and he set out after them, blindly in his exhaustion, yet no longer worried or afraid. His running was detached, all but the torment of pain in his chest, and though below his waist there was nothing but fringe, he somehow found himself thinking with a curious clarity that explained many things in that last mile.

It was the cheering that started those thoughts. The sound of his name, like the pounding of rain, refreshing him, beating out a monotone of encouragement. "Burke . . . Burke . . . Burke!"

He remembered the cheering back in Framingham, the vague sounds of applause and enthusiasm that had accompanied him mile after mile. Not a brief, concerted cheer for a stretch run and victory that he had so often heard, but something new and different that he had never before experienced. For more than two hours he had heard these sounds, and the thought of this helped carry him now, filling him with wonderment until, struggling closer to those twin bobbing figures up ahead, the question came to him—how did they know him, this crowd? They had never seen him before. His name was in the papers' starting line-up. Number 18. Johnny Burke. And then, all at once, he knew. Those half million along the course who cheered were cheering a name, the memory of a name, the memory of other races back through the years. Not him, but his father, whom they had known and loved as a great competitor who always gave his best.

There were twin shadows at his shoulder now and the blood was boiling into his eyes along with the tears, and under his heart were red-hot coals. Loose bird shot filled his throat and the faces of the crowd went swimming by like painted faces in a dream. He lifted his elbows a little higher to give his lungs more clearance. He made a staggering turn into Exeter Street for the last hundred yards, and the sound of his name beat against his eardrums and he knew, finally, why his father had come back to run for nineteen years, why the others, not the clowns but the good competitors, came out on this day each year. Whether he finished first or fifty-first, each heard, for a little while, the sound of his name, a bit of acclaim to treasure secretly, to set him apart from his fellow man and make brighter an existence that otherwise was humdrum and monotonous; not an easy thing for any man to give up, for there is a need of such tribute in all men of heart and spirit, and each must find his little share in whatever way he can.

They said it was the closest finish in many years, but Johnny Burke did not know it. He did not feel the tape at his chest and would have run on had not strong hands grabbed him, supporting his arms so that he stood straddle-legged in the street with a sick stupor enveloping him until someone threw water in his face. Gradually then, the opaque shutter of his vision lifted and he straightened, seeing other faces about him and the cameras of the press photographers. When he felt someone prying at his hand he opened it and looked down and found the lemon, now squeezed to yellow pulp.

The reporters were kind to him as he stretched out on the white-sheeted cot in the basement of the old brick building. They stood about patiently until his heart had slowed and the strength began to flow again along his muscles. When he sat up someone put the laurel wreath upon his head. He had to keep it on while the flash bulbs popped, and then he had to talk, though there was little he could say except that he was glad he'd won and knew his father would be pleased.

Later, under the shower, he thought of all the things he might have said, and of them all the thing he wanted most to say could be told to no one but his father. He knew how it would sound to those reporters

—falsely modest, pretentious; corny, they'd call it. How could he tell them that he had not won this race alone, could not have won but for his father? Oh, it was his legs and lungs that did the job, but, faltering back there in the hills of Newton, it was Bronson who had pulled him through. Bronson, talking to him, getting water from the official car and reviving him. Not because Bronson liked him or cared particularly whether he finished or not, but because in him he saw the other Johnny Burke. And Tom Reynolds, taunting him into matching strides when he started to lag again, reminding him always of his father so that he would not quit.

These two who had helped him had been thinking of his father, and yet, even with their help, he could not have won without the lemon that stilled his nausea and comforted him. Now, letting the cold water play along his spine, he had to know whether this, too, had been offered because of his father or whether that gesture Kay Reynolds had made was in some part for him alone.

Upstairs in the corridors of the old clubhouse the wives and mothers and families of those who had already finished clustered about their men; others, still waiting, gathered round to greet the front runners with the camaraderie born of good-natured competition. None seemed disgruntled, and when Johnny Burke appeared they came to him with their congratulations as though he had long been one of them. He thanked them as best he could, the cords in his throat tightening as he spoke of his father and parried questions he could not answer.

How long he stood there he was never sure; he only knew that it was an anxious time because always he was looking over heads and shoulders for a dark head and a heather-colored suit. Then, finally, he was by himself and an official had come up to ask him how the cup and medal were to be engraved.

"The way the entry read," Johnny Burke said, and the official, not understanding, smiled.

"But you're Johnny Burke, junior, aren't you?"

"Yes," Johnny said, and could neither explain nor say he wanted his father's record to read an even twenty races run. "Yes," he said again, "but I don't use the junior much. John Burke is the way I want it."

Then a soft voice was at his elbow, and his heart skipped and went racing on as he turned and saw Kay Reynolds' friendly smile. He had to clear his throat before he could reply to her congratulations, but there was a curious glow in his breast now; for as he took her offered hand in his he found something in her eyes that made him forget New York, something that told him from here on he was on his very own.

LOVE

---

by GUY DE MAUPASSANT

(1885)

With very few exceptions, the short stories of Guy de Maupassant, the French master of that literary form, exhibit a wry, detached and unsentimental attitude toward the world. Love is one of the exceptions. It is by a younger De Maupassant, much more impressionable, far more emotional. This is one of the surprises of his charming story of a hunting trip. The ending, so swiftly turned and so suddenly right, supplies another, though it is much more tender than the usual twist at the end of De Maupassant stories.

I HAVE JUST READ among the general news in one of the papers a drama of passion. He killed her and then he killed himself, so he must have loved her. What matters He or She? Their love alone matters to me; and it does not interest me because it moves me or astonishes me, or because it softens me or makes me think, but because it recalls to my mind a remembrance of my youth, a strange recollection of a hunting adventure where Love appeared to me, as the Cross appeared to the early Christians, in the midst of the heavens.

I was born with all the instincts and the senses of primitive man, tempered by the arguments and the restraints of a civilized being. I am passionately fond of shooting, yet the sight of the wounded animal, of the blood on its feathers and on my hands, affects my heart so as almost to make it stop.

That year the cold weather set in suddenly toward the end of autumn, and I was invited by one of my cousins, Karl de Rauville, to go with him and shoot ducks on the marshes, at daybreak.

My cousin was a jolly fellow of forty, with red hair, very stout and bearded, a country gentleman, an amiable semi-brute, of a happy disposition and endowed with that Gallic wit which makes even mediocrity agreeable. He lived in a house, half farmhouse, half château, situated in a broad valley through which a river ran. The hills right and left were covered with woods, old manorial woods where magnificent trees still remained, and where the rarest feathered game in that part of France was to be found. Eagles were shot there occasionally, and birds of passage, such as rarely venture into our overpopulated part of the country, invariably lighted amid these giant oaks, as if they knew or recognized some little corner of a primeval forest which had remained there to serve them as a shelter during their short nocturnal halt.

In the valley there were large meadows watered by trenches and separated by hedges; then, farther on, the river, which up to that point had been kept between banks, expanded into a vast marsh. That marsh was the best shooting ground I ever saw. It was my cousin's chief care, and he kept it as a preserve. Through the rushes that covered it, and made it rustling and rough, narrow passages had been cut, through which the flat-bottomed boats, impelled and steered by poles, passed along silently over dead water, brushing up against the reeds and making the swift fish take refuge in the weeds, and the wild fowl, with their pointed, black heads, dive suddenly.

I am passionately fond of the water: of the sea, though it is too vast, too full of movement, impossible to hold; of the rivers which are so beautiful, but which pass on, and flee away; and above all of the marshes, where the whole unknown existence of aquatic animals palpitates. The marsh is an entire world in itself on the world of earth— a different world, which has its own life, its settled inhabitants and its passing travelers, its voices, its noises, and above all its mystery. Nothing is more impressive, nothing more disquieting, more terrifying occasionally, than a fen. Why should a vague terror hang over these low plains covered with water? Is it the low rustling of the rushes, the strange will-o'-the-wisp lights, the silence which prevails on calm nights, the still mists which hang over the surface like a shroud; or is it the almost inaudible splashing, so slight and so gentle, yet sometimes more terrifying than the cannons of men or the thunders of the skies, which makes these marshes resemble countries one has dreamed of, terrible countries holding an unknown and dangerous secret?

No, something else belongs to it—another mystery, perhaps the mystery of the creation itself! For was it not in stagnant and muddy water, amid the heavy humidity of moist land under the heat of the sun, that the first germ of life pulsated and expanded to the day?

I arrived at my cousin's in the evening. It was freezing hard enough to split the stones.

During dinner, in the large room whose sideboards, walls, and ceiling were covered with stuffed birds, with wings extended or perched on branches to which they were nailed—hawks, herons, owls, nightjars, buzzards, tiercels, vultures, falcons—my cousin, who, dressed in a sealskin jacket, himself resembled some strange animal from a cold country, told me what preparations he had made for that same night.

We were to start at half past three in the morning, so as to arrive at the place which he had chosen for our watching place at about half past four. On that spot a hut had been built of lumps of ice, so as to shelter us somewhat from the trying wind which precedes daybreak, a wind so cold as to tear the flesh like a saw, cut it like the blade of a knife, prick it like a poisoned sting, twist it like a pair of pincers, and burn it like fire.

My cousin rubbed his hands: "I have never known such a frost," he said; "it is already twelve degrees below zero at six o'clock in the evening."

I threw myself onto my bed immediately after we had finished our meal, and went to sleep by the light of a bright fire burning in the grate.

At three o'clock he woke me. In my turn, I put on a sheepskin, and found my cousin Karl covered with a bearskin. After having each swallowed two cups of scalding coffee, followed by glasses of liqueur brandy, we started, accompanied by a gamekeeper and our dogs, Plongeon and Pierrot.

From the first moment that I got outside, I felt chilled to the very marrow. It was one of those nights on which the earth seems dead with cold. The frozen air becomes resisting and palpable, such pain does it cause; no breath of wind moves it, it is fixed and motionless; it bites you, pierces through you, dries you, kills the trees, the plants, the insects, the small birds themselves, who fall from the branches onto the hard ground, and become stiff themselves under the grip of the cold.

The moon, which was in her last quarter and was inclining all to one side, seemed fainting in the midst of space, so weak that she was unable to wane, forced to stay up yonder, seized and paralyzed by the severity of the weather. She shed a cold, mournful light over the world, that dying and wan light which she gives us every month, at the end of her period.

Karl and I walked side by side, our backs bent, our hands in our pockets and our guns under our arms. Our boots, which were wrapped in wool so that we might be able to walk without slipping on the frozen river, made no sound, and I looked at the white vapor which our dogs' breath made.

We were soon on the edge of the marsh, and entered one of the lanes of dry rushes which ran through the low forest.

Our elbows, which touched the long, ribbonlike leaves, left a slight noise behind us, and I was seized, as I had never been before, by the powerful and singular emotion which marshes cause in me. This one was dead, dead from cold, since we were walking on it, in the middle of its population of dried rushes.

Suddenly, at the turn of one of the lanes, I perceived the ice hut which had been constructed to shelter us. I went in, and as we had nearly an hour to wait before the wandering birds would awake, I rolled myself up in my rug in order to try and get warm. Then, lying on my back, I began to look at the misshapen moon, which had four horns, through the vaguely transparent walls of this polar house. But the frost of the frozen marshes, the cold of these walls, the cold from the firmament penetrated me so terribly that I began to cough. My cousin Karl became uneasy.

"No matter if we do not kill much today," he said: "I do not want you to catch cold; we will light a fire." And he told the gamekeeper to cut some rushes.

We made a pile in the middle of our hut, which had a hole in the middle of the roof to let out the smoke, and when the red flames rose up to the clear, crystal blocks they began to melt, gently, imperceptibly, as if they were sweating. Karl, who had remained outside, called out to me: "Come and look here!" I went out of the hut and remained struck with astonishment. Our hut, in the shape of a cone, looked like an enormous diamond with a heart of fire, which had been suddenly planted there in the midst of the frozen water of the marsh. And inside, we saw two fantastic forms, those of our dogs, who were warming themselves at the fire.

But a peculiar cry, a lost, a wandering cry, passed over our heads, and the light from our hearth showed us the wild birds. Nothing moves one so much as the first clamor of a life which one does not see, which passes through the somber air so quickly and so far off, just before the first streak of a winter's day appears on the horizon. It seems to me, at this glacial hour of dawn, as if that passing cry which is carried away by the wings of a bird is the sigh of a soul from the world!

"Put out the fire," said Karl, "it is getting daylight."

The sky was, in fact, beginning to grow pale, and the flights of ducks made long, rapid streaks which were soon obliterated on the sky.

A stream of light burst out into the night; Karl had fired, and the two dogs ran forward.

And then, nearly every minute, now he, now I, aimed rapidly as soon as the shadow of a flying flock appeared above the rushes. And Pierrot and Plongeon, out of breath but happy, retrieved the bleeding birds, whose eyes still, occasionally, looked at us.

The sun had risen, and it was a bright day with a blue sky, and we were thinking of taking our departure, when two birds with extended necks and outstretched wings glided rapidly over our heads. I fired, and one of them fell almost at my feet. It was a teal, with a silver breast, and then, in the blue space above me, I heard a voice, the voice of a bird. It was a short, repeated, heart-rending lament; and the bird, the little animal that had been spared, began to turn round in the blue sky, over our heads, looking at its dead companion which I was holding in my hand.

Karl was on his knees, his gun to his shoulder watching it eagerly, until it should be within shot. "You have killed the duck," he said, "and the drake will not fly away."

He certainly did not fly away; he circled over our heads continually, and continued his cries. Never have any groans of suffering pained me so much as that desolate appeal, as that lamentable reproach of this poor bird which was lost in space.

Occasionally he took flight under the menace of the gun which followed his movements, and seemed ready to continue his flight alone, but as he could not make up his mind to this, he returned to find his mate.

"Leave her on the ground," Karl said to me, "he will come within shot by and by." And he did indeed come near us, careless of danger, infatuated by his animal love, by his affection for his mate, which I had just killed.

Karl fired, and it was as if somebody had cut the string which held the bird suspended. I saw something black descend, and I heard the noise of a fall among the rushes. And Pierrot brought it to me.

I put them—they were already cold—into the same gamebag, and I returned to Paris the same evening.

THE MAN FROM
CAP D'AMOUR

by *THOMAS H. RADDALL*

(1943)

Hockey is one of those sports which apparently lend themselves better to conversation than to writing. There is, in any event, a dearth of good hockey stories, and even that fine Canadian novelist, Hugh McLennan, who has written the definitive essay on the game, has never written hockey fiction. After a long investigation, we came across The Man from Cap D'Amour, *a fresh and unpretentious story whose wonderful avoidance of cliché raised it, we thought, well above the other candidates we were considering. It is set in Canada, naturally, in one of those provincial reaches where life boils down to its real essentials: one's work, the other sex, and hockey.*

CARIBOU," said Maling, who was fond of epigrams, "is where good wireless operators go when they die—and bad ones while they live."

Dolly Hershman tied the lace of her skating boot firmly and sat back in the chair under the switchboard, thrusting out her long legs with the confidence of a woman who knows they will bear inspection. "That sounds like a libel," she said, running an approving eye over the high-laced boots and the stockings that vanished smoothly under her short pleated skirt.

"And a bit sacrilegious," added MacOdrum with a smug look.

"I don't like it either," Mrs. Maling said vigorously. "Explain your-self."

"Speakin' professionally, sweetheart, professionally. Caribou is a wireless operator's paradise, therefore I assume the good ones come here when they dot-an'-dash their last 'SK' upon this mortal coil. The bad ones, like the poor, we have with us always. Consider a moment. When a benign Government seized on Mr. Marconi's astonishin' invention back in 1904 the apparatus was crude an' the range was short. So they set up a flock of little stations about the shores of the Gulf an' upon the islands thereof as a brand-new aid to navigation. Government is sensitive about navigation in the Gulf. The St. Lawrence is the mouth of Canada, highly important to the digestive organs between Montreal an' Fort William."

"What does that make Vancouver?" demanded Blackburn, who was a West Coast man and sensitive about it.

"He sounds like a traveling medicine show," Mrs. Maling said tartly.

"Now, since the Gulf is icebound four or five months a year there's no point in keepin' all those wireless stations goin' in winter. Hence the hegira, a lot of high-spirited young Crusoes descendin' upon the peace of Montreal an' Halifax every fall. What to do with 'em? That was a problem. Some could be laid off, true enough. But the wireless operator is a peculiar animal with rovin' instincts, an' findin' him again in spring—all of him—would have buffaloed Sherlock Holmes an' a whole army of Watsons. So they parked 'em for the winter at various all-year-round stations where they could make 'emselves useful an' keep in practice. Now, down at this end of the Gulf there was a large fishin' population on the Millstones, cut off by ice all winter. Benign Government decided to keep the Millstones' wireless station goin' the year around, which meant also a station on the mainland within range. Mark the finger of Destiny writin' Caribou on the map."

"Ancient history," yawned young Blackburn at the phones. He gave the crystal detector an expert rap, listened a moment, and scribbled an entry on the long yellow procès-verbal sheet.

"I'm sick of history," murmured Dolly Hershman, for she was a teacher at the Academy. "But don't consider my feelings."

"Now, Caribou had another geographical advantage. An easy rail journey to Halifax or Saint John——"

"Canada's great winter ports," boomed MacOdrum, striking a political pose, "ice-free the year around, through which the mighty commerce of this rising nation——"

"Where there is an intermittent demand for ship wireless operators. See the beauty of it? They could park some of the seasonal men at Caribou, sendin' 'em off to join ships whenever the need arose, or to coast stations in Nova Scotia for reliefs."

The door opened and more skaters came in from the ice under the aerial mast, bringing a blast of cold air. They tramped noisily on their skates toward the stove, tearing off gloves and warming their hands. Joram and Parrish were wireless operators. Ruth Boland was the daughter of a Caribou merchant, Isobel M'Rae another teacher from the Academy, and there was a red-cheeked blonde girl known for some obscure reason as Jimsie. They said "Brrrr" and "Gosh, my feet are cold," and then, noticing Maling's pipe still waving in mid-air, paused politely.

"What's this?" demanded Jimsie. "A game?"

"A game," Blackburn said. "The boss is playing charades."

"And the answer," Mrs. Maling said, "is a lemon. Go on, darling."

Her husband put the pipe in his teeth with a snap. "The answer is a lot of brash undisciplined youngsters driftin' through Caribou every winter, an' Satan findin' mischief still for idle hands to do. They can make dots an' dashes. They can make a fist at repairs. They can read magazines half the night watch"—looking at Joram—"an' doze the rest"—this to Parrish—"an' turn in a log sheet in the mornin' as plausible as gospel. But they haven't the responsibility of a Labrador pup. That's why I say all the bad operators come to Caribou. Sometimes I think I'm runnin' a kindergarten. It was different in the old days. Now when I was at Cape Torrent in 1908——"

"There were giants in those days," murmured Mrs. Maling.

"But see how you've improved your position," urged Isobel M'Rae. "Here you are, temporary Saint Peter of a temporary heaven for wireless operators. That makes you enormously important to the lovelorn gals of Caribou."

Dolly Hershman threw a red wool mitten at her. "Bella, please! Have you no shame? And while we're on the subject, Saint Peter, I'd like to point out that Paradise is going to the dogs. There hasn't been a new operator for two weeks."

"Only night before last," Art Joram said pensively, "at the Hockey Club Dance, she looked in my eyes an' said she'd love me forever."

"The ravenous women of Caribou," observed Parrish, a cynic of twenty-one, "are a tradition up the Gulf."

Maling tapped the pipe on his boot. "I do my best, girls, but I have to take things as they come. As a matter of fact there's a new operator on his way from Cap D'Amour, but you won't like him at all. He's a son of Hamish MacNeill, the operator in charge up there."

"Cap D'Amour," repeated Jimsie. "Sounds very nice."

"And very misleading," Mrs. Maling said. "The early French explorers had a lot of fun naming points along the coast. Just a succession of black crags and barren hills, and the worse they look the better the name: Belle Isle, Point Riche, Bonne Bay, Cap D'Amour— just a lot of Norman jokes that sound very flat after two or three centuries. But these MacNeills, darling; isn't there something I've heard —MacNeill, MacNeill—Cap D'Amour——?"

"They're a legend," Maling said. "Hamish MacNeill went up there when they built the station in 1904 and he's been there ever since, raising a family of redheaded boys. It's a wild inaccessible place, an' the only human life they see is the lighthouse staff an' once a year the crew of a supply steamer. There used to be two other operators, but MacNeill taught his boys the business, an' Cap D'Amour's been a family affair since the war broke out. This is the oldest boy; somewhere about nineteen, I think; a great redheaded gawk, I fancy, with rock moss in his hair an' bake-apples growin' out of his ears."

Isobel M'Rae wrinkled her nose. "Probably thinks a foxtrot is something to do with fur-trapping." Jimsie stood up on her skates, tucked her lower lip inside her mouth, and gave a one-minute sketch of a gawk from Cap D'Amour.

"You mean to say he's never seen a woman?" Dolly Hershman said incredulously.

"His mother, that's all," Maling said. "He was about four when the MacNeills went up there. Been holdin' down a watch at Cap D'Amour since operators got scarce in the early days of the war. It's an all-year-round station—heaven knows why."

"This," MacOdrum mused, "is goin' to be fun."

"Fun," agreed the girls.

Hennessy, MacOdrum, Ishway, and Blackburn met the newcomer at the railway station. They had to wait until midnight; for the Caribou hockey team had gone to play at Starborough accompanied by a large crowd of supporters, and the return journey always delayed the train. It came rocking into the station at last and stopped in a cloud of steam and a great whistling of air brakes. The Caribou players jumped to the platform in a swarm of yelling citizens and moved off with song. The wireless committee of welcome, huddled in the lee of a freight shed, saw nothing of a redheaded gawk from Cap D'Amour. The jubilation of Caribou died away toward Main Street, and a frosty silence hung over the train. They went aboard to investigate and found a young man sitting calmly by the stove in an empty second-class carriage. He was well over six feet tall, with a girlish complexion and a swollen eye rapidly turning black.

"You the fella from Cap D'Amour?" Ishway said.

The tall young man stood up. "I am," he said precisely. "Who are you?"

"We," MacOdrum said, "are the fellas from Caribou. Why didn't you get off the train?" He called off names and they shook hands all round.

"I wanted to be sure," said the man from Cap D'Amour. "They said Caribou was at the end of the line, so I waited a while."

"Where'd you get the shiner?" demanded Hennessy.

The tall young man put up a hand and prodded his eye in a gingerly way. "There were a lot of people having a noisy time in the other carriage. There seemed to be a celebration. Some of them had been drinking, I think. Some of them got to fighting. They broke two of the train windows. One fellow asked me where I was going, and I told him the wireless station at Caribou, and he hit me in the eye."

"What did you do?" blurted Hennessy. He was Irish and blood-thirsty.

"I got up and went into the second-class carriage. It was quiet in here. There was a squaw smoking a pipe and spitting at the stove."

The delegation regarded each other in silence. "Let me get this straight," MacOdrum said patiently. "You said you were goin' to the wireless station an' this guy hit you in the eye. Then—correct me if I'm missin' anything—you got up an' went into the second-class carriage. Right?"

"Right," said young MacNeill. "I've been told about that kind of thing. No gentleman lets himself get mixed up in a brawl."

"Who told you that?" gasped Hennessy.

"My mother."

"You're a credit to her," MacOdrum said heavily. "Where's your baggage?"

Next morning Maling sat the newcomer in the operator's chair and explained the apparatus in simple words and at great length. He had received the report of the welcome committee and feared the worst. At last he said, "Have I made it clear?"

"Yes, sir."

Maling coughed. He could not remember being addressed as "Sir" in fifteen hard-bitten years. "Any questions you'd like to ask?" he said kindly.

MacNeill slid a phone off his left ear. "Well, nothing much, sir. It's queer old stuff, isn't it? I thought these ten-inch coil sets were used only for emergency apparatus aboard ship. I guess they're not much good for anything else. On a coast station! Fancy that!"

"It was good stuff in 1904 when this station was built," Maling said defensively. "Caribou's been passed by the march of time. Matter of fact, the station's usefulness is over. I don't think they'll open it another year. Millstone's got a new three-kilowatt transmitter an' he can make himself heard all over the Gulf."

"Yes," murmured the man from Cap D'Amour in his precise way. "We've talked to them from Cap D'Amour. I guess the time is coming when most of the Gulf stations will be closed down or turned into direction-finders. They're putting out receivers now with vacuum-tube detectors and amplifiers, and you can sit and listen to the whole world. No need for these little short-range stations any more. Your battery-charging outfit—that's interesting. Rectifying the town's account with a vacuum tube. A lot better than running a big gasoline engine and dynamo like we had to do at Cap D'Amour."

"Where'd you learn about vacuum tubes an' direction-finders?" Maling said curiously, for this was in 1919, when such things were still new.

MacNeill stirred in the chair. "Books," he said diffidently. "Father sent for all the latest technical books and magazines. We had little classes four times a week. That was in addition to Mom's school classes. I stopped in Halifax for a while after I got off the boat, and took my examinations for a first-class certificate. At the wireless office in the Navy Yard. The examining officer said he had to send the papers to Ottawa, but in the meantime I could consider myself passed by acclamation. What did he mean?"

"A new technical term, I fancy," Maling said hurriedly. "Find the exams hard?"

"No. I was surprised. It was just a lot of old stuff. He examined me on a 1½-K.W. standard ship set—the old British type, with converter and fixed spark gap."

"Had you ever seen one before?"

"No, but I learned about it in Hawkhead and Dowsett's book. I took it all apart and put it together again. I wanted to dismantle the converter and show how to wind a new armature, but the officer said 'Good God, no,' and passed on to the Postmaster-General's Regulations." He sat up alertly in the chair and settled the phones firmly over his ears. "Millstone's calling, sir. Asking QRU?"

"Tell him 'Yes.' " Maling took a clip from the wall. "Here's a couple of day letters."

MacNeill threw the transmitting switches expertly, and the old-fashioned open spark leaped and crackled like a machine gun. The messages were long. There was a cheap rate between Caribou and the Millstones for the benefit of people from the islands who wintered on the mainland. He finished and threw the send-receive switches. Across the silent room Maling could hear the whine of Millstone's transmitter in the phones. " 'Send slower!' " uttered the man from Cap D'Amour, surprised. He repeated the messages laboriously. As the crash of the blue electric snake subsided there was a hush, painful by sheer contrast, and Maling heard the curt "R. SK." from Millstone. MacNeill took his pencil and marked the time of transmission on the messages, made an entry on his log sheet, and sat back in the chair, slipping the phone from his left ear. "Funny," he said. "The air is clear as a bell, but they couldn't get me the first time and asked me to send slower."

"Listen," Maling said. "I timed some of that first transmission by the clock. You were poundin' brass at somethin' like thirty words a minute. Those day letters were in French full of family names an' bits of *patois*. This plain-aerial spark makes a sound in the other fella's phones like somebody tearin' a shirt. Have a heart. Just because you've pounded a brass key since you were old enough to learn the alphabet, you mustn't think you've got to show off your speed. Some day an old hand will get you on the receivin' end an' roast your ears off."

The man from Cap D'Amour sat up stiffly. "I wasn't showing off, sir. That's my normal speed. I made errors in that repeat because I'm not used to sending slow."

Maling gave him a hard look. The black eye made a caricature of the recruit's right profile, but from the left his face was handsome. The long sweep of his jaw was just saved from ruthlessness by a deep cleft in the chin, but he had the fresh complexion of a girl. His visible eye was large and a very dark brown, a soulful eye. His mouth was wide, the upper lip molded in fine curves such as women achieve by pencil marks, and his teeth were square and white. It came to Maling as a revelation that the man from Cap D'Amour was the answer to almost any maiden's prayer; and because he did not look for beauty in his operators and indeed disliked extreme good looks in any man, the next thought popped into his mind with a fitness little short of diabolical.

"Do you skate, MacNeill?"

"Yes, sir. Very well."

"Play hockey?"

"Hockey? We never had enough for a team at Cap D'Amour. We used to fool around with sticks and a puck, though, my brothers and the lighthouse men. I guess you'd call it pretty crude. But Dad taught us the fine points. You've got enough for a team here, haven't you?"

Maling nodded. "We've got a schedule with the town team, too. Caribou at present is a sort of clearinghouse for spare operators, so our team changes rapidly; but we've managed to keep our end up. There's quite a rivalry. The Caribou girls seem to like wireless operators, which adds to the fun."

MacNeill frowned. "What's that got to do with it?"

Maling gave him another hard look, but the recruit's face was innocent. "Let it go. The point is, we've got a game on next week, an' Ishway's a bit lame. Got a hard body check into the boards in our last game. What position d'you play?"

"Oh, anything. I'm not a bad goal tender. I can play a pretty fair game on defense, too. But if I had my choice, I guess I'd rather play right wing."

"Good!" Maling's voice was grim. "The boys are going down to the rink this afternoon for practice, so you'd better plan to go along. Got skates?"

"Oh, yes, sir!"

When Maling repeated this conversation to his wife she bristled at once. "Pete! don't you dare let that boy play against Town. They'll kill him. You ought to be ashamed of yourself."

Maling set his jaw defiantly. "He's too cocky, darlin'. About everything. Needs takin' down a peg or two. They'll knock some of the stuffin' out of him. Good for him."

Hennessy's reaction was like Mrs. Maling's. "Say! That pretty boy won't last a minute. It'll be murder. Listen! Somebody smacked him on the train an'——"

"I know, I know. Nevertheless, Mick, he plays next week. He's six-foot-one an' healthy, an' it's time he learned there isn't any Santa Claus. He wants to play right wing."

Hennessy shrugged. "Well, it's his funeral, not mine. But he won't play long, Pete. The Town bunch are mostly just outa the army, an' they play like they were still hustlin' Fritz along the road to Mons. Bayonet drill has given 'em some fancy new ideas about a hockey stick. Besides, the crowd likes rough stuff."

Maling went down to the rink in the afternoon and watched Hennessy put the team through their paces. A number of Caribou idlers joined him at the boards. The man from Cap D'Amour played very well. He moved like the wind, using a good choppy stride; his stick-handling was good, his pass shots were well timed, and his goal shots hard and accurate. Hennessy, at the goal, found himself sprawling, diving, and exerting all his tricks to keep the puck out of the net. When they paused for a spell, Hennessy skated over to the boards, his short legs muffled in goal tender's pads. He was grinning. "What d'ye think of him, Pete?"

"Not bad. But anybody can do that stuff with no opposition. What's your idea?"

Hennessy rested his arms on the boards and wrinkled his snub nose. "You said it. He plays like a perfect gentleman, if you get what I mean. One hoist from those gorillas on the Town defense an' he'll be listenin' to the birdies. We got to pray for Ishway's ankle. He's our only spare unless some more ops drift in."

In the bungalow on the hill Mrs. Maling admitted a breathless troop of girls. They draped themselves over the furniture, flinging skating boots on the floor, and burst into voice.

"One at a time," Mrs. Maling said crisply. "What do you think of the gawk from Cap D'Amour?"

Jimsie had the grace to blush. "There's only one word. He's divine."

"Did you ever see a boy so good-looking?" demanded Dolly Hershman.

"And," moaned Bella M'Rae, "he's never been anywhere and
doesn't know anything, the darling! Where's he been all my life?
When I look at him I feel funny all over."

"He's really handsome," said Ruth Boland, the sedate one. "And
he has the quaintest old-fashioned manners. We—happened—to be
skating in the rink when the boys came down for practice, so we
paired off for a few turns around the ice. Dolly, the hussy, got to him
first."

Dolly rolled her large blue eyes. "My dear, you've no idea. At
first he wouldn't touch me. And when I pointed out Bella and Art
Joram, and Ruth waltzing with Bob MacOdrum, he drew in a deep
breath like a swimmer heading into cold water and put his arm
around my waist as if it were a roll of barbed wire. Darling, I could
have screamed! When I slid my arm around his waist he shuddered
like a fly-bitten horse. He went three times around the rink with me,
wearing a we-who-are-about-to-die expression, and then dropped me
like a hot brick when Hennessy came on wearing his goal pads. It was
too delicious. And that black eye!"

Jimsie's mouth was set firmly. "We might as well have everything
open and aboveboard. I want to say here and now that I saw him
first."

"Nonsense!" Dolly Hershman said. "My arm was around his waist
when you others were gasping for breath. That gives me a first mortgage."

"Pooh!" poohed Isobel M'Rae. "Anyone could see you scared him
out of his wits. The poorest technique I ever saw. And his hair goes
so nicely with my new sweater."

"I think," Ruth Boland said in her slow warm voice, "you'd better
leave him to me. You're all in too much of a rush. You frighten him.
If he's got to learn about women he might as well learn quietly. I'm
a perfectly nice girl and I'm sure his mother would approve of me. I
think I'll teach him to dance, first."

"That," Mrs. Maling observed with approval, "is a perfectly nice
way for a perfectly nice girl to get a perfectly nice man's arms
around her. First, though, you'd better learn to sing 'The Flowers of

the Forest,' all of you. Pete's putting him in as right wing against Town next Friday night. He'll make a beautiful corpse."

The babel of protest still echoed plaintively in the little parlor when Maling walked in to face the wifely music.

The week passed pleasantly enough. There was strenuous daily practice in the Town rink. There was a sleigh drive, a moonlight snowshoe hike, and a tobogganing party, each of which ended in the warmth and glow of a Caribou home with noise and refreshments. In all of them the man from Cap D'Amour was a cynosure. He had smitten feminine Caribou like a new and feverish disease. Flappers paused and stared after him, goggle-eyed, on the street. Old ladies backed him into parlor chairs and asked kindly after that perfect stranger, his mother, and remembered gustily the days of their youth. The more eligible females buzzed about him like flies. When they found he could not dance and would not try, they sat out with him in relays on the stairs. He had no stock of small talk and understood very little of theirs, but they found him keen on his work and drew him on that, listening with rapt faces while his eager baritone explained inductance, rheostats, condensers, electromotive force, and the theory of the Heaviside layer. When he appeared in church on Sunday morning he was conducted to a front pew, and the young ladies of the choir, facing him from high stalls under the palisade of organ pipes, rolled soulful eyes to the roof and chanted the anthem at him like a personal hymn of praise; and after the service the minister's wife invited him to teach a class at Sunday School, which, with great embarrassment, he declined.

The young men of the town regarded him with puzzled hate. They knew the episode of the train in all its shameful detail, and they had various appropriate names for a young man who would not smoke, drink, or fight, who referred openly to his mother as "Mom," and was rumored to be in the habit of saying his prayers every night. But somehow these terms did not fit a man who stood six feet in his socks, turned flying somersaults on snowshoes, and skated like a bullet. He should have lisped in a treble key, but his voice had a hard ring like a steel rail under the section man's hammer. He should have had fluttering lids and downcast eyes in the presence of men and an assured dancing-master manner in the company of women; but he looked men straight in the eye like a child and was uneasy and diffident with girls. Maling, who had seen him pick up a 250-pound condenser with ease, informed an astonished barber's shop that the man from Cap

D'Amour was "strong as a bull moose." The young men went about with bewildered frowns, and told each other darkly that there would be an open hunting season in the rink on Friday night.

Maling went down to the rink on the fateful night full of guilt. Ishway, his ankle bandaged under the long wool stockings, sat at the phones in the wireless station in full panoply—padded shorts, sweater, boots, and skates. It was agreed that Maling should run up in a car and take over the watch if his services were needed. Ordinarily the crowd for Wireless-versus-Town games was small, because wireless teams were always scratch crews, often dependent on town men for substitutes, and the scores were one-sided. Tonight the rink was packed. The long plank seats groaned under a mass of rugs and humanity, and the standing room behind was rapidly filling up. Tobacco smoke curled upward from the packed tiers and joined an increasing cloud under the rafters. There was something savage in the roar of conversation that filled the place.

"It's like a——" Mrs. Maling paused. She was going to say "bull-fight," but that seemed inadequate. "It's like one of those old Roman arenas, Pete."

Maling nodded grimly. "Yeah. An' here's the Early Christian."

The Wireless team came on the ice amid shouts, whistles, and applause. Their sweaters were shabby relics of obscure teams in which they had played. Hennessy's was blue, with "Glace Bay Wolves" in white letters; Joram's red-and-green said "Halifax Hurricanes"; Parrish wore a simple and ambiguous "Montreal"; and MacOdrum, who had joined an infantry battalion in Canada before transferring to the field telegraphs, announced "Seventy-fifth." The sweaters of young Blackburn and MacNeill were unadorned. The overhead lights struck bright gleams of bronze from MacNeill's bare head. A male voice, pitched in a pseudo-feminine key, cried, "Oh, you kid with the red hair!" and everybody laughed. The Town team appeared in a tumult of approval. They wore white sweaters with broad red stripes and looked very large and confident.

"Who's the referee?" demanded Mrs. Maling.

Her husband stretched his short neck and did some bobbing and twisting. "Skid Lepreau and—ah-hah!—Bucky MacDonald."

Mrs. Maling pursed her lips and glared. "I thought so. It's deliberate. Lepreau wears a pair of mental blinkers and Bucky MacDonald simply loves a fight on the ice. The man's notorious."

"Aw now, sweetheart. He's just broad-minded, that's all."

She caught sight of Dolly Hershman, Bella M'Rae, Jimsie, and the Boland girl sitting opposite center ice, and stood up, waving. They saw her and fluttered their hands, pointing to the burly figure of Bucky MacDonald and rolling their eyes toward the rafters.

The teams faced off. Bucky MacDonald, barrel-chested and important in white sweater and cap, dropped the puck and skated aside. Play began with a clatter of sticks and a tangle of scrambling forwards. From this tangle the puck shot suddenly over the Wireless blue line, and Joram and MacOdrum moved promptly to meet it. There was another scramble as they met the Town forwards in hot pursuit, with Blackburn, Parrish, and MacNeill back-skating rapidly to join battle. The puck, lost for a moment in flying ice dust and a whirl of gleaming skates, appeared outside the melee, a lonely black dot. It was a tempting shot to the Wireless goal, where Hennessy waited tensely, trying to make himself as large as possible in the vulnerable side of his cage. The crowd yelled. Four players thrust at it, sticks clashing. The puck moved a few feet toward the boards and stopped again. This time five sticks scooped at it hungrily and it went clear, and young Blackburn pounced on it and fled up the ice, followed by the pack. MacNeill flew up along the right boards for a pass, but the Town defense men stopped Blackburn's rush, and their center player, hook-checking smartly, rapped the puck toward the left boards, where it bounced and disappeared in a flurry of wildly ducking spectators.

The teams settled down. The forward lines from time to time broke away toward the opposing goal, but seldom got past the defense for a hard shot. Joram and MacOdrum were playing a stout game on the Wireless defense. Blackburn at left wing and Parrish at center did very well against the heavier Town forwards. The man from Cap D'Amour was the doubtful quantity. At times his speed was brilliant, his stick-handling was good, and he could rush the puck without yielding to that amiable weakness of amateur forwards, the thrill of a lone attack. But his play generally was erratic. Maling put it down to lack of experience in team play. His wife, with feminine instinct, diagnosed it more accurately as plain stage fright. At the end of the first period the scoreboard was blank. The Town goalie had stopped eight shots, Hennessy twelve. As the players trooped off the ice, Maling relaxed.

"See, sweetheart? You got the boys all wrong. Good clean play throughout, no trippin' an' very little body checkin'. Why, it's positively dull."

"Wait and see," his wife said ominously. She wriggled her chilled feet inside the heavy black overshoes and wished she had brought another rug.

The game went into the second period in the same gentlemanly scramble. This time the Town forwards carried the puck away, working a perfect three-man combination. MacNeill, back-skating like a demon, swung in toward the Town center and poke-checked shrewdly. Center feinted a left pass. The man from Cap D'Amour made a lightning sweep to block it. At the same moment he backed into Joram, and as they sprawled, MacNeill's stick went between the legs of the Town center. The man fell heavily, followed in quick succession by Blackburn, Parrish, and Town's right wing, who were skating in at speed. The crowd stood up with a single motion as the human heap untangled, and saw the Town center, a popular man named Muir, lying inert on the ice. He was carried off awkwardly by a trio of rink attendants and Caribou's one-man police force, and Bucky MacDonald waved MacNeill off the ice for a major penalty. At once the crowd broke into catcalls. The man from Cap D'Amour stood uncertainly for a moment and then followed the direction of MacDonald's jerking thumb toward the penalty box. He stood there like a prisoner at the bar, surrounded by a booing chorus, and his amazement gave place slowly to a deep blush that spread up to the roots of his tousled hair.

"Accident!" Maling objected. His voice was lost in the uproar. So was a shrill chorus of "No fair! No fair!" from utterly biased feminine voices all over the benches.

"It looked bad, just the same," Mrs. Maling said reluctantly.

Town substituted a gaunt rangy man at center, and play was resumed. The Wireless team, one man short, promptly found itself on the defensive. There was some body checking, in which Joram and Bob MacOdrum joined readily, but nothing bad enough to warrant interference from the referees. Sticks were carried higher, though, and elbows were suddenly prominent. Maling noted these ominous signs and glanced at his wife. She was looking at her watch, timing MacNeill's penalty. The Wireless team fought a delaying action, but Town was not to be denied. Hennessy performed brilliant antics in his cage, stopped a barrage of shots, but twice there was a flurry in front of the goal and a puck that appeared in the corner of the net as if by magic. The second was an absurd rolling shot, and Hennessy looked sheepish as the crowd cheered.

When MacNeill resumed his place he was booed again vigorously. The team took up the attack again in good heart. Parrish caught a loose puck and got into his stride, with MacNeill racing up the right ice for a pass. Town's right wing, at Parrish's heels, hooked the puck nicely. MacNeill, coming in fast, met the heavy Town defense men. They caught him between them and swung their shoulders together in that bruising operation known as "the hoist." It was legitimate but deliberate. MacNeill picked himself up quickly, wiping ice dust from his face, and plunged back to join the play. Then a remarkably accidental skate caught his own in mid-career and he took a header, sliding along on his chest.

"They're roughing him," Mrs. Maling hissed. Maling watched a stick butt connect with MacNeill's ribs and thought of Hennessy on bayonet drill. Soon the man from Cap D'Amour was white from head to foot with ice dust. Town ran up another goal as the period closed, and Maling went down to comfort a grim team.

"The party's gettin' rough," Hennessy grinned.

"Givin' as good as we get, though," Joram said stoutly.

"They're pickin' on the kid," Hennessy said. "Maybe you better run up for Ishway. Talk the kid into callin' it a night."

Maling walked over to MacNeill and turned his back on the rest of the team.

"Listen, son. You've played a good game for your first appearance, but there's a time to quit, an' this is it. I'll put Ishway on defense an' send Joram up to right wing in your place." MacNeill said nothing for a moment. His left cheek was swelling and a thin trickle ran like a red pencil mark from a cut on his forehead.

He blurted, "Look here, sir. They're not playing hockey at all."

"Sure, sure," Maling soothed. "Now Ishway's used to this kind of play—and——"

"They're playing just the way Father told me not to play!"

Maling paused. "What d'you mean, son?"

"Well, up at Cap D'Amour Father'd get us all down on the pond back of the wireless station and show us the right way. Then some days, when Mom was busy at the house, he'd take us down and show us how not to play. It was kind of fun, for a change. We were all big strong boys and we could take it. So could Father."

Maling's eyes widened. "You mean high-stickin'?"

"And tripping."

"Body checkin'? Elbowin'?"

"Yes. And how to rush the puck and jump into the air straight at the defense man and make him drop aside to avoid your skates."

"Phew! Anything else?"

"Yes. He showed me how to swing a fist so as to get all the speed of my skating into it."

"What did your mother say?"

"Well, I don't think she liked it very much. The day I blacked Father's eye and young Ian got a sprained ankle, she said she guessed Father would never outgrow his Cape Breton upbringing."

"An' what did Father say to that?"

"He said it was more blessed to give than to receive sometimes, and an old Highland custom."

Maling put hands in overcoat pockets and rocked back and forth on heel and toes, meditatively. "Son, this is interestin'. Did Hamish MacNeill, by any chance, tell you 'When in Rome, play your hockey Roman style'?"

MacNeill regarded him with surprised brown eyes. "Rome? Why, I never knew they——"

"Let it go, son; let it go. I was thinkin' of arenas an' Early Christians, I guess. The point is, the local boys are moppin' up the ice with your gentlemanly person. The point is, I'm afraid you're goin' to get hurt."

"I can take it!" snapped the man from Cap D'Amour. There was a glow in the dark eyes.

"Sure! But I can't. Conscience doth make cowards of us all. I've got a conscience named Helena A. Maling, an' it's gonna hurt me plenty if the boys hurt you."

MacNeill's eyes were like molten bronze now. There were red glints. "You talk in riddles, sir. Do you mean I should play hockey the way Father taught me not to play just because these fellows got a little rough?"

"That's the general idea, son."

"Very well." The man from Cap D'Amour breathed deeply. "But you understand, sir, it isn't quite fair. I mean, these fellows never knew Father."

The bell rang. Maling choked and tottered back to his seat.

"Pete, you're still playing that boy!" said the Voice of Conscience.

"Sweetheart," he confessed, "curiosity got the best of me."

The final period opened smartly with the Town forwards breaking away in a smooth combination. Center, poke-checked furiously by Parrish and Blackburn, passed to Right Wing. MacOdrum and Joram moved up slowly to meet Right Wing, who passed to Left Wing, a quick clean shot across the ice. MacNeill, back-skating like a whirl-wind, bumped Left Wing hard and hooked busily. Left Wing rapped the puck against the boards, eluded MacNeill with a passing elbow thrust for good measure, picked up the rubber again on the re-bound, and headed for the Wireless goal through the wide-open de-fense. The crowd came to its feet roaring, while Hennessy performed the quaint bear dance of a goalie facing a terrific shot at close quarters. At this point the man from Cap D'Amour appeared to trip. He came down on one knee and then slid headlong, arms outthrust, and the tip of his stick pulled Left Wing's skate from under him. It was neatly timed and executed. Left Wing fell, thrusting out gloved hands to break the force of his descent. Hennessy cleared the puck easily, even nonchalantly, and a second later Left Wing slid into the cage on his chest. A wit in the stands shouted "Goal!" and there was a laugh from that quarter. There were shouts of "Penalty!" from seats near the boards, but the referees had noticed nothing.

There followed some jockeying near the Wireless blue line. Then Parrish broke away with the puck, received a stiff body check, and went down, scooping the rubber blindly toward right ice. MacNeill was at his post, traveling fast. He caught the puck neatly and rushed for the Town goal. The heavy Town defense appeared like Nemesis before him, skating slowly toward him. The stage was set for another "hoist," and a brutal one, for the man from Cap D'Amour was racing at top speed. Mrs. Maling closed her eyes. She did not see MacNeill leap high in air. She missed the startled looks of the defense men, their instinctive dives to avoid the oncoming skates, and the presence of mind with which they tried to hook the flyer's feet with their sticks. She did see MacNeill make a perfect landing, flipping the puck to the left, where young Blackburn promptly shot it home. The Town goalie had moved out to meet MacNeill, and a high shot to the corner caught him flat-footed. She was astonished to hear the crowd cheer-ing, for her opinion of a Caribou hockey crowd was low. Maling was rubbing his hands.

Play resumed with a rising tempo. Hard body checks became a commonplace. Sticks were carried higher and so were tempers. Mac-

Neill was in the thick of it. Things happened wherever he went. In his astonishing metamorphosis the experts perceived a certain deadly science which gave more punishment than it took. And the crowd loved it. They had come to see an execution; they were seeing a one-man riot. Caribou liked its hockey rough.

The referees hesitated. Skid Lepreau saw things in spite of his mental blinkers. A quiet easygoing man, he had sensed the injustice of MacNeill's penalty in the second period, and he believed in the compensation of errors. Bucky MacDonald, an old hockey player who had never asked or given quarter in his own day, believed that frequent whistling made a dull game. These consonant beliefs ignored the fact that the man from Cap D'Amour was running amuck. The Town players, aroused, began to seek him out with vengeful purpose, and in this amiable distraction Parrish and the speedy Blackburn found profit, rushing the Town goal again and again. The goalie performed miracles. Presently, inevitably, a shot went home. The crowd cheered, and went on yelling as the Wireless forwards strove for another to even the score. MacNeill redoubled his efforts. Players went down in mutual disaster, arose, and scattered after the puck, met and fell again. In the tangled heaps of white-powdered men fists worked busily with short stiff jabs too quick and too vague for even-handed justice from the referees. Lepreau frowned and MacDonald glared, but they were helpless. Finally a heap disintegrated near the left boards with fists flying openly. Sticks were dropped. Ten men smote and slithered in a fierce ecstasy, while the two goalies looked upon the fight with longing eyes and stared at each other down the length of the rink. Bucky MacDonald sailed into the melee, whistle in teeth, blowing furiously. In the midst of it raged the man from Cap D'Amour. His bronze locks were wet with sweat and melted ice dust. His large eyes burned. His fists shot out with speed and accuracy. The referee thrust a purple face at him, whistled at him shrilly, and swiftly MacNeill's busy knuckles came up. There was no malice about it. He was striking out impartially at a shifting ring of hostile faces, and the new face suffered with the rest.

War is a contagious thing. The ice was suddenly populated by men pouring out of the stands, eager to smite somebody, anybody. Wary wives and sweethearts seized their companions and dragged them away from that seductive spectacle. The game broke up in mass disorder. Through the aggressive assembly waded Caribou's police force, a giant man in blue, leaving a sort of armed peace in his wake.

The word passed before him. "John Angus! Here's John Angus!" He came to the center of the battle like an ambulatory Gibraltar. The warring players stumbled apart, grinning sheepishly.

"Boys," rumbled John Angus calmly, "I guess that'll be all for to-night."

In the bare little dressing room MacNeill put off his skate boots with a gesture of disgust. The room was full of people talking furiously and patting him on the back. He was silent and unappreciative, and once he wriggled his shoulders in a shuddering almost feminine way, as if the touch of strange hands were distasteful. As he put on his overcoat he spoke. "Out of my way, you! I've got to relieve Ishway."

"Here's with you, son," Maling said. They walked up the hill in silence, Mrs. Maling between them, and found a grim young man at the phones perspiring in hockey kit. Ishway ignored MacNeill's battered face. He thrust a message form at Maling and said—

"Read that!"

Mrs. Maling recognized the narrow, canary-yellow service form, used for official business. "Bad news?" she blurted, eyes very wide.

"For somebody!" Ishway said meaningly. Maling studied the penciled words.

"Well?" cried his wife.

" 'Send operator immediately Cape Rip. Supply ship sails from Halifax tomorrow night. This post requires fast operator with thorough experience shore-station work. Acknowledge.' "

He read it aloud slowly and looked up.

"What's bad about that?" Mrs. Maling said.

Ishway breathed heavily through his nostrils. "Everything! It's like transportation for life. A barren pile of rock, the loneliest station on the coast. Once they get you there, nothing but death or a writ of habeas corpus will ever set you free."

"Let's see," Maling said slowly. "Parrish? Blackburn? Hennessy? None of these boys can handle a fast wire. That leaves it up to you, Joram or MacOdrum."

"I," said Ishway thickly, "spent three years up there, which is plenty for one man's lifetime. I got away on the flat of my back with ptomaine poisoning. You can count Joram out, too. He came here from a ship with no previous shore-station experience." He looked up at the ancient apparatus and smiled grimly. "You can't get 'thorough experience' with this junk."

"What about MacOdrum?"

"All kinds of experience—includin' three years in France with a trench set. That's just behind him. Mac wants to see some life."

"We can't all do what we want," Maling said levelly, "even in these queer times."

"He'll resign first," Ishway said. "So would I."

Wise in his generation, Maling sighed. The colts must be gentled. Young men with a long war behind them were in no mood for discipline of any sort. They did their work efficiently, and they liked Pete Maling because he was a good fellow, but they would not be ordered anywhere if they did not want to go. In another year or two perhaps, when this intoxicating freedom had grown stale—but in the meantime there were jobs to burn. Ships laid down under wartime building programs were taking the water from every yard in North America. An operator with a first-class ticket could get a job anywhere, and in the States wages were high. Since the whole purpose in running this bull pen at Caribou was to keep a supply of operators on hand, a sudden irruption of resignations would attract some cold notice from headquarters. Why, it would be asked, was Maling unable to get along with his men?

His wife, pretending to read a copy of *Jack Canuck* in the corner, thought suddenly of young MacNeill. How nice that he was so inexperienced! He had just come out of the wilderness, and a return to it would mean the best years of his life wasted in desert air. There was something repellent about the mere thought. He was too fresh and burning, too utterly attractive, for a fate like that. In a perfectly virtuous way she was half in love with him. All the women of Caribou were in love with him. There was something about his monastic background that captured the feminine imagination. His good looks, his modesty, his athletic frame, his naïve mind, all added to the fascination, and his droll preference for the society of men made him irresistible. Women were all eager, too eager, to be charming to him.

And the curious thing was that men liked him. They had come to the rink prepared to see him bumped into unconsciousness, had swarmed upon the ice howling for a chance to beat his head off, but they had gone away in reluctant admiration. That hard-fisted, hot-eyed passion on the ice had caught their respect, just as it stirred in respectable matrons and spinsters the most unaccountable yearnings. And apart from his physical charm were his rare intelligence and the unusual education hammered into it by that prim schoolma'am his mother. He would go far. The world lay at the feet of such a young man.

"I'll go," said young MacNeill.

"But you can't!" gasped Mrs. Maling.

"I've had a lifetime of experience," he added calmly. "I've passed for a first-class ticket. I can send and receive at thirty words a minute and keep it up all day. I've heard Cape Rip a thousand times, and I can say without boasting that I'm as good as any operator they've got."

It was the perfect solution to Maling's problem. He opened his mouth to take up the young idiot before something changed his mind, but Mrs. Maling caught his eye. He hesitated a moment, licking his lips.

"Look here, MacNeill. You don't want to go up there. It's worse than Cap D'Amour."

MacNeill stiffened. "What's wrong with Cap D'Amour?"

"What's wrong with Caribou?" demanded Mrs. Maling. She was getting angry. "Do you realize every girl in the place is mad about you? Is it possible you don't know that women, women everywhere, are ready to grovel at the feet of a man like you? Doesn't that mean anything to you?"

MacNeill regarded her with puzzled resentment. "You're joking, Mrs. Maling. But women are the trouble—saving your presence, ma'am. There are too many. I never—my mother told me to keep away from women, but how can I when the world is full of them? She told me not to use my fists on other men, too, and I've been brawling. I want to go to Cape Rip and kind of sort myself out."

"Haven't you any ambition?" Mrs. Maling said. It was incredible.

"Yes," said the man from Cap D'Amour. "I want to be the best operator on the coast."

Maling pursed his lips, raised his eyebrows, and shrugged. Under the sardonic eyes of Ishway he reached for a service message pad and scrawled the fateful words. His wife sank back in the shabby armchair and closed her eyes. Whatever the future held for the young god from Cap D'Amour, it was clear that Peter Maling was in for an uncomfortable night.

LIGHT TACKLE

———◆———

by *PHILIP WYLIE*

(1940)

The Crunch and Des deep-sea fishing stories have been delighting Saturday
Evening Post *readers for almost two decades now. After four collections of
these stories had been brought out in book form, Philip Wylie's publisher made
a grand compilation,* The Best of Crunch and Des, *and mentioned plaintively in his jacket blurb how difficult it had been to select the best stories, for
he honestly loved them all. How much more difficult for us to select only one!*
Light Tackle, *however, struck us as a most representative choice, combining, as
it does, the rugged good humor and warmth of the protagonists along with some
of Wylie's knowledgeable and felicitous descriptions of fishing off Miami.*

MISS JONES reached her favorite "spot" on the County Causeway
after supper but before all the color had gone from the sky.
The tide was coming in, which was good, and the breeze was dropping. Unmindful of the trucks, the squealing trolleys and the horde of
automobiles which streamed from Miami to Miami Beach and
from the beach to the mainland, she unwrapped a paper bundle, took
out a neatly wound hand line which was equipped with a sinker, a
short wire leader, and a hook, and she carefully pressed the hook into
the body of a dead, rather overdead, shrimp. She threw the assemblage into the flowing salt water, watched it drift out from the
masonry that supported the bridge, and felt the lead touch bottom.
She began her wait.

The sky flamed and bleached itself. The drawbridge lifted and settled ponderously many times—to the impatient accompaniment of the horns and voices of motorists. Ranged along the cement railing beside Miss Jones were scores of other fishermen—old men and young, women and children; some with rods and reels and pails of live bait, but most with less ostentatious gear: hand lines, or bamboo poles innocent of reels. Miss Jones fished hopefully, but without success.

It was dark and the distant beach had turned on the full glamour of its neon skyline when she noticed that the man nearest her was catching quite a few fish. Grunts and sand perch and an occasional snapper. He, too, was using a hand line, but he threw it farther than she could and in a diagonal direction. His bait was different. His manner of waiting after a nibble, and striking hard, was not the technique she had used. At last, though the act was unprecedented for her, she decided to speak to him; he was not well-dressed, but he looked nice.

"I guess," she said, "you're having the luck for the whole causeway." She smiled while she spoke—a little ruefully.

Crunch Adams had not even noticed his neighbor. Now, in the light of the street lamp, he could see a pretty girl, maybe twenty-three or -four, a bit thin; a girl with a mighty nice voice—sincere and curiously vibrant. Miss Jones was further illuminated by the headlight of a passing car. A blonde, Crunch perceived; one of the maple-fudge kind, and with gray eyes. No man—not even a happily married man —wantonly rebuffs the Miss Joneses of this world.

"The people," Crunch began, "who fish the causeways hardly ever bother to think about the bottom. But it's the bottom that determines where the fish are. If you come up here at slack tide on a calm day you can see that right where I'm throwing my rig there's a mess of rock. A barge sank there during the '26 blow. Here!"

The word meant that he had reached out for her line. She yielded it without a word and let him throw. He handed it back to her. She thanked him—and waited—and presently she felt a jiggle.

"Let him run with it a second," Crunch said, watching critically. "Now! Yank!"

The girl yanked. A yank answered her. The fish ran through the careening tide and the line slid through her fingers. She caught it up and pulled in, hand over hand. There was a white splash far below. She felt the fish wriggling in the air. Then Crunch reached down and tossed it onto the sidewalk, where it began to spring into the air.

"Snapper," he said. "Nice one, too. Ought to go a pound and a half."

Miss Jones looked at the fish with shining eyes. "Would you . . . would you . . . kill it for me? Before it gets under somebody's car?"

Crunch picked up the fish, carefully avoiding its clicking teeth, and he dispatched it. He regarded Miss Jones's excitement with understanding, and threw his own line.

"Snappers are so darned good to eat," she said, wrapping the fish in paper.

"You bet they are. And people leave 'em lying around here to rot, sometimes." Crunch jerked his line, brought up a grunt, and dropped it—alive—into a pail of water.

"Once, right here," Miss Jones continued, "I got a grouper. Quite a big one." Success seemed to have made her talkative. "Two pounds, the man at the bait place said. I made chowder out of him—and it was simply delicious! Tasted like cinnamon." She began winding up her line. "And once I caught a jack—but he wasn't very good."

Crunch baited again—with a cubical chunk of purple meat cut from a bonita. It occurred to him that the young lady was more interested in her catch from the gastronomic standpoint than from the aspect of sport. He peered through the night. She was pretty thin—although not that thin. "You better keep right on fishing," he said. "We ought to be able to get you a dozen of those."

She shook her head. "I haven't any place to keep 'em. I—well—I sort of get 'em as I need 'em. *If* I'm lucky, that is." She looked into his bucket, where six or eight fish were swimming and panting. "They wouldn't keep—like that—I mean for days, would they?"

He was thinking about her—a pretty girl, a nice one, who fished for food and didn't even have an icebox to preserve her catch. He answered rather absently. "In a pail? I'm afraid not. Die in an hour or two. My mate'll be along to get these soon—and put 'em in our live well. They're for bait. We've got an open party slated to fish amberjack tomorrow." His line tugged, and that kept him from seeing her face.

But her voice turned him around. It was stunned. "You mean—you're a charter-boat captain?"

"Uh-uh."

"Which one?"

"The *Poseidon*."

"Then—" she swallowed—"then . . . you're Crunch Adams! Last

winter I used to go down to buy fish from the boatmen. Mackerel—
and pieces of kingfish—and dolphin—and I've often seen your boat
come in!"

Crunch knew what it was like to be poor. He also knew what it
was like to be proud. But he took a chance. "You're kind of—
stranded down here—Miss—?"

The girl supplied her name quietly. She finished wrapping her fish
and her line in newspaper before she continued. She had been thinking it over. It was all right for her to tell him. Everybody knew that
Crunch Adams was a perfectly swell person. And you had to talk to
somebody—sometimes. "Not exactly," she said at last. "I—I've got
my rent paid for all summer. And a little money—if I stretch it. I've
been looking for a job, but things kind of drop off here in the spring.
I've got one promised—if I can wait till fall. You see . . . I'm a
librarian. That is, I was—up north. I got arthritis and came down
here for two months. I was fine—but when I went back, I got sick
again. So . . ."

Desperate came along the causeway with a fresh pail of water.
Not realizing that his skipper was engaged in conversation, he
broached the only subject on his mind at the moment: "I got one
more guy for tomorrow. That makes three. And guess who? Thornton
Denby, no less! Wanted to weasel in for five bucks, as usual, but I
made him pay six. He also wanted to fish the stream—but I said it
was the reef or no dice."

Somewhat to Desperate's surprise, a response came from a lady
standing beside Crunch. "You mean—you mean people can actually
go out in a charter boat for as little as six dollars?"

Scenting a customer, Desperate lost no time. "Sure! When business
is slack we split the summer price four ways and get four people to
go. Twenty-five bucks divided by four is six and a quarter—and we
knock off the two bits for luck."

"Could I be the fourth? Do you take—women? I've been absolutely out of my mind to go fishing on one of those boats ever since I
got here!"

Crunch, upon seeing Miss Jones about to spend six dollars she
couldn't conceivably afford, tried to think of something. The best idea
—which he voiced—was hardly polite. "We can't take a dame—a
woman. We don't know the first two guys very well—and this Denby
is the stickiest fishing man in Florida. Besides—"

"We took that Mrs. Hoag with three men," Des countered, "and

she caught a tuna!" His only alert instinct at the moment was the instinct for trade and commerce. "Crunch and I can look out for you. If
you've got six bucks handy? . . ."

The *Poseidon*'s skipper was stammering. Miss Jones hesitated and
then produced a small pocketbook. Crunch heard her murmur, "I
shouldn't do it! But I've just got to!" He didn't interfere, because his
mate, with a smirk of triumph, was reaching for the money. Instead,
he began to think of how he could return the six dollars to the girl.

Des glanced at the fish in the pail and said, "We'll need that many
more, easy." He started off with them, giving Crunch a wink to indicate it took a go-getter to nail the business. "Be at the dock at eight,"
he said to Miss Jones. "This Denby likes to start early."

Crunch and Miss Jones were left alone—except for the noisily
passing thousands. "You shouldn't have done that," he said.

She nodded. "I know it. But a time comes in your life when you've
got to do at least something rash!" She began to unwrap her line. "I
might as well help, now, hadn't I, since I'm going to use some of that
live bait? Golly! Can you imagine *me* in a charter boat!"

The morning was halcyon—soft as the spring always is in south
Florida; sun-drenched, cloud-shaded, perfumed. A light breeze shattered the water outside the jetties into millions of bright facets; the
sharp bow of the *Poseidon* divided a moving pattern of foam that was
like etching on glass.

Miss Jones—she had been reticent about her first name—lay on
the warm canvas deck forward, where Crunch had put her so that
the men could get acquainted, tell their jokes, and pass around an eye
opener if they wished. She watched the changing blues of the bottom
under the ship's keel—the light blue made by the sand and the dark
patches where the rocks were. She watched the hawks tower and the
gulls dive and the pelicans volplane. Inside her mind, she talked to
herself.

I shouldn't have come, she thought. Those two men—Mr. Porter
and Mr. Welch—didn't want me much. And Mr. Denby didn't want
me at all! I never saw such a fussy person! A bachelor, I'll bet! All
that tackle! And all that talk! You'd think fishing was as important
and as difficult as a surgical operation! Mr. Porter and Mr. Welch
didn't seem to like him much. Which makes things just lovely! And I
can afford six bucks about as well as I can afford platinum shoes!

Crunch came and sat down beside her. She was wearing the same
slacks—pink—purchased, no doubt, when she'd still had that librari-

an's job. Her pink and blue scarf fluttered in the air. Her eyes were dark gray; only, the water made them seem blue. And her hair, although of a maple-fudge blondness, had lemon-colored glints in it. "I'm sorry my mate hooked you for that money," Crunch began. "I'd have been darned glad—in your case—to take you out . . ."

Miss Jones flushed. "I wouldn't think of going any other way!"

"Yeah. I suppose not." He, also, flushed a little. "Those guys weren't rude to you when we started, were they? I had to be on top . . ."

The girl grimaced a little. "They weren't overjoyed at the prospect of a woman being along."

Crunch nodded. "Welch and Porter work in town—and have families. They can only afford to go out this way—once in a while—in the summer. They're both pretty good guys, really. As for Denby—he has plenty of dough. Stays here year around. Owns a house on the beach. He fishes light tackle—he's an expert at it—but he's stingy."

"A bachelor, I bet," she said.

Crunch chuckled. "For reasons too numerous to mention! Tell you what. He'll fish on top—always does. I'll put Porter up here, too. You and Mr. Welch can sit below. Ask him about his kids—he has five and he's proud of 'em all—and he'll be your friend."

"You're sweet," Miss Jones said gratefully. "I'll go through his kids from infant diseases to marks in arithmetic!"

So they began to fish. In the lazy morning, with Mr. Welch pouring out proud-parent anecdotes and beginning to think that the female passenger was not altogether a washout. Overhead, Mr. Porter was silent, sitting in a little chair on the edge of the canopy. Miss Jones held her rod tremblingly and watched the water. But Mr. Denby really provided the thematic monologue for the trip. He would have had a pleasant voice, she thought, if he had not kept it high and penetrating. He might have had pleasant manners, too—but fishing seemed to make manners inaccessible to him.

"Crunch," he said loudly, "you missed some rather good weeds about a hundred yards off the port quarter! . . . There's a rock bed just off the lighthouse that you completely overlooked! . . . Don't see how you fellows take any pleasure in fishing with that rope . . . Look at my gear: a four-ounce tip—a six-thread line that breaks with a strain of eighteen or twenty pounds—and a hook with the barb filed off! Now—that's what I call fishing! Give the fish a chance! . . . Most men don't realize that even with reef fish there's often the problem of a drop back—very slight, mind you, but real. You do it with your rod, and everything depends on feel. Though I can't see why anybody wants to fish the reef. Let me show you, Porter. . . . Crunch! Don't you think we're going about half a knot too fast? And look at that bait! It turned over three times while I was letting it back! It'll unwind my whole line, if you don't trim it! I tell you, nobody knows how to cut a bait out here. . . . Now here's another thing, Porter. You fish a number ten hook and a 6/0 reel. It's a crime, actually! Take a squint at this 3/0 of mine. Had it built specially. Isn't geared up like that thing of yours. Winds in a ratio of 1 to 1. The reason for that . . ."

"That guy," Mr. Welch murmured to Miss Jones, "knows all about fishing. *He* knows he knows it. And *we* know he knows. Why in hell doesn't he shut up?"

Miss Jones giggled. Then she had a strike.

For months she had watched them bring in the "big ones." Months of living alone in a one-room apartment with a bed that folded into the wall and an electric plate for cooking. Months of being lonely. Of going to "free" things—concerts and lectures and the fishing docks. Months of being ill—and then better—but always poorer and more worried. Now—a "big one" had hit her line. She could see the welter in the ocean, feel the jerk in her arms, hear the reel's unforgettable sound as the fish ran—a harsh and heady whir. She had always imagined that it would be exciting; she had never guessed that it would have that particular quality of thrill—of wildness, violence, fury and fight.

She became aware of Crunch beside her. "Barracuda," he said quietly. Then she heard Mr. Denby's voice. It was an anxious staccato of advice. His heart was in it—and his whole nervous system—as if he were catching the fish by talk: "Keep the rod tip up, Miss Jones! But not too high! That's it! Now! Reel! He's going to broach! Bad! Very bad! You gave him slack! Better tighten the drag, Crunch. With a telegraph pole like that, she can stand more strain! Besides— she's keeping the rest of us from fishing! Come on! Wind, woman! Drop the tip and pick up what you gain that way! Then back—and do it over!"

Crunch cast toward his passenger a glance around which were invisible brass knuckles. Denby did not even notice. But Miss Jones was aware of his words, and, consciously or not, she began to follow each suggestion. Almost to her annoyance, she observed a change in his tone: "Fine! That's right! Never saw a man who could get the idea so quickly!"

In a few minutes, Crunch made a swoop with a big gaff—although Denby protested at gaffing a 'cuda—and brought aboard a silver fish about four feet long. It was mottled with black and Crunch spread its jaws with pliers for the girl to see. "Teeth like a wolf," he said. "Look!"

Miss Jones was panting delicately. Tendrils of her hair were stuck upon her brow. Her eyes were dilated. "Imagine," she whispered. *"Me!* I caught it! *Think of it!"*

Mr. Porter spoke rather petulantly: "Let's go fishing."

Des gunned the motors. The *Poseidon* moved along again. "On six-thread," Mr. Denby said good-humoredly, "that would have been quite a little scrap."

There are many sorts of fishing along the Florida coast. Trolling in the Gulf Stream is one. Trolling on the "reef" is another. The "reef" is a generic name for the shoal water along that edge of the Atlantic. It is clear water—green, sometimes, more often pale blue—and it varies in depth from coral emergences to more than a hundred feet. In that relatively shallow territory lie thousands of square miles of underwater wilderness—forests of coral, caverns, blind valleys, stone flowers and stone trees; and hundreds of square miles of submarine desert—regions of bare sand, rippled and duned, like the Sahara. There are lunar places in it—plains and abysses of raw rock—and places where colored vegetation grows in weird, uncouth jungles.

The reef is to fish what the primeval forest is to mammalian game. Not the streamlined, purple creatures of the gulf current live there— not sailfish and marlin and tunas and dolphins—but other fish which are strong, more numerous, and also, perhaps, hungrier. Jacks inhabit that fantastic land, and the groupers, which are bass, the many snappers, parrots, yellowtail, ordinary mackerel, triggers, countless small fish that travel in butterfly-bright schools, 'cudas, and, of course, all the rays together with a large variety of sharks. More fish are caught, as a rule, on a given day on the reef than are caught in a day on the Stream.

The *Poseidon's* mixed party began to catch fish. Mr. Porter boated a twenty-pound grouper. Mr. Welch hung and lost a hard-running fish of uncertain identity. Miss Jones caught another barracuda. Mr. Denby managed to bring to gaff a small jack after a battle; he stood on his feet, with his light rod bowed in a U, and kept his line taut with a skill that was admired even by Crunch.

Then Miss Jones hung a small mackerel and when she had it close to the boat, something tore it from her hook. For a moment line ripped from the reel. Then it went slack in the water.

Crunch, who had been at her side, acted swiftly. "An amberjack took that fish," he said. "Let's go!" He lifted the cover from the live-bait well. With a dip net, he took out one of the fish he had caught on the night before. Quickly he fixed it to a hook—with string. He chose the handiest hook—which was Mr. Welch's. He threw the fish overboard. "Watch it," he said to Miss Jones. "Watch it as long as you can."

So she stood up and leaned over the stern. The *Poseidon* was drifting, her motors stopped. She could see the little fish swim down in spirals, carrying the shiny leader. Then she saw something else. Around it loomed shapes—big, tan-colored shapes—and one of them shot toward it. She could actually see the big fish grab the little one and she bit the back of her hand. "He's got it!" she said sharply. "There's a dozen of them down there!"

"Let him run till he swallows it!" Crunch advised Mr. Welch. "All right! Sock him!"

Mr. Welch "socked." His reel wailed. Miss Jones sat back in her chair. She watched him hang on while the fish ran, watched him pump and perspire when the amberjack paused to consider, listened to him swear when the fish took off again, and looked at the expression on his face—an expression of concentration, jubilance, and anxiety which would have been funny if she had not shared every second of that mood. After fifteen minutes the fish was close to the boat. She saw that Crunch had gone to the bait well. He had another grunt in his hand. He peered up to the canopy. "Mr. Denby! Like to try one on light tackle? They're pretty big in this school."

Miss Jones hadn't guessed that there would be another chance. But now, looking into the water, she could see Mr. Welch's fish being hoisted to the surface, inch by inch, and around it was the school to which it had belonged. Big, shooting shapes following along beside their hooked companion, trying from time to time to make a grab at whatever it had in its mouth.

The small fish on Mr. Denby's line swam down toward what would obviously be a horrid reception, and while Miss Jones still looked, she saw one of the big fish spot the new arrival, wheel, and torpedo toward it. Then she heard Mr. Denby's reel purr interminably. She wondered how such a thin line could hold so huge a fish.

For a while she forgot Mr. Denby. They boated Mr. Welch's fish. "Go sixty, easy," Des said, grinning. But Miss Jones just stared. She'd only seen dead big fish until then. It was a beautiful thing alive: opalescent, silver, bronze—from that color came its name—and full of dazzling, almost tangible vitality.

Mr. Denby called attention to himself, presently: "Crunch! This devil's got nearly all my line! Guess you better head around!"

So Crunch ran to the controls and started the boat. He chased the amberjack while the angler gathered back line on his little reel. That was the beginning of a long session. Very long, as Mr. Porter and Mr. Welch began to hint. A half hour; then an hour. And it was Denby, they said in guarded tones, who had complained that Miss Jones was taking so long to get in her fish!

When an hour and a half had passed and Mr. Denby was still battling—still reeling with rapid endurance—still bracing himself against the hurtling runs of his quarry, Mr. Porter's patience snapped. "Really, man," he said in a tone of suppressed anger, "you're taking up our day! You shouldn't have used that light rig! It's not fair!"

But Denby fished on as if he had not heard.

Miss Jones began to look, not at the water and the thin line cutting through it, but at the man on the canopy. He wasn't exactly selfish, consciously. He was just determined. Terribly determined. He fought his fish as if he were fighting something much more important. She wondered about that. And when, after nearly two hours, Denby's line broke, she did not feel furious, like the other two men. She felt sad. She looked at Denby to see how he was taking it. For a minute—a short part of a minute—she thought he was going to cry. But, then, he smiled. He smiled distinctly. "Part of the game," he said quietly. "Must have been a whopper. Sorry I held you up so long, fellows."

That was all he did say. Miss Jones felt like crying herself. She caught Crunch staring up at his finicky passenger and in Crunch's startling blue eyes there was a gleam; the kind of gleam anybody would like to be responsible for. But Mr. Denby didn't seem to see that either.

They came in late that afternoon, when the sun was shooting bars of radiance halfway to the zenith. Miss Jones was on the forward deck again. She had been there ever since the fish had been lost. She'd protested that she was tired—though she wasn't. And Crunch had supplied her with an abundant lunch, having suspected that she would not know it was the duty of the passengers to bring lunch for the ship's crew. Somehow, she hadn't wanted to fish any more that day—partly for fear that she would hang a big one and annoy the others by taking too long, and partly for some inner reason she couldn't analyze.

By and by—to her surprise—Mr. Denby came up and sat beside her. "I never quit until we get in past the bell buoy," he said. "Sorry I wasn't more sociable today. Your first trip? Thought so. You did well."

She thanked him. At close range, he looked different. He had direct, hazel eyes and a high forehead. His skin was sunburned a rather silly pink but, near to, that didn't matter. And his voice, when he lowered it, was shy. "It's too bad," she said, "you lost that big amberjack. I saw him take the bait, and he surely was a monster."

The two men in the cockpit invited them to have a drink, but Miss Jones's companion said he never touched the stuff, and, evidently, he assumed that she didn't either.

"I . . ." he began presently—and was not satisfied with whatever opener he had in mind. "You see, Miss Jones—I'm a fanatic about fishing. I wasn't athletic in school or college. Quite the reverse. Kind of a—a coward. But after I grew up I got the idea that someday I could hang up a light-tackle record fishing—if I stuck to it. I love to fish, you know. I release most of the ones I get. Hate a meat hog."

She understood the look in his eye—then. The frantic determination. He had been fighting—not a fish, but himself. Old wounds, old feelings of inferiority. "Did you ever break a record?" she asked.

He smiled, a crinkly smile, as if he were looking into the future and seeing himself with the record broken. "Not yet. But—of course —I've only been after one for twelve years."

Then they were nearing the dock. Mr. Denby tried to seem offhand. "Well . . . another time! I hope you'll be a member of some party that I'm on one of these days." He was earnest and worried, as if he wanted to say more and did not know how.

Miss Jones looked at him and smiled. "Thanks. I'm afraid not, though. It's a bit too expensive for me. I'm strictly a causeway Waltonian, and this was just a . . ."

"A binge?" He was chuckling sympathetically.

"Yes. For me—a binge. But I did enjoy it. And I think you're a terribly good sport."

They were throwing the stern lines aboard the *Poseidon* then. People on the dock crowded through the vermilion sunlight to see what wonders had been wrenched from the sea that day. Miss Jones made ready to go ashore. And Crunch came up to her. He was uncomfortable. "Look," he said. "One thing—I mean . . . Well . . ." He tried to thrust six dollars into her hand. But she stepped lightly on the fish box, laughed at him, smiled at Mr. Denby, and was gone.

Some nights later, just as Miss Jones was on the point of throwing her rig into the running tide, Crunch came along the luminous, thunderous causeway. He had a rod in his hand—a rod with a shiny reel and agate-lined guides. "Hello," he said.

Miss Jones grinned. "After more bait? You know, I still dream about my day at sea! It was just gorgeous! And I was probably an awful nuisance!"

"Not to one man," Crunch answered. "You made quite a hit with Denby, I guess. He's been hanging around for days—and I didn't know why until this afternoon. He came down with this rod. For you. He said it was an old one that he didn't use any more."

She was embarrassed—and touched. "I couldn't think of taking it!"

"Why not? He can afford it. You're fishing for serious out here— and I know what that's like. This rod'll help you. You can cast a mile with it—after a little practice. Look."

Crunch whipped the rod in an arc. The reel sang. The bait went flying through the twilight like a driven golf ball. It splashed far out beyond the other lines that sagged down from the causeway. "He was afraid you'd refuse," Crunch continued. "So he made me take it to you. The old hundred-percenter had a barbless hook and three-thread line on it. I changed the three-thread to twelve—you can't handle that fine stuff on a rocky bottom. But it's a nice rig. I'd take it."

"He's kind of a cute guy," she said.

Crunch eyed her as he handed over the rod. "I bet you didn't talk that way in the library!"

"Even a librarian," she answered, with an assumption of mock dignity, "has access to the vernacular."

"Denby said—if you ever got anything good—to let him know."

"Oh?" She pursed her lips. "A string attached, hunh? Well—I must say—that if I were going to sell my soul—I think deep-sea fishing whenever you wanted to go, would be a fair price. I loved it!"

He stood beside her for a while. A hell of a nice girl, he thought; if she were a boy I could get her a job as a mate; she'd be a cracker-jack, I'll bet. He knew how it was to want things and not have them. He could imagine her "efficiency" apartment, her regular diet of fish, and her feelings, when she watched the fishing fleet go out and come in.

She reeled in and was getting ready to cast. He showed her how to thumb the reel, how to use her wrists, and, a moment later, how to pick out a backlash when you did it wrong. After a dozen tries, she had grasped the fundamentals. Maybe, Crunch began thinking, Sari could do something about her.

His eyes were fixed on the dark waters of the bay—somberly—because his thoughts made him unhappy. Then his eyes flickered and focused. There had been a roll—a shimmer—a silhouette of a fin—out on the inky surface. He knew what that was. If he could get it—or them—to hit, that would be another happy experience for Miss Jones. But he had no plug. They came through often—under the arches of the causeway—in the spring. Sometimes they wouldn't strike a diamond brooch, but sometimes they would take anything.

At Miss Jones's feet was the newspaper that contained her shrimp, and the string that had been around it. The paper was white and it would stay white in the water for a while. He tore off several strips and picked up the string. "Wind in," he said. "Let me have that hook for a second!"

Puzzled, she obeyed. Crunch fixed the strips of paper around the hook as much as possible in imitation of a feather lure. Then he scanned the water again. "Now," he said. "Yonder—just in line with the bow of that yacht! Cast as far as you can and don't let it sink! Instead, reel in slowly and jerk your rod a bit. If anything hits, hit back as hard as you can—and fast!"

She caught the excitement in his voice. "But—did you see something?"

"Go ahead! Cast! Exactly the way I said!"

Doubtfully, she cast the impromptu bait. It arced through the evening and hit the water. Crunch could see it there—a white dot. He saw it start to wiggle toward them. "That's it!" Then he saw the heavy surge under the paper lure.

Miss Jones struck. She pressed on the thumbstall hard. But something—something like lightning—was on that line. It ran as if she had hooked into a passing automobile. Then it stopped. "Wind!" Crunch yelled. "Wind as you never did in your life! It's going to jump!"

"But what is it?" she gasped.

"Look!"

She was barely able to manage her rod and to look. Out in the light of the electric signs and the buildings and the radiance from the causeway she saw a silverish-white fish crash up into the air, hang for a second, somersault completely, and vanish. "Oh, my," she murmured.

"Tarpon!" he yelled. "A beauty! If you get him—you'll really have something!" He raced along the sidewalk past the other fishermen. He bawled at the top of his lungs. "Pull in your lines, everybody, please! We've hung a big tarpon here! Hey! You with the big stomach! Pull in that line! The lady'll foul you if you don't!" His voice changed to an ominous roar: "And if you don't think I can make you, wise guy! . . . Well . . . that's better!"

He ran back to Miss Jones. "Keep the line tight! After we wear him down, we'll lead him along the causeway to shore and beach him! Boy! That's it!" He ran off to warn more distant anglers.

Miss Jones was thinking. Thinking of the fish she had promised to bring to her neighbors the day she had gone out to sea. Fish she had not provided because she had caught only two barracudas. She was thinking of the size of the tarpon, and of poor old Mrs. Wilmot, and of Mr. Treelman who was out of work, and the Berkimer kids. She also thought, for a flash, of Mr. Denby and his tragic desire to break a record. Then she had no more time for thinking. The tarpon ran under the causeway and shot out—miraculously without cutting the line—and it began to leap and pinwheel in the air.

Around Miss Jones the other causeway fishermen gathered, but she did not notice them. She did not hear their shouts of advice. Behind her, a car stopped and a man in a white dinner jacket hopped out to look. He hurried back to a woman in the car and said rather dazedly, "Some girl has hung a walloping big tarpon on a casting outfit! Let's watch!" He helped from the car a woman in evening clothes. Behind them, another car stopped. A truck driver headed for the beach peered, slowed, and pulled up his brake. Horns began to blow. The crowd bulged out on the street. From Miami, a motorcycle policeman cut through the snarl with a braying siren and began to yell questions: "What's going on? Where's the accident? Did some half-wit go through the railing?"

Then, he too, saw the great silver king plunging in the night, and because many—perhaps most—of the people of Miami are fisher-men, he forgot his duty, pushed to the rail, and bellowed, "Lady, you better watch out on those jumps! Come back farther with the rod!"

Miss Jones didn't notice him. But she did notice that the thumb-stall—rotten by long sitting in Mr. Denby's tackle closet—was wear-ing thin. Her finger became hot. A chunk of leather tore away. Her bare thumb hit the wet and racing spool. She shut her jaws. When pain shot into her arms, she used the other thumb, although it was awkward. Then she found that by pressing against the metal side of the spinning spool, less heat was generated. When her left thumb grew slippery, she knew it was bleeding. But she did not care. The tarpon was not leaping quite as high or quite as often. Crunch had cleared away all the dangling lines and was beside her again.

The fish sank below the surface and she could feel the slow, steady beat of its tail.

"Sulking," Crunch said. "Let's start leading him. Every time you come to a post, get all set and pass the rod around it from your left hand to your right. If he starts to leap or run—stop and fight him!"

So they began to move along the causeway. Miss Jones passed the rod around obstructions. Crunch followed, coaching. And the crowd followed, too, yelling, encouraging and voicing envy. Traffic behind them was a hopeless tangle and traffic was piling up ahead. From one of the stalled cars came a man with a camera to which was attached a bulb. Its soundless light broke over the mob.

Miss Jones found that by pulling steadily, she could tow the tarpon in the desired direction. Her fingers bled. Her wrists ached. Her shoul-der joints felt separated. But she kept on. When they came around the end of the causeway, she was groggy. She tripped on some weeds and stumbled over a pile of rubble. The crowd stayed above her, looking down, and the man with the camera kept shooting pictures. But Crunch was at her side.

"Just get out there on that bare spot—and pump," he said. "The way you did the 'cudas."

So she pumped. She was out of breath and wet with perspiration. But she kept pulling. And suddenly, to her vague amazement, Crunch waded into the water. He bent over. He groped. Then he half threw up on the land a prodigious, glittering fish which flopped heavily in the red glare of a big electric sign. "Got it," Crunch said.

Miss Jones didn't exactly faint, but her knees gave way and she sat down.

Twenty minutes later she was ensconced in the stern of the *Poseidon*. Traffic had been restored on the causeway. There was only a small crowd on the Gulf Stream Dock—perhaps a couple of hundred people—and out of it came the fishing editor of the *Dispatch* to interview her. The tarpon was hanging on the rack. He stopped to look at it. He whistled. Then he said, "You're Miss Jones?"

She was about to reply. But another person broke through the awed spectators. It was Mr. Denby—without a hat—with staring eyes. He charged up to the fishing editor. "On three-thread!" he yelled. "Three-thread, old man! A world's record!"

Miss Jones, who had felt her heart bounce at the sight of Mr. Denby, now felt that same organ wither and grow ashamed. "On twelve-thread," she said quietly. "Crunch changed it. I'm afraid, Mr. Denby, we're still as far from that record as ever."

The skipper came up from below in dry shoes and trousers. He heard her words and took in the disappointment on the expert's face. "Yeah," he said slowly. "She couldn't handle three-thread on that bottom, Denby. Another thing—your thumbstall wore out and she's torn her fingers all up. Maybe it wasn't a world's record—but it's a new high for grit!"

Mr. Denby still seemed bogged in disappointment.

"Anyway," Miss Jones said sorrowfully, "it'll make up for the meal I promised the Wilmots and the Treelmans and the Berkimers. Not to mention myself. I've got the use of an icebox now."

Crunch gulped.

Mr. Denby stared.

"But," the fishing editor said, "tarpon are no good to eat! They're muddy."

Denby grabbed Crunch's arm and pulled him aside. "You mean to say—a lovely girl like that—fishes because she needs food?"

"Lots of people do," Crunch replied laconically. "Nice people."

Denby gulped.

"Our cameraman happened to be going over the causeway—" the fishing editor felt compelled to lighten a pall he could not fathom—

"and he says he got some elegant stuff! We'll give you a spread on the sports page! . . ."

He went on talking. But the situation was not relieved then. Not wholly relieved later—when Mr. Denby insisted that as soon as Miss Jones's hands were healed she should be his guest for a day "outside."

It is that day which changed everything.

A day like all the other days of spring on the Florida coast. The *Poseidon* was moving smoothly out toward the purple edge of the Gulf Stream. Desperate was at the controls. Crunch was rigging up Mr. Denby's four-six outfit. And Mr. Denby detached himself from an animated conversation with Miss Jones. "Not the light outfit, Crunch!" he said in a low voice. "Give me the heaviest stuff you have. Thirty-nine thread, if you've got it. And tell Des not to head for the Stream. I want to fish the reef."

Crunch was startled. "Thought you hated the reef?"

Mr. Denby's mouth was firm. "We're fishing for groupers, today. Groupers for the Wilmots and the Treelmans and those other people. Big, delicious groupers. Dozens of them! I don't want to take a chance on losing anything we hang."

Crunch put down the light outfit. There was written on his face a masterpiece of mixed moods. Surely, he reflected, Denby has changed. Maybe Miss Jones was right. Maybe he was at bottom a good egg. "Head for Fowey Rock," he yelled to Des. He fixed two big rigs.

Mr. Denby had returned to the cockpit with a pillow. "This," he said, "will make you more comfortable—ah—Miss Jones. I wish I knew your first name."

"If I told you you'd be shocked. My mother had imagination, she was practically reckless."

There was amusement in his eyes—and affection. "I'll find out," he said. "You only gave your initials in the newspaper story. But I'm a determined man. Very determined!"

"Yes. I know." She said that earnestly.

"My own," he continued, "is Thornton. Does that give you courage?"

Miss Jones blushed. "You won't believe it—but it's Scheherazade."

Mr. Denby peered at the radiant sea. "It's beautiful," he murmured.

Crunch gazed at Mr. Denby and Miss Jones. Then he ducked out through a window and joined Desperate.

The mate started below to replace him, but Crunch caught his arm. "As much as possible," he said, "I think we'll both stay up on top today. We may get some fish—but mostly, we're just a gondola."

Des thought that over and understood. "I hope she'll teach him not to tell everybody how to fish," he finally said.

At that instant, Mr. Denby called, "I've got a strike! Nope! Missed him!"

Crunch leaned over the canopy edge.

"You hit too hard," Scheherazade said sweetly but firmly.

There was utter devotion in Thornton's response. "So I did! Much too hard."

THE MALTESE CAT

---

by RUDYARD KIPLING

(1895)

The narrator of this well-known story, in the event you are meeting him for the first time, is a polo pony. Endowing animals with human emotions and the power of human speech usually results in a fatal mawkishness. One of Kipling's gifts is that he can not only get away with this; he can make it extraordinarily acceptable. The Maltese Cat is as typical of Kipling as a story can be. It is set in the old colonial India which spawned that special breed of British army men, and the author, extolling such old-fashioned virtues as courage, pours a tremendous amount of heart into his up-beat tale. He is, to be sure, a romantic writer, but he is a good romantic writer, which is a rare thing. Incidentally, among the tricks which Kipling attempts and pulls off in this story is to give more than a dozen polo ponies individual "personalities" so you can keep them apart. He also manages to explain clearly and excitingly, without ever sounding like a sports manual, what polo is all about.

THEY HAD good reason to be proud, and better reason to be afraid, all twelve of them; for though they had fought their way, game by game, up the teams entered for the polo tournament, they were meeting the Archangels that afternoon in the final match; and the Archangels' men were playing with half a dozen ponies apiece. As the game was divided into six quarters of eight minutes each, that meant a fresh pony after every halt. The Skidars' team, even supposing there were no accidents, could only supply one pony for every other

249

change; and two to one is heavy odds. Again, as Shiraz, the gray Syrian, pointed out, they were meeting the pink and pick of the polo ponies of Upper India, ponies that had cost from a thousand rupees each, while they themselves were a cheap lot gathered, often from country carts, by their masters, who belonged to a poor but honest native infantry regiment.

"Money means pace and weight," said Shiraz, rubbing his black-silk nose dolefully along his neat-fitting boot, "and by the maxims of the game as I know it——"

"Ah, but we aren't playing the maxims," said The Maltese Cat. "We're playing the game; and we've the great advantage of knowing the game. Just think a stride, Shiraz! We've pulled up from bottom to second place in two weeks against all those fellows on the ground here. That's because we play with our heads as well as our feet."

"It makes me feel undersized and unhappy all the same," said Kittiwynk, a mouse-colored mare with a red brow-band and the cleanest pair of legs that ever an aged pony owned. "They're twice our style, these others."

Kittiwynk looked at the gathering and sighed. The hard, dusty polo ground was lined with thousands of soldiers, black and white, not counting hundreds and hundreds of carriages and drags and dog carts, and ladies with brilliant-colored parasols, and officers in uniform and out of it, and crowds of natives behind them; and orderlies on camels, who had halted to watch the game, instead of carrying letters up and down the station; and native horse dealers running about on thin-eared Biluchi mares, looking for a chance to sell a few first-class polo ponies. Then there were the ponies of thirty teams that had entered for the Upper India Free-for-All Cup—nearly every pony of worth and dignity, from Mhow to Peshawar, from Allahabad to Multan; prize ponies, Arabs, Syrian, Barb, country-bred, Deccanee, Waziri, and Kabul ponies of every color and shape and temper that you could imagine. Some of them were in mat-roofed stables, close to the polo ground, but most were under saddle, while their masters, who had been defeated in the earlier games, trotted in and out and told the world exactly how the game should be played.

It was a glorious sight, and the come and go of the little, quick hoofs, and the incessant salutations of ponies that had met before on other polo grounds or racecourses were enough to drive a four-footed thing wild.

But the Skidars' team were careful not to know their neighbors, though half the ponies on the ground were anxious to scrape acquaintance with the little fellows that had come from the North, and, so far, had swept the board.

"Let's see," said a soft gold-colored Arab, who had been playing very badly the day before, to The Maltese Cat; "didn't we meet in Abdul Rahman's stable in Bombay, four seasons ago? I won the Paikpattan Cup next season, you may remember?"

"Not me," said The Maltese Cat, politely. "I was at Malta then, pulling a vegetable cart. I don't race. I play the game."

"Oh!" said the Arab, cocking his tail and swaggering off.

"Keep yourselves to yourselves," said The Maltese Cat to his companions. "We don't want to rub noses with all those goose-rumped half-breeds of Upper India. When we've won this Cup they'll give their shoes to know *us*."

"We shan't win the Cup," said Shiraz. "How do you feel?"

"Stale as last night's feed when a muskrat has run over it," said Polaris, a rather heavy-shouldered gray; and the rest of the team agreed with him.

"The sooner you forget that the better," said The Maltese Cat, cheerfully. "They've finished tiffin in the big tent. We shall be wanted now. If your saddles are not comfy, kick. If your bits aren't easy, rear, and let the *saises* know whether your boots are tight."

Each pony had his *sais*, his groom, who lived and ate and slept with the animal, and had betted a good deal more than he could afford on the result of the game. There was no chance of anything going wrong, but to make sure, each *sais* was shampooing the legs of his pony to the last minute. Behind the *saises* sat as many of the Skidars' regiment as had leave to attend the match—about half the native officers, and a hundred or two dark, black-bearded men with the regimental pipers nervously fingering the big, beribboned bagpipes. The Skidars were what they call a Pioneer regiment, and the bagpipes made the national music of half their men. The native officers held bundles of polo sticks, long cane-handled mallets, and as the grandstand filled after lunch they arranged themselves by ones and twos at different points round the ground, so that if a stick were broken the player would not have far to ride for a new one. An impatient British Cavalry Band struck up "If you want to know the time, ask a p'leeceman!" and the two umpires in light dust coats

danced out on two little excited ponies. The four players of the
Archangels' team followed, and the sight of their beautiful mounts
made Shiraz groan again.

"Wait till we know," said The Maltese Cat. "Two of 'em are playing in blinkers, and that means they can't see to get out of the way of
their own side, or they *may* shy at the umpires' ponies. They've *all*
got white web reins that are sure to stretch or slip!"

"And," said Kittiwynk, dancing to take the stiffness out of her,
"they carry their whips in their hands instead of on their wrists. Hah!"

"True enough. No man can manage his stick and his reins and
his whip that way," said The Maltese Cat. "I've fallen over every
square yard of the Malta ground, and I ought to know."

He quivered his little, flea-bitten withers just to show how satisfied
he felt; but his heart was not so light. Ever since he had drifted into
India on a troopship, taken, with an old rifle, as part payment for a
racing debt, The Maltese Cat had played and preached polo to the
Skidars' team on the Skidars' stony polo ground. Now a polo pony is
like a poet. If he is born with a love for the game, he can be made. The
Maltese Cat knew that bamboos grew solely in order that polo balls
might be turned from their roots, that grain was given to ponies to
keep them in hard condition, and that ponies were shod to prevent
them from slipping on a turn. But, besides all these things, he knew
every trick and device of the finest game in the world, and for two
seasons had been teaching the others all he knew or guessed.

"Remember," he said for the hundredth time, as the riders came
up, "you *must* play together, and you *must* play with your heads.
Whatever happens, follow the ball. Who goes out first?"

Kittiwynk, Shiraz, Polaris, and a short high little bay fellow with
tremendous hocks and no withers worth speaking of (he was called
Corks) were being girthed up, and the soldiers in the background
stared with all their eyes.

"I want you men to keep quiet," said Lutyens, the captain of the
team, "and especially not to blow your pipes."

"Not if we win, Captain Sahib?" asked the piper.

"If we win you can do what you please," said Lutyens, with a
smile, as he slipped the loop of his stick over his wrist, and wheeled
to canter to his place. The Archangels' ponies were a little bit above
themselves on account of the many-colored crowd so close to the
ground. Their riders were excellent players, but they were a team of
crack players instead of a crack team; and that made all the differ-

ence in the world. They honestly meant to play together, but it is very hard for four men, each the best of the team he is picked from, to remember that in polo no brilliancy in hitting or riding makes up for playing alone. Their captain shouted his orders to them by name, and it is a curious thing that if you call his name aloud in public after an Englishman you make him hot and fretty. Lutyens said nothing to his men, because it had all been said before. He pulled up Shiraz, for he was playing back, to guard the goal. Powell on Polaris was half-back, and Macnamara and Hughes on Corks and Kittiwynk were forwards. The tough, bamboo ball was set in the middle of the ground, one hundred and fifty yards from the ends, and Hughes crossed sticks, heads up, with the Captain of the Archangels, who saw fit to play forward; that is a place from which you cannot easily control your team. The little click as the cane shafts met was heard all over the ground, and then Hughes made some sort of quick wrist stroke that just dribbled the ball a few yards. Kittiwynk knew that stroke of old, and followed as a cat follows a mouse. While the Captain of the Archangels was wrenching his pony round, Hughes struck with all his strength, and the next instant Kittiwynk was away, Corks following close behind her, their little feet pattering like raindrops on glass.

"Pull out to the left," said Kittiwynk between her teeth; "it's coming your way, Corks!"

The back and halfback of the Archangels were tearing down on her just as she was within reach of the ball. Hughes leaned forward with a loose rein and cut it away to the left almost under Kittiwynk's foot, and it hopped and skipped off to Corks, who saw that if he was not quick it would run beyond the boundaries. That long bouncing drive gave the Archangels time to wheel and send three men across the ground to head off Corks. Kittiwynk stayed where she was; for she knew the game. Corks was on the ball half a fraction of a second before the others came up, and Macnamara, with a backhanded stroke, sent it back across the ground to Hughes, who saw the way clear to the Archangels' goal, and smacked the ball in before any-one quite knew what had happened.

"That's luck," said Corks, as they changed ends. "A goal in three minutes for three hits, and no riding to speak of."

" 'Don't know," said Polaris. "We've made 'em angry too soon. Shouldn't wonder if they tried to rush us off our feet next time."

"Keep the ball hanging, then," said Shiraz. "That wears out every pony that is not used to it."

Next time there was no easy galloping across the ground. All the Archangels closed up as one man, but there they stayed, for Corks, Kittiwynk, and Polaris were somewhere on top of the ball, marking time among the rattling sticks, while Shiraz circled about outside, waiting for a chance.

"We can do this all day," said Polaris, ramming his quarters into the side of another pony. "Where do you think you're shoving to?"

"I'll—I'll be driven in an *ekka* if I know," was the gasping reply, "and I'd give a week's feed to get my blinkers off. I can't see anything."

"The dust is rather bad. Whew! That was one for my off-hock. Where's the ball, Corks?"

"Under my tail. At least, the man's looking for it there! This is beautiful. They can't use their sticks, and it's driving 'em wild. Give old Blinkers a push and then he'll go over."

"Here, don't touch me! I can't see. I'll—I'll back out, I think," said the pony in blinkers, who knew that if you can't see all round your head, you cannot prop yourself against the shock.

Corks was watching the ball where it lay in the dust, close to his near foreleg, with Macnamara's shortened stick tap-tapping it from time to time. Kittiwynk was edging her way out of the scrimmage, whisking her stump of a tail with nervous excitement.

"Ho! They've got it," she snorted. "Let me out!" and she galloped like a rifle bullet just behind a tall lanky pony of the Archangels, whose rider was swinging up his stick for a stroke.

"Not today, thank you," said Hughes, as the blow slid off his raised stick, and Kittiwynk laid her shoulder to the tall pony's quarters, and shoved him aside just as Lutyens on Shiraz sent the ball where it had come from, and the tall pony went skating and slipping away to the left. Kittiwynk, seeing that Polaris had joined Corks in the chase for the ball up the ground, dropped into Polaris' place, and then "time" was called.

The Skidars' ponies wasted no time in kicking or fuming. They knew that each minute's rest meant so much gain, and trotted off to the rails, and their *saises* began to scrape and blanket and rub them at once.

"Whew!" said Corks, stiffening up to get all the tickle of the big vulcanite scraper. "If we were playing pony for pony, we would bend those Archangels double in half an hour. But they'll bring up fresh ones and fresh ones and fresh ones after that—you see."

"Who cares?" said Polaris. "We've drawn first blood. Is my hock swelling?"

"Looks puffy," said Corks. "You must have had rather a wipe. Don't let it stiffen. You'll be wanted again in half an hour."

"What's the game like?" said The Maltese Cat.

" 'Ground's like your shoe, except where they put too much water on it," said Kittiwynk. "Then it's slippery. Don't play in the center. There's a bog there. I don't know how their next four are going to behave, but we kept the ball hanging, and made 'em lather for nothing. Who goes out? Two Arabs and a couple of country-breds! That's bad. What a comfort it is to wash your mouth out!"

Kitty was talking with a neck of a lather-covered soda-water bottle between her teeth, and trying to look over her withers at the same time. This gave her a very coquettish air.

"What's bad?" said Gray Dawn, giving to the girth and admiring his well-set shoulders.

"You Arabs can't gallop fast enough to keep yourselves warm— that's what Kitty means," said Polaris, limping to show that his hock needed attention. "Are you playing back, Gray Dawn?"

" 'Looks like it," said Gray Dawn, as Lutyens swung himself up. Powell mounted The Rabbit, a plain bay country-bred much like Corks, but with mulish ears. Macnamara took Faiz-Ullah, a handy, short-backed little red Arab with a long tail, and Hughes mounted Benami, an old and sullen brown beast, who stood over in front more than a polo pony should.

"Benami looks like business," said Shiraz. "How's your temper, Ben?" The old campaigner hobbled off without answering, and The Maltese Cat looked at the new Archangel ponies prancing about on the ground. They were four beautiful blacks, and they saddled big enough and strong enough to eat the Skidars' team and gallop away with the meal inside them.

"Blinkers again," said The Maltese Cat. "Good enough!"

"They're chargers—cavalry chargers!" said Kittiwynk, indignantly. *"They'll* never see thirteen-three again."

"They've all been fairly measured, and they've all got their certificates," said The Maltese Cat, "or they wouldn't be here. We must take things as they come along, and keep your eyes on the ball."

The game began, but this time the Skidars were penned to their own end of the ground, and the watching ponies did not approve of that.

"Faiz-Ullah is shirking—as usual," said Polaris, with a scornful grunt.

"Faiz-Ullah is eating whip," said Corks. They could hear the leather-thonged polo quirt lacing the little fellow's well-rounded barrel. Then The Rabbit's shrill neigh came across the ground.

"I can't do all the work," he cried, desperately.

"Play the game—don't talk," The Maltese Cat whickered; and all the ponies wriggled with excitement, and the soldiers and the grooms gripped the railings and shouted. A black pony with blinkers had singled out old Benami, and was interfering with him in every possible way. They could see Benami shaking his head up and down, and flapping his under lip.

"There'll be a fall in a minute," said Polaris. "Benami is getting stuffy."

The game flickered up and down between goal post and goal post, and the black ponies were getting more confident as they felt they had the legs of the others. The ball was hit out of a little scrimmage, and Benami and The Rabbit followed it, Faiz-Ullah only too glad to be quiet for an instant.

The blinkered black pony came up like a hawk, with two of his own side behind him, and Benami's eye glittered as he raced. The question was which pony should make way for the other, for each rider was perfectly willing to risk a fall in a good cause. The black, who had been driven nearly crazy by his blinkers, trusted to his weight and his temper; but Benami knew how to apply his weight and how to keep his temper. They met, and there was a cloud of dust. The black was lying on his side, all the breath knocked out of his body. The Rabbit was a hundred yards up the ground with the ball, and Benami was sitting down. He had slid nearly ten yards on his tail, but he had had his revenge, and sat cracking his nostrils till the black pony rose.

"That's what you get for interfering. Do you want any more?" said Benami, and he plunged into the game. Nothing was done that quarter, because Faiz-Ullah would not gallop, though Macnamara beat him whenever he could spare a second. The fall of the black pony had impressed his companions tremendously, and so the Archangels could not profit by Faiz-Ullah's bad behavior.

But as The Maltese Cat said when "time" was called, and the four came back blowing and dripping, Faiz-Ullah ought to have been kicked all round Umballa. If he did not behave better next time The Maltese Cat promised to pull out his Arab tail by the roots and—eat it.

There was no time to talk, for the third four were ordered out.

The third quarter of a game is generally the hottest, for each side thinks that the others must be pumped, and most of the winning play in a game is made about that time.

Lutyens took over The Maltese Cat with a pat and a hug, for Lutyens valued him more than anything else in the world; Powell had Shikast, a little gray rat with no pedigree and no manners outside polo; Macnamara mounted Bamboo, the largest of the team; and Hughes Who's Who, alias The Animal. He was supposed to have Australian blood in his veins, but he looked like a clotheshorse, and you could whack his legs with an iron crowbar without hurting him.

They went out to meet the very flower of the Archangels' team; and when Who's Who saw their elegantly booted legs and their beautiful satin skins, he grinned a grin through his light, well-worn bridle.

"My word!" said Who's Who. "We must give 'em a little football. These gentlemen need a rubbing down."

"No biting," said The Maltese Cat, warningly; for once or twice in his career Who's Who had been known to forget himself in that way.

"Who said anything about biting? I'm not playing tiddly-winks. I'm playing the game."

The Archangels came down like a wolf on the fold, for they were tired of football, and they wanted polo. They got it more and more. Just after the game began, Lutyens hit a ball that was coming toward him rapidly, and it rolled in the air, as a ball sometimes will, with the whirl of a frightened partridge. Shikast heard, but could not see it for the minute, though he looked everywhere and up into the air as The Maltese Cat had taught him. When he saw it ahead and overhead he went forward with Powell as fast as he could put foot to ground. It was then that Powell, a quiet and level-headed man, as a rule, became inspired, and played a stroke that sometimes comes off successfully after long practice. He took his stick in both hands, and, standing up in his stirrups, swiped at the ball in the air, Munipore fashion. There was one second of paralyzed astonishment, and then all four sides of the ground went up in a yell of applause and delight as the ball flew true (you could see the amazed Archangels ducking in their saddles to dodge the line of flight, and looking at it with open mouths), and the regimental pipes of the Skidars squealed from the railings as long as the pipers had breath.

Shikast heard the stroke; but he heard the head of the stick fly off at the same time. Nine hundred and ninety-nine ponies out of a thousand would have gone tearing on after the ball with a useless player pulling at their heads; but Powell knew him, and he knew Powell; and the instant he felt Powell's right leg shift a trifle on the saddle flap, he headed to the boundary, where a native officer was frantically waving a new stick. Before the shouts had ended, Powell was armed again.

Once before in his life The Maltese Cat had heard that very same stroke played off his own back, and had profited by the confusion it wrought. This time he acted on experience, and leaving Bamboo to guard the goal in case of accidents, came through the others like a flash, head and tail low—Lutyens standing up to ease him—swept on and on before the other side knew what was the matter, and nearly pitched on his head between the Archangels' goal posts as Lutyens kicked the ball in after a straight scurry of a hundred and fifty yards. If there was one thing more than another upon which The Maltese Cat prided himself, it was on this quick, streaking kind of run half across the ground. He did not believe in taking balls round the field unless you were clearly overmatched. After this they gave the Archangels five-minuted football; and an expensive fast pony hates football because it rumples his temper.

Who's Who showed himself even better than Polaris in this game. He did not permit any wriggling away, but bored joyfully into the scrimmage as if he had his nose in a feedbox and was looking for something nice. Little Shikast jumped on the ball the minute it got clear, and every time an Archangel pony followed it, he found Shikast standing over it, asking what was the matter.

"If we can live through this quarter," said The Maltese Cat, "I shan't care. Don't take it out of yourselves. Let them do the lathering."

So the ponies, as their riders explained afterward, "shut up." The Archangels kept them tied fast in front of their goal, but it cost the Archangels' ponies all that was left of their tempers; and ponies began to kick, and men began to repeat compliments, and they chopped at the legs of Who's Who, and he set his teeth and stayed where he was, and the dust stood up like a tree over the scrimmage until that hot quarter ended.

They found the ponies very excited and confident when they went to their *saises;* and The Maltese Cat had to warn them that the worst of the game was coming.

"Now *we* are all going in for the second time," said he, "and *they* are trotting out fresh ponies. You think you can gallop, but you'll find you can't; and then you'll be sorry."

"But two goals to nothing is a halter-long lead," said Kittiwynk, prancing.

"How long does it take to get a goal?" The Maltese Cat answered. "For pity's sake, don't run away with a notion that the game is half won just because we happen to be in luck *now!* They'll ride you into the grandstand, if they can; you must not give 'em a chance. Follow the ball."

"Football, as usual?" said Polaris. "My hock's half as big as a nose bag."

"Don't let them have a look at the ball, if you can help it. Now leave me alone. I must get all the rest I can before the last quarter."

He hung down his head and let all his muscles go slack, Shikast, Bamboo, and Who's Who copying his example.

"Better not watch the game," he said. "We aren't playing, and we shall only take it out of ourselves if we grow anxious. Look at the ground and pretend it's fly time."

They did their best, but it was hard advice to follow. The hoofs were drumming and the sticks were rattling all up and down the ground, and yells of applause from the English troops told that the Archangels were pressing the Skidars hard. The native soldiers behind the ponies groaned and grunted, and said things in undertones, and presently they heard a long-drawn shout and a clatter of hurrahs!

"One to the Archangels," said Shikast, without raising his head. "Time's nearly up. Oh, my sire—and *dam!*"

"Faiz-Ullah," said The Maltese Cat, "if you don't play to the last nail in your shoes this time, I'll kick you on the ground before all the other ponies."

"I'll do my best when my time comes," said the little Arab, sturdily.

The *saises* looked at each other gravely as they rubbed their ponies' legs. This was the time when long purses began to tell, and everybody knew it. Kittiwynk and the others came back, the sweat drip- ping over their hoofs and their tails telling sad stories.

"They're better than we are," said Shiraz. "I knew how it would be."

"Shut your big head," said The Maltese Cat; "we've one goal to the good yet."

"Yes; but it's two Arabs and two country-breds to play now," said Corks. "Faiz-Ullah, remember!" He spoke in a biting voice.

As Lutyens mounted Gray Dawn he looked at his men, and they did not look pretty. They were covered with dust and sweat in streaks. Their yellow boots were almost black, their wrists were red and lumpy, and their eyes seemed two inches deep in their heads; but the expression in the eyes was satisfactory.

"Did you take anything at tiffin?" said Lutyens; and the team shook their heads. They were too dry to talk.

"All right. The Archangels did. They are worse pumped than we are."

"They've got the better ponies," said Powell. "I shan't be sorry when this business is over."

That fifth quarter was a painful one in every way. Faiz-Ullah played like a little red demon, and The Rabbit seemed to be every- where at once, and Benami rode straight at anything and every- thing that came in his way; while the umpires on their ponies wheeled like gulls outside the shifting game. But the Archangels had the better mounts—they had kept their racers till late in the game— and never allowed the Skidars to play football. They hit the ball up and down the width of the ground till Benami and the rest were out- paced. Then they went forward, and time and again Lutyens and Gray Dawn were just, and only just, able to send the ball away with a long, spitting backhander. Gray Dawn forgot that he was an Arab; and turned from gray to blue as he galloped. Indeed, he forgot too well, for he did not keep his eyes on the ground as an Arab should, but stuck out his nose and scuttled for the dear honor of the game. They had watered the ground once or twice between the quarters, and a careless water man had emptied the last of his skinful all in one place near the Skidars' goal. It was close to the end of the play, and for the tenth time Gray Dawn was bolting after the ball, when his near hind foot slipped on the greasy mud, and he rolled over and over, pitching Lutyens just clear of the goal post; and the triumphant Archangels made their goal. Then "time" was called—

two goals all; but Lutyens had to be helped up, and Gray Dawn rose with his near hind leg strained somewhere.

"What's the damage?" said Powell, his arm around Lutyens.

"Collarbone, *of* course," said Lutyens, between his teeth. It was the third time he had broken it in two years, and it hurt him.

Powell and the others whistled.

"Game's up," said Hughes.

"Hold on. We've five good minutes yet, and it isn't my right hand. We'll stick it out."

"I say," said the Captain of the Archangels, trotting up, "are you hurt, Lutyens? We'll wait if you care to put in a substitute. I wish— I mean—the fact is, you fellows deserve this game if any team does. 'Wish we could give you a man, or some of our ponies—or something."

"You're awfully good, but we'll play it to a finish, I think."

The Captain of the Archangels stared for a little. "That's not half bad," he said, and went back to his own side, while Lutyens borrowed a scarf from one of his native officers and made a sling of it. Then an Archangel galloped up with a big bath sponge, and advised Lutyens to put it under his armpit to ease his shoulder, and between them they tied up his left arm scientifically; and one of the native officers leaped forward with four long glasses that fizzed and bubbled.

The team looked at Lutyens piteously, and he nodded. It was the last quarter, and nothing would matter after that. They drank out the dark golden drink, and wiped their mustaches, and things looked more hopeful.

The Maltese Cat had put his nose into the front of Lutyens' shirt and was trying to say how sorry he was.

"He knows," said Lutyens, proudly. "The beggar knows. I've played him without a bridle before now—for fun."

"It's no fun now," said Powell. "But we haven't a decent substitute."

"No," said Lutyens. "It's the last quarter, and we've got to make our goal and win. I'll trust The Cat."

"If you fall this time, you'll suffer a little," said Macnamara.

"I'll trust The Cat," said Lutyens.

"You hear that?" said The Maltese Cat, proudly, to the others. "It's worth while playing polo for ten years to have that said of you. Now then, my sons, come along. We'll kick up a little bit, just to show the Archangels this team haven't suffered."

And, sure enough, as they went on to the ground, The Maltese Cat, after satisfying himself that Lutyens was home in the saddle, kicked out three or four times, and Lutyens laughed. The reins were caught up anyhow in the tips of his strapped left hand, and he never pretended to rely on them. He knew The Cat would answer to the least pressure of the leg, and by way of showing off—for his shoulder hurt him very much—he bent the little fellow in a close figure-of-eight in and out between the goal posts. There was a roar from the native officers and men, who dearly loved a piece of *dugabashi* (horse-trick work), as they called it, and the pipes very quietly and scornfully droned out the first bars of a common bazaar tune called "Freshly Fresh and Newly New," just as a warning to the other regiments that the Skidars were fit. All the natives laughed.

"And now," said The Maltese Cat, as they took their place, "remember that this is the last quarter, and follow the ball!"

"Don't need to be told," said Who's Who.

"Let me go on. All those people on all four sides will begin to crowd in—just as they did at Malta. You'll hear people calling out, and moving forward and being pushed back; and that is going to make the Archangel ponies very unhappy. But if a ball is struck to the boundary, you go after it, and let the people get out of your way. I went over the pole of a four-in-hand once, and picked a game out of the dust by it. Back me up when I run, and follow the ball."

There was a sort of all-round sound of sympathy and wonder as the last quarter opened, and then there began exactly what The Maltese Cat had foreseen. People crowded in close to the boundaries, and the Archangels' ponies kept looking sideways at the narrowing space. If you know how a man feels to be cramped at tennis—not because he wants to run out of the court, but because he likes to know that he can at a pinch—you will guess how ponies must feel when they are playing in a box of human beings.

"I'll bend some of those men if I can get away," said Who's Who, as he rocketed behind the ball; and Bamboo nodded without speaking. They were playing the last ounce in them, and The Maltese Cat had left the goal undefended to join them. Lutyens gave him every order that he could to bring him back, but this was the first time in his career that the little wise gray had ever played polo on his own responsibility, and he was going to make the most of it.

"What are you doing here?" said Hughes, as The Cat crossed in front of him and rode off on an Archangel.

"The Cat's in charge—mind the goal!" shouted Lutyens, and bowing forward hit the ball full, and followed on, forcing the Archangels toward their own goal.

"No football," said The Maltese Cat. "Keep the ball by the boundaries and cramp 'em. Play open order, and drive 'em to the boundaries."

Across and across the ground in big diagonals flew the ball, and whenever it came to a flying rush and a stroke close to the boundaries the Archangel ponies moved stiffly. They did not care to go headlong at a wall of men and carriages, though if the ground had been open they could have turned on a sixpence.

"Wriggle her up the sides," said The Cat. "Keep her close to the crowd. They hate the carriages. Shikast, keep her up this side."

Shikast and Powell lay left and right behind the uneasy scuffle of an open scrimmage; and every time the ball was hit away Shikast galloped on it at such an angle that Powell was forced to hit it toward the boundary; and when the crowd had been driven away from that side, Lutyens would send the ball over to the other, and Shikast would slide desperately after it till his friends came down to help. It was billiards, and no football, this time—billiards in a corner pocket; and the cues were not well chalked.

"If they get us out in the middle of the ground they'll walk away from us. Dribble her along the sides," cried The Maltese Cat.

So they dribbled all along the boundary, where a pony could not come on their right-hand side; and the Archangels were furious, and the umpires had to neglect the game to shout at the people to get back, and several blundering mounted policemen tried to restore order, all close to the scrimmage, and the nerves of the Archangels' ponies stretched and broke like cobwebs.

Five or six times an Archangel hit the ball up into the middle of the ground, and each time the watchful Shikast gave Powell his chance to send it back, and after each return, when the dust had settled, men could see that the Skidars had gained a few yards.

Every now and again there were shouts of "Side! Off side!" from the spectators; but the teams were too busy to care, and the umpires had all they could do to keep their maddened ponies clear of the scuffle.

At last Lutyens missed a short easy stroke, and the Skidars had to fly back helter-skelter to protect their own goal, Shikast leading. Powell stopped the ball with a backhander when it was not fifty yards from the goal posts, and Shikast spun round with a wrench that nearly hoisted Powell out of his saddle.

"Now's our last chance," said The Cat, wheeling like a chockchafer on a pin. "We've got to ride it out. Come along."

Lutyens felt the little chap take a deep breath and, as it were, crouch under his rider. The ball was hopping toward the right-hand boundary, an Archangel riding for it with both spurs and whip; but neither spur nor whip would make his pony stretch himself as he neared the crowd. The Maltese Cat glided under his very nose, picking up his hind legs sharp, for there was not a foot to spare between his quarters and the other pony's bit. It was as neat an exhibition as fancy figure skating. Lutyens hit with all the strength he had left, but the stick slipped a little in his hand, and the ball flew off to the left instead of keeping close to the boundary. Who's Who was far across the ground, thinking hard as he galloped. He repeated stride for stride The Cat's maneuvers with another Archangel pony, nipping the ball away from under his bridle, and clearing his opponent by half a fraction of an inch, for Who's Who was clumsy behind. Then he drove away toward the right as The Maltese Cat came up from the left; and Bamboo held a middle course exactly between them. The three were making a sort of Government-broad-arrow-shaped attack; and there was only the Archangels' back to guard the goal; but immediately behind them were three Archangels racing all they knew, and mixed up with them was Powell sending Shikast along on what he felt was their last hope. It takes a very good man to stand up to the rush of seven crazy ponies in the last quarters of a Cup game, when men are riding with their necks for sale, and the ponies are delirious. The Archangels' back missed his stroke and pulled aside just in time to let the rush go by. Bamboo and Who's Who shortened stride to give The Cat room, and Lutyens got the goal with a clean, smooth, smacking stroke that was heard all over the field. But there was no stopping the ponies. They poured through the goal posts in one mixed mob, winners and losers together, for the pace had been terrific. The Maltese Cat knew by experience what would happen, and, to save Lutyens, turned to the right with one last effort that strained a back sinew beyond hope of repair. As he did so he heard the right-hand goal post crack as a pony cannoned into it—crack, splinter and fall like a mast. It had been sawed three parts through in case of accidents, but it upset the pony nevertheless, and he blundered into another, who blundered into the left-hand post, and then there was confusion and dust and wood. Bamboo was lying on the ground, seeing stars; an Archangel pony rolled beside him, breathless and angry; Shikast had sat down dog-fashion to avoid falling over the others, and was sliding along on his little bobtail in a cloud of dust; and Powell was sitting on the ground, hammering with his stick and trying to cheer. All the others were shouting at the top of what was left of their voices, and the men who had been spilled were shouting too. As soon as the people saw no one was hurt, ten thousand native and English shouted and clapped and yelled, and before anyone could stop them the pipers of the Skidars broke onto the ground, with all the native officers and men behind them, and marched up and down, playing a wild Northern tune called "Zakhme Bagán," and through the insolent blaring of the pipes and the high-pitched native yells you could hear the Archangels' band hammering, "For they are all jolly good fellows," and then reproachfully to the losing team, "Ooh, Kafoozalum! Kafoozalum! Kafoozalum!"

Besides all these things and many more, there was a Commander-in-chief, and an Inspector-General of Cavalry, and the principal veterinary officer of all India standing on the top of a regimental coach, yelling like schoolboys; and brigadiers and colonels and commissioners, and hundreds of pretty ladies joined the chorus. But The Maltese Cat stood with his head down, wondering how many legs were left to him; and Lutyens watched the men and ponies pick themselves out of the wreck of the two goal posts, and he patted The Maltese Cat very tenderly.

"I say," said the Captain of the Archangels, spitting a pebble out of his mouth, "will you take three thousand for that pony—as he stands?"

"No, thank you. I've an idea he's saved my life," said Lutyens, getting off and lying down at full length. Both teams were on the ground too, waving their boots in the air, and coughing and drawing deep breaths, as the *saises* ran up to take away the ponies, and an officious water carrier sprinkled the players with dirty water till they sat up.

"My aunt!" said Powell, rubbing his back, and looking at the stumps of the goal posts. "That was a game!"

They played it over again, every stroke of it, that night at the big dinner, when the Free-for-All Cup was filled and passed down the table, and emptied and filled again, and everybody made most eloquent speeches. About two in the morning, when there might have been some singing, a wise little, plain little, gray little head looked in through the open door.

"Hurray! Bring him in," said the Archangels; and his *sais,* who was very happy indeed, patted The Maltese Cat on the flank, and he limped in to the blaze of light and the glittering uniforms, looking for Lutyens. He was used to messes, and men's bedrooms, and places where ponies are not usually encouraged, and in his youth had jumped on and off a mess table for a bet. So he behaved himself very politely, and ate bread dipped in salt, and was petted all round the table, moving gingerly; and they drank his health, because he had done more to win the Cup than any man or horse on the ground.

That was glory and honor enough for the rest of his days, and The Maltese Cat did not complain much when the veterinary surgeon said that he would be no good for polo any more. When Lutyens married, his wife did not allow him to play, so he was forced to be an umpire; and his pony on these occasions was a flea-bitten gray with a neat polo tail, lame all round, but desperately quick on his feet, and, as everybody knew, Past Pluperfect Prestissimo Player of the Game.

THE ZEALOTS OF
CRANSTON TECH

---

by *ARCHIE OLDHAM*

(1956)

*Considering that basketball has become firmly entrenched as the American
winter-season game, there is a remarkable paucity of basketball stories. Further-
more, few of them manage to be much more than another romantic account
of how the hero went off on a record-breaking scoring spree that won the big
game and the heart of the prettiest majorette in the whole school. The humor
and dimension which make* The Zealots of Cranston Tech *a stand-out among
basketball stories undoubtedly derive from the author's intimate knowledge of
the game and its environment. Archie Oldham is a basketball coach who writes
on the side. Last winter, after several successful seasons at Oswego State
Teachers College—this is not a fictional school, by the way—Oldham was
appointed the new head coach at Columbia University.*

I T WASN'T exactly that I wanted to be an immediate hero. I hadn't
expected the college band to meet me at the station or anything.
After all, I was the one who had decided to trade big-time basketball
for the special degree in geology, so that was that. But I had counted
on *someone* being around to say hello. The third-leading scorer from
the Midwest doesn't hike himself off to a hick school like Cranston
Tech every day in the week. And no one around even to shake
hands.

The thing was, it got worse. When I reached the campus and checked in with the registrar, still nothing. Pick out any joker on the bus in Chicago or leaving a drugstore in South Bend and say, "John Yeabsley," and right away they'll tell you about the 34 points I scored against Illinois and the hook shot I beat DePaul with in that double overtime. But this Cranston Tech. No one had even heard of me. In New England, they probably think the Big Ten were the signers of the Versailles Treaty.

After a week, I went to see the coach. I'd looked up his record in one of those basketball magazines on the train. According to the magazine, he'd won only eight games in the last three years, but he was supposed to be optimistic because he had nine lettermen returning. I laughed over that for about an hour and a half. From Philadelphia to New York. Most coaches out home would have already taken the gas pipe if they had won only eight games in *one* year. But this fellow Sorenson was feeling his oats because he had nine of his world-beaters coming back for an encore. Why, if the morons had taken just eight games over all that time, they should have been stood against a wall and put out of their misery. And he was optimistic.

Anyway, I went over to see him at his office. He was stocky, with silky white hair. He put down his pen and reached across the desk, grabbing my hand in a vise. There was a loud crunch as the bones cracked. You could see from his chest and shoulders and the erect way he held himself that he had spent three quarters of his life working out with gym apparatus, and now that he was getting old he wanted to make sure everyone knew he was still hale and hearty.

"What can I do for you, son?" he asked, all business.

Here I walk into his office 6-foot-6 with a 17-point average, and he wants to know what *he* can do for *me*.

"I'm John Yeabsley," I said. I waited for a minute. "Jumping John Yeabsley," I added.

"Oh," he said, "a track man."

"Well, not exactly," I replied. "I've played some basketball. I'm a senior transfer."

"I see," he nodded, looking serious. He pursed his lips and eyed me thoughtfully. "I suppose you know we have a veteran line-up back this year, all used to my brand of play."

"You must be loaded," I said.

"But don't let it discourage you," he put in generously. "You're welcome to try out for the team as long as you understand I can't carry any deadwood. There's always the intramural league."

I walked out into the hall in sort of a daze. No one had ever talked to me like that before. Deadwood yet. I was just getting my bearings when someone came flying around the corner of the corridor at me, her books and papers sailing all over in the collision, some blond hair right in the middle of everything.

I went for my knee, the one that slips out sometimes, but I could feel that it was all right.

"I guess I'm still John Yeabsley, single and available evenings," I said, looking up. I gave her the smile my sister calls my wholesome, I'll-mow-the-wheat-today-Father smile.

She giggled. She was a real towhead, tall and flushed from the outdoors, and her giggle wasn't a silly one, but the kind of intelligent giggle that girls with nice straight noses have.

"I'm awfully sorry I ran you down, and I'm still Isabelle Sorenson," she replied brightly. She was standing there smiling back and not at all worried about her books lying around. "Are you going to be on Daddy's basketball team?" she asked.

"That's the sixty-four-thousand-dollar question," I answered. "Daddy doesn't seem to be staking his life on it." I began picking up the debris. "Say, how's for a little knife-and-fork scrimmage tonight, Isabelle? While we have dinner, you can teach me about basketball."

"You're tall enough to get rebounds for Daddy," the girl mused, ignoring my question. She was still smiling, though. "Penobscot can hurt us underneath."

"This can't be my day to win over the Sorensons," I sighed. "I suppose if I make All-American, you'll wave to me from the stands."

"You're not doing so badly," she grinned, taking her things and starting down the hall. "I'll be watching the tryouts!"

There were a few things that were different about the tryouts at Cranston Tech. First, we didn't do any actual playing. Not even half-court scrimmage. To tell the truth, we didn't even do any shooting. You see, there weren't any balls.

The first day I walked out on the court I saw most of the fellows jogging around taking laps and doing push-ups in the middle of the floor. I walked over to the manager, who was sitting in the stands. He was a young kid wearing a freshman cap.

"Has someone gone for the balls?" I said.

"What?" he asked.

"The balls," I repeated. "Where are the practice balls?"

"Oh, we don't use any until the cuts are made," the kid answered.

"Look, Son," I snapped, "if you're going to be lazy, you'll never make the grade here. Now go pump up some balls."

The boy looked scared. "Honest, I can't do it," he insisted. "Coach Sorenson would have my scalp if I threw out any balls today."

I marched over to Wally Lang, the captain. He was busy doing push-ups.

"Wally," I said, "I'm itching to get started. Where do they keep the ammunition?"

"Now just hold your horses, John," he replied. He got up. "There'll be plenty of balls out here as soon as you make the team."

"But how can I show you what I can do without a ball?" I exploded.

"You'll see," Wally said, doing a deep knee-bend. "You'll see."

I saw. Coach Sorenson finally came out on the court carrying a big box. The manager helped him put it down and then they began handing out ropes to everyone there. They all started skipping rope.

"I'm not very good at this," I said to Wally. Wally was skipping away like a whiz.

"Well, you'd better be," Wally advised, skipping along smoothly. "This is the coach's rebound test."

"His rebound test!" I said, getting the rope all tangled up around my feet and ankles. "Suppose you can rebound, but you can't skip rope?"

"Oh, it doesn't work that way," Wally explained, never missing his timing. "The coach's tests are foolproof. You can depend on them."

"I wish you could say as much for the coach's teams," I replied, losing my balance and stumbling backward.

When we put the ropes back in the box, I peeked at a big, typewritten sheet the manager was keeping for old man Sorenson. Next to my name was the entry: *Rebounding—extremely poor.*

The next one was a real corker. It was the coach's reflex test. They put three teacups behind you on the floor and gave you a penny. One teacup was white, one was red, and one was blue. The manager would call out one of the three colors and you were expected to wheel and drop the penny in the right cup like a flash. They had a stop watch to clock your speed. To tell the truth, I couldn't wheel and drop the penny in *any* of the cups at any speed. There's just something about standing out in the middle of a basketball court and trying to drop a penny in the right-colored teacup that doesn't appeal to me. Even if I could do it, I wouldn't like it.

Out of 47 teacup candidates, I trailed the field by a wide margin.

By 5:30, after four more foolproof tests, I trailed the field by the widest of all wide margins.

I was just trudging off the court for the locker room when I spied Isabelle over in the stands.

"If they use teacups for baskets at Penobscot, I'm licked," I said, sitting down on the railing.

"After the cuts, that may be an academic question," she laughed. But she said it in a nice way, and now she was looking at me very closely. That is, she was looking me *over,* sizing me up. I felt embarrassed.

"I had a cousin who could grow warts when he wanted," I said.

"You've got nice definition," she replied.

"What?" I asked.

"Your muscles," she said. "Your legs have especially good tone to them. It's just your deltoids. They're very weak."

I looked around to see if anyone was still in the gym.

"Your deltoids are up here," she explained, smiling and putting her hands on my shoulders. "Right along here." She ran her hands along the top of my shoulders. Her fingers were strong.

"Say, that's all right," I said, closing my eyes and getting into the swing of things. "How come you learned all this?"

"Oh, I had to," said Isabelle. "I teach health education down at the high school."

"What do you think of those muscles behind my neck?" I asked. "Right . . . right . . . there! Those right there." Brother, did that feel good.

"Very weak," Isabelle said in a low voice. She was pretty close now with her arms around my shoulders and didn't have to speak too loud. "Very, very weak," she whispered. Suddenly she pulled up. "I'll give you some exercises, and in a few days we can start on light dumbbells," she announced brightly.

That brought me to. "Hey, hold on, now!" I said in alarm. "I mean, it's not that I wouldn't want to have stronger deltoid muscles and work with light dumbbells or anything. Don't think that. It's just— well, I don't want to get tight for basketball!"

She patted my cheek. "Don't worry about a thing, poor John. I'm afraid that's not going to be a problem at all."

She was right. I was cut from the squad the next day. The coach was pretty nice about it, though. He took me over into a corner where no one could hear.

"John," he said, looking grave, "I want to commend you for your spirit in trying out for the team. It takes a lot of courage for those of us with meager ability to compete with the advanced few. However, we may as well face the fact here and now—you'll never make a basketball player."

"I'm not much with teacups, either," I said.

"You'll get a world of benefit out of the intramural program," he promised.

I looked at him. The whole thing was so absurd it wasn't worth bothering about. But at the same time, I could feel a rising irritation stir inside me.

"Coach Sorenson," I protested, "you just don't know about my background. Let me explain . . ."

"There's no need to explain, John," he said reassuringly. "Some of us have the ability and receive the right kind of coaching early. Others, like yourself, never get the chance." He reached out and grabbed me by the hand. "All the more credit that you gave all you had." He gave all *he* had, and there was a pathetic crack just before my fingers lost their feeling.

I was still soaking my hand under the hot water in the shower when Wally came in. "Too bad, John," he said. "Thanks for giving it a try anyway, fella."

"Oh, well, I came here for the studies and not the basketball," I said truthfully enough. "Besides, I've picked up another extracurricular interest in the meantime."

"I hope it's not Isabelle Sorenson," Wally said.

"What do you mean?"

"I mean you better stay away from her," said Wally. "First thing you know, she'll be inviting you over for a home-cooked meal."

"She already has," I said. "Tonight."

"Well, you'd better call it off while you can. For your own good, steer clear."

"She seems awfully friendly," I said, excited.

"I know all about it," he replied. "She gets you over there alone for the home-cooked meal. It seems innocent enough."

"She's nice and tall," I said, turning the shower to cold and jumping around. I was pretty keyed up.

"All right," sighed Wally, "but don't forget that I warned you."

I arrived at Isabelle's a half-hour early. She was in a soft green sweater and slacks and moccasins. She was wearing perfume, and her blond hair looked lovely on her shoulders against the green sweater.

She was solicitous about my being dropped from the team. She took my arm and leaned close as we went back to the kitchen. All the frustration of the afternoon was melting away. She had set table out in the kitchen and I sat down at my place rubbing my hands, suddenly hungry.

Isabelle opened the icebox and took out a tall glass of some strange liquid and set it down in front of me. I sniffed at it.

"Hey, what is this stuff?" I asked, grinning.

"Turnip juice," Isabelle answered.

"You're kidding," I said, amused.

"It's packed with vitamins," she replied.

"That's nice," I said easily, "but I don't happen to care for turnips. Let's throw in a substitute from the bench."

Isabelle shook her head. "If we're to start on those light dumbbells soon, you have to eat a nutritious diet."

"All right, then," I said, a slight edge in my voice, "what's wrong with orange juice or tomato juice? The point is, I don't *want* turnip juice!"

"Try it and you'll like it," she said, turning away.

I was losing some of my good humor, but it seemed like a fool thing to make an issue of. I choked down the awful slop. I was just beginning to feel ill, when Isabelle wheeled up with the next course. It was a deep dish.

"Lamb stew?" I said hopefully.

"No," she answered, "beef hearts, calves' brains, and kidney stew."

"What!" I said, starting to get up.

"None of us eat enough organ meats," Isabelle put in quickly, "and they're so tasty once we get used to them. See how good!" She had begun spooning out the steaming entrails on my plate.

I put down my napkin. "What had you fixed for dessert?" I asked very quietly.

"A pie," she replied, noticing the change in my voice. She looked nervous.

"What sort of pie?" I continued.

"A nice pie," Isabelle said, backing away.

"What *kind?*"

"A liver-and-lung pie," she said in panic, as I pushed aside my chair. "With blackstrap molasses sauce!" she raced. "You'd think it was a mince pie it tastes so good! Really, Johnny, you'll—"

"I believe I can find my own coat," I said evenly. I marched out to the hall closet, Isabelle running after me. "No wonder Wally warned me away! You try to convert anyone you can get your nutritious, dumbbell-strengthened hands on."

"But it's different in your case, Johnny!" she pleaded, close to tears. "Wally's on the team; I'm interested in you because—because I'm fond of you!"

For a moment, I almost weakened. She looked very cute standing there with the little apron over her slacks, still holding the bubbling stew in front of her and getting ready to cry.

But reason prevailed. "If you're fond of me, it would only be worse," I sighed, pulling on my overcoat. "Let's face it once and for all, Isabelle—you and your father are zealots. There's only one way to do anything: the Sorenson way." I opened the front door. "Well, the fads and the formulas won't work on me. I'm too much of an individualist!"

"It's not fair to call Daddy a zealot just because you can't play basketball!" she wailed in a high, squeaky voice.

That did it. Holding myself erect, I strode into the night, promptly ramming my head against the top of the doorway.

"Oh, your poor head!" Isabelle cried, starting after me.

"And you're not going to change the shape of my head, either!" I shouted, feeling for the bump. I had several other things to say, too, but the turnip juice was starting to act up again, and I rushed down the front walk before my role as individualist became further jaded by a state of complete nausea.

After that, I wasn't too happy at Cranston. It gets pretty cold and windy in New England around December and January. A lot of snow, also. My marks got better and better, but my morale was way down. I was the only one on campus over the Christmas holidays. Even old man Sorenson and Isabelle took off. They flew down to Florida for two weeks, and Isabelle came back with her nice, straight nose all suntanned.

The basketball team charged through January undefeated. I stopped off at a few of the home games and found out why. The schools we played were all pretty small and the material was as mediocre as our own. Then I started dropping around to our practices. It was a stupid thing to do, but I couldn't help myself. I had a lot of spare time and my last year of college was passing by and I was homesick for the game I'd been raised on.

The worst part of Sorenson's practice sessions were the shooting drills. Rightly, Sorenson figured that if the ball had a nice arch on it, its chances of going in the basket were increased. An extremist to the end, though, he carried the idea one step further. Wrongly, he figured the higher you could propel the ball upward, the surer you were to score each time. It was quite something to watch when all his boys started shooting together. Their arms were so high in the air on the follow-through it looked like a mass ascension of Mount Everest.

Three days before the Penobscot game, one of the forwards twisted his ankle in scrimmage. Some of the others on the squad were tied up with exams, and only nine men were left on the floor.

One minute I was sitting there in my old suntans and sneakers watching, and the next I was out on the court. I don't know how I got there; it just happened.

The coach looked up, startled. Then he realized who I was. "Sorry, John," he said, shaking his head, "but I couldn't do it. You might be injured."

Wally came over. "We sure need the practice, Coach," he said. "We'd be careful not to hurt him."

Old man Sorenson was biting his lip.

"I'll chance it because the Penobscot game is bigger than any of us," I vowed, getting into the spirit of things.

The coach turned with that look in his eye, but before he could mangle me with a grateful handshake, I raced off to the other end of the court.

We played for five minutes before anyone even looked my way. I guess they thought if they passed the ball, I'd try to eat it or something. Anyway, when they finally took the plunge, this big football player, Abernathy, was guarding me. I gave a little head feint and the pigskin kid went up 10 feet in the air. He must have thought he was blocking that kick. I drove around to the right hard, someone else picked me up, I changed direction shaking him, too, and banked in a running left-hand hook high off the backboard.

There was quite a silence. Everyone stopped and stood where they were. Wally looked over at the coach with his mouth open. The coach fumbled in his jacket and came out with a pair of silver-rimmed glasses.

The next time down, you could see old hit-the-line Abernathy steeling himself to play it cagey. You couldn't fake him out of his uniform more than a dozen times. So I changed up a little. I gave him the long, driving step to the right, and he fell back fast to stop me from going around again. Only thing, I wasn't going around again, but faking. I snapped back to set position, and he knew he was a goner unless he rushed up fast. So *now* I gave the head feint, and it was an impressive thing to see, Abernathy taking to the air like a great bird. I let him sail by, and then I drove in and layed it up.

They stopped the practice.

Old man Sorenson walked over to me stiffly like a man in a dream. He put both his hands on my shoulders. "All this time," he said. His voice almost broke. "All this time on your own—you've been practicing!"

I nearly had a stitch. He really thought I'd gone off alone and transformed myself into a polished basketball player by sheer will power.

He dismissed the whole team. Then he took me by the arm and led me up the stairs to the auxiliary gym.

"You see that rope we have up there?" he said, pointing at the ceiling. About 30 feet above there was a hemp rope stretched from wall to wall. "I want you to spend the rest of the afternoon shooting at the far basket, but all your shots must go over that rope. This is the scientific way I develop the Sorenson arch."

"That's a wonderful idea," I said, looking away from the rope. I was getting a little dizzy. "I'm afraid it won't work for me, though. I mean, I don't think my arms are strong enough."

"You'll get it, John," the coach grinned, supremely confident. After all, he'd seen me work a miracle already. "Stick with it, boy, and you'll get it."

By six o'clock when the janitor came around to close, it was obvious that if I was ever to develop the Sorenson arch, the balls would have to be pumped up with helium. The coach's spirits sagged to an all-time low. You could see how he was thinking. His way to shoot was the only sure way, so how could he gamble with me in the most important game of the year? I was an unorthodox freak who'd made a few lucky plays in a scrimmage.

I was on the squad, though, and it felt pretty good to be handed a uniform again. They were taking me down to Penobscot, too. I decided to come all the way out of my cocoon. I called up Isabelle.

"Hello?" she said.

"Hello, Isabelle," I said. "This is John. John Yeabsley."

"Oh," she said.

"How's tricks?"

"Do you wish to speak to my father?" she asked.

"What's the matter? You don't sound too happy."

"I'm all right," she said. "I'm just not speaking to you, that's all."

"Sure you are," I said. "I'm calling to tell you I forgive you."

"Good-by."

"Hey, hold on there!" I shouted. "What I mean is, I'm ready to compromise. If you'll give in on the turnip juice, I'll take a crack at that other junk. And even the light dumbbell exercises. Now, you can't ask for much more than that, can you?"

"Are you finished?" she said coolly. This certainly wasn't the old, carefree Isabelle I'd barged into in the hall that day.

"I guess so," I said, "but I don't understand. It was all right when I didn't make the team in the beginning; now that I'm finally on it, you're angry."

"You just didn't have the ability in the tryouts," Isabelle explained shortly. "Now you've developed the ability, but you're too stubborn and pigheaded to learn Daddy's foolproof way of shooting and help the school. Well, I hope you'll be very happy watching the game from the bench, Mister Know-it-all! You—you—individualist!"

As soon as we took the court at Penobscot for lay-ups, we felt that something was wrong. You couldn't put your finger on it, but we all sensed it. Penobscot's new field house was beautiful. The floor felt good under us, and the stands, already packed to the rafters, were set far enough back from the outside lines. The length of the court was fine, too. But, still, something was different.

Then the manager threw out the balls for shooting warm-up, and it happened. All the shots. Not one of them went in. Not one of them ever reached the basket. It was the ceiling of the new field house. It was too low. Or at least it was too low for the Sorenson arch. And that was all our gang had been using for four years. Every shot they took caromed off the ceiling and fell dismally short.

The first four minutes of the game were a nightmare. Our whole team was jittery. Wally threw two passes away, and George Abernathy fell all over his own feet trying a dribble.

At 12-0, we called time out.

"Coach, you know what you have to do?" Wally shouted. The Penobscot stands were going wild yelling, "Roll-it-up! Roll-it-up!" and pounding their feet on the new stands of the new field house.

"I'm going to write the rules committee about this low ceiling!" the coach shouted back.

"No," said Wally, "you have to put John in."

I got up and started to take off my warm-up pants.

"I don't know," the coach said. He was awfully nervous. "He's untested in competition."

"It's our only chance," Wally said. "He's the only one who can shoot here!"

I went over and reported to the scorer's table and came back.

"It's too much pressure to put on his shoulders," the coach was arguing. He looked pretty panicky.

"Coach," I said, "I'm already in the game. Now you just go on back to your seat and enjoy yourself."

As a matter of fact, I was a little cold at first. I missed my first two shots. Old man Sorenson had his head in his hands over on the bench. Then I began to click. I banged away on a couple of jump shots and a one-hand push from behind the circle. I got down on a fast break, driving all the way in for a lay-up, and when I was hit from behind, I made it a three-point play.

After that, the game broke open. They came out to pick me up early, so I went to the head feints and the drives. By the end of the half, they had two men playing me, and I started feeding off to Wally or anyone else who was free.

In the dressing room, the coach was jumping all over. His hand was shaking as he held the scoring book. He'd never had anyone score 27 points in a whole game before; I'd done it in less than a half.

He was still full of the jitters, though. Just before we went out again, he tried to sober us up.

"A nineteen-point lead is nothing against a team as strong as Penobscot," he said, pacing up and down. "They have poise and spirit and a world of bench strength. They're the kind of ball club that likes to be behind by nineteen points at the half."

Everyone was quiet. "Coach," I said, "wish them a lot of luck."

I almost didn't go to practice Monday. I'd caught a little cold riding down Main Street with the mayor in that open car. Then, I'd been out late with Isabelle Sunday night. But at the last minute, I decided to go. It might look as though I were pulling rank if I didn't show up.

I got into my sweat suit and started down the hall to the main gym. There was an awful racket going on in there. A lot of banging and sawing and hammering. I went through the door. Coach Sorenson was standing out in the middle of the court with some carpenters. They were just finishing the framework of what looked like a giant wooden tower with steps. It went almost to the ceiling.

"Surprise, John," the coach said, a twinkle in his eye. "This is all for you!" He pointed at the structure.

"It's *what?*"

"I should have thought of it from the start," he explained easily. "We have to correct your bad shooting habits gradually. So, we put you at the top of the ladder here and let you shoot your normal way for a while. Then, each day, we bring you down one step at a time, adding a little more arch as you go. When you reach the floor in a week, you'll have a foolproof Cranston shot."

I began to laugh and then I stopped, and then I just wanted to sit down and hold on to something.

"Mr. Sorenson," I said finally, "I'm afraid I'll never understand you. I just got finished scoring forty-three points in the big game of the year. The mayor of Cranston presented me with the keys to the city. Your daughter even promised to let me eat what I want from now on. Do you mean to tell me you still want to change my shooting?"

"But don't you see?" Sorenson said eagerly, grabbing me by the arm. "If you can score forty-three points the wrong way, think how many you can get when you learn to do it right!"

I picked up a ball and went over to the tower. Just as I was going up, I heard someone calling my name. Isabelle was running across the court toward me, clattering in her high heels. She looked all right running up out of breath and bright-eyed with my pin on her sweater.

I came down a step. "Take this before you begin, Johnny," she whispered, reaching up and giving my hand a squeeze. Then I realized she was slipping something to me. I opened my palm and looked. It was a yeast cake.

"It's good for your pituitary gland," she said fondly.

I drew in a deep breath. In the Midwest, they teach you to accept defeat stoically.

"If there's anything I ever wanted," I said, starting back up the ladder with the basketball in one hand and the yeast cake in the other, "it's a foolproof pituitary gland."

YOU COULD LOOK IT UP

———◆———

by *JAMES THURBER*

(1941)

James Thurber, who often dips into the world of fantasy in his stories and books, was doing so when he wrote this wild baseball yarn in 1941. Ten years passed, and on August 19, 1951, Mr. Thurber suddenly appeared to be clair-voyant, for the St. Louis Browns actually bobbed up with a midget in their line-up, to bat against the Detroit Tigers! It turned out to be more farce than fantasy. In any case, if you haven't been introduced before, meet all thirty-five inches of one of the most amusing characters in sports fiction, Pearl du Monville.

IT ALL BEGUN when we dropped down to C'lumbus, Ohio, from Pitts-burgh to play a exhibition game on our way out to St. Louis. It was gettin' on into September, and though we'd been leadin' the league by six, seven games most of the season, we was now in first place by a margin you could 'a' got it into the eye of a thimble, bein' only a half a game ahead of St. Louis. Our slump had given the boys the leapin' jumps, and they was like a bunch a old ladies at a lawn fete with a thunderstorm comin' up, runnin' around snarlin' at each other, eatin' bad and sleepin' worse, and battin' for a team average of maybe .186. Half the time nobody'd speak to nobody else, without it was to bawl 'em out.

Squawks Magrew was managin' the boys at the time, and he was darn near crazy. They called him "Squawks" 'cause when things was goin' bad he lost his voice, or perty near lost it, and squealed at you like a little girl you stepped on her doll or somethin'. He yelled at everybody and wouldn't listen to nobody, without maybe it was me. I'd been trainin' the boys for ten year, and he'd take more lip from me than from anybody else. He knowed I was smarter'n him, anyways, like you're goin' to hear.

This was thirty, thirty-one year ago; you could look it up, 'cause it was the same year C'lumbus decided to call itself the Arch City, on account of a lot of iron arches with electric-light bulbs into 'em which stretched acrost High Street. Thomas Albert Edison sent 'em a telegram, and they was speeches and maybe even President Taft opened the celebration by pushin' a button. It was a great week for the Buckeye capital, which was why they got us out there for this exhibition game.

Well, we just lose a double-header to Pittsburgh, 11 to 5 and 7 to 3, so we snarled all the way to C'lumbus, where we put up at the Chittaden Hotel, still snarlin'. Everybody was tetchy, and when Billy Klinger took a sock at Whitey Cott at breakfast, Whitey throwed marmalade all over his face.

"Blind each other, whatta I care?" says Magrew. "You can't see nothin' anyways."

C'lumbus win the exhibition game, 3 to 2, whilst Magrew set in the dugout, mutterin' and cursin' like a fourteen-year-old Scotty. He bad-mouthed everybody on the ball club and he bad-mouthed everybody offa the ball club, includin' the Wright brothers, who, he claimed, had yet to build a airship big enough for any of our boys to hit it with a ball bat.

"I wisht I was dead," he says to me. "I wisht I was in heaven with the angels."

I told him to pull hisself together, 'cause he was drivin' the boys crazy, the way he was goin' on, sulkin' and bad-mouthin' and whinin'. I was older'n he was and smarter'n he was, and he knowed it. I was ten times smarter'n he was about this Pearl du Monville, first time I ever laid eyes on the little guy, which was one of the saddest days of my life.

Now, most people name of Pearl is girls, but this Pearl du Monville was a man, if you could call a fella a man who was only thirty-four, thirty-five inches high. Pearl du Monville was a midget. He was part French and part Hungarian, and maybe even part Bulgarian or somethin'. I can see him now, a sneer on his little pushed-in pan, swingin' a bamboo cane and smokin' a big cigar. He had a gray suit with a big black check into it, and he had a gray felt hat with one of them rainbow-colored hatbands onto it, like the young fellas wore in them days. He talked like he was talkin' into a tin can, but he didn't have no foreign accent. He might 'a' been fifteen or he might 'a' been a hundred, you couldn't tell. Pearl du Monville.

After the game with C'lumbus, Magrew headed straight for the Chittaden bar—the train for St. Louis wasn't goin' for three, four hours—and there he set, drinkin' rye and talkin' to this bartender.

"How I pity me, brother," Magrew was tellin' this bartender. "How I pity me." That was alwuz his favorite tune. So he was settin' there, tellin' this bartender how heartbreakin' it was to be manager of a bunch of blindfolded circus clowns, when up pops this Pearl du Monville outa nowheres.

It give Magrew the leapin' jumps. He thought at first maybe the D.T.s had come back on him; he claimed he'd had 'em once, and little guys had popped up all around him, wearin' red, white and blue hats.

"Go on, now!" Magrew yells. "Get away from me!"

But the midget clumb up on a chair acrost the table from Magrew and says, "I seen that game today, Junior, and you ain't got no ball club. What you got there, Junior," he says, "is a side show."

"Whatta ya mean, 'Junior'?" says Magrew, touchin' the little guy to satisfy hisself he was real.

"Don't pay him no attention, mister," says the bartender. "Pearl calls everybody 'Junior,' 'cause it alwuz turns out he's a year older'n anybody else."

"Yeh?" says Magrew. "How old is he?"

"How old are you, Junior?" says the midget.

"Who, me? I'm fifty-three," says Magrew.

"Well, I'm fifty-four," says the midget.

Magrew grins and asts him what he'll have, and that was the beginnin' of their beautiful friendship, if you don't care what you say.

Pearl du Monville stood up on his chair and waved his cane around and pretended like he was ballyhooin' for a circus. "Right this way, folks!" he yells. "Come on in and see the greatest collection of freaks in the world! See the armless pitchers, see the eyeless batters, see the infielders with five thumbs!" and on and on like that, feedin' Magrew gall and handin' him a laugh at the same time, you might say.

You could hear him and Pearl du Monville hootin' and hollerin' and singin' way up to the fourth floor of the Chittaden, where the boys was packin' up. When it come time to go to the station, you can imagine how disgusted we was when we crowded into the doorway of that bar and seen them two singin' and goin' on.

"Well, well, well," says Magrew, lookin' up and spottin' us. "Look who's here. . . . Clowns, this is Pearl du Monville, a monseer of the old, old school. . . . Don't shake hands with 'em, Pearl, 'cause their fingers is made of chalk and would bust right off in your paws," he says, and he starts guffawin' and Pearl starts titterin' and we stand there givin' 'em the iron eye, it bein' the lowest ebb a ball-club manager'd got hisself down to since the national pastime was started.

Then the midget begun givin' us the ballyhoo. "Come on in!" he says, wavin' his cane. "See the legless base runners, see the outfielders with the butter fingers, see the southpaw with the arm of a little chee-ild!"

Then him and Magrew begun to hoop and holler and nudge each other till you'd of thought this little guy was the funniest guy than even Charlie Chaplin. The fellas filed outa the bar without a word and went on up to the Union Depot, leavin' me to handle Magrew and his new-found crony.

Well, I got 'em outa there finely. I had to take the little guy along, 'cause Magrew had a holt onto him like a vise and I couldn't pry him loose.

"He's comin' along as masket," says Magrew, holdin' the midget in the crouch of his arm like a football. And come along he did, hollerin' and protestin' and beatin' at Magrew with his little fists.

"Cut it out, will ya, Junior?" the little guy kept whinin'. "Come on, leave a man loose, will ya, Junior?"

But Junior kept a holt onto him and begun yellin', "See the guys with the glass arm, see the guys with the cast-iron brains, see the fielders with the feet on their wrists!"

So it goes, right through the whole Union Depot, with people starin' and catcallin', and he don't put the midget down till he gets him through the gates.

"How'm I goin' to go along without no toothbrush?" the midget asts. "What'm I goin' to do without no other suit?" he says.

"Doc here," says Magrew, meanin' me—"doc here will look after you like you was his own son, won't you, doc?"

I give him the iron eye, and he finely got on the train and prob'ly went to sleep with his clothes on.

This left me alone with the midget. "Lookit," I says to him. "Why don't you go on home now? Come mornin', Magrew'll forget all about you. He'll prob'ly think you was somethin' he seen in a nightmare maybe. And he ain't goin' to laugh so easy in the mornin', neither," I says. "So why don't you go on home?"

"Nix," he says to me. "Skiddoo," he says, "twenty-three for you," and he tosses his cane up into the vestibule of the coach and clam'ers on up after it like a cat. So that's the way Pearl du Monville come to go to St. Louis with the ball club.

I seen 'em first at breakfast the next day, settin' opposite each other; the midget playin' "Turkey in the Straw" on a harmonium and Magrew starin' at his eggs and bacon like they was a uncooked bird with its feathers still on.

"Remember where you found this?" I says, jerkin' my thumb at the midget. "Or maybe you think they come with breakfast on these trains," I says, bein' a good hand at turnin' a sharp remark in them days.

The midget puts down the harmonium and turns on me. "Sneeze," he says; "your brains is dusty." Then he snaps a couple drops of water at me from a tumbler. "Drown," he says, tryin' to make his voice deep.

Now, both them cracks is Civil War cracks, but you'd of thought they was brand-new and the funniest than any crack Magrew'd ever heard in his whole life. He started hoopin' and hollerin', and the midget started hoopin' and hollerin', so I walked on away and set down with Bugs Courtney and Hank Metters, payin' no attention to this weak-minded Damon and Phidias acrost the aisle.

Well, sir, the first game with St. Louis was rained out, and there we was facin' a double-header next day. Like maybe I told you, we lose the last three double-headers we play, makin' maybe twenty-five errors in the six games, which is all right for the intimates of a school for the blind, but is disgraceful for the world's champions. It was too wet to go to the zoo, and Magrew wouldn't let us go to the movies, 'cause they flickered so bad in them days. So we just set around, stewin' and frettin'.

One of the newspaper boys come over to take a pitture of Billy Klinger and Whitey Cott shakin' hands—this reporter'd heard about the fight—and whilst they was standin' there, toe to toe, shakin' hands, Billy give a back lunge and a jerk, and throwed Whitey over his shoulder into a corner of the room, like a sack a salt. Whitey come back at him with a chair, and Bethlehem broke loose in that there room. The camera was tromped to pieces like a berry basket. When we finely got 'em pulled apart, I heard a laugh, and there was Magrew and the midget standin' in the door and givin' us the iron eye.

"Wrasslers," says Magrew, cold-like, "that's what I got for a ball club, Mr. du Monville, wrasslers—and not very good wrasslers at that, you ast me."

"A man can't be good at everythin'," says Pearl, "but he oughta be good at somethin'."

This sets Magrew guffawin' again, and away they go, the midget taggin' along by his side like a hound dog and handin' him a fast line of so-called comic cracks.

When we went out to face that battlin' St. Louis club in a double-header the next afternoon, the boys was jumpy as tin toys with keys in their back. We lose the first game, 7 to 2, and are trailin', 4 to 0, when the second game ain't but ten minutes old. Magrew set there like a stone statue, speakin' to nobody. Then, in their half a the fourth, somebody singled to center and knocked in two more runs for St. Louis.

That made Magrew squawk. "I wisht one thing," he says. "I wisht I was manager of a old ladies' sewin' circus 'stead of a ball club."

"You are, Junior, you are," says a familyer and disagreeable voice.

It was that Pearl du Monville again, poppin' up outa nowheres, swingin' his bamboo cane and smokin' a cigar that's three sizes too big for his face. By this time we'd finely got the other side out, and Hank Metters slithered a bat acrost the ground, and the midget had to jump to keep both his ankles from bein' broke.

I thought Magrew'd bust a blood vessel. "You hurt Pearl and I'll break your neck!" he yelled.

Hank muttered somethin' and went on up to the plate and struck out.

We managed to get a couple runs acrost in our half a the sixth, but they come back with three more in their half a the seventh, and this was too much for Magrew.

"Come on, Pearl," he says. "We're gettin' outa here."

"Where you think you're goin'?" I ast him.

"To the lawyer's again," he says cryptly.

"I didn't know you'd been to the lawyer's once, yet," I says.

"Which that goes to show how much you don't know," he says.

With that, they was gone, and I didn't see 'em the rest of the day, nor know what they was up to, which was a God's blessin'. We lose the nightcap, 9 to 3, and that puts us into second place plenty, and as low in our mind as a ball club can get.

The next day was a horrible day, like anybody that lived through it can tell you. Practice was just over and the St. Louis club was takin' the field, when I hears this strange sound from the stands. It sounds like the nervous whickerin' a horse gives when he smells somethin' funny on the wind. It was the fans ketchin' sight of Pearl du Monville, like you have prob'ly guessed. The midget had popped up onto the field all dressed up in a minacher club uniform, sox, cap, little letters sewed onto his chest, and all. He was swingin' a kid's bat and the only thing kept him from lookin' like a real ballplayer seen through the wrong end of a microscope was this cigar he was smokin'.

Bugs Courtney reached over and jerked it outa his mouth and throwed it away. "You're wearin' that suit on the playin' field," he says to him, severe as a judge. "You go insultin' it and I'll take you out to the zoo and feed you to the bears."

Pearl just blowed some smoke at him which he still has in his mouth.

Whilst Whitey was foulin' off four or five prior to strikin' out, I went on over to Magrew. "If I was as comic as you," I says, "I'd laugh myself to death," I says. "Is that any way to treat the uniform, makin' a mockery out of it?"

"It might surprise you to know I ain't makin' no mockery outa the uniform," says Magrew. "Pearl du Monville here has been made a bone-of-fida member of this so-called ball club. I fixed it up with the front office by long-distance phone."

"Yeh?" I says. "I can just hear Mr. Dillworth or Bart Jenkins agreein' to hire a midget for the ball club. I can just hear 'em." Mr. Dillworth was the owner of the club and Bart Jenkins was the secretary, and they never stood for no monkey business. "May I be so bold as to inquire," I says, "just what you told 'em?"

"I told 'em," he says, "I wanted to sign up a guy they ain't no pitcher in the league can strike him out."

"Uh-huh," I says, "and did you tell 'em what size of a man he is?"

"Never mind about that," he says. "I got papers on me, made out legal and proper, constitutin' one Pearl du Monville a bone-of-fida member of this former ball club. Maybe that'll shame them big babies into gettin' in there and swingin', knowin' I can replace any one of 'em with a midget, if I have a mind to. A St. Louis lawyer I seen twice tells me it's all legal and proper."

"A St. Louis lawyer would," I says, "seein' nothin' could make him happier than havin' you makin' a mockery outa this one-time baseball outfit," I says.

Well, sir, it'll all be there in the papers of thirty, thirty-one year ago, and you could look it up. The game went along without no scorin' for seven innings, and since they ain't nothin' much to watch but guys poppin' up or strikin' out, the fans pay most of their attention to the goin's-on of Pearl du Monville. He's out there in front a the dugout, turnin' handsprings, balancin' his bat on his chin, walkin' a imaginary line, and so on. The fans clapped and laughed at him, and he ate it up.

So it went up to the last a the eighth, nothin' to nothin', not more'n seven, eight hits all told, and no errors on neither side. Our pitcher gets the first two men out easy in the eighth. Then up come a fella name of Porter or Billings, or some such name, and he lammed one up against the tobacco sign for three bases. The next guy up slapped the first ball out into left for a base hit, and in come the fella from third for the only run of the ball game so far. The crowd yelled, the look a death come onto Magrew's face again, and even the midget quit his tomfoolin'. Their next man fouled out back a third, and we come up for our last bats like a bunch a schoolgirls steppin' into a pool of cold water. I was lower in my mind than I'd been since the day in nineteen-four when Chesbro throwed the wild pitch in the ninth inning with a man on third and lost the pennant for the Highlanders. I knowed something just as bad was goin' to happen, which shows I'm a clairvoyun, or was then.

When Gordy Mills hit out to second, I just closed my eyes. I opened 'em up again to see Dutch Muller standin' on second, dustin' off his pants, him havin' got his first hit in maybe twenty times to the plate. Next up was Harry Loesing, battin' for our pitcher, and he got a base on balls, walkin' on a fourth one you could 'a' combed your hair with.

Then up come Whitey Cott, our lead-off man. He crotches down in what was prob'ly the most fearsome stanch in organized ball, but all he can do is pop out to short. That brung up Billy Klinger, with two down and a man on first and second. Billy took a cut at one you

could 'a' knocked a plug hat offa this here Carnera with it, but then
he gets sense enough to wait 'em out, and finely he walks, too, fillin'
the bases.

Yes, sir, there you are; the tyin' run on third and the winnin' run
on second, first a the ninth, two men down, and Hank Metters comin'
to the bat. Hank was built like a Pope-Hartford and he couldn't run
no faster'n President Taft, but he had five home runs to his credit for
the season, and that wasn't bad in them days. Hank was still hittin'
better'n anybody else on the ball club, and it was mighty heartenin',
seein' him stridin' up toward the plate. But he never got there.

"Wait a minute!" yells Magrew, jumpin' to his feet. "I'm sendin' in
a pinch hitter!" he yells.

You could 'a' heard a bomb drop. When a ball-club manager says
he's sendin' in a pinch hitter for the best batter on the club, you know
and I know and everybody knows he's lost his holt.

"They're goin' to be sendin' the funny wagon for you, if you don't
watch out," I says, grabbin' a holt of his arm.

But he pulled away and ran out toward the plate, yellin', "Du Monville battin' for Metters!"

All the fellas begun squawlin' at once, except Hank, and he just
stood there starin' at Magrew like he'd gone crazy and was claimin'
to be Ty Cobb's grandma or somethin'. Their pitcher stood out there
with his hands on his hips and a disagreeable look on his face, and
the plate umpire told Magrew to go on and get a batter up. Magrew
told him again Du Monville was battin' for Metters, and the St. Louis
manager finely got the idea. It brung him outa his dugout, howlin' and
bawlin' like he'd lost a female dog and her seven pups.

Magrew pushed the midget toward the plate and he says to him,
he says, "Just stand up there and hold that bat on your shoulder.
They ain't a man in the world can throw three strikes in there 'fore
he throws four balls!" he says.

"I get it, Junior!" says the midget. "He'll walk me and force in the
tyin' run!" And he starts on up to the plate as cocky as if he was Willie Keeler.

I don't need to tell you Bethlehem broke loose on that there ball
field. The fans got onto their hind legs, yellin' and whistlin', and everybody on the field begun wavin' their arms and hollerin' and
shovin'. The plate umpire stalked over to Magrew like a traffic cop,
waggin' his jaw and pointin' his finger, and the St. Louis manager
kept yellin' like his house was on fire. When Pearl got up to the plate

and stood there, the pitcher slammed his glove down onto the ground and started stompin' on it, and they ain't nobody can blame him. He's just walked two normal-sized human bein's, and now here's a guy up to the plate they ain't more'n twenty inches between his knees and his shoulders.

The plate umpire called in the field umpire, and they talked a while, like a couple doctors seein' the bucolic plague or somethin' for the first time. Then the plate umpire come over to Magrew with his arms folded acrost his chest, and he told him to go on and get a batter up, or he'd forfeit the game to St. Louis. He pulled out his watch, but somebody batted it outa his hand in the scufflin', and I thought there'd be a free-for-all, with everybody yellin' and shovin' except Pearl du Monville, who stood up at the plate with his little bat on his shoulder, not movin' a muscle.

Then Magrew played his ace. I seen him pull some papers outa his pocket and show 'em to the plate umpire. The umpire begun lookin' at 'em like they was bills for somethin' he not only never bought it, he never even heard of it. The other umpire studied 'em like they was a death warren, and all this time the St. Louis manager and the fans and the players is yellin' and hollerin'.

Well, sir, they fought about him bein' a midget, and they fought about him usin' a kid's bat, and they fought about where'd he been all season. They was eight or nine rule books brung out and everybody was thumbin' through 'em, tryin' to find out what it says about midgets, but it don't say nothin' about midgets, 'cause this was somethin' never'd come up in the history of the game before, and nobody'd ever dreamed about it, even when they has nightmares. Maybe you can't send no midgets in to bat nowadays, 'cause the old game's changed a lot, mostly for the worst, but you could then, it turned out.

The plate umpire finely decided the contrack papers was all legal and proper, like Magrew said, so he waved the St. Louis players back to their places and he pointed his finger at their manager and told him to quit hollerin' and get on back in the dugout. The manager says the game is percedin' under protest, and the umpire bawls, "Play ball!" over 'n' above the yellin' and booin', him havin' a voice like a hog-caller.

The St. Louis pitcher picked up his glove and beat at it with his fist six or eight times, and then got set on the mound and studied the situation. The fans realized he was really goin' to pitch to the midget, and they went crazy, hoopin' and hollerin' louder'n ever, and throwin' pop bottles and hats and cushions down onto the field. It took five, ten minutes to get the fans quieted down again, whilst our fellas that was on base set down on the bags and waited. And Pearl du Monville kept standin' up there with the bat on his shoulder, like he'd been told to.

So the pitcher starts studyin' the setup again, and you got to admit it was the strangest setup in a ball game since the players cut off their beards and begun wearin' gloves. I wisht I could call the pitcher's name—it wasn't old Barney Pelty nor Nig Jack Powell nor Harry Howell. He was a big right-hander, but I can't call his name. You could look it up. Even in a crotchin' position, the ketcher towers over the midget like the Washington Monument.

The plate umpire tries standin' on his tiptoes, then he tries crotchin' down, and he finely gets hisself into a stanch nobody'd ever seen on a ball field before, kinda squattin' down on his hanches.

Well, the pitcher is sore as a old buggy horse in fly time. He slams in the first pitch, hard and wild, and maybe two foot higher'n the midget's head.

"Ball one!" hollers the umpire over 'n' above the racket, 'cause everybody is yellin' worsten ever.

The ketcher goes on out toward the mound and talks to the pitcher and hands him the ball. This time the big right-hander tries a undershoot, and it comes in a little closer, maybe no higher'n a foot, foot and a half above Pearl's head. It would 'a' been a strike with a human bein' in there, but the umpire's got to call it, and he does.

"Ball two!" he bellers.

The ketcher walks on out to the mound again, and the whole infield comes over and gives advice to the pitcher about what they'd do in a case like this, with two balls and no strikes on a batter that oughta be in a bottle of alcohol 'stead of up there at the plate in a big-league game between the teams that is fightin' for first place.

For the third pitch, the pitcher stands there flat-footed and tosses up the ball like he's playin' ketch with a little girl.

Pearl stands there motionless as a hitchin' post, and the ball comes in big and slow and high—high for Pearl, that is, it bein' about on a level with his eyes, or a little higher'n a grown man's knees.

They ain't nothin' else for the umpire to do, so he calls, "Ball three!"

Everybody is onto their feet, hoopin' and hollerin', as the pitcher sets to throw ball four. The St. Louis manager is makin' signs and faces

like he was a contorturer, and the infield is givin' the pitcher some
more advice about what to do this time. Our boys who was on base
stick right onto the bag, runnin' no risk of bein' nipped for the last
out.

Well, the pitcher decides to give him a toss again, seein' he come
closer with that than with a fast ball. They ain't nobody ever seen a
slower ball throwed. It come in big as a balloon and slower'n any
ball ever throwed before in the major leagues. It come right in over
the plate in front of Pearl's chest, lookin' prob'ly big as a full moon
to Pearl. They ain't never been a minute like the minute that followed
since the United States was founded by the Pilgrim grandfathers.

Pearl du Monville took a cut at that ball, and he hit it! Magrew
give a groan like a poleaxed steer as the ball rolls out in front a the
plate into fair territory.

"Fair ball!" yells the umpire, and the midget starts runnin' for
first, still carryin' that little bat, and makin' maybe ninety foot an
hour. Bethlehem breaks loose on that ball field and in them stands.
They ain't never been nothin' like it since creation was begun.

The ball's rollin' slow, on down toward third, goin' maybe eight,
ten foot. The infield comes in fast and our boys break from their
bases like hares in a brush fire. Everybody is standin' up, yellin' and
hollerin', and Magrew is tearin' his hair outa his head, and the midget
is scamperin' for first with all the speed of one of them little dash-
hounds carryin' a satchel in his mouth.

The ketcher gets to the ball first, but he boots it on out past the
pitcher's box, the pitcher fallin' on his face tryin' to stop it, the shortstop sprawlin' after it full length and zaggin' it on over toward the
second baseman, whilst Muller is scorin' with the tyin' run and Loesing is roundin' third with the winnin' run. Ty Cobb could 'a' made a
three-bagger outa that bunt, with everybody fallin' over theirself tryin'
to pick the ball up. But Pearl is still maybe fifteen, twenty feet
from the bag, toddlin' like a baby and yeepin' like a trapped rabbit,
when the second baseman finely gets a holt of that ball and slams it
over to first. The first baseman ketches it and stomps on the bag, the
base umpire waves Pearl out, and there goes your old ball game, the
craziest ball game ever played in the history of the organized world.

Their players start runnin' in, and then I see Magrew. He starts
after Pearl, runnin' faster'n any man ever run before. Pearl sees him
comin' and runs behind the base umpire's legs and gets a holt onto
'em. Magrew comes up, pantin' and roarin', and him and the midget

plays ring-around-a-rosy with the umpire, who keeps shovin' at Magrew with one hand and tryin' to slap the midget loose from his legs with the other.

Finely Magrew ketches the midget, who is still yeepin' like a stuck sheep. He gets holt of that little guy by both his ankles and starts whirlin' him round and round his head like Magrew was a hammer thrower and Pearl was the hammer. Nobody can stop him without gettin' their head knocked off, so everybody just stands there and yells. Then Magrew lets the midget fly. He flies on out toward second, high and fast, like a human home run, headed for the soap sign in center field.

Their shortstop tries to get to him, but he can't make it, and I knowed the little fella was goin' to bust to pieces like a dollar watch on a asphalt street when he hit the ground. But it so happens their center fielder is just crossin' second, and he starts runnin' back, tryin' to get under the midget, who had took to spiralin' like a football 'stead of turnin' head over foot, which give him more speed and more distance.

I know you never seen a midget ketched, and you prob'ly never even seen one throwed. To ketch a midget that's been throwed by a heavy-muscled man and is flyin' through the air, you got to run under him and with him and pull your hands and arms back and down when you ketch him, to break the compact of his body, or you'll bust him in two like a matchstick. I seen Bill Lange and Willie Keeler and Tris Speaker make some wonderful ketches in my day, but I never seen nothin' like that center fielder. He goes back and back and still further back and he pulls that midget down outa the air like he was liftin' a sleepin' baby from a cradle. They wasn't a bruise onto him, only his face was the color of cat's meat and he ain't got no air in his chest. In his excitement, the base umpire, who was runnin' back with the center fielder when he ketched Pearl, yells, "Out!" and that give hysteries to the Bethlehem which was ragin' like Niagry on that ball field.

Everybody was hoopin' and hollerin' and yellin' and runnin', with the fans swarmin' onto the field, and the cops tryin' to keep order, and some guys laughin' and some of the women fans cryin', and six or eight of us holdin' onto Magrew to keep him from gettin' at that midget and finishin' him off. Some of the fans picks up the St. Louis pitcher and the center fielder, and starts carryin' 'em around on their shoulders, and they was the craziest goin's-on knowed to the history of organized ball on this side of the 'Lantic Ocean.

I seen Pearl du Monville strugglin' in the arms of a lady fan with a ample bosom, who was laughin' and cryin' at the same time, and him beatin' at her with his little fists and bawlin' and yellin'. He clawed his way loose finely and disappeared in the forest of legs which made that ball field look like it was Coney Island on a hot summer's day.

That was the last I ever seen of Pearl du Monville. I never seen hide nor hair of him from that day to this, and neither did nobody else. He just vanished into the thin of the air, as the fella says. He was ketched for the final out of the ball game and that was the end of him, just like it was the end of the ball game, you might say, and also the end of our losin' streak, like I'm goin' to tell you.

That night we piled onto a train for Chicago, but we wasn't snarlin' and snappin' any more. No, sir, the ice was finely broke and a new spirit come into that ball club. The old zip come back with the disappearance of Pearl du Monville out back a second base. We got to laughin' and talkin' and kiddin' together, and 'fore long Magrew was laughin' with us. He got a human look onto his pan again, and he quit whinin' and complainin' and wishtin' he was in heaven with the angels.

Well, sir, we wiped up that Chicago series, winnin' all four games, and makin' seventeen hits in one of 'em. Funny thing was, St. Louis was so shook up by that last game with us, they never did hit their stride again. Their center fielder took to misjudgin' everything that come his way, and the rest a the fellas followed suit, the way a club'll do when one guy blows up.

'Fore we left Chicago, I and some of the fellas went out and bought a pair of them little baby shoes, which we had 'em golded over and give 'em to Magrew for a souvenir, and he took it all in good spirit. Whitey Cott and Billy Klinger made up and was fast friends again, and we hit our home lot like a ton of dynamite and they was nothin' could stop us from then on.

I don't recollect things as clear as I did thirty, forty year ago. I can't read no fine print no more, and the only person I got to check with on the golden days of the national pastime, as the fella says, is my friend, old Milt Kline, over in Springfield, and his mind ain't as strong as it once was.

He gets Rube Waddell mixed up with Rube Marquard, for one thing, and anybody does that oughta be put away where he won't bother nobody. So I can't tell you the exact margin we win the pennant by. Maybe it was two and a half games, or maybe it was three and a half. But it'll all be there in the newspapers and record books of thirty, thirty-one year ago and, like I was sayin', you could look it up.

ALI THE TERRIBLE TURK

from

NIGHT AND THE CITY

———◆———

by GERALD KERSH

(1946)

*Is professional wrestling a sport? Television watchers today have good reason
to think it's a vaudeville act. But there were giants in other days, and wrestling,
even though it may have been the most brutal of sports, was a sport and one
that was on the level. Even then, however, wrestlers (like Ali, the hero of this
excerpt) seem to have been born to be exploited by villains, and Harry Fabian,
the central figure of Gerald Kersh's incisive picture of slum and gangster
London, is surely one of the most loathsome characters in modern fiction. There
is more than a little of Dickens in Kersh's stories of the London underworld a
century later.*

FROM THE GYMNASIUM came the noise of two men shouting together. Kration was roaring with laughter, while Ali grunted with
rage. Adam stood between them.

"What's the trouble?" said Fabian.

Ali replied: "There is only two kinds of Cypriot. There is the Cypriot who always giggles, and the Cypriot who never smiles."

"Hoh-hoh-hoh!" laughed Kration.

"The first kind laughs all the time because he is too stupid to see

296

that he is really something to weep at; the other frowns all the time, because he is too foolish to see how ridiculous he is."

Kration still laughed. Ali went on, at the top of his voice: "They all wave their hair. They have only three trades. There is no Cypriot who is not a barber, a tailor, or a kitchen boy. In the end they all call themselves wrestlers. But damn it, their national sport is dominoes. They bang down the dominoes, and shout—that is the game. They make love to servant girls who take them to the pictures. Then they are national heroes. And they all fight like slaves. *Ptoo,* and *ptoo* on the Cypriot!"

"Big belly!" laughed Kration, showing twenty brilliant teeth. When Kration laughed he looked like a man who was completely satisfied with himself. The expression of his smiling face said: "If I were not Kration, I should be God Almighty." But as soon as his mouth closed his face changed. Savagery came into it. He looked strong and ferocious enough to tear himself apart. His hair crouched low on his forehead, trying to obliterate his eyebrows; his eyebrows, colliding over his nose in a spray of black hair, endeavored to smother his eyes; and only the flat, heavy prow of his nose kept his eyes apart—otherwise, they would have snapped at each other. Meanwhile they waited, smoldering; while his upper lip snarled in triumph over the lower, which, from time to time, jumped up and clamped down on it. Turkey, Greece, and Africa waged war in his veins. Even his hair carried on ancient warfare. There was antagonism in his very follicles, and the hair writhed out, enormously thick, twisted, rebellious, kinked, frizzled, and dried up.

He said to Adam: "He too old to hit. I hit him once, he die. One finger enough. Tiss finger: look!" He wagged a forefinger.

"Lay off!" said Fabian.

"He said I was old! He said I was fat."

Fabian grinned. "Old? Fat? Hell, can't we all see you're a two-year-old? Ain't you wasting away to a shadow?"

"You may joke, yes. But let me fight him. I will show him how old I am. . . . *Tfoo,* I say! Didn't your grandmother learn that a Turk was a better man than a Cypriot while your grandfather hid under the bed? Mongrel!"

"You—"

"Hold um!" yelled Fabian, and attached himself, like a mosquito, to Ali's wrist, while Adam threw his arms round Kration and held him. The Cypriot shook himself. Adam's feet left the floor.

"Listen! Listen!" shouted Fabian. "What's the excitement? You two are having a chance to fight it out in the ring. I'm billing you as a surprise item for next show. Why waste your energy down here, mugs? Ali is making a comeback, see? Ali the Terrible Turk, and Kration. See?"

"Good," said Ali.

"No," said Kration, "my friends will laugh at me for fighting an old man."

"Two guineas apiece!" said Fabian.

"No," said Kration.

Ali suggested: "Give him four, my two and his two. I will fight him for nothing."

"Well?" said Fabian.

"Right," said Kration.

Ali sneered. "They can be bought, these champions. *Ptoo!* He would sell his brother and sister for a small cup of coffee. His friends would laugh at him! Hou! They will laugh all the more when I tie him up like a brown-paper parcel."

Kration replied, over his shoulder: "Fat guts, say your prayers."

Adam took Fabian aside, and said:

"Seriously, are you going to let those two fight?"

"Why not?"

"It's a crime! Ali's nearly seventy; Kration's not yet thirty. Ali's old, but he won't admit it. And he's sick."

"Boloney! He's a tiger."

"But—"

"What are you worrying about? Afraid he'll drop dead, or something?"

"I'm afraid he'll take a beating, and I don't want to see it."

"Then stay away."

"I'll give you a fiver if you'll call the fight off."

"Are you trying to offer me money to interfere with sport? Besides, there's more than that in it for me."

"Oh, go and drown yourself." Adam went to the dressing room, and found Ali. "Ali, do me a favor. Call this crazy fight off."

"Why?"

"Why? You get nothing for it, and besides, Kration's not a wrestler; he's a rough-house specialist; a killer."

"Yah? And I am a hangman."

"But, Ali!"

Ali turned with bulging eyes. "Go to the devil! Leave me alone!" he said.

Adam and Nosseross walked through the sharp air of the morning, to the Corner House.

"Oh, my Christ," said Nosseross, "look who's here!"

It was Fabian, somewhat flushed with excitement, drinking coffee at an adjacent table. Even as Nosseross spoke, Fabian cried: "Oh, boy, oh, boy, do my eyes deceive me?" and came to their table. "What, Phil Nosseross, you old crook, you! Listen, Phil, if you wanna see a show, come and see the one I'm running. Listen, Phil, you've heard of Ali the Terrible Turk? He's making a comeback. And is that man in form or is he in form? I'll tell you—he's in form. Is this gonna be a needle fight or is this gonna be a needle fight? Boy, will they tear lumps out of each other!"

Adam said: "I have half a mind to smack you on the nose."

"Go on, then, smack me on the nose!" said Fabian. "Am I supposed to be scared?"

"What is all this, anyway?" asked Nosseross.

"The fight of the century. Ali the Terrible Turk against Kration. Coming?"

"What, old Ali? He must be getting on for seventy. I saw him thirty years ago, and he wasn't anybody's chicken then. But what a fighter!" said Nosseross. "Not much skill, mind you, and no psychology; but what a terror! Heart of a lion, and about as strong as a bear. Is he still alive?"

"You'll see," said Fabian.

"Listen," said Adam, "let me referee that fight."

"I'm refereeing it myself," said Fabian. He grinned at Nosseross: "He's scared in case Ali—"

"It's not that. Poor old Ali's finished, and you know it. He can't win. About the only thing he's got left is his pride. He's only got one eye. The only thing that keeps him going is the fact that he's never been defeated. And now you match him against a man forty years younger. You ought to be ashamed of yourself!"

"Any betting on this fight?" asked Fabian, grinning.

"With you refereeing it?" said Adam. "Thanks."

"Betting?" said Nosseross. "You're crazy. Dog racing is dirty; boxing isn't clean; racing stinks a bit: but wrestling! There hasn't been a straight match in forty years."

Fabian grinned in Adam's face. "I thought you'd be scared to bet on Ali," he said.

"What odds are you laying?"

"Twenties on Kration."

"I'll take you," said Adam. "Give me forty pounds to two."

"You're on."

"Idiot," said Nosseross, when Fabian had gone. "Why d'you let him rib you into giving him two pounds?"

"I'm not so sure. Old Ali'll never lie down while there's breath in him. But I'd give a tenner to have this fight called off," said Adam.

Here, in one of the dressing rooms, Ali was preparing for the fight. Ali was fat, fantastically fat. When he was naked, one could see how malevolently time had dealt with him; blowing him up like a balloon, and dragging him down like a bursting sack. His pectorals hung flabbily, like the breasts of an old woman. His belly sagged!

He brushed his mustache, pinched out a length of Hungarian Pomade, and molded the ends to needle points with a dexterous twirl.

"Kration'll try and grab that," said Adam, "just to give the lads a laugh."

"Let him try!"

"Ali, why not trim it down?"

Ali swore that he would as soon trim down another essentially masculine attribute. He put on a curious belt, nearly a foot wide, made of canvas and rubber. "Pull this tight, please; as tight as you can," he said; and muttered, with an apologetic look: "I do not want the people to be under an impression that I have been getting a leetle bit fat. . . ."

Adam pulled at the straps, and, like toothpaste in a tube, soft fat oozed up above Ali's waistline.

"Ali, is this wise? This belt squeezes your guts together. If Kration hits you, or kicks you there—"

"Let him try." Ali writhed into a set of long black tights, and pulled over them a pair of red silk shorts. "Now, help me with this sash." He held up a long band of frayed red satin, embroidered with Arabic characters. "This was a present from Abdul Hamid. . . ."

"Ali, you're crazy to press your belly in like that!"

"*Ptah!*" Ali drew himself up, and stood with folded arms. "Tell me, do I look good?"

Adam felt an impulse to shed tears. "Fine!"

"One day, I let you sculpture me."

"Thanks, Ali. Listen, Ali; be cautious, for heaven's sake."

"My little friend, you forget that I have won hundreds of fights—that I have never been beaten!"

"I know. But I should hate like hell to see you hurt."

Ali laughed. "Professor Froehner tore one of my ribs right out of the skin, but I beat him; and I fought again next day. In all my life, nobody ever heard me cry out! Nobody ever saw me tap the mat. Leblond had me by the foot in a jujitsu hold. 'Give in, or I break your ankle,' he said. I said: 'Break on, Leblond: Ali never gives in.' And he broke my ankle, and I got up on one foot, and pinned him. I said: 'You cannot hurt Ali. But he whom Ali grips, God forgets!' That is me!"

"Oh, I'm sure you'll win. I've betted on you."

"Good boy! What odds did they lay against me?"

"Very small."

"You're lying. They think I'm an old man. They laugh. Good, let them. And in the end, when they laugh on the other side of the face, I shall laugh, too—I shall laugh right into their eyes, and say: 'The old wolf still has teeth.' Do I look good?"

"You look like a champion, Ali, you really do."

Ali laughed, until the fat on his stomach bounced like a cat in a sack. "Ha-ha-ha! I surprised you, eh? . . . They think I'm going to fool about with this Greek, this Cypriot. No. I shall walk in—one, two, three; up with the legs, back with the head—dash him down, pick him up like a child, shake him like a kitten; then over my head, bim-bam, and pin him. Back again—forward with his head, under my arm with it, and *khaaa!* my old stranglehold, until his eyes pop out. Then I shall pick him up like a dumbbell, and hold him above my head, and say to the crowd: 'This is the man who thought he could beat Ali the Turk!' Then—"

An open door let in the shouting of a crowd. Legs Mahogany came through, bleeding from the nose, followed by the Black Strangler, who staggered as he walked. An attendant came in, and said:

"Ali!"

Ali put on a dressing gown of quilted red silk, thirty years old, and eroded by moths. "Smart, eh? A woman gave me this in Vienna, in . . . I forget the date. . . ."

Adam whispered: "Give me your glass eye: it's madness to wrestle in one of those things."

"Rubbish! And let him see I have a blind side?"

"Give it to me, I tell you!"

"If you insist, then, take it." Ali slid out his left eye, and gave it to Adam, who put it in his waistcoat pocket. Then he strode, with slow dignity, out to the ringside, while through his head ran the cheerful rhythm of the *March of the Gladiators,* the tune to which the old wrestlers at the International Tournaments had strutted in glory round the arenas.

There was a roar of applause. Ali raised his hands to acknowledge it, when he saw Kration, already in the ring, bowing and smiling. Ali grasped the ropes and swung himself up. There was a pause. A little trickle of clapping broke out; then laughter, which rose and swelled, pierced by high catcalls and shrill whistles. . . .

"Hoooi! Laurel and 'Ardy!"

"Where d'you get them trousis?"

"Take yer whiskers orf! We can't see yer!"

Somebody began to sing, in a good tenor voice: "It happened on the beach at Belly-Belly!"

Figler's friend, Lew, rose and shouted, in a voice trained in the market places of the earth: "Good old Ali! We remember you!"

Ali tore off his dressing gown, and threw it to Adam.

"Go on, laugh!" he cried.

They laughed.

Fabian shrieked into a megaphone: "Ladies and gentlemen! On my right, two hundred and forty pounds of bone, muscle, brain, and nerve, Kration of Cyprus, contender for championship honors! . . . On my left—"

"Father Christmas!" said a voice; and there was another shout of laughter.

"Ali the Terrible Turk, ex-heavyweight champion of the world, now making a sensational comeback—"

"Champion of wot world?" yelled a thin, Cockney voice.

"Lad-eez and gentlemen! The name of Ali the Terrible Turk was a household word at the beginning of the century—"

"Wot century?"

("That's what you get, if you get old without any money," said Lew to Figler.)

Fabian stepped back. Kration and Ali went to their corners. Kration still smiled. It was best, he decided, to let it seem that this affair was an elaborate joke. Ali was as grim as death.

"Now don't forget—take it easy!" whispered Adam.

Ali replied: "I shall have pinned him within twenty seconds. Count twenty, slowly—"

The gong clanged.

The wrestlers went out into the ring.

Kration advanced with the grace of a dancer. Ali moved slowly, jaws clamped, chin down. They circled about each other, feinting. Then there was a sound like the crack of a whip. Before Ali's fat-clogged, time-laden muscles could co-ordinate in a counterattack, Kration had slapped him on the buttocks.

"Get 'im by the 'orns!" somebody shouted.

"Right," said Kration, and grabbed at Ali's mustache. But next moment, a grip like pincers closed on his wrist, a force like an earthquake twirled him round, and his hand went back over his head toward his shoulder blades.

Kration broke out into a sweat. It occurred to him that Ali was in savage earnest. He had not sufficient skill to break the hold. Resisting Ali's pressure with all his strength, he butted backwards with his head. The hard, round skull, padded with kinky black hair, jolted against Ali's jaw. The Turk snarled, and tried to knock Kration's feet from under him; but between himself and his opponent, his vast abdomen stood like a wall. Kration's head jerked back again. In Ali's nose, something like a lever in a pump, and bright red blood began to run on to his mustache.

Kration broke away, whirled round, and, in turning, struck Ali on the jaw with his forearm. It seemed to Ali that the Cypriot was swimming in a sea of red water reticulated with a network of dazzling light; and that the voice of this sea was laughter. But even as his brain wavered, his ancient instincts were sending him lumbering after Kration, while his consciousness automatically juggled with the logic of a hundred different forms of attack. . . .

He's too fast: Waste no strength chasing! Get close and crush! His huge right hand hooked Kration's neck. Kration's fingers, forked like a snake's tongue, flickered toward his eyes. Ali ducked. Kration's nails scratched his forehead. Then Ali had his right hand in an irresistible grip. Adam saw his back quiver.

"Flying mare!" screamed a woman's voice.

Ali heaved Kration off his feet by his right arm; stooped to throw him over his shoulder; then stopped. The edge of his belt had cut him short. They stayed, for a moment, in this ignominious posture. Then Kration, wriggling like a python, caught Ali's throat between his biceps and forearm, twisted a leg between Ali's thighs, grunted, tugged; then writhed away as they fell. The Turk's body struck the mat with the dead thud of a falling tree. Something snapped: his belt had burst. Kration uttered a triumphant yell, and pulled it away; leaped back, and held it over his head.

Laughter roared through the spectators like a wind through trees. Ali was up, growling. Fabian took the belt from Kration's hands, muttering, as he did so: "Liven it up a bit, can't you, you two? Don't play about like kids in a bloody nursery! Come on, now!"

Kration evaded Ali's slashing right hand, threw himself back against the ropes, and fired himself across the ring like a stone from a catapult. His right shoulder struck Ali in the abdomen. Ali fell backwards, with a tremendous gasp, but even as he fell, rolled over with a grunt and caught Kration below the ribs in a scissorshold.

Kration felt like a man in a train smash, pinned by a fallen ceiling. He writhed, but Ali held fast. The crowd screamed. Kration breathed in short coughs—*Asssss. . . .Asssss. . . . Assssss.* He tensed all the iron muscles of his stomach. Ali still struggled for breath: every exhalation, blowing through the blood which still ran from his nose, spattered the mat with red drops: *Prup-aghhh . . . prup-aghhh,* . . . He realized that he could not hold Kration for more than another ten seconds. Cramp crawled in the muscles of his thighs.

Kration ground the heel of his hand into Ali's mouth, and broke loose; leaped high in the air, and came down backside first. Ali saw him coming, but could not move quickly enough. Kration's two hundred and forty pounds dropped, like a flour sack falling from a loft, on to Ali's chest. Wind rushed out—*Ahffffffffff!*—with a fine spray of blood. Darkness descended on the Turk; for perhaps one second, he became unconscious. His mind floundered up out of a darkness as deep and cold as Siberian midnight. He found himself struggling to his feet.

Adam's voice reached his ears as from an immense distance: "Careful, Ali, careful!" Kration was upon him again, on his blind side, and had caught him in a wristlock.

Ali's brain flickered and wavered like a candle flame in a draft. There was a countermove; something . . . something . . . he could not remember. He put out all his might, and caught one of the Cyp-

riot's wrists; grunted: "Hup!" like a coal heaver, and used his tremendous weight to spin Kration round and swing him off his feet. As
Kration staggered, Ali caught one of his ankles; twirled him round,
six inches off the mat, in the manner of an acrobatic dancer, then let
go. The Cypriot fell on his face, kicking and heaving like a wounded
leopard. "Ahai!" yelled Ali, springing forward as Kration rose to his
hands and knees. "Waho!"

"Nice work!" screamed Adam.

Ali had Kration in a headlock. Kration crouched, gathering his
strength; then began to strain left and right, in spasmodic jerks. Blood
from Ali's nose fell like rain on Kration's back. Both men were red to
the waist, slippery with blood. Ali's grip was slipping: Kration was as
hard to hold as a flapping sail in a raging wind. . . . Kration's head
was free. Ali caught a glimpse of his face, purple, swollen, split by a
grin of anger that displayed all his teeth, white as peeled almonds.
Then Kration swung his left arm. His hard, flat palm struck Ali in the
face: one of his nails scraped the surface of Ali's eye.

A blank, bleak horror came into the heart of the Turk. *My eye!
My last eye! If I lose this eye, too!* Then he roared like a maddened
lion, buried his fingers in the softer flesh above Kration's hips, lifted
him above his head by sheer force, threw him across the ring, and
followed him, growling unintelligible insults and spitting blood—

Clang! went the gong.

Ali groped his way back to his corner, and sat limply. Adam
sponged him with cold water, adjusted his sash, and wiped the blood
from his face.

"My eye," said Ali, "my eye!"

"It's badly scratched," said Adam.

Ali's eye was closing. The lids, dark and swollen, were creeping together to cover the blood-colored eyeball.

The crowd shouted. One voice screamed: "Carm on, Nelson! Carm
on, whiskers!"

Ali sucked up a mouthful of water and, like a spouting whale,
sprayed it toward the crowd. "Cowards!" he shouted. "Cowards!"

Figler muttered: "This is disgusting. Let's go."

Lew, shaken by emotion, did not answer, but raised his piercing
voice and called to Ali: "Good work, Ali! I've not seen anything
better since you beat Red Shreckhorn in Manchester!"

Ali called back: "Thank you for that!"

"Go easy, for God's sake, go easy," said Adam.

The gong sounded. Kration advanced, smiling. To Ali, he looked like a man half formed out of red dust. He thought: *If I do not get him within five minutes, this eye will close, and then I shall be a man fighting in the dark.* This thought was indescribably terrifying. The curtain of mist was darkening. Now, by straining the muscles of his forehead and cheeks, and holding his mouth wide open, he could barely manage to see.

A voice cried: "Look out, Kration! He's going to swallow you!" Another shouted: "Oo-er! Look at 'is whiskers! They're coming unstuck!"

Ali's mustache had, indeed, fallen into a ludicrous Nietzschean droop, matted to a spiky fringe with congealing blood. Kration snarled, leaped in, struck Ali across the neck with a flailing arm, and seized his mustache. He tugged. If the hair had not been slippery with the blood from Ali's nose, Kration might have pulled it out. But it slid through his fingers. Ali, weeping huge tears of pain, grasped blindly, and caught the Cypriot by the biceps of his right arm. The darkness had come. He knew that if he relaxed that grip, he was lost. As Kration jerked back, Ali followed. The Cypriot began to gasp with pain: *Esss-ha; esss-ha. . . .* Everything in Ali's body and soul focused in the five small points of his finger tips. He was blind, now, utterly blind, lost in a roaring, spinning ring, dumb with agony, choked with blood, deafened with howls of derision and encouragement which seemed to have no end—and in this world of sickening pain, there was only one real thing, and that was the arm of his enemy, in which he was burying his fingers. . . .

They clung together, spinning round and round like two twigs in a whirlpool; the Cypriot groaning, now; Ali silent. He felt cold. A ring post ground into his back. He groped with his other hand, and found nothing. The noise of the crowd was becoming fainter; his face seemed to be swelling and swelling, while in his breast his heart thundered like horses galloping over a wooden bridge. Something knocked his feet from the mat. He fell, still clutching Kration's arm. The Cypriot said: "For Christ's sake!" Ali replied: "You feel my grip, eh?"

Voices were shouting: "Stop the fight! Stop it!"

Out of his midnight, Ali roared: "Stop nothing! Ali never stops!"

Suddenly, he released Kration's biceps, slid his hand down until it reached the wrist, where it shut like a bear trap; swung his other hand to the elbow. The Cypriot's arm broke. Ali heard his scream of pain, but still held on. Kration became limp. Ali held his eye open, with the first and second fingers of his free hand. He could see nothing except an interminable, fiery redness. Somebody tried to prize open his fingers, which still gripped Kration's wrist. Ali struck out blindly. A voice said: "Stop! You've won! It's me, Adam!"

"By God," said Ali, "that Greek went down like bricks."

The crowd was delirious. Fabian said: "You certainly gave those sons of bitches their money's worth."

Adam led him back to the dressing room.

Ali found his voice: "Did you see how I beat him? Did you see how I broke him up? Did you see how I pulled him down? Did you see how his arm went? Did you see my grip? I could have beaten him in the first ten seconds, only I wanted the public to see a *fight*. Did you see my grip? What Ali grips, God forgets!"

"You were great, Ali."

"Now am I fat?"

"No, Ali."

"Now am I old?"

"No, Ali."

"Now have I no teeth?"

"Teeth like a tiger."

"Now can I wrestle?"

"Better than ever, Ali."

"Now am I undefeated?"

"Still undefeated, Ali."

Ali raised his head, brushed back his mustache, twirled it again to fine points, and said: "Nobody on God's earth ever beat me. Nobody ever will. Look at me. If he hadn't scratched my eye, I should be as right as rain."

"Have a rest, Ali."

"Close the windows," said Ali, "there's a devil of a cold wind."

The windows were already closed.

Ali muttered: "I wonder if my eye is badly damaged? Get me some boracic acid crystals and a little warm water——" He stopped abruptly and said: "Put your hand on my chest!"

Adam did so. In Ali's chest, he felt something rattling, like a loose plate in a racing engine.

Ali exclaimed, with an astounded expression: "The clock is stopping!"

"Nonsense, Ali! Rest."

Ali struck his vast belly with a colossal fist, and murmured: "What a meal for the worms!"

Those were the last words he ever uttered.

That night he died.

FIFTY AND EIGHT

from

EQUINOX

———◆———

by *A L L A N   S E A G E R*

(1943)

*Swimming is not one of those sports which one usually thinks of as involving
its followers in a passion bordering on the fanatic. Be that as it may, early in
his life swimming has come to mean the world to Stanley Dinsmore, the young
man described in this excerpt from Allan Seager's* Equinox. *Stanley is only a
secondary character in the novel, the young man who falls in love with the
daughter of the central character, Richard Miles. Pitifully unsure of himself in
many salient respects, Stanley is at home when swimming as he is at no other
time. All of his dreams of glory, consequently, run in that direction, and fore-
most is his obsession to better Johnny Weissmuller's record of 50.8 seconds for
the hundred.*

H E WAS twenty-two years old and all he wanted to do was swim.
He had been on the team at Detroit Northwestern High School
and he had been the number-two sprint man for three years at the
University of Michigan. He was not really very good. At public bath-
ing beaches, where he did not like to swim, a crowd would always
gather to watch him and even the lifeguards would nod to each other,
but in the Payne Whitney pool or the Iowa pool, other swimmers

would take one look at him and go on talking. He was strong in the shoulders but had little natural buoyancy, and he was as good as he would ever be in his senior year at Michigan, when he swam the last leg of a medley relay in :52.2 against Ohio State. This is fast time even considering the relay start which allows you to time your arm swing smoothly by watching the man coming in at your feet. It was fast enough to have made him the number-one sprint man at any college in the country but Yale, Michigan, and perhaps Northwestern or Ohio State in the odd years. He was not a great swimmer though.

He was six feet two inches tall and weighed a hundred and ninety in his silk tank suit, and when he was swimming the muscles of his upper arms and shoulders looked huge through the breaks in the foam. He carried a Spalding annual around with him, and the page was very dirty where the world's records were listed, and he had drawn a ring around the line where it said: *100 yds.* (*75-foot pool*), *51 seconds—John Weissmuller.* He had never doubted that someday he would climb out of a pool, everyone shouting and his chest aching, and an assistant timer would run up to him and scream in his ear, "Fifty and eight! Fifty and eight!" He had decided to try his first champagne on that night, but in the showers immediately afterward he would be modest, merely saying thanks and sticking out his soapy hand. He was sure he could break the record if he worked hard enough and so was his girl, Joan Hinkman, a Delta Gamma at Michigan, but nobody else considered it probable.

When he was in high school and in his freshman year at Michigan his family sat in the reserved seats at swimming meets, with splash curtains drawn up over their laps, very proud of their son. His father wrote down the first, second, and third places and the time for every race in pencil and kept the programs in a drawer in his bureau. His mother, when she caught a glimpse of his face as he turned his head to breathe, would repeat softly to herself, "That is my son, the flesh of my flesh," and a heaving, swelling feeling would come inside her breast as if he were in danger, and she would twist her handkerchief into a knot in her lap. She also kept a scrapbook of newspaper clippings for him with great neatness, spreading the newspaper out on the dining-room table and cutting the story or the photograph out of it with her best dressmaking shears, to paste carefully in the scrapbook. With a deprecatory manner, she would get it out of the bookcase and show it to anyone who came to call. Once she showed it to the iceman. Her son, Stanley, was a marvel to her, she said, because no one in her family or on Mr. Dinsmore's side either had ever taken to the water, and when they had lived in Adrian before Mr. Dinsmore had gone into the automobile business, Stanley was forever running off to swim in the Raisin River. It was a very treacherous stream and a great many people, some of them grown men, drowned in it every year. But even when Stanley was a little boy, not more than eight or nine, he had shown this mysterious ability in the water. Then she would lean forward toward the visitor and point out the photograph taken of Stanley after he had won the fifty-yard dash in the city high-school championships.

After his freshman year at Michigan, his family's pride in his swimming grew less. They stopped driving out to Ann Arbor for the home meets, and Mrs. Dinsmore began to let the scrapbook go. She saved the newspapers that contained the clippings just as faithfully but she let them pile up in the bookcase. Both of them wanted to see signs of a talent in Stanley or at least an inclination toward some profession. (Mrs. Dinsmore yearned for him to become a professional man, a doctor or a lawyer, because it had—a word she now hesitated to use publicly—more *class*. Mr. Dinsmore, who had never heard his wife's hopes even when they were talking in bed at night, assumed that Stanley would get a job as a service man at the Rouge plant in the summer before his senior year and go into the sales end when he was graduated.) Stanley was a constant disappointment. He talked only of swimming and he went into the bathroom every few minutes to wet his hair and comb it.

Mr. Dinsmore was fifty years old. When he was forty, he was making twenty-five thousand dollars a year as a lesser member of the Ford hierarchy and his salary had not been cut during the depression. He spoke easily of "Edsel," "Sorenson," and "Harry Bennett," although he never spoke to them or they to him because they did not know who he was, and the Founder was always "Mr. Ford." After his salary was raised, before Mrs. Dinsmore really knew about Grosse Pointe, he bought a new house on Oakman Boulevard, a red brick, "Georgian-type" with an arch of brick thrown out over the driveway that led to the garage in back. They sold nearly all the old furniture they brought from Adrian and bought new. It was heavily overstuffed and there were seven floor lamps on the ground floor. Mr. Dinsmore was very happy in the new house, yet it seemed to lack something, a last touch of the opulence it deserved. One day he had an electric organ delivered and installed. He was unable to say why he wanted it, as neither he nor his wife could play it, and Stanley had gone no further than Chaminade's *Scarf Dance* in his piano lessons. Yet there it was standing at one end of the living room, its console a soft gleaming mahogany. No one touched it except to polish it, but occasionally when Mr. Dinsmore had some of the boys from the plant in for a drink, he would solemnly pull out all the stops and lay his forearm on the keyboard and press down. A vast blurred sound would shake the house. "Cost me fifteen hundred. Makes a hell of a racket, don't it?" he would say proudly. At such moments he felt that he stood on the pinnacle of life and he would urge everybody to finish their drinks so they could have another.

He drove a Lincoln Zephyr. He belonged to the D.A.C. and he lunched there as often as he could, eating tenderloin steak and deep-dish apple pie, smoking rich Corona cigars and reciting the lore of the automobile business with his peers. He owned a summer cottage at Pointe aux Barques. He had fifty thousand dollars' paid-up insurance. His wife had a mink coat and a God-awful number of dresses. His son was in college and belonged to a fraternity—not one of the best, maybe, but Calvin Coolidge had been a Phi Gam—and the boys at the house were such fine fellows that Mr. Dinsmore was a little afraid of them when he went out there on football Saturdays. Or if it rained, him and Mrs. Dinsmore listened to the game over the radio. It cost seven hundred and fifty. They didn't have to go out in the sopping wet. They could take it easy. That was the point: they weren't rich but they could take it easy. And while he did not know that he regarded his wife and son as scarcely sentient trophies wrung from a life to which he owed a duty to embellish further, he waited and searched to see if his son would not spontaneously discover the virtue of his life and begin to emulate his father on his own hook. There was nothing else the boy could really want, was there? But Stanley was apathetic to the point of defiance.

His father sounded him shrewdly to find out if any of those long-haired professors out at Ann Arbor had been putting funny ideas in his head, radical ideas about unions and things. Stanley said they hadn't. Mr. Dinsmore asked him if he didn't want to transfer to the Engineering School. Stanley said, no, he didn't think he did. He was getting along all right in the Lit School.

"Have you been thinking what department you want to get into when you graduate? They could probably use a college man in Sales."

"Why, I sort of thought of going to New York if I could."

"Hell, they wouldn't put you in the New York office right away. You got to learn the business first, boy. N-o-o, sir," he chuckled. "Start at the bottom of the ladder, that's what you'll do. Then if you work and keep your nose clean, why, five, six, eight years, you might make Export and you can go to New York or China or any damn place you want."

"I wasn't thinking about Ford's necessarily."

Cunningly, Mr. Dinsmore did not explode. "What were you thinking about? What's New York got that we haven't got?"

"The New York Athletic Club for one thing."

"And what's the matter with the Detroit Athletic Club?"

"I'm getting tired of Pinkston. He always wants to develop a diver. He doesn't give me any coaching."

In the effort to keep his temper, Mr. Dinsmore nearly bit through the end of the unlit cigar he had in the side of his mouth. "Oh, so you want to keep on swimming?" he said. "You've been swimming in meets for ten years, ever since you were twelve years old. Don't you think it's time you started figuring how to make some money?"

"Oh, I intended to get a job there. I didn't mean you had to keep up my allowance. I'll get a job somewhere and work days and swim in the evenings."

"Swim in the evenings, huh?" Mr. Dinsmore had been right for so many years that he could not admit suddenly that he had been wrong in the way he had handled his son. Yet the idea was there. This smooth tanned face was the face of a stranger. "When I was your age, I'd been working five years painting screen doors at the Prentice Screen Door factory in Adrian. I had four hundred and twenty-three dollars in the bank saved up."

"I'd just as soon save all the money I could."

"But, for the love of God, how long you going to keep on swimming?"

"I've got five or six good years yet. Look at Walter Spence. I bet he was thirty-five years old before he quit. That record of Weissmuller's can't last forever."

Mr. Dinsmore could see they didn't mesh. And worse than that they weren't going to mesh. His only ace was to order him to go to work at the plant. Stanley would do it. He had always been obedient, but he bet, by Christ, that if he did get him a job in the Service Department, he would swim noon hours in the Rouge itself, eat in ten minutes, swim twenty in the dirty little river in the mud and muck and coke dust. He bet, by God, he would.

Mr. Dinsmore hated to argue. He hated people who knew their own minds when their minds were different from his. He wanted things neat, not wishy-washy. He gave the order. After all, when you consider it, he made twenty-five thousand dollars a year. He knew best.

"Well, young man, you're going to work in the Service Department. When's graduation?"

"June seventeenth."

"June eighteenth there'll be a job waiting for you. New York's out." Mr. Dinsmore stood up and walked quickly out of the room. Since his son was a possession that represented a sizable investment, he suffered no hesitation in commanding him to work at Ford's. And having commanded he was sure obedience would be forthcoming and he thought no more about it.

When he is seventeen, a boy has done nothing. All things are possible. And out of all the possibilities he will, with the natural optimism of youth or maybe the natural optimism of American youth, pick the things he wants the most. The future will bring him wealth and honor. He will never, in rags, shoot snipes in the gutter or go to jail and yell out of a cell window at a passing seventeen-year-old boy, "Hey, bud, go get me a deck of butts, will you?" Since these things are certain—the honor, the money, and the great abilities—in the future, in just a little while now, can he be blamed for borrowing ahead of time some of the prestige, a touch of the arrogance, that, granting only the accomplishment, will come along pretty soon? Young kids are snotty bastards. They don't treat their elders with respect. They are contemptuous of people who work at dull jobs because they know themselves are princes.

Stanley Dinsmore was twenty-two years old. Out of the zodiacal scheme of possibilities that lay before him, he had adopted one. He had not chosen it exactly. As a skinny little boy, he thought swimming was the only activity worth putting any time on, and in the heel of boyhood, when the choice or the strong, strong wish is made, with his voice changing and the first light beard hairs shining on his face, scarcely knowing he did it, drifting easily into it as if he were borne on water, he became a swimmer and he did not wholly know or his father at all that he had chosen anything or how deep the choice was.

For there was nothing for him that was not linked with swimming, nothing desirable. If he thought of money, having a lot of money, it was only to use to pay Matt Mann or Bob Kiphuth for coaching him privately, and once having broken the record, he could use money for railroad tickets and steamship passages to cities where he could swim and conquer other lesser champions. Fame was the flash of the bulbs of news cameras (the water of the pool would show at his feet) and columns in the newspapers about him, his stroke analyzed, his kick admired by Corum, Cunningham, and Salsinger. Fame was also the dull gleam and distorted bas-reliefs on medals, big as silver dollars. Health when he thought about it at all was a little vague anxiety about the tone of his muscles—he often rolled his shoulders as if he were trying to settle his coat collar or he would stretch out his arms and shake his hand loosely at the end of it. Girls would like him automatically when he was the champion, tanned, modest, dressed in a white jacket with a wine-colored bow tie and a boutonnière to match. It would be simple to take them out on the verandas of a dozen country clubs and kiss them, beautiful girls like Gloria Callen. Of when he grew old, when his wind went back on him and the fat set in his muscles, he seldom thought.

In the history lectures at college, France held his attention briefly as a small area, almost square, filled with trenches and cathedrals, in whose porches stood, meek and awe-struck, the great personages all together, the Henry kings, the Louis kings, Joan of Arc on a white horse, the cardinals each in his scarlet biretta, Richelieu and Mazarin, Napoleon, Pasteur (with Paul Muni's face), Mme Curie, Charles Boyer, and foreground, front, and center, in a glow of brightness, larger than all these was Jean Taris, the Olympic 400-meter swimmer, in a water-polo cap with his ears sticking out. On the English cliffs, Drake did not bowl, rather, at the foot of the cliffs, Captain Webb was forever setting out for Calais swimming breaststroke. The rest of the island was a jumble of relics, ghosts, and dates to remember. Germany was a dark vicious plain and on it in a clump stood Bismarck, Kant, Beethoven, Hitler, Göring, and Goebbels, and Henry the Fowler, all drinking steins of beer, and at the rear a file of persecuted Jews slunk heavily away, but again in the foreground, clad only in a swimming jockstrap, was the stocky frame of Erich Rademacher who won the breaststroke at Amsterdam in 1928. Before the town hall of Stockholm (a picture of which he had seen in the *National Geographic*), Charles XII, the Bernadotte family, Gustavus

Adolphus, and Garbo feasted at a table laden with smörgåsbord (which he had eaten at the Stockholm Restaurant on East Jefferson in Detroit) and at the head of the table, gaunt and lean, sat the great Arne Borg who had once held every world's record from the 220 to the mile. The other nations of the earth were dim and dull except for Japan, where Koike, Makino, and the others came from, the tireless children, fourteen years old, who dishonestly pumped themselves up with oxygen at the Los Angeles Olympics, and winning, received congratulations from the Tenno. Stanley Dinsmore, if anyone had cared to ask him, could have explained that his geography and history were mixed and spangled. He could not help it. He would not have apologized for it because his education had not led him to think that his aims were mean or petty. He would have explained it all with dignity and confidence, knowing he was not ignorant because he was a college man, and with a certain earnest charm.

What he could not explain, what he knew with sureness, as his blood knew the pipes of his body, in the way his eye picked out near from far, as real as his teeth and never thought upon, was himself in water, himself before water, himself after water, water and he. Solemn, fascinated, a fat baby, he had sat in a white tub slowly opening and shutting his fingers upon the slender, the beautiful, the wild, wild water, trying to grab it. Older and under it, holding the willow roots against the haul of the current, frightened of the silence as if it had a secret in it, he had opened his eyes and looked out through the still brown murk toward the light glow where the sunlight struck the surface and bent, descending, diffused. And in the circle against the darkness he saw a fish, his companion, swimming to stand still, he and the fish, alone, he king over the fish and the flow, and he had come up breathless with his eyelids stinging and full of mud among the dull grasses of the riverbank.

And now. The coach sang, ". . . a nice easy hundred, Stanley. Keep y'head up. Get 'em in and get 'em out and re-lax, boy," and lifting his bare feet up and down nervously, curling his toes over the edge of the tiles to get a firm grip, he would be thinking how he would launch himself outward over the water at the coach's signal, duck his head as he entered, and after he had glided for a second, start his kick and lift his head and when he felt it break water, pull one arm down under him in a strong sweep. From then on he would keep his head high, and fling his arms loosely and accurately in front of him, not pulling hard, relaxed, breathing seven times in the

twenty-five yards between turns, and when he rolled his head side-
ward to breathe, he would see the coach running naked along the
edge of the pool, sweeping his arm forward to make him go faster,
his mouth round, tense, shouting but unheard in the thunder of the
foam.

Almost smiling at this unseemly superficial commotion he was making on the surface of the green water, almost but never quite knowing
that it was unseemly, superficial, he would finish the distance and
hang onto the edge of the slop trough, panting and tossing his head
to throw the long yellow hair out of his eyes, looking anxiously at the
coach to hear how long it had taken him, how long over fifty-two
seconds. But if he could have only the water, the green water, this
fluid mirror of breaking images, always bearing him softly with minute and gentle pressure or flowing past him or above him as he sank
with his hair waving a little, as he sank alone, given this, he would
never have cared to race anyone, a man or a watch. He would not
have agreed that this was true. When he talked of swimming to a girl
or to other swimmers, he said he wanted to race, he wanted to beat
the record more than anything else in the world. But it was not true
and he almost knew it, for the water was his own place, and at night
in dreams he owned it all, pond, pool, lake, and the little elbow
reaches of the sea. Neptune he did not believe in, one of those old
Greek gods in white statuary, in hard poems. The myths and stories
of water were nothing to him. Water was a place, a kingdom where he
could live, solemn, fascinated, a secret in it, alone, without sound or
time or anyone to bother him.

One day at the end of summer, he met his father near the Ro-
tunda. They drove home together every day.

"Payday, huh?" his father asked.

"Yes." He held out a folded wad of money he had been carrying
in his hand. "I've just quit." He looked straight ahead through the
windshield at the road. "I'm going to New York."

A SESSION IN
STILLMAN'S GYM

from

THE HARDER THEY FALL

———————◆———————

by *BUDD SCHULBERG*

(1947)

Beginning with his first novel, What Makes Sammy Run?, *Budd Schulberg has been an author who builds his stories on long and penetrating firsthand research. He takes his readers inside certain distinct, almost separate worlds, which he exposes for the sordid microcosms they are.* What Makes Sammy Run? *dealt with a Hollywood success story;* Waterfront *with people caught in the underworld of the New York docks. In* The Harder They Fall, *Schulberg goes intimately behind the curtain of just about the most seamy sector of American sports, the fight racket. You don't need any further background to understand what is going on in this episode.*

AMERICANS are still an independent and rebellious people—at least in their reaction to signs. Stillman's gym, up the street from the Garden, offers no exception to our national habit of shrugging off small prohibitions. Hung prominently on the gray, nondescript walls facing the two training rings a poster reads: "No rubbish or spitting on the floor, under penalty of the law." If you want to see how the boys handle this one, stick around until everybody has left the joint and see what's left for the janitor to do. The floor is strewn with cigarettes smoked down to their stained ends, cigar butts chewed to soggy pulp, dried spittle, empty match cases, thumbed and trampled copies of the *News, Mirror* and *Journal,* open to the latest crime of passion or the race results, wadded gum, stubs of last night's fight at St. Nick's (managers comps), a torn-off cover of an Eighth Avenue restaurant menu with the name of a new matchmaker in Cleveland scrawled next to a girl's phone number. Here on the dirty gray floor of Stillman's is the telltale debris of a world as sufficient unto itself as a walled city of the Middle Ages.

You enter this walled city by means of a dark, grimy stairway that carries you straight up off Eighth Avenue into a large, stuffy, smoke-filled, hopeful, cynical, glistening-bodied world. The smells of this world are sour and pungent, a stale gamey odor blended of sweat and liniment, worn fight gear, cheap cigars and too many bodies, clothed and unclothed, packed into a room with no noticeable means of ventilation. The sounds of this world are multiple and varied, but the longer you listen, the more definitely they work themselves into a pattern, a rhythm that begins to play in your head like a musical score: The trap-drum beating of the light bag, counterpointing other light bags; the slow thud of punches into heavy bags; the tap-dance tempo of the rope skippers; the three-minute bell; the footwork of the boys working in the ring, slow, open-gloved, taking it easy; the muffled sound of the flat, high-laced shoes on the canvas as the big name in next week's show at the Garden takes a sign from his manager and goes to work, crowding his sparring partner into a corner and shaking him up with body punches; the hard-breathing of the boxers, the rush of air through the fighter's fractured nose, in a staccato timed to his movements; the confidential tones the managers use on the matchmakers from the smaller clubs spotting new talent. *Irving, let me assure you my boy loves to fight. He wants none of them easy ones. Sure he looked lousy Thursday night. It's a question of styles. You know that Ferrara's style was all wrong for him. Put 'em in with a boy who likes to mix it an' see the difference;* the deals, the arguments, the angles, the appraisals, the muted Greek chorus, muttering out of the corner of its mouth with a nervous cigar between its teeth; the noise from the telephones; the booths "For Out-going Calls Only," *Listen, Joe, I just been talking to Sam and he says okay for two hundred for the semi-final at* . . . the endless ringing of the "Incoming Calls Only"; a guy in dirty slacks and a cheap yellow sports shirt, cupping his hairy hands together and lifting his voice above the incessant sounds of the place: *Whitey Bimstein, call for Whitey Bimstein, anybody seen Whitey . . ."*; the garbage-disposal voice of Stillman himself, a big, authoritative, angry-looking man, growling out the names of the next pair of fighters to enter the ring, loudly but always unrecognizably, like a fierce, adult babytalk; then the bell again, the footwork sounds, the thudding of gloves against hard bodies, the routine fury.

The atmosphere of this world is intense, determined, dedicated. The place swarms with athletes, young men with hard, lithe, quick bodies under white, yellow, brown and blackish skins and serious, concentrated faces, for this is serious business, not just for blood, but for money.

I was sitting in the third row of the spectators' seats, waiting for Toro to come out. Danny McKeogh was going to have him work a couple of rounds with George Blount, the old Harlem trial horse. George spent most of his career in the ring as one of those fellows who's good enough to be worth beating, but just not good enough to be up with the contenders. Tough but not too tough, soft but not too soft—that's a trial horse. Old George wasn't a trial horse any more, just a sparring partner, putting his big, porpoise body and his battered, good-natured face up there to be battered some more for five dollars a round. There were sparring partners you could get for less, but George was what Danny called an honest workman; he could take a good stiff belt without quitting. To the best of his ring-wise but limited ability he obliged the managers with whatever style of fighting they asked for. He went in; he lay back; he boxed from an orthodox stand-up stance, keeping his man at distance with his left; he fought from out of a crouch and shuffled into a clinch, tying his man up with his clublike arms and giving him a busy time with the in-fighting. Good Old George, with the gold teeth, the easy smile and the old-time politeness, calling everybody mister, black and white alike, humming his slow blues as he climbed through the ropes, letting himself get beaten to his knees, climbing out through the ropes again and picking up the song right where he had left it on the apron of the ring. That was George, a kind of Old Man River of the ring, a John Henry with scar tissue, a human punching bag, who accepted his role with philosophical detachment.

In front of me, sparring in the rings and behind the rings, limber-
ing up, were the fighters, and behind me, the nonbelligerent echelons,
the managers, trainers, matchmakers, gamblers, minor mobsters, kib-
itzers, with here and there a sports writer or a shameless tub-thumper
like myself. Some of us fall into the trap of generalizing about races:
the Jews are this, the Negroes are that, the Irish something else again.
But in this place the only true division seemed to be between the flat-
bellied, slender-waisted, lively-muscled young men and the men with
the paunches, bad postures, fleshy faces and knavish dispositions
who fed on the young men, promoted them, matched them, bought
and sold them, used them and discarded them. The boxers were of all
races, all nationalities, all faiths, though predominantly Negro, Italian,
Jewish, Latin-American, Irish. So were the managers. Only those with
a bigot's astigmatism would claim that it was typical for the Irish to
fight and Jews to run the business, or vice versa, for each fighting
group had its parasitic counterpart. Boxers and managers, those are
the two predominant races of Stillman's world.

I have an old-fashioned theory about fighters. I think they should
get paid enough to hang up their gloves before they begin talking to
themselves. I wouldn't even give the managers the 33⅓ per cent allowed by the New York Boxing Commission. A fighter only has about
six good years and one career. A manager, in terms of the boys he can
handle in a lifetime, has several hundred careers. Very few fighters
get the consideration of race horses which are put out to pasture
when they haven't got it any more, to grow old in dignity and comfort like Man o' War. Managers, in the words of my favorite sports
writer, "have been known to cheat blinded fighters at cards, robbing
them out of the money they lost their eyesight to get."

I still remember what a jolt it was to walk into a foul-smelling men's
room in a crummy little late spot back in Los Angeles and slowly
recognize the blind attendant who handed me the towel as Speedy
Sencio, the little Filipino who fought his way to the top of the bantam-
weights in the late twenties. Speedy Sencio with the beautiful footwork, who went fifteen rounds without slowing down, an artist who
could make a fight look like a ballet, dancing in and out, side to side,
weaving, feinting, drawing opponents out of position and shooting
short, fast punches that never looked hard, but suddenly stretched
them on the canvas, surprised and pale and beyond power to rise.
Little Speedy in those beautiful double-breasted suits and the cocky,
jaunty but dignified way he skipped from one corner to the other to

shake hands with the participants in a fight to decide his next victim. Speedy had Danny McKeogh in his corner in those days. Danny looked after his boys. He knew when Speedy's timing was beginning to falter, when he began running out of gas around the eighth, and when the legs began to go, especially the legs. He was almost thirty, time to go home for the fighting man. One night the best he could get was a draw with a tough young slugger who had no business in the ring with him when Speedy was right. Speedy got back to his corner, just, and oozed down on his stool. Danny had to give him smelling salts to get him out of the ring. Speedy was the only real money-maker in Danny's stable, but Danny said no to all offers. As far as he was concerned, Speedy had had it. Speedy was on Danny all the time, pressing for a fight. Speedy even promised to give up the white girl he was so proud of if Danny would take him back. With Danny it was strike three, you're out, no arguments. Danny really loved Speedy. As a term of endearment, he called him "that little son-of-a-bitch." Danny had an old fighter's respect for a good boy, and, although it would make him a little nauseous to use a word like dignity, I think that is what he had on his mind when he told Speedy to quit. There are not many things as undignified as seeing an old master chased around the ring, easy to hit, caught flat-footed, old wounds opened, finally belted out. The terrible plunge from dignity is what happened to Speedy Sencio when Danny McKeogh tore up the contract and the jackals and hyenas nosed in to feed on the still-warm corpse.

Strangely enough, it was Vince Vanneman who managed Speedy out of the top ten into the men's can. Vince had him fighting three and four times a month around the small clubs from San Diego to Bangor, any place where "former bantamweight champion" still sold tickets. Vince chased a dollar with implacable single-mindedness. I caught up with him and Speedy one night several years ago in Newark, when Speedy was fighting a fast little southpaw who knew how to use both hands. He had Speedy's left eye by the third round and an egg over his right that opened in the fifth. The southpaw was a sharpshooter and he went for those eyes. He knocked Speedy's mouth-piece out in the seventh and cut the inside of his mouth with a hard right before he could get it back in place. When the bell ended the round Speedy was going down and Vince and a second had to drag him back to his corner. I was sitting near Speedy's corner, and though I knew what to expect from Vince I felt I had to make a pitch in the right direction. So I leaned over and said, "For Christ sake, Vince, what do you want to have, a murder? Throw in the towel and stop the slaughter, for Christ's sweet sake."

Vince looked down from the ring where he was trying to help the trainer close the cuts over the eyes. "Siddown and min' your own friggin' business," he said while working frantically over Speedy to get him ready to answer the bell.

In the next round Speedy couldn't see because of the blood and he caught an overhand right on the temple and went down and rolled over, reaching desperately for the lowest strand of the rope. Slowly he pulled himself up at eight, standing with his feet wide apart and shaking his head to clear the blood out of his eyes and his brain. All the southpaw had to do was measure him and he was down again, flat on his back, but making a convulsive struggle to rise to his feet. That's when Vince cupped his beefy hands to his big mouth and shouted through the ropes, "Get up. Get up, you son-of-a-bitch." And he didn't mean it like Danny McKeogh. For some reason known only to men with hearts like Speedy Sencio's, he did get up. He got up and clinched and held on and drew on every memory of defense and trickery he had learned in more than 300 fights. Somehow, four knockdowns and six interminable minutes later, he was still on his feet at the final bell, making a grotesque effort to smile through his broken mouth as he slumped into the arms of his victorious opponent in the traditional embrace.

Half an hour later I was having a hamburger across the street, when Vince came in and squeezed his broad buttocks into the opposite booth. He ordered a steak sandwich and a bottle of beer. He was with another guy, and they were both feeling all right. From what Vince said I gathered he had put up five hundred to win two-fifty that Speedy would stay the limit.

When I paid my check I turned to Vince's booth because I felt I had to protest against the violation of the dignity of Speedy Sencio. I apologize to anybody who might have been in that short-order house and overheard me. The only thing I can say in my defense is that if you are talking to an Eskimo it is no good to speak Arabic. But what I said didn't even make Vince lose a beat in the rhythmical chewing of his steak.

"Aaah, don't be an old lady," Vince said. "Speedy's never been kayoed, so why should I spoil his record?"

"Sure," I said, "don't spoil his record. Just spoil his face, spoil his head, spoil his life for good."

"Go away," Vince said, laughing. "You'll break my frigging heart."

The bell brought me back from Newark, from Speedy Sencio with his lousy job in that crapper and, I thought, from Vince Vanneman. Then I saw Vince himself coming in. I realized this must have been one of those times when the mind seems to sense someone before the image strikes the eye so that it appears a coincidence when the very man you're thinking about comes in the door. He was wearing a yellow linen sports shirt, open at the neck, worn outside his pants. He came up behind Solly Prinz, the matchmaker, and gave him the finger. Solly seemed to rise up off the ground and let out an excited, girlish scream. Everybody knew Solly was very goosey. It got a good laugh from the circle Solly was standing with. With the rest of his fingers bent toward his palm, Vince held the assaultive middle finger lewdly.

"See that, girls?" he said. "That's what a Chicago fag means when he says he'll put the finger on you." That got a laugh too. Vince was a funny guy, a great guy for laughs, just a big fun-loving kid who never grew up.

Vince came over and ran his hand over my hair.

"Hello, lover," he said.

"Balls," I said.

"Aw, Edsie," Vince pouted, "don't be that way. You've got it for me, baby." He threw his head back in an effeminate gesture, flouncing his fat body with grotesque coyness.

It was another Vanneman routine, always good for laughs. Humor was intended to lie in the margin of contrast between the fag act and Vince's obvious virility. I used to wonder about it.

"Seen him box yet?" Vince said.

"He'll be out in a minute," I said. "Danny's having Doc look him over."

"When you gonna break somethin' in the papers about him?"

"When Nick and I figure it's time," I said.

"Get him, get him!" Vince said. "What are ya, a goddam primmerdonner? Damon Runyon or something? I got a right to ask. I'm a partner, ain't I?"

Edwin Dexter Lewis, I mused, born in Harrisburg, Pa., of respectable churchgoing Episcopalians, nearly two years in the Halls of Nassau with First Group in English and a flunk in Greek, the occasional companion, intellectual and otherwise, of a Smith graduate and *Life*

Magazine researcher, an imminent playwright, clearly a man of breeding and distinction—if not of honor. At what point in what I smilingly refer to as my career was it decided that I was to become a business associate of Vincent Vanneman, two hundred and fifteen pounds of Eighth Avenue flotsam, graduate of Blackwell's Island, egger-onner of beaten fighters, contemporary humorist and practical joker.

"This isn't a partnership," I said. "It's a stock company. Just because we both have a couple of shares of the same stock doesn't make us brothers."

"What'sa matter, Eddie, can't you take a rib any more?" Vince grinned, wanting to be friends. "I just thought maybe when you put something in the paper you c'n drop in a line about me, you know, how it was me discovered the big guy."

"You mean how you muscled in on Acosta?"

"I don't like them words," Vince said.

"Forgive me," I said. "I didn't know you were so sensitive."

"What the hell you got on me?" Vince wanted to know. "Why you always try to give me the business?"

"Take it easy, Vince," I said. "I'll give you a nice big write-up some day. All you've got to do is drop dead."

Vince looked at me, spat on the floor, leaned back on his fat rump and opened his *Mirror* to the double-page spread on the Latin thrush who beat up the bandleader's wife when she surprised them in a West Side hotel.

Behind me a familiar voice was saying, "I wouldn't kid ya, Paul, I've got a bum what'll give yer customers plenty of action. Never made a bad fight in his life."

I looked around to see Harry Miniff talking to Paul Frank, match-maker for the Coney Island Club. Harry's hat was pushed back on his head as usual and a dead cigar hung between his lips as he talked.

"You don't mean that dog Cowboy Coombs, for Chrisake?" Paul said.

Miniff wiped the perspiration from his lip in a nervous gesture. "Whaddya mean, dog? I'll bet ya fifty right now Coombs c'n lick that Patsy Kline who's supposed to be such a draw out at Coney."

"I need somebody for Kline a week from Monday," Paul admitted. "But Patsy figures to murder an old man like Coombs."

"Whaddya mean, old?" Miniff demanded. "Thirty-two! You call that old? That ain't old. Fer a heavyweight that ain't old."

"For Coombs it's old," Paul said. "When you been punched around fifteen years, it's old."

"I tell ya, Coombs is in shape, Paul," Miniff insisted, but the desperate way he said it made it sound more like a plea than a statement of fact. "And win or lose, he's a crowd-pleaser. Ya know that, Paul. Kline'll know he's been in a fight."

"What about that last one up in Worcester?" Frank said.

"T'row that one out," Miniff dismissed it, reaching quickly into his coat pocket and coming up with a handful of worn newspaper clippings. "Sure, sure, in the record book it's a TKO for La Grange. But read what they said about us in the Worcester papers. Coombs woulda gone for a win if he hadn't busted his hand on the other bum's head. Here, you c'n read about it right here!"

He held the clippings up in front of Paul's face, but the matchmaker waved them away.

"How's the hand now?" Paul said.

"Good's new, good's new," Miniff assured him. "You don't think I'd send one of my boys in with a bum duke, do ya?"

"Yes," Paul said.

Miniff wasn't hurt. There was too much at stake to be hurt: five hundred dollars if he talked Paul Frank into using the Cowboy with Patsy Kline. One sixty-six for Miniff's end. And he could improve that a little if he held out a few bucks on Coombs' share of the purse. Miniff could use that kind of money. The Forrest Hotel, on 49th Street, had put up with Miniff's explanations for six or seven months.

"I'll tell you what I'll do with you, Paul," Miniff said. "If you want to be absolutely sure that your customers get their money's worth before Kline puts the crusher on Coombs . . ." He paused and looked around with a conspirator's discretion. "Come on out'n the sidewalk," he said, "where we can talk private."

"Awright," Paul agreed, unenthusiastically. "But cut it off short."

Relaxed and poker-faced, Paul moved toward the wide doorway with the undersized, overanxious director of the destiny of Cowboy Coombs hanging onto his arm and talking up into his face, sweating to make a buck.

Toro had to duck his head to fit through the doorway from the locker room. Usually the boys were so absorbed in their own workouts that they hardly looked up. I've seen the biggest draws in the business working shoulder to shoulder with some fifty-buck preliminary boy and nobody seeming to know the difference. But when Toro came in, everything seemed to stop for a second. He was dressed in black— long black tights and a black gym shirt which would have reached the ankles of the average Stillman boxer. In his clothes, which had been at best haphazardly fit, he had loomed to elephantine proportions. One felt overawed by a shapeless mass. But stripped down to gym clothes, the mass became molded into an immense but well-proportioned form. The shoulders, growing out of the long, muscular neck, were a yard wide but tapered sharply to a lean, firm waist. The legs were massive, with tremendously developed calves, and biceps the size of cantaloupes stood out in his arms. The short-legged Acosta, Danny, and Doc Zigman, the hunchbacked trainer, coming out of the locker room with Toro, looked like stubby tugs escorting a giant steamer. Danny, the tallest of the three, a man of average height, only reached his shoulder.

Toro moved into the big room slowly, shyly, and again I had the impression of a great beast of burden moving along with an obedient eye on its master. Acosta looked up and said something to Toro, and he began to go through warming-up calisthenics. He bent at the waist and touched his toes. He sat on the floor and raised his enormous torso until his head was between his legs. He was limber and, for a man of his size, surprisingly agile, though he didn't perform his exercises with the authority, the zip, of the boxers around him. Again I had the image of an elephant that performs its feats in the circus ring. Slowly, mechanically and with a sullen acquiescence, it executes every command its trainer gives it.

When Danny thought he had warmed up enough, Acosta and Doc prepared him for the ring. They fastened around his neck the heavy leather headgear that protected the fighter's ears and the vulnerable areas of the brain. They fitted over his teeth the hard, red rubberized mouthpiece. With the big sixteen-ounce training gloves on his hands he climbed up to the ring; the bulky headgear and the way the mouthpiece exaggerated the already abnormal size of his mouth gave him the frightening appearance of an ogre from some childhood fairy tale. On the apron, just before climbing through the ropes, he paused a moment and looked over the hundred-odd spectators staring up at him with casual curiosity. He would never face a more critical audience. Some of them were Eighth Avenue *aficionados* who paid four bits to Curley at the door for the privilege of seeing some favorite scrapper knock his sparring partners silly. But most of Toro's audience were professional appraisers who chewed their cigars with cold disdain and sized up the newcomers with shrewd eyes.

"Moliner," Stillman said matter-of-factly, his gravel voice lost in the general hubbub, and Toro climbed into the ring. Toward the ring at a shuffling pace came big, easy-natured George, muttering one of his favorite songs:

> *"Give me a big fat woman with the meat shakin' on her*
>   *bones* . . .
> *Give me a big fat woman with the meat shakin' on her*
>   *bones* . . .
> *And every time she shakes it some skinny woman loses her*
>   *home."*

Danny put his hand on George Blount's heavy forearm to give him last-minute instructions on how he wanted him to fight Toro, the different points of Toro's style he wanted George to test. I saw the Negro nod with his warm, good-humored smile. "You get it like you want it, Mr. McCuff," George said, climbing up into the ring with the businesslike air of a laborer punching in for a hard day's work.

The bell rang and George shuffled toward Toro amiably. He was a big man himself, six foot two and around two fifteen, but he fought from a crouch, hunching his head down into his thick shoulders to present a difficult, weaving target. He could be a troublesome fighter, though men who knew what they were doing straightened him up with right-hand uppercuts, reached through his short, clublike arms to score with stiff jabs and stopped him with a hard right-hand over the heart every time he flat-footed in for his roundhouse, haphazard attack. Toro held his long left hand out as Acosta had undoubtedly schooled him and pushed his glove toward George's face in what was supposed to be a jab. But there was no snap to it. George waded in, telegraphing a looping left, and Toro moved as if to avoid it, but his timing was off and he caught it on the ribs. George walked around Toro, giving him openings and feeling him out, and Toro turned with him awkwardly, holding out that left hand, but not knowing what to do with it. George brushed it aside and threw another left hook. It caught Toro in the pit of the stomach, and he grunted as they went into a clinch.

Acosta was leaning against the ropes just below them, tensed as if this was for the championship of the world and not just the warm-up round of a training workout. He shouted something up to Toro in shrill Spanish. Toro charged in, moving his body with awkward desperation, and hit George with a conventional one-two, a left to the jaw and a right to the body. George just shook them off and smiled. Despite the size of the body from which they came, there was no steam to Toro's punches. His fists shot out clumsily without the force of his body behind them. George moved around him again, ducking and weaving in the old-time Langford style, and Toro tried his one-two again, but George easily slipped his head out of reach of the left, caught the slow right on his glove and drew Toro into a clinch again, tying him up with his left hand and his right elbow, but managing to keep his right glove free to work into Toro's stomach.

The bell rang and Toro walked back to his corner, shaking his head. Acosta jumped into the ring, talking and gesticulating excitedly, jabbing, uppercutting, knocking George down in pantomime. Toro looked at him gravely, nodding slowly and occasionally looking around in bewilderment, as if wondering where he was and what was happening.

The second round was no better for Toro than the first. George was moving around him with more confidence now, cuffing him almost at will with open-gloved lefts and rights. Acosta cupped his hands to his mouth and shouted, *"Vente, El Toro, vente!"* Toro lunged forward with all his might, swinging so wildly with his huge right arm that he missed George completely and plunged heavily into the ropes. Some of the spectators laughed. It made them feel better.

Just before the round ended, Danny caught George's eye and nodded. George closed his gloves and crowded Toro into a corner, where he feinted with his left, brought Toro's guard down and cracked a hard right to the point of Toro's jaw. Toro's mouth fell open and his knees sagged. George was going to hit him again when the bell rang. Like a man who drops his hammer at the first sound of the whistle, George automatically lowered his hands, ambled back to his corner, took some water from the bottle, rolled it around in his mouth, spat it out, and, with the same easygoing smile with which he had entered the ring, climbed out again.

Toro leaned back against the ropes and shook his head in a gesture of confusion. For two rounds his giant's body had floundered as if it had lost all connection with the motor impulses in his brain.

Acosta was at Toro's side quickly, wiping the sweat from his large, solemn face while Doc Zigman kneaded the long thick neck with his capable fingers. Then, while Acosta held the ropes apart for him, Toro climbed ponderously out of the ring.

"Didja see that big bastard?" a regular behind me said. "Couldn't lick a postage stamp."

"From one of them chile-bowl countries," said his companion. "El Stinkola, if you understan' Spanish."

I turned to Vince, who was quiet for a change. "You sure know how to pick them," I said.

"Don't jump me," he said. "Nick's the brain and he thinks he can build 'im."

"If we could only get them to decide the championship on form like a beauty contest, Toro would walk away with it. But how can a guy who looks so invincible when he's standing still turn into such a bum when he starts moving?"

"Danny can teach him plenty," Vince said.

"Danny's the best," I agreed. "But if Danny knows how to make a silk purse out of a sow's ear, he's been holding out on us."

"Why don't you try talkin' like everybody else?" Vince said. "All them five-dollar expressions, nobody knows what the futz you're talkin' about."

"In other words, you become nobody by self-appointment," I said. "You got something there, Vince."

George was leaning against the wall near the ring, waiting to go another round with a new Irish heavyweight from Newark, just up from the amateurs. I could recognize a couple of lines of the song that seemed to play continually in his head.

> *"Gimme a fat woman for a pillow where I can rest my*
> > *head . . .*
> *Gimme a fat woman for a pillow where I can rest my*
> > *head . . .*
> *A fat woman knows how to rock me till my face is cherry*
> > *red."*

"How do *you* do, Mr. Lewis?" George said when I came up. He always asked it as if it were really a question.

"How do you feel, George?"

"Ready to go," George said. I had never known him to give any other answer. The night Gus Lennert banged him out in one round, when Gus still had something, and George hadn't come to until he was back in his dressing room, that had still been his answer to "How do you feel?"—"Ready to go."

"What do you think of Molina, George?"

"Big man," George said.

George never put the knock on anyone. Anger seemed unknown to him and the common expressions of derision and contempt in which nearly all of us indulge were never his way. I've often wondered if George hadn't fought all the meanness and bad temper out of his system, if it hadn't all been blotted up in the canvas along with his sweat and his blood.

"Think he'll ever make a fighter, George?"

His black face creased in a wise smile. "Well, I'll tell you, Mr. Lewis. I'd like to have the job of working out with him all the time. I'd like that fine."

As I went into the dressing rooms, George was squaring off with the Irish heavyweight. The big Irish kid fought with a set sneer on his face and neither knew how to nor wanted to pull his punches. He tore into George at the bell and whacked him a terrible punch under the right eye. I saw George smile and work his way into a clinch as the door swung closed behind me.

Inside, Toro was stretched out on one of the rubbing tables and Sam, a bald-headed, muscular fat man was working him over. Toro was so oversized for the ordinary rubbing table that his knees reached the end and his legs dangled down over the side. Danny, Doc, Vince and Acosta were standing around. Acosta turned to me and began a long-winded, excitable explanation. "El Toro, today you do not see him on his best. It is perhaps the excitement of his first appearance before such important people. Since the climate is very different from when he fight in Buenos Aires, I think . . ."

"I theenk," said Vince, exaggerating Acosta's accent, "he's a bum. But don't worry, chumo. We've made a dollar with bums before."

"All right. Out of here! I want everybody out of here," Danny said. The only way you could tell he had been at the bottle was that his voice was pitched a little louder than usual. But it wasn't only the bottle talking. It was Vince, to whom he had given the silent treatment ever since that Sencio affair. It was Acosta, who was getting on Danny's edgy nerves. It was Toro, this Gargantuan excuse for a fighter.

Nobody moved. Danny became petulant. "You think I'm talking for my health? I want everybody the hell out of here!"

Acosta drew himself up to his full five-feet-five. "Luis Acosta is not accustom to such insult," he said. "El Toro Molina is my discovery. Wherever El Toro is, I must be also."

"Nick Latka owns the biggest piece of this boy," Danny said flatly. "I work for Nick. A boy can only have one manager telling him what to do. I don't want to hurt no feelings, but I'll see you outside."

Acosta puffed up as if he were going to do something, but he only bowed his head stiffly and went out.

"That's puttin' the little spic in his place," Vince said.

"I said I want everybody out," Danny snapped.

"Listen, I'm one-a the partners, ain't I?" Vince demanded.

Danny never addressed him directly. "I'm responsible to Nick for his fighters' condition. I don't want to have to tell him people are getting in my way."

The word "Nick" dropped on Vince like a sandbag. "Okay, okay, the bum is yours," he said and sauntered out.

"I think I better go take a look at Grazelli's hand," Doc Zigman said. He and Danny were old friends. He knew the order hadn't been for him. "See you later, Danny."

I started to follow him out, but Danny said, "Stick around, laddie. You handle this boy's lingo, don't you?"

I went over to the table and looked down at Toro. *"¿Puede usted entenderme en español?"* I said.

Toro looked up at me. He had large, liquid, dark-brown eyes. *"Si, señor,"* he said respectfully.

"Good," Danny said. "I've got a few things I want to tell him about that workout before I forget. But we'll wait till Sam gets through. A boy's got to be relaxing completely when he's being rubbed down. That's why I ran those guys out of here."

After Sam finished up, Toro raised himself to a sitting position and looked around. "Where is Luis?" he said in Spanish.

"He is outside," I said. "You will see him soon."

"But why is he not here?" Toro said.

I nodded toward Danny. "He is your manager now," I said. "Danny will take very good care of you."

Toro shook his head and, with wide, thick lips in a child's pout, he said, "I want Luis."

"Luis will continue to stay on with you," I managed to say. "Luis is not going to leave you. But to be a success here you must have an American manager."

Toro shook his head sullenly. "I want Luis," he said. "Luis is my *jefe*."

It's time he heard, I thought. Time for this great hulk of an adopted son to learn the pugilistic facts of life. Better to hear them from me with all the cushion I could give them in my limited Spanish than to pick them up from the gutter talk of Vince and his brothers, as he was sure to do.

"Luis no longer owns you," I said, wishing I had more words with which to make the subtle shadings. "Your contract is divided up among a group of North Americans, of whom Mr. Latka has the largest share. You must do everything he says, just as if he were Luis. He knows much more about boxing than Luis or your Lupe Morales, and can teach you many things."

But Toro just shook his head again. "Luis tells me to fight," he said. "Luis takes me to this country. When we have enough money to build my big house in Santa Maria, Luis will take me home again."

I looked at Danny. "Maybe we better get Acosta back in here to straighten him out," I said.

"Okay," he said. "Call him in. What I got to tell the boy will still be good tomorrow."

I found Luis pacing up and down on the spectator's side of the rings. From the way he looked at me I could see his insides were tied into knots. "Your boy is all mixed up," I said. "He doesn't know what's happening to him. You better go in and get him straightened out."

"You are all jealous of me," Acosta said as we walked back toward the dressing rooms. "You are all jealous because it is Luis who has discover El Toro and so you want to separate us. You do not understand that I am the only one who can make El Toro fight."

"Look, Luis," I said, "you're a nice little guy, but you might as well get straightened out yourself. You can't make Toro fight. There's nobody in the world who can make Toro fight. If anybody comes close, it's Danny, because there isn't a better teacher in the business than Danny McKeogh."

"But Luis Firpo himself has tol' me how magnificent is my El Toro," Acosta said.

"Luis," I said, "on Sunday I listened to all this crap, because I was trying to be polite. And because I hadn't seen this overgrown peasant of yours yet. But now you might as well have it between the eyes. Even your Luis Firpo was a bum. All he had was a Sunday punch. He didn't know enough boxing to get out of his own way."

Acosta looked at me as if I had insulted his mother. "If you will pardon me," he said, "how do I know that is not just your North American arrogance? Actually Firpo has knock out the great Dempsey that day, but the judges did not want to let the title go to the Argentine."

"If you will pardon me," I said, "that is just pure Argentine horse manure."

Acosta sighed. "For me this is very sad," he said. "Always I dream of New York. And from the first moment I see El Toro . . ."

"I know, I know," I cut in impatiently. "We've had all that." And then I thought of that epic figure of a man and that big trusting puss being cuffed around by an old pro like George Blount and I was seized by the indignity of it and I said, "Goddamit, Luis, you've pulled him out by his roots. You should've left him there in Santa Maria, where he belongs."

Acosta shrugged. "But it was for his own good that . . ."

"Oh, if you will pardon me," I said, "balls! All your life you were a little frog in a little pool. A little frog with big dreams. And all of a sudden you saw a chance, saddled yourself on Toro's back, to make a big splash in a big pool."

"In my country," Acosta said pompously, "such a remark can lead to a duel."

"Don't take me too seriously, Luis," I said. "In your country I hear some of you like to shoot off guns. Here most of us just like to shoot off our mouths."

We had reached the door to the rubbing room. "Now go in there and explain to Toro how Danny is the boss," I said. You could almost hear the air rushing from his deflated ego as he went in. He barely nodded to Danny, who joined me in the hall.

"Luis, *¿qué pasa?* What happened? Explain to me. I do not understand," I could hear Toro saying as the door closed.

VRONSKY'S
STEEPLECHASE

from

ANNA KARENINA

───────◆───────

by LEO TOLSTOY

(1875)

*Very little recapitulation of the plot need be supplied to give the reader suffi-
cient background for full enjoyment of this excerpt from* Anna Karenina. *Anna,
the wife of an older and pompous government official, falls violently in love
with Count Alexey Vronsky, a dashing, arrogant, handsome army officer. When
he joins his regiment, she follows him. Vronsky's thoughts are naturally on
Anna, first, but they are diverted by the steeplechase for which he has been
preparing for weeks. This exciting account of that race is just one of the many
extended episodes in the novel in which Tolstoy extols the multiple satisfac-
tions of vigorous outdoor activity, be it an early-morning shoot or an arduous
session scything fields of hay.*

WHEN Vronsky looked at his watch on the Karenins' balcony, he
was so greatly agitated and lost in his thoughts that he saw the
figures on the watch's face, but could not take in what time it was. He
came out onto the highroad and walked, picking his way carefully
through the mud, to his carriage. He was so completely absorbed in

his feeling for Anna, that he did not even think what o'clock it was, and whether he had time to go to Bryansky's. He had left him, as often happens, only the external faculty of memory, that points out each step one has to take, one after the other. He went up to his coachman, who was dozing on the box in the shadow, already lengthening, of a thick lime tree; he admired the shifting clouds of midges circling over the hot horses, and, waking the coachman, he jumped into the carriage and told him to drive to Bryansky's. It was only after driving nearly five miles that he had sufficiently recovered himself to look at his watch, and realize that it was half-past five and he was late.

There were several races fixed for that day: the Mounted Guards' race, then the officers' mile-and-a-half race, then the three-mile race, and then the race for which he was entered. He could still be in time for his race, but if he went to Bryansky's he could only just be in time, and he would arrive when the whole of the court would be in their places. That would be a pity. But he had promised Bryansky to come, and so he decided to drive on, telling the coachman not to spare the horses.

He reached Bryansky's, spent five minutes there, and galloped back. This rapid drive calmed him. All that was painful in his relations with Anna, all the feeling of indefiniteness left by their conversation, had slipped out of his mind. He was thinking now with pleasure and excitement of the race, of his being anyhow, in time, and now and then the thought of the blissful interview awaiting him that night flashed across his imagination like a flaming light.

The excitement of the approaching race gained upon him as he drove farther and farther into the atmosphere of the races, overtaking carriages driving up from the summer villas or out of Petersburg.

At his quarters no one was left at home; all were at the races, and his valet was looking out for him at the gate. While he was changing his clothes, his valet told him that the second race had begun already, that a lot of gentlemen had been to ask for him, and a boy had twice run up from the stables. Dressing without hurry (he never hurried himself and never lost his self-possession), Vronsky drove to the sheds. From the sheds he could see a perfect sea of carriages, and people on foot, soldiers surrounding the racecourse, and pavilions swarming with people. The second race was apparently going on, for just as he went into the sheds he heard a bell ringing. Going toward the stable, he met the white-legged chestnut, Mahotin's Gladiator, being led to the racecourse in a blue forage horsecloth, with what looked like huge ears edged with blue.

"Where's Cord?" he asked the stableboy.

"In the stable, putting on the saddle."

In the open horse box stood Frou-Frou, saddled ready. They were just going to lead her out.

"I'm not too late?"

"All right! All right!" said the Englishman; "don't upset yourself!"

Vronsky once more took in in one glance the exquisite lines of his favorite mare, who was quivering all over, and with an effort he tore himself from the sight of her and went out of the stable. He went toward the pavilions at the most favorable moment for escaping attention. The mile-and-a-half race was just finishing, and all eyes were fixed on the horse guard in front and the light hussar behind, urging their horses on with a last effort close to the winning post. From the center and outside of the ring all were crowding to the winning post, and a group of soldiers and officers of the horse guards were shouting loudly their delight at the expected triumph of their officer and comrade. Vronsky moved into the middle of the crowd unnoticed, almost at the very moment when the bell rang at the finish of the race, and the tall, mud-spattered horse guard who came in first, bending over the saddle, let go the reins of his panting gray horse that looked dark with sweat.

The horse, stiffening out its legs, with an effort stopped its rapid course, and the officer of the horse guards looked round him like a man waking up from a heavy sleep and just managed to smile. A crowd of friends and outsiders pressed round him.

Vronsky intentionally avoided that select crowd of the upper world, which was moving and talking with discreet freedom before the pavilions. He knew that Madame Karenina was there, and Betsy, and his brother's wife, and he purposely did not go near them for fear of something distracting his attention. But he was continually met and stopped by acquaintances, who told him about the previous races, and kept asking him why he was so late.

At the time when the racers had to go to the pavilion to receive the prizes, and all attention was directed to that point, Vronsky's elder brother, Alexander, a colonel with heavy fringed epaulets, came up to him. He was not tall, though as broadly built as Alexey, and handsomer and rosier than he; he had a red nose, and an open, drunken-looking face.

"Did you get my note?" he said. "There's never any finding you."

Alexander Vronsky, in spite of the dissolute life, and in especial the drunken habits, for which he was notorious, was quite one of the court circle.

Now, as he talked to his brother of a matter bound to be exceedingly disagreeable to him, knowing that the eyes of many people might be fixed upon him, he kept a smiling countenance, as though he were jesting with his brother about something of little moment.

"I got it, and I really can't make out what *you* are worrying yourself about," said Alexey.

"I'm worrying myself because the remark has just been made to me that you weren't here, and that you were seen in Peterhof on Monday."

"There are matters which only concern those directly interested in them, and the matter you are so worried about is—"

"Yes, but if so, you may as well cut the service."

"I beg you not to meddle, and that's all I have to say."

Alexey Vronsky's frowning face turned white, and his prominent lower jaw quivered, which happened rarely with him. Being a man of very warm heart, he was seldom angry; but when he was angry, and when his chin quivered, then, as Alexander Vronsky knew, he was dangerous. Alexander Vronsky smiled gaily.

"I only wanted to give you Mother's letter. Answer it and don't worry about anything just before the race. *Bonne chance,*" he added, smiling, and he moved away from him. But after him another friendly greeting brought Vronsky to a standstill.

"So you won't recognize your friends! How are you, *mon cher?*" said Stepan Arkadyevitch, as conspicuously brilliant in the midst of all the Petersburg brilliance as he was in Moscow, his face rosy, and his whiskers sleek and glossy. "I came up yesterday, and I'm delighted that I shall see your triumph. When shall we meet?"

"Come tomorrow to the mess room," said Vronsky, and, squeezing him by the sleeve of his coat, with apologies, he moved away to the center of the racecourse, where the horses were being led for the great steeplechase.

The horses who had run in the last race were being led home, steaming and exhausted, by the stableboys, and one after another the fresh horses for the coming race made their appearance, for the most part English racers, wearing horsecloths, and looking with their drawn-up bellies like strange, huge birds. On the right was led in

Frou-Frou, lean and beautiful, lifting up her elastic, rather long pasterns, as though moved by springs. Not far from her they were taking the rug off the lop-eared Gladiator. The strong, exquisite, perfectly correct lines of the stallion, with his superb hindquarters and excessively short pasterns almost over his hoofs, attracted Vronsky's attention in spite of himself. He would have gone up to his mare, but he was again detained by an acquaintance.

"Oh, there's Karenin!" said the acquaintance with whom he was chatting. "He's looking for his wife, and she's in the middle of the pavilion. Didn't you see her?"

"No," answered Vronsky, and without even glancing round toward the pavilion where his friend was pointing out Madame Karenina, he went up to his mare.

Vronsky had not had time to look at the saddle, about which he had to give some direction, when the competitors were summoned to the pavilion to receive their numbers and places in the row at starting. Seventeen officers, looking serious and severe, many with pale faces, met together in the pavilion and drew the numbers. Vronsky drew the number seven. The cry was heard: "Mount!"

Feeling that, with the others riding in the race, he was the center upon which all eyes were fastened, Vronsky walked up to his mare in that state of nervous tension in which he usually became deliberate and composed in his movements. Cord, in honor of the races, had put on his best clothes, a black coat buttoned up, a stiffly starched collar, which propped up his cheeks, a round black hat, and top boots. He was calm and dignified as ever, and was with his own hands holding Frou-Frou by both reins, standing straight in front of her. Frou-Frou was still trembling as though in a fever. Her eye, full of fire, glanced sideways at Vronsky. Vronsky slipped his finger under the saddle girth. The mare glanced aslant at him, drew up her lip, and twitched her ear. The Englishman puckered up his lips, intending to indicate a smile that anyone should verify his saddling.

"Get up; you won't feel so excited."

Vronsky looked round for the last time at his rivals. He knew that he would not see them during the race. Two were already riding forward to the point from which they were to start. Galtsin, a friend of Vronsky's and one of his more formidable rivals, was moving round a bay horse that would not let him mount. A little light hussar in tight riding breeches rode off at a gallop, crouched up like a cat on the saddle, in imitation of English jockeys. Prince Kuzovlev sat with a white face on his thoroughbred mare from the Grabovsky stud, while an English groom led her by the bridle. Vronsky and all his comrades knew Kuzovlev and his peculiarity of "weak nerves" and terrible vanity. They knew that he was afraid of everything, afraid of riding a spirited horse. But now, just because it was terrible, because people broke their necks, and there was a doctor standing at each obstacle, and an ambulance with a cross on it, and a sister of mercy, he had made up his mind to take part in the race. Their eyes met, and Vronsky gave him a friendly and encouraging nod. Only one he did not see, his chief rival, Mahotin, on Gladiator.

"Don't be in a hurry," said Cord to Vronsky, "and remember one thing: don't hold her in at the fences, and don't urge her on; let her go as she likes."

"All right, all right," said Vronsky, taking the reins.

"If you can, lead the race; but don't lose heart till the last minute, even if you're behind."

Before the mare had time to move, Vronsky stepped with an agile, vigorous movement into the steel-toothed stirrup, and lightly and firmly seated himself on the creaking leather of the saddle. Getting his right foot in the stirrup, he smoothed the double reins, as he always did, between his fingers, and Cord let go.

As though she did not know which foot to put first, Frou-Frou started, dragging at the reins with her long neck, and as though she were on springs, shaking her rider from side to side. Cord quickened his step, following him. The excited mare, trying to shake off her rider first on one side and then the other, pulled at the reins, and Vronsky tried in vain with voice and hand to soothe her.

They were just reaching the dammed-up stream on their way to the starting point. Several of the riders were in front and several behind, when suddenly Vronsky heard the sound of a horse galloping in the mud behind him, and he was overtaken by Mahotin on his white-legged, lop-eared Gladiator. Mahotin smiled, showing his long teeth, but Vronsky looked angrily at him. He did not like him and regarded him now as his most formidable rival. He was angry with him for galloping past and exciting his mare. Frou-Frou started into a gallop, her left foot forward, made two bounds, and fretting at the tightened reins, passed into a jolting trot, bumping her rider up and down. Cord too scowled, and followed Vronsky almost at a trot.

There were seventeen officers in all riding in this race. The race-course was a large three-mile ring of the form of an ellipse in front of the pavilion. On this course nine obstacles had been arranged: the stream, a big and solid barrier five feet high just before the pavilion, a dry ditch, a ditch full of water, a precipitous slope, an Irish barricade (one of the most difficult obstacles, consisting of a mound fenced with brushwood, beyond which was a ditch out of sight for the horses, so that the horse had to clear both obstacles or might be killed); then two more ditches filled with water, and one dry one; and the end of the race was just facing the pavilion. But the race began not in the ring, but two hundred yards away from it, and in that part of the course was the first obstacle, a dammed-up stream, seven feet in breadth, which the racers could leap or wade through as they preferred.

Three times they were ranged ready to start, but each time some horse thrust itself out of line, and they had to begin again. The umpire who was starting them, Colonel Sestrin, was beginning to lose his temper, when at last for the fourth time he shouted "Away!" and the racers started.

Every eye, every opera glass, was turned on the brightly colored group of riders at the moment they were in line to start.

"They're off! They're starting!" was heard on all sides after the hush of expectation.

And little groups and solitary figures among the public began running from place to place to get a better view. In the very first minute the close group of horsemen drew out, and it could be seen that they were approaching the stream in twos and threes and one behind another. To the spectators it seemed as though they had all started simultaneously, but to the racers there were seconds of difference that had great value to them.

Frou-Frou, excited and overnervous, had lost the first moment, and several horses had started before her, but before reaching the stream, Vronsky, who was holding in the mare with all his force as she tugged at the bridle, easily overtook three, and there were left in front of him Mahotin's chestnut Gladiator, whose hindquarters were moving lightly and rhythmically up and down exactly in front of Vronsky, and in front of all the dainty mare Diana bearing Kuzovlev more dead than alive.

For the first instant Vronsky was not master either of himself or his mare. Up to the first obstacle, the stream, he could not guide the motions of his mare.

Gladiator and Diana came up to it together and almost at the same instant; simultaneously they rose above the stream and flew across to the other side; Frou-Frou darted after them, as if flying; but at the very moment when Vronsky felt himself in the air, he suddenly saw almost under his mare's hoofs Kuzovlev, who was floundering with Diana on the farther side of the stream. (Kuzovlev had let go the reins as he took the leap, and the mare had sent him flying over her head.) Those details Vronsky learned later; at the moment all he saw was that just under him, where Frou-Frou must alight, Diana's legs or head might be in the way. But Frou-Frou drew up her legs and back in the very act of leaping, like a falling cat, and, clearing the other mare, alighted beyond her.

"Oh, the darling!" thought Vronsky.

After crossing the stream Vronsky had complete control of his mare and began holding her in, intending to cross the great barrier behind Mahotin, and try to overtake him in the clear ground of about five hundred yards that followed it.

The great barrier stood just in front of the imperial pavilion. The Tsar and the whole court and crowds of people were all gazing at them—at him, and Mahotin a length ahead of him, as they drew near the "devil," as the solid barrier was called. Vronsky was aware of those eyes fastened upon him from all sides, but he saw nothing except the ears and neck of his own mare, the ground racing to meet him, and the back and white legs of Gladiator beating time swiftly before him, and keeping always the same distance ahead. Gladiator rose, with no sound of knocking against anything. With a wave of his short tail he disappeared from Vronsky's sight.

"Bravo!" cried a voice.

At the same instant, under Vronsky's eyes, right before him flashed the palings of the barrier. Without the slightest change in her action his mare flew over it; the palings vanished, and he heard only a crash behind him. The mare, excited by Gladiator's keeping ahead, had risen too soon before the barrier and grazed it with her hind hoofs. But her pace never changed, and Vronsky, feeling a spatter of mud in his face, realized that he was once more the same distance from Gladiator. Once more he perceived in front of him the same back and short tail, and again the same swiftly moving white legs that got no farther away.

At the very moment when Vronsky thought that now was the time to overtake Mahotin, Frou-Frou herself, understanding his thoughts, without any incitement on his part, gained ground considerably and began getting alongside of Mahotin on the most favorable side, close to the inner cord. Mahotin would not let her pass that side. Vronsky had hardly formed the thought that he could perhaps pass on the outer side, when Frou-Frou shifted her pace and began overtaking him on the other side. Frou-Frou's shoulder, beginning by now to be dark with sweat, was even with Gladiator's back. For a few lengths they moved evenly. But before the obstacle they were approaching, Vronsky began working at the reins, anxious to avoid having to take the outer circle, and swiftly passed Mahotin just upon the declivity. He caught a glimpse of his mud-stained face as he flashed by. He even fancied that he smiled. Vronsky passed Mahotin, but he was immediately aware of him close upon him, and he never ceased hearing the even-thudding hoofs and the rapid and still quite fresh breathing of Gladiator.

The next two obstacles, the watercourse and the barrier, were easily crossed, but Vronsky began to hear the snorting and thud of Gladiator closer upon him. He urged on his mare and to his delight felt that she easily quickened her pace, and the thud of Gladiator's hoofs was again heard at the same distance away.

Vronsky was at the head of the race, just as he wanted to be and as Cord had advised, and now he felt sure of being the winner. His excitement, his delight, and his tenderness for Frou-Frou grew keener and keener. He longed to look round again, but he did not dare do this and tried to be cool and not to urge on his mare, so as to keep the same reserve of force in her as he felt that Gladiator still kept. There remained only one obstacle, the most difficult; if he could cross it ahead of the others, he would come in first. He was flying toward the Irish barricade, Frou-Frou and he both together saw the barricade in the distance, and both the man and the mare had a moment's hesitation. He saw the uncertainty in the mare's ears and lifted the whip but at the same time felt that his fears were groundless; the mare knew what was wanted. She quickened her pace and rose smoothly, just as he had fancied she would, and as she left the ground gave herself up to the force of her rush, which carried her far beyond the ditch; and with the same rhythm, without effort, with the same leg forward, Frou-Frou fell back into her pace again.

"Bravo, Vronsky!" he heard shouts from a knot of men—he knew they were his friends in the regiment—who were standing at the obstacle. He could not fail to recognize Yashvin's voice though he did not see him.

"O my sweet!" he said inwardly to Frou-Frou, as he listened for what was happening behind. "He's cleared it!" he thought, catching the thud of Gladiator's hoofs behind him. There remained only the last ditch, filled with water and five feet wide. Vronsky did not even look at it but, anxious to get in a long way first, began sawing away at the reins, lifting the mare's head and letting it go in time with her paces. He felt that the mare was at her very last reserve of strength; not her neck and shoulders merely were wet, but the sweat was standing in drops on her mane, her head, her sharp ears, and her breath came in short, sharp gasps. But he knew that she had strength left more than enough for the remaining five hundred yards. It was only from feeling himself nearer the ground and from the peculiar smoothness of his motion that Vronsky knew how greatly the mare had quickened her pace. She flew over the ditch as though not noticing it. She flew over it like a bird; but at the same instant Vronsky, to his horror, felt that he had failed to keep up with the mare's pace, that he had, he did not know how, made a fearful, unpardonable mistake, in recovering his seat in the saddle. All at once his position had shifted and he knew that something awful had happened. He could not yet make out what had happened, when the white legs of a chestnut horse flashed by close to him, and Mahotin passed at a swift gallop. Vronsky was touching the ground with one foot, and his mare was sinking on that foot. He just had time to free his leg when she fell on one side, gasping painfully, and, making vain efforts to rise with her delicate, soaking neck, she fluttered on the ground at his feet like a shot bird. The clumsy movement made by Vronsky had broken her back. But that he only knew much later. At that moment he knew only that Mahotin had flown swiftly by, while he stood staggering alone on the muddy, motionless ground, and Frou-Frou lay gasping before him, bending her head back and gazing at him with her exquisite eyes. Still unable to realize what had happened, Vronsky tugged at his mare's reins. Again she struggled all over like a fish and, her shoulders setting the saddle heaving, she rose on her front legs; but, unable to lift her back, she quivered all over and again fell on her side. With a face hideous with passion, his lower jaw trembling, and his cheeks white, Vronsky kicked her with his heel in the stomach and again fell to tugging at the rein. She did not stir, but thrusting her nose into the ground, she simply gazed at her master with her speaking eyes.

"A—a—a!" groaned Vronsky, clutching at his head. "Ah! what have I done!" he cried. "The race lost! And my fault! shameful, unpardonable! And the poor darling, ruined mare! Ah, what have I done!"

A crowd of men, a doctor and his assistant, the officers of his regiment, ran up to him. To his misery he felt that he was whole and unhurt. The mare had broken her back, and it was decided to shoot her. Vronsky could not answer questions, could not speak to anyone. He turned and without picking up his cap, which had fallen off, walked away from the racecourse, not knowing where he was going. He felt utterly wretched. For the first time in his life he knew the bitterest sort of misfortune, misfortune beyond remedy, and caused by his own fault.

Yashvin overtook him with his cap and led him home, and half an hour later Vronsky had regained his self-possession. But the memory of that race remained for long in his heart, the cruelest and bitterest memory of his life.

ABOUT THE EDITORS

PETER SCHWED *attended Lawrenceville and Princeton largely as a result of the sporting and literary tastes indoctrinated into him by the time he was twelve by his father. That worthy not only owned a small stable of race horses but also loved the Owen Johnson Lawrenceville stories and ranked Sammy White, of the Princeton backfield of 1911, alongside Theodore Roosevelt as his heroes of the early part of the century. At school and college Schwed played a good brand of tennis (he still does), competed with enthusiastic mediocrity at other sports, managed cross-country and track teams, and went on to become a tournament badminton player and an ardent spectator and fan of the entire sporting scene. In recent years, slowed up by the heavy impost of a wife and four small children, he does not attend every sporting event which takes his fancy, but he keeps abreast of the sports world by editing a number of sports books, as part of his job as editor and executive of a major book-publishing house.*

HERBERT WARREN WIND, *like Mr. Schwed, has spent a good part of his life in and around sports, playing them, watching them, coaching them, reading and writing them. In the 1920s and early 30s, Brockton, Massachusetts, his home town, was, as he recalls it fondly, a wonderful place for a boy to grow up: there was a basketball court in every third back yard, the playing fields at the Fair Grounds were five minutes away, the golf course was ten, and Fenway Park was close enough to get into in under an hour whenever the Red Sox went tearing off on a two-game winning streak. A fairly respectable all-round athlete, Mr. Wind played some industrial-league baseball, varsity basketball at Yale, college rugby at Cambridge University, and has competed in a number of other sports with occasional glimmers of competence. At present an associate editor of* Sports Illustrated, *he is best known for his articles and his books on golf, but he has covered all sports at one time or another since breaking in with the* Brockton Enterprise *twenty-odd years ago.*